C000301824

AN IMPROBABLE SPY

BOOK ONE OF THE CHARLES BOWATER SERIES

JAMES WITHINGTON

Jay Books

To Margaret with grateful thanks

PART 1: VISIONS

ONE

The West Berlin early summer evening was clear and balmy. The air was still but the constant hum of traffic was always there as this beleaguered city continued to recover apace from the devastation wrought upon it by Russian forces 27 years previously. The garden terrace of the Officers' Mess in Smuts Barracks, with its high, stout and barbed-wire-topped walls secreted behind trees and clipped hedges, was protected from this constant growl of German energy and provided an oasis of calm for those within. The ever foreboding and silent presence of Spandau Prison situated to one side of the barracks, with its rotational allied guard force of 120 soldiers guarding the one remaining inmate, provided further soundproofing from the external drone of traffic.

This perfect evening was indeed made for a civilised and enjoyable black-tie al fresco dinner and thereafter dancing, and the officers' mess terrace was laid out with that in mind. The Mess Sergeant and his willing and not so willing staff of regular mess staff and a number of co-opted soldiers, masquerading as suitably attired waiters, barmen and assistants, had laboured through the afternoon to ensure that all the details and style required of an occasion such as this were just so. The sweating chefs in the mess kitchen had been busy producing a three-course meal that would prove to be a culinary delight. The 40 or so officers and their wives, girlfriends and other assorted hopefuls, along with a number of invited guests, would be nudged to drink champagne on arrival, be seated around six immaculately prepared and silvered tables and thereafter, when suitably copious of amounts of excellent food and fine wine had been consumed, dance the night away. It was a Saturday and all bode well for a very good party. Sunday was another day.

The tables on the terrace had been arranged as a group at the back of the spacious terrace and close to the mess entrance, which led into the ante-room beyond. In front of the tables was the dance floor which consisted of a slightly raised platform, and beyond that a podium from which music would be played. This consisted of a string quartet for when dining took place, and for the less formal post-dinner shenanigans a band made up of several musically inclined tank crew. Their desire to occasionally break away from the musically stringent and, at times, stultifying requirements of a military Squadron band was plainly obvious. They really wanted to be like The Who and managed their act rather well. However, they could not smash up their equipment at the end of the show because they had no means of replacing it on army pay, and their short haircuts were rather incongruous. The string quartet was made up of rather ancient Polish gentlemen who had, at the end of the war and as part of the enormous tide of human flotsam that spread across Europe, found themselves in the British Sector of Berlin which then became the British Sector of West Berlin. All were disinclined to return to their native Poland. They had served with the British Army during the war and a return could spell trouble for them and their families. The mess had hired these gentlemen from the Officers' Club in the British Sector and their music was sublime.

Army etiquette demanded a seating plan for formal and not so formal social occasions and this was no exception. A prominently displayed seating plan at the terrace entrance showed where the partygoers would be sitting on the six tables of six. In a close-knit environment such as the army, amplified by the parochial and claustrophobic military environment of West Berlin, ensuring everybody was happy to sit where they had been placed was near impossible. Local disagreements, dislikes, feuds, illicit love affairs and other human emotions, good and bad, had all to be taken into account. However, the Mess Secretary, a rather mischievous young Captain, had decided on this occasion to throw caution to the wind and place people wherever. For each setting on each table, a name card was placed. No escaping the possibility of sitting next to an admired, loved, despised or even hated neighbour.

The Regimental silver was out in force on starched white tablecloths. Each place was carefully set out and contained the requisite cutlery, side plate, napkin and exquisite wine glasses. Candelabras provided the necessary candle-lit glow that always seemed to generate all types of human emotions, especially when wine had been partaken.

The Mess Sergeant, a soldier of immense experience who had fought in Korea and won a Military Medal for valour, conducted a final check of all. He was a man of classic military bearing and self-discipline for whom the army had been a life and who had decided that at his age, and with obligatory retirement looming, he would volunteer for the then vacant post of Mess Sergeant of the Officers' Mess in West Berlin. The pull of operational soldiering had waned and he found this new, very different and relatively sedentary challenge much more to his liking. He was a happy man, but this did not preclude him from continuing his career-long attention to detail and his often-stentorian approach to those under him. Firm but fair, he never let his standards slip.

His impressive row of medals had many a young officer and soldier agog with admiration.

The Mess Sergeant placed his staff at their designated posts. Waiters were positioned at the entrance with trays of glasses filled with champagne and others were discreetly dotted around the terrace. The final result was splendid in the soft summer evening air.

SECOND LIEUTENANT CHARLES BOWATER, along with the other young and unmarried officers who lived in the officers' mess, strolled onto the terrace. All were attired in the obligatory black tie and they had been instructed by the Mess Secretary to act as initial hosts to those married officers and their wives, as well other guests, who were due to arrive very soon. Some of the young officers had girlfriends who were also due to arrive. Charles did not, which was unusual given the plethora of real and potential female company that existed in West Berlin, either from within British and other military social circles, or from the German population. There was never any shortage for young British officers to indulge in those heady and halcyon days in West Berlin in the early seventies, and in the middle of a very real Cold War.

The guests began to arrive and soon the terrace had filled with an elegantly dressed gathering of officers and their ladies, as well as the invited guests. The military men tended to all look more or less the same – apart from the Officer Commanding who was a most ugly man; short, overweight, almost entirely bald and with a face ravaged by years of over-indulgence. Rather surprisingly his wife, who was no doubt long-suffering, was petite and attractive. No one knew what really went on behind closed doors but there was much tittle-tattle and speculation. What everyone did know was that she was, when warmed by wine, prone to take undue interest in young men, and particularly young men in uniform. This further fuelled speculation and the secret hope for scandal.

All this, in part, was driven by the almost universal hatred of the Officer Commanding, in both a professional and social sense, and the desire to see him fall. He was known appropriately within the Squadron as 'Buttocks' on account of his ridiculously fat and wobbly arse. The soldiers also approved of this nickname but it was never voiced aloud. All in the Squadron were well aware of the Officer Commanding's uncontrollable temper and vindictive nature. If he could throw the Army Manual of Military Law at you, he would – with relish.

The remaining eight officers of the Squadron were all career soldiers. Of these, the two captains were married and the remainder, all lieutenants but known as subalterns, lived in the mess and were single. Marriage before a certain age, and certainly not before the age of 27, was discouraged and frowned upon within certain regiments in the army. Young officers were expected to devote their energies towards the Regiment and the army and get married later. Both the captains' wives caused the subalterns some considerable disquiet and chiefly in the form of lascivious sexual thoughts. Not only did they both possess considerable good looks and charm, but both deliberately teased men to distraction, sometimes in unison.

The girlfriends of those subalterns who could be bothered to engage, or were lucky enough to be successful in the never-ending quest for female company, also arrived. One was the daughter of a British military doctor stationed in Berlin with the British Brigade. She rode horses and rumour had it that she enjoyed using her riding crop not only on horses. No wonder George, her current beau, always looked so pleased with himself but never went sunbathing at the Wannsee. The others were German and most were young and beautiful. They were all confident and engaging and they did not hesitate to use their good or not-so-good English.

They had all enthusiastically participated in many an unplanned and wildly drunken night in the mess where, following the inevitable formal or semi-formal dinner, military and national inhibitions would be thrown to the wind. Champagne would be drunk in copious quantities and games would be played and clothes discarded. Smuggling the young ladies out of the mess and the barracks very early the next morning could be tricky, especially with a monumental hangover, but luckily 'Buttocks' had not yet caught wind of these activities and the guard force were well used to these events, which always brightened up what was normally a dull guard-duty.

The guests that evening were a mixed bag. 'Buttocks' had decreed that the Officers' Mess must entertain guests that might have a positive bearing on his non-existent career. This meant a heavy emphasis on inviting staff officers from the British Berlin Brigade Headquarters, as well as a smattering from American and French force officers serving in West Berlin. 'Buttocks' also liked to impress diplomats and other worthies from the West Berlin expatriate community.

On this occasion, the Brigade was represented by the Brigade Major, a man stultifying, bland and boring, and his dowdy and nodding wife; and a junior staff officer who was so wet that you could shoot duck off him, and his nervous and nodding wife. Both could think and talk about nothing other than military matters and their wives nodded in unison. Those who had been placed next to any of them could look forward to an evening of unmitigated tedium. 'Buttocks' would never have considered to try to broaden the scope of invitations to include cultured, artistic, witty, politically astute and entertaining people who could engage in a wide variety of interesting topics and be prepared to argue the toss on any matter over the dinner table or on the dance floor.

There were two American guests and one French. The American colonel and his wife were well known to the Squadron's officers through professional and social contact. They were engaging and amusing, as well as being the most generous hosts at their home. The other American officer, whose name was Brad, was not known to the Squadron but proved to be the life and soul of the party; drinking for both America and Europe, recounting risqué and improbable stories of his adventures in Vietnam, dancing with every unsuspecting lady he could persuade, mainly ignoring the lady who had accompanied him, and finally falling asleep in the early hours in an armchair in the mess.

However, it was the lady he bought on his arm that caused a stir. She was stunningly beautiful as well as being socially very assured. She did not seem to mind the behaviour of her escort and was happy to dance and talk the night away with others, and with obvious enjoyment. The French officer was prim and correct, immaculately turned out and sipped his champagne and wine with a disdainful, somewhat sinister air of superiority. His wife was attractive in a very French way, slim but not thin and beautifully dressed. The make-up must have taken hours to apply.

Diplomats from various western consulates and a number of expatriates and local worthies made up the numbers. The champagne was flowing and the conversation animated and gaining in volume by the minute. Suddenly a loud and stentorian voice rose above the hubbub. 'Ladies and Gentlemen, dinner is served. Please take your seats.' No one could argue with the tall, immaculate, imposing and bemedaled soldier, whose authority was evident.

When the three ladies on his table were seated, Charles sat down and surveyed the scene. The noisy young American officer and his beautiful friend were on his table, as was the young British staff officer and his nodding wife. The table was completed with the presence of Giles Hackett, the squadron second in command who had invited Brad and his partner. Casting a furtive look at Brad's partner as she took her seat next to him, he realised that she was indeed very good looking. Charles then looked at her escort and could plainly see he was not much interested in engaging her in conversation.

Charles turned to introduce himself to the young and beautiful woman seated on his left.

'Good evening. I'm Charles.'

'Good evening. My name is Greta Meier.'

Her accent was heavily German but her mastery of English faultless.

'Welcome to the mess. I do hope that you have an enjoyable evening.'

He stole another look at her face, a look she noticed, and she turned and smiled at him. This time he studied her more closely and could see that she was indeed beautiful. A perfectly formed face, lovely mouth, perfect teeth, startling blue, blue eyes and hair a rich blonde mane falling to bare shoulders. Her skin, almost translucent, glowed in the evening air.

She told him that she had been born in Dresden during the last few desperate years of the Third Reich. Her father had been in the Wehrmacht, her mother a housewife, and she had an elder sister. She chose not to elaborate on what happened to them when the Red Army entered Germany and occupied Dresden, only to say that their father returned and that they all survived and continue to live in that city. She did not appear to be evasive about this time but rather talked quietly in a measured and practical tone. She told him that in 1952, at the insistence of their parents, she was moved by them to live with an aunt in a small village near Osnabrück in West Germany. Her sister refused to leave her parents and remained in East Germany. Living with her aunt, she completed her secondary education and found a position as an administrator with a small, local agricultural company. There she led a humdrum existence, fending off a constant stream of enthusiastic potential suitors, most of whom she found dull, oafish and intent on one thing only.

What she did not tell Charles was that aside from these irritating interludes, she used her looks and charm to target and seduce a number of what she considered more worthy men. This meant travelling into Osnabrück and sitting in bars and restaurants until she noticed a likely candidate. A smile was normally enough and over the years she became adept at using her looks and body, enjoying varied and energetic sex, but never allowing herself to be drawn into a serious relationship. She loved sex and although she was not endeared to those who supplied it, this gave her experience and expertise. She learnt quickly how she could dominate men and use them for her own ends if necessary.

In the meantime, the 'iron curtain' had descended and the Berlin Wall was erected in 1961, effectively cutting her off from her parents and sister whom she had not seen for 20 years. She added that her life represented nothing more than that experienced by many young Germans in those years after the war and that pity was the last thing they needed. Young Germans in the west wanted to concentrate on the present and future, and place the past firmly behind them, even to the point of denial. Glancing up at the forbidding walls of Spandau Prison, she smiled at the irony of her remark.

Charles leaned forwards. 'What brings you to West Berlin and how did you meet our charming American friend sitting opposite us?'

'I responded to an advertisement for a chief administrator at a pharmaceutical company and amazingly got the job! I like working for them and the conditions are very good. As for the American, I would describe him as an acquaintance rather than a friend. He is quite nice when he is sober, which is not very often. I am tiring of his antics and his performance this evening seems to be no exception.'

'What will you do?'

'I will go home alone to my comfortable little apartment in Charlottenburg and think about what a lovely evening I hope that I will have in your mess. So far, so very good!'

They ate and drank, exchanged pleasantries with the others on the table, and continued to explore each other's lives. He told her a little about himself. He was an only child and his parents what he called a classically English couple. He was sent to a good school which he loved and then joined the army and went to Sandhurst. He told her that he was considered average academically, excelled at sport by his own admission and generally enjoyed his five years there despite the physical rigours imposed on the boys. These included a distinct lack of heating or hot water, especially during the long winter months where it was not uncommon to wake in the 30-strong dormitory and discover a thin layer of ice on the sheets, and where the flat-plate electric heaters were placed on the dormitory ceiling, thus offering warmth and comfort six feet above your head. Infrequent washing was supplemented by being forced, with a literal pistol, into the school swimming pool where one could compete with frogs and other unknown aquatic creatures in the dark green water. But after the first freezing and miserable winter he had found it all to his liking and the longer he stayed and the more senior he became the easier was life in general, especially when he was introduced to the delights of female company.

She appeared most interested in all these tales, laughed frequently and their conversation was animated and comfortable. He really did like her very much but also realised that compared to what she and her family had probably been through his tales of youthful trials and tribulations probably seemed insignificant, even pathetic to her.

He also told her that despite the ardent attempts by a sixth-form boy to lure him to his private cubicle, he discovered girls during his last two years at school. Weekend forays to the local town, which contained a girls' public school and a convent, became frequent and distracting from the important matters of studies and sport. Girls were dated, he fell in love frequently, wanted to get married, fell out of love, found someone else, fumbled and only at the last moment discovered sex, although it proved at the time to be most disappointing and unsatisfactory. He also discovered beer and cider. For two and sixpence, you could buy a pint of the local scrumpy which would ensure that you spent the next 24 hours not knowing where you were and wondering how you would manage to get back to school in one piece.

All of these stories she found both amusing and baffling – a world that was wholly alien to her and of which she had no knowledge or real understanding.

If he thought her face sublime, then when she rose from the table at his polite request for a dance, he was ill-prepared for the perfection of her body. Discussions in the mess sometimes centred on the preferred perfect woman's body. Some liked the thinner elf-like type; another an ample figure; others tall and still others short, whilst Charles always liked the rounded type and on the shorter side. They often wondered if women had the same sort of discussion about their perfect man. Greta met his criteria absolutely and as he took her in his arms, he was almost overwhelmed by the sensuality emanating from her body. One dance turned into ten and when they returned to their table for a much-needed drink, the American had reached the point of no return and had retired to a comfortable armchair inside the mess for a much deserved and lengthy sleep, whilst the others had drifted onto other tables, the dance floor or had left. They had the table to themselves.

He looked into her eyes and smiled. She seemed gentle, kind and decent, highly intelligent and socially relaxed and engaging. She was never short of conversation or an amusing riposte. She was elegant, well-mannered and poised. Could there be anything wrong with her, he wondered? If he got to know her intimately, might he find some weakness?

He ventured to suggest that he would like it very much if they could meet again. Her response was positive and keen. They agreed to meet that next morning at a small coffee house in the Tiergarten which Greta knew of and for which she gave him directions. They wandered out onto the street and hailed a taxi.

'Well, I shall say good night and it was so good to meet you.'

'Thank you for a lovely evening, Charles, and I look forward to seeing you tomorrow at eleven.'

Their lips brushed and she was gone. For a moment he stared after the taxi and then returned to the mess garden. A few determined remaining young officers occupied one of the tables and he joined them. Drink had been partaken and they were overly and noisily interested in the lady that Charles had taken such an interest in. Charles, wisely, decided to keep his powder dry, downed a final glass and went to his room upstairs, passing the snoring American who would remain in situ until morning and awake wondering where he was. Charles thought in passing that if he was still there in the morning, he would invite him to breakfast.

TWO

The next morning, he rose early and went for his customary 5km run followed by a shower before venturing downstairs to the dining room for breakfast. The American had skulked off and no one else was around.

Charles prepared himself with care and arrived far too early at the agreed rendezvous. Rather than sit in the café, he positioned himself on a bench with a view to the entrance. With good German timing, she arrived at eleven. In the warm spring air she was wearing a light dress with a broad belt that accentuated her figure and she looked radiant and lovely. He felt a tingling of excitement at what might follow.

They sat outside and talked incessantly over coffee. As on the previous evening, she was engaging, interesting herself and always interested in what he had to say. She made him feel comfortable and relaxed and they decided that they would move on to have lunch elsewhere. The small restaurant she chose was perfect. Animated conversation continued over a light but delicious lunch accompanied by a bottle of excellent wine. That bottle turned into two and although this made him feel drowsy and replete, it did not seem to affect her at all.

She asked if he would like to come back to her flat and he readily agreed. He felt himself falling for this bewitching woman and made no effort to resist. They wandered slowly back to her flat which proved to be as charming and elegant as she. It was small but tastefully decorated and furnished in light and refreshing colours, and everything was neat, tidy and clean. He did, however, notice that there were no family pictures on display, or indeed any other pictures at all. But this only distracted him for a moment in passing and he thought little more of it.

She prepared wine and put on some music. Both could sense a charged atmosphere of anticipation and coming pleasure but it seemed neither was willing to make the first move. The soft music did the trick and with the wine they came together, as they had done the evening before, and danced closely. The wine had loosened his inhibitions and his hands began to explore her body through the thin material of her dress. He caressed her back and then her bottom and there was no resistance; rather a pressing willingness for him to go further. They kissed long and deep and his mind swam with desire for her and his hardness pressed against her, a hardness she could surely feel.

Without further ado she led him by the hand to the bedroom and they sat on the bed together. They fell back kissing fervently and he put his hand up her thigh to her knickers whilst she undid his belt and felt for him.

He undressed completely and lay on the bed. He experienced a flashback to the few delightful hours with that Dutch woman in Amsterdam on his way to Germany from England, but it was short-lived as Greta appeared completely naked before him. Her body was all that he imagined it would be and he gazed at her whilst she gazed back at him. He had always been described as 'well endowed' by countless envious school and army friends and acquaintances where taking communal showers in communal changing rooms and getting dressed and undressed in communal dormitories or at Sandhurst was a way of life. By the look on Greta's face, she obviously agreed.

Over the next two hours, they utterly sated each other with their bodies. She was passionate, tender, experienced and expert in all, and at times he found it difficult to keep up. But as the passion and almost frantic energy from both of them increased, the more they found harmony. It was almost all too perfect.

He had never experienced anything like this before and their crossing of the finishing line was spectacular and all consuming. At the end, they slept exhausted and replete and only woke when the evening sun crept into the room.

They showered together, another first for Charles as she put her arms around his neck, their soapy bodies intertwined and there was no holding back this time. They climaxed simultaneously in a very short time. After dressing, he felt no desire to leave so she happily cooked supper whilst chatting away and telling him about her move to West Berlin and the setting up of her flat. She was an easy conversationalist with her sometimes amusing but flawless English and he was happy to listen, eat and take her all in in the fullest possible way. He felt a calmness and contentment.

Her telephone rang. It was the American and she listened intently as he spoke. It seemed to Charles that he was attempting to explain away his behaviour of the evening before but she cut him off, and in a voice that was in every way different to way she had always spoken to Charles, told the American in clear, short and harsh tones that she no longer wished to see him again and he was not to contact her. His audible protests were cut short as she put the telephone down. Her face immediately softened and she smiled that sweet smile at him.

'I do not think that he will contact me again. At any rate, I have you now and that makes me very happy. Would you like to spend the night with me?'

'I would love to but I will have to leave early tomorrow as we have a squadron church parade in uniform and I will need to get my act together.'

The night's lovemaking was gentler, more measured and less frenetic but nonetheless just as passionate. There was time to explore, to talk quietly and to discover all the erogenous quirks, likes and dislikes of each other's bodies. She was soft and pliable, but at the same time always seemed to be able to control their lovemaking with an almost authoritarian ease. He now had time to ponder on this and was not sure whether he liked it or not. But she was undoubtably beautiful and such good company, in and out of bed, that he decided that he did not really care and that he was happy to be taken in hand.

He left early the next morning, their farewells fond and intimate. They would meet again that coming Wednesday. He set off and decided that as the weather was so perfect he would walk some of the way and then find a taxi back to the barracks. His thoughts were full of her and of the evening and night they had spent together, but at the back of his mind was a nagging doubt. On reflection, he thought he may have noticed a degree of hardness and of a controlling nature under that sweet and delightful exterior. He wondered about the lack of family pictures in her flat given how she had talked so lovingly about them. He also mused on her apartment – the lack of warmth and homeliness, no indication of other lives and a seeming obsession with neatness and cleanliness. It was sterile and cold. She was even at pains to make the bed when they got up. He thought that maybe he was being too critical and decided to ride with it and see how things developed between them in the coming weeks, now he was back in the land of the army and a church parade where he could spend a moment of quiet thanking God for meeting her.

SOPHIA CLOSED the door of her flat, made herself a cup of coffee. It was time to make a call from the phone box down the street.

THREE

The squadron settled further into life in West Berlin, a regular routine based on hard and persistent training, continuous education and knowledge of the operational requirement of their mission at squadron, brigade and tripartite levels. In maintaining a level of readiness that could not afford any misunderstandings or material gap, this existence could have lapsed into a state of humdrum. This could not be allowed to happen and this demand, even at the lowest tank troop level, meant that Charles and his fellow troop leaders were kept very busy.

As the weeks and months passed, often at a hectic pace both professionally and socially, Charles and Greta's relationship not only survived but blossomed. He came to accept that something in her past was perhaps the reason why, at times, she could display a less endearing side. She remained very interested in him, demure and as always beautiful and engaging. Why look a gift horse in the mouth? It was of interest to him that although she was in his thoughts constantly, he did not think he was in love with her or loved her. He had dwelt on this and came to conclusion that he did not really know what being in love was, and that apart from his mother he certainly had no idea what it meant to love someone. He was an only child and as a boy and young man was used to getting his own way. He had always been at heart a loner amongst male company. Outwardly he was engaging, social, amusing and highly competent, but he sought to be on his own whenever possible. Not an easy thing in the army. Although he had many male friends, they were never really friends in the truest sense of the word, rather acquaintances. He respectfully kept them all at arm's length.

The conclusion to all this was that he thought it best that the relationship was kept at a fun, light and breezy level with no complications. It seemed to him that Greta was content with this unspoken arrangement and so they carried on leading a hectic social life within the West Berlin social scene, attending parties and balls, having dinner out or with friends or in the mess or officers' club, going to the cinema and theatre, exploring intimately a West Berlin where recent history constantly bore down on them, and going for long walks in the Tiergarten, the Grunewald or by the lakes.

Equally hectic was their sex life which alternated between frantic lovemaking, not only in her bedroom but in all rooms of her flat, with the kitchen table being her favourite, as well as outside in hopefully secluded spots during their long walks – and long, gentle nights in bed where sleep normally took precedence. Both seemed happy but the question of a possible future together was never broached. He often ruminated about why neither he or she ever went beyond the present and why there was never any talk of plans for their future together, pillow or otherwise. He had not asked her this question but for him, as it was during their first intimate time together where the first seeds of doubt had emerged, there was always something missing. As a young man with no real experience of being in love, or what loving someone actually meant, he thought often about these matters. She was stunningly beautiful, highly intelligent and an engaging and wonderful companion but still there was something not quite right. He found it difficult to comprehend but in order not to break the spell of her presence and continued interest in him, he placed it at the back of his mind and focussed entirely on the present.

CHARLES WAS PROMOTED from Second Lieutenant to Lieutenant, and he felt grander than he really was. His position as a Troop Leader remained and the only discernible difference was that his pay increased fractionally, though not enough to make inroads into his constant and nagging overdraft.

At around the same time, the squadron said goodbye to Major 'Buttocks' as he was to be posted to a run-of-the-mill staff job at the headquarters of British Army of the Rhine in West Germany. His dream of being promoted had been dashed, so whilst he fumed and moaned his officers smirked and tittered. The officers' mess held a dinner in his honour where, following a pleasant farewell speech from the second-in-command which was full of ill-disguised platitudes, he took the unprecedented step of refusing to rise to his feet and reply. It all went down like a lead balloon and although 'Buttocks' was well oiled by the end of the evening, none of the other officers were anything other than stone-cold sober.

The squadron also held a farewell party for him. The sergeant major and his sergeants were placed on high alert and forbidden to drink more than two beers. Their task for the evening was clear; any signs of abuse, verbal or physical, towards the outgoing major and immediate ejection and punishment would take place. There persisted throughout an atmosphere of people not wanting to be there and it was, and remains, the shortest and most sober squadron party ever held.

His successor could not have been more different. Tall, lean and handsome with a penchant for hard physical exercise, he was engaging, civilised, sensible, amiable with a thoughtful air and highly professional. Obviously, a man heading for the top. Everyone took to him and although he was single, he decided not to live in the mess but take the allocated married quarter that his predecessor had lived in, thus giving thoughtful latitude to the living-in officers.

FOUR

One of the favourite commitments that the officers of the squadron were required to undertake were flag tours into East Berlin. Travelling in pairs in a designated Brigade-allotted vehicle with appropriate markings including a Union Jack flag, they were given the unique opportunity to represent the Western Allies in the diplomatic and military right to access the Soviet Sector of Berlin. This undertaking was vitally important in ensuring that all the occupying forces of Berlin worked in a spirit of co-operation, although in reality the Cold War at that time was very cold, threatening and highly dangerous to world peace, and Berlin represented the apex of that confrontation. They were young men thrust into a situation that was illuminating but fraught with possible misunderstanding and danger.

Charles always sought Jamie Buckingham, the young officer with whom he had grown up with in the army, to pair up for flag tours, and normally he was successful.

The annual May Day parade in East Berlin to celebrate the continued success of the workers' paradise was due and during the period immediately prior to the parade the British, American and French military authorities increased their flag tours to the maximum allowed. On the day of their tour, Charles and Jamie were duly inspected by the Squadron Leader before their designated car was due to pick them up at Smuts Barracks. As representatives of the British Army's presence in that divided city they had to be immaculate in their turnout, but they also were keen to show their new Squadron Leader that they were on top of their game.

The gleaming black staff car arrived and the young officers were pleased to see the Royal Corps of Transport driver, one Corporal Hancock who had taken them on a previous tour into East Berlin. Corporal Hancock was a man of many parts. He had been in the army since he was a 15-year-old boy and in his long but not so illustrious career he had gone up and down the rank structure on a far too frequent basis, alternating between displaying excellent soldiering qualities, professional knowledge and leadership, and causing alcohol-induced mayhem when it was least expected. He had once reached the dizzy heights of Staff Sergeant. His marriage record was equally turbulent and unpredictable, but it was generally assumed that he did not have a current wife. With his posting to West Berlin, he had settled into his role of driver and was content with his current rank and status.

Over the 18 months he had been with the Brigade Transport Squadron he had made a point of becoming an excellent driver, highly trained in the art of evasive and defensive driving techniques, and of possessing an encyclopaedic knowledge of the layout and street systems of East Berlin. Everybody wanted him as their driver on flag tours. A loyal and sometimes dedicated soldier, he respected those officers whom he saw as competent and human. He did not question orders, but preferred that situations and decisions taken were explained to him as a matter of professional courtesy. Corporal Hancock and Charles formed an easy relationship based on mutual professional respect.

He drove them to Brigade Headquarters at the Olympic Stadium where they received their obligatory briefing from a spotty staff officer. The briefing included times to enter East Berlin and when to return by, suggested routes and points where they could leave the car, although these were few and confined to places of public interest such as museums and the Alexanderplatz in the centre, and significant scope as to gaining of any information on preparations for the forthcoming May Day parade. Corporal Hancock smiled when he heard that as he knew exactly where they needed to go, both to gain useful information and to irritate the Soviets and East Germans. Here stood the difference between the formal briefing and the reality on the ground, which Corporal Hancock knew all about.

And on they went to Checkpoint Charlie, the iconic crossing point into East Berlin and the place where east really did meet west. On the American side, the checks were cursory but designed to ensure that the paperwork was in order and that timings in and out were strictly adhered to. Within the short distance between the American checkpoint and the East German checkpoint, the whole atmosphere changed as the grim reality of the wholly state-controlled Workers' Paradise bore down on them. Against the bustle and brightness of the west only metres behind, everything seemed grey on this sunny late spring day. Faceless tenement buildings stretched before them into the heart of East Berlin and there, to left and right, the reality of the meaning of the Cold War for all to see; the two walls and between them the 'death strip' with watchtowers, the carefully raked mine-field strip, tank traps at key points, razor wire everywhere, dog runs, powerful searchlights, and the patrolling East German soldiers who had orders to shoot to kill any person trying to escape to the west. By 1972 this scar had been developed to a point where it was almost impossible to escape, but attempts still took place. Most were unsuccessful and some lethal.

The Stasi-controlled guard, masquerading as a Grenztruppen der DDR soldier, inspected their papers, went into the guardhouse and after an age, whilst others circled the vehicle with dogs, he reappeared, presented their papers and the barrier was opened. It felt like this was a first foray into enemy territory but there were many of these flag tours happening every week, in both directions. Through the Quadripartite Agreement, flag-tour vehicles were not permitted to be interfered with or searched at any time, but this did not stop the adrenalin from running at a higher level than normal. Corporal Hancock, a man of few words, had said nothing during the crossing, but as they pulled away from the checkpoint he told the two young officers that they were now being followed by a black car in which sat three men in homburgs and presumably, if you had read enough literature on this subject and imagined them as the successors of the Gestapo, long, bulky leather overcoats with the collars turned up.

'This is normal procedure. They will attempt to remain with us throughout the tour and my job is to shake them off so that we can go and visit places more interesting than museums and other so-called tourist attractions,' said Corporal Hancock.

'But we need to first visit the normal spots such as Alexanderplatz and the Pergamon Museum where we can get out, do some walking and rubber-necking and show ourselves,' said Charles. 'After that, we can hopefully do a bit of information gathering in your safe hands.'

They pulled up outside the main entrance to the Pergamon Museum and, leaving Corporal Hancock with the car, sauntered up the impressive steps. They noticed that the dark car was parked a short distance away. A steady pace, both in the car and on foot, was the order of the day for flag tours. The more East Germans who saw this display of Western Allied presence in East Berlin, the better. In their immaculate service uniforms, these two good-looking young officers caused an immediate stir amongst those people who were in the museum at the time; a drab, badly dressed, grey-faced and sallow people against which they shone. Some looks were scornful and dismissive but others, and in particular from those that were younger and female, showed interest and admiration. A group of schoolgirls giggled and whispered amongst themselves. No one was disrespectful. The museum housed a spectacular display of antiquity, Middle Eastern and Islamic art, none of which were of any interest to Charles.

Having firstly noticed that they seemed to be being followed by a man in a homburg and long dark coat, and whilst viewing with ill-disguised disinterest the Pergamon Altar, Charles noticed a young woman on her own and taking a great interest in the Altar. At first sight and from the side she seemed to be remarkably attractive but when she turned towards him and, meeting his eyes, looked directly at him, he felt his heart skip a beat and his throat constrict. At that moment, all thoughts of Greta, which were normally somewhere towards the front of his mind, were banished. He stared unashamedly at her and she at him.

He just enough time to appraise her and see that she was of medium height and with blonde straight hair and a petite and shapely figure from what he could see. But it was her face that transfixed him. Calm, serene and beautiful in a very Eastern European way, and with skin that glowed with a translucence that was mesmerising. His mother would call it a 'peaches and cream' complexion. Brown eyes and a mouth that was perfection. He jumped out of his trance and realised that unless he did something now, the moment would be lost forever and he would never see her again. Talking to a stranger would not be dangerous for him but it could be dangerous for her and he did not want that. He was mindful of the monkey following.

In near desperation, he turned to a pillar and from his wallet took an old receipt and scribbled 'Come here every day at 10 o'clock.' Folding it, he looked around. She was standing there looking at him and he smiled, walked slowly past her and put the note in her gloved hand. He knew that the chances of seeing her again were slim, if not zero, but if he could secure another flag tour in the near future there might be a chance. All he knew was that when their eyes met and held, there existed an immediate bond between them that was difficult to fathom but hopeless to deny.

Back in the car they moved to Alexanderplatz where they strolled in the sunshine amongst a throng of inquisitive people, had a cup of tasteless coffee in a shabby café and strolled slowly back to the car. In the sunshine they noticed with some amusement the reflection from the bright sunshine of a reflected cross on the Fernsehturn, or TV tower, often referred to by Berliners as the 'Pope's Revenge', and an obvious irritation to leaders of the Workers' Paradise. They could not change nature but perhaps they might wish to change that hideous tower?

Once they had left the Alexanderplatz, Corporal Hancock's first mission was to shake off the monkeys behind who had stuck to them like glue throughout. He informed the officers of his intention and then headed east into an increasingly drab and almost desolate urban maze of unknown streets flanked on all sides by grey slabs of tenement blocks, hastily constructed after the war and which looked barely capable of sustaining human life. Few people walked the streets and the roads were almost completely devoid of traffic. This, and not Alexanderplatz and the Mitte, was the reality of the Workers' Paradise. A few trees strove forlornly to provide a splash of spring colour. As he drove into this maze of streets, he increased his speed and used many small side streets, most of which he negotiated through a series of very quick and sudden turns, turned back on himself on a number of occasions and finally came to a halt up a quiet and narrow lane. He had shown undoubted driving skills of the highest order and at no time did Charles or Jamie feel unsafe. Corporal Hancock explained that they would wait there for ten minutes to see if the tail had been shaken off. If not he would repeat the process using different routes until, hopefully, they were successful. After ten minutes no tail appeared, so Corporal Hancock suggested that he could take them to a place where they would be able to enjoy a grandstand view of the Soviet Army's preparations for the forthcoming May Day parade. This was agreed, although Charles' mind was almost completely elsewhere.

The street that they slowly drove down was flanked on one side by the ubiquitous tenements but on the other was a very extensive open area which was protected by a substantial fence, topped with barbed wire. This was obviously a military barracks as beyond the grassed area there was a large expanse of concrete which was obviously a parade ground, and beyond that barracks blocks and hangers. And there on the parade ground sat a large number of Soviet Army vehicles of all descriptions; tanks, armoured personnel carriers, artillery pieces and anti-aircraft weapons, as well a variety of support vehicles. Crawling all over these was at least five hundred Russian soldiers intent on cleaning and polishing and preparing these vehicles for the parade. Corporal Hancock slowed even further so that Jamie could take pictures with the brigade-issued camera. Suddenly there was a shout and within seconds the five hundred came rushing down the slope towards their car, shouting angrily and shaking their fists. They had been seen and it was time to leave but not before a final picture of a furious Russian officer at the fence displaying for convenience his unit's insignia. A most useful piece of intelligence.

The high-speed 'escape' was successful and feeling that they had had enough excitement for one day, and without further incident, they made their way back to Checkpoint Charlie, the inevitable grim guards and sniffer dogs, and then into the west with a feeling of both relief and release.

The flag-tour team were debriefed at Brigade Headquarters and the staff officer was pleased indeed with their report and the photographs they produced, particularly the one showing the insignia of the unit. Charles thanked Corporal Hancock for his outstanding driving and said that they hoped to work with him again soon, all the while thinking of the woman in the museum.

FIVE

Anna Nazarov was an exceptionally gifted and beautiful child who, in her home city of Leningrad, grew into an exceptionally gifted and beautiful young woman. She lived with her parents and twin sister throughout her childhood, during her five years of training to be a doctor and for a final year learning German and English at a language college. A child living with her or his parents in the Soviet Union for this length of time was not usual. The Soviet system placed the needs of the state before that of the family and this meant families were often separated according to the demands of the state and the careers of the parents. Highly qualified parents often worked in 'closed' cities within the Soviet Union and this could mean separation, sometimes for years, from their families. If both parents were highly qualified, it could be that they worked in different cities and away from their children. Grandparents and other relatives took on a far greater significance and influence in children's lives than would generally be the case in the west.

Mikhail and Aleksandra Nazarov were scions of the Soviet state. He was a Political Commissar with the Red Army during the Great Patriotic War and as a young woman she fought with the partisans in the Pripet Marshes in Belarus. Both were lucky to survive the ruthless and barbaric German onslaught through to their subsequent final defeat in Berlin. This personal history imbued each of them with a fierce patriotism and belief in the Soviet state and systems which would stay with them for the rest of their lives. He trained as a scientist and she became a communist party official and they were happy together in a relationship that would endure for as long as their belief in communism. They lived and worked in some privilege, their small apartment was always neat and clean to a fault and they were intensely proud of their two daughters. They were loyal party members who towed the line and always attended the right events in Leningrad. They had no recollection, records or knowledge, nor did they wish to have, of their family history or status before 1917. Before the revolution, their family were minor aristocrats who were erased from history by the Bolsheviks as a matter of policy. This policy was initiated and led by Lenin who was, ironically, a minor aristocrat himself, and furthered by Stalin. They inhabited the present and not the past or future, and they lived for the Soviet state and their daughters. They worked hard and long but knew that they could look forward to a peaceful retirement where they would enjoy all the benefits that the state promised them as loyal and patriotic workers; a generous pension, a home, free medical care and annual holidays on the Black Sea.

Anna, unlike her sister who was compliant and accepting of the system in which she worked as a translator for the party in the Polish and Czech languages and always lived at home, was not so convinced about all this. She possessed a sweet and kind persona combined with a fierce intelligence and determination to progress and be successful within a system which, below the surface, was riddled with corruption, nepotism and, where necessary, brutality. Unlike her parents and sister, she viewed life in terms of where she would like to be, rather than living just for the present and being fearful of the future. She was also interested in her family's past but her few attempts to find out more through conversations with a number of elderly aunts who had survived the trials and tribulations of the twentieth century were met with eyes tinged with sadness but with no information forthcoming.

Anna had grown into a passionate, impetuous and internally rebellious young woman, although like most Soviet citizens, she was expert in the art of keeping one's thoughts to oneself; indeed showing little or no emotion or behaviour that would make a person stand out in a crowd. Still, she often harboured questions on the sustainability and legitimacy of the system of which she was fully a part.

On graduation and the learning of languages, she worked as a junior doctor in a hospital in Leningrad. This further added to her unease. Although the doctors, nurses, auxiliary and administrators were generally highly trained and the equipment and medical methods they used were modern; incompetence, laziness, disregard for patient aftercare and well-being, corruption and interference from above were endemic. She concentrated only on working hard and to the highest standards possible in that unprincipled atmosphere. Her father, by now a man well respected within the party, sensed her unhappiness and made enquiries as to the possibility of her joining the government as a doctor in some capacity. With her father's influence, her undoubted ability and intelligence, her languages and her seeming devotion to the Soviet cause, she was invited to interview for the post of Assistant Medical Officer at the Soviet Union's embassy in East Berlin. There followed an exhaustive process of background vetting of her and her family, medical checks and administrative procedures so lengthy and bureaucratic as to make the most ardent of adherents weep. So it was that in January of 1972 she said goodbye to her parents and sister and travelled to

East Berlin by train, the first time she had left Leningrad in her life.

SHE SOON BEGAN to realise that to be a member of the Soviet Ministry of Foreign Affairs working in an embassy bought some distinct advantages. She travelled first class by train and in a closed carriage, was met at the Ostbahnhof in East Berlin by an embassy driver and taken to the embassy in the Unter den Linden in the Mitte. She was registered and shown to her own apartment which was small but comfortably furnished with a sitting room, bedroom and bathroom. She was informed by the housekeeper that her manager, the embassy doctor, would meet her in his office at 08:30 hours the next morning. Meals were to be taken in the embassy staff canteen downstairs.

To Anna, all of this was quite unexpected and most agreeable. All her life she had shared a bedroom with her sister and now she had independence – and her own apartment!

From the beginning of their relationship, Anton Orlov, the embassy doctor, proved to be a decent, kind and considerate man, as well as being an excellent doctor who had laboured all his professional life under the dead hand of Soviet bureaucratic inertia, incompetence and slovenliness. He held no illusions about the system for which he worked and therefore his attitude towards it was ambivalent. Over the years, he had mastered the art of carefully disguising his inner feelings as to what he considered was a system with no moral compass, whilst at the same time portraying a confident and competent persona who held the best interest of the health of the embassy staff at heart. Even in the early 1970s, this ability to compartmentalise one's life was a growth industry within the Soviet system, and strongest amongst those who had enjoyed the benefits of an extensive education. And it was certainly much more prevalent within the populations of Eastern Europe. To keep one's mouth shut no matter what your inner feelings and thoughts might be, and be a good, loyal citizen, seemed the only way forward.

Being solely dedicated to the embassy staff and their families meant the clientele base was small; but this did not mean that Anna and Anton did not face on a daily basis a wide range of common complaints, illnesses, imaginary or otherwise, and an occasional serious case where immediate repatriation by air back to Russia was needed. The days were always busy either clinically or in ensuring that all records were kept up to date and the ambassador fully briefed on a weekly basis as to health, or otherwise, of his flock. In general, the embassy staff and their families were not healthy in a robust sense but there was never any shortage of treatments and medicines to cure or ward off diagnosed illnesses. This abundance of medical supplies was in direct contrast to the daily dire shortages that existed for the general population of East Berlin, and plainly evident as soon as you stepped outside the embassy gates.

Anton soon recognised Anna's intelligence, knowledge, dedication and work ethic and as their professional relationship developed, he was able to delegate more responsibility to her in the clinic. This was very unusual within the Soviet system where delegation of any kind was considered risky, both for the delegator and the nominee. Fear of failure and consequent retribution meant that delegation was avoided and decision-making remained at the top of the management tree, meaning that normally things were put off or never happened. Everyone within the Soviet system had someone above them. A common joke, never voiced aloud, was that even Stalin had had someone above him – himself.

The busy daily routine of the clinic did not mean that evenings could be spent relaxing at home. There were many social events to attend, both in the embassy and to other delegations in East

Berlin. Both Anton and Anna were normally required to attend and these could be in the form of a cocktail party or a dinner preceded by a reception. Anna suspected, and Anton knew, that her presence was probably because the ambassador found her decorative and elegantly dressed with beautiful manners. She did not demur, not because these events were fun, interesting or glamorous, but because it offered her an insight into the culture of others, something she was keen to develop.

On the rare occasions when she did find herself with a little free time, and taking advantage of the concession that walking out was allowed, she began to geographically and historically piece together East Berlin through walking the streets of the centre, a centre still displaying the evidence of the destruction wrought by Allied bombing and the Red Army in 1945.

To Anna, it seemed that alcohol played a significant role in oiling the diplomatic machine. She found it alarming how much alcohol the embassy staff were happy to drink, whether it be at an official reception where numerous toasts with vodka were proposed, in private rooms and apartments, at home in the married quarters compound if you lived there, or in the barracks where the guards and drivers lived. She soon identified a number of staff who were alcoholics, and many more who habitually drank too much. As far as she could ascertain no one was ever removed from their post, but many of them were regular visitors to the clinic with alcohol-induced illnesses and injuries. Drunkenness also bought unwelcome advances by men who during the day would ignore her. The ambassador was one such hopeful and the other a senior figure who worked as head of the Economics Department. It was, however, an open secret within the embassy that his real position was as head of the KGB and that his role was to head up espionage and counter-espionage activities and operations against the allies in West Berlin and, where there was an overlap, West Germany. His name was Victor Sokolov and he was a bull of a man, a prodigious drinker and womaniser. He had attempted several passes at her but she had managed to adroitly avoid or evade his confident but boorish efforts. She spoke to Anton about it and he advised her that she use avoidance and evasion as her main weapons against this unwanted attention. A delicate balancing act was required. The KGB wielded real power, much more so than the ambassador.

She was also required to attend numerous evening and weekend briefings and lectures. These included those on how to be and remain a good, loyal communist; history lessons on the Great Patriotic War and the Warsaw Pact; briefings on the quadripartite agreement and what it contained including flag tours; general lectures on the inequities of the west in general, and NATO in particular; as well as cultural briefings on East Berlin. Some were interesting but some were excruciatingly tedious, especially those designed to keep you in line. Throughout it all she remained poised, calm and smiling.

Her posting with the embassy was for two years so despite the negatives, and she was mature and sensible enough to know from the beginning that there would always be some, she was determined to use her time well, make a name for herself and where possible enjoy life. She had no interest in men and in those first few months no one amongst the younger members of the embassy staff generated in her any interest at all.

If the effect of the meeting of those eyes and the passing of the furtive note in the Pergamon Museum was remarkable for Charles, for Anna it was a revelation. But their reactions to this event were entirely different. Although generally sensible and straightforward in his manner of thinking and acting Charles was a romantic at heart and, because of his youth and inexperience, weak and naïve when it came to affairs of the heart. He believed that given enough focus and effort everything was possible. He understood that to be able to see her again at the museum would be a very long shot indeed given the restricted number of times he would be able to secure a place on a flag tour, and the highly unlikely chance of her being there when he was. The fact that there was zero opportunity to communicate and that to be seen openly speaking together could place her in danger was not lost on him. But he remained overly optimistic and was determined to see her again. To that end, he typed a carefully prepared note to give her should they meet again. It occured to him that by doing this, he was probably breaking every restriction in the book concerning the passing of personal information to the 'enemy'. In the meantime, he both carried on as normal at work and in the mess and in the evenings rushed into the arms of Greta where the lovemaking sometimes became more frenetic than normal. It was disconcerting that as he made love to her and looked into her face, he could only see that of the woman in the Pergamon.

Unlike Charles, Anna worked on the basis that nothing was possible in a system that was devoid of encouraging any form of initiative or sense of responsibility, and that did not consider romance as especially useful to the furtherance of the socialist cause. Living at home and working hard did not help her interest in the opposite sex, and the few hopelessly fumbling spotty and underfed youths who made a forlorn attempt to kiss her and put their hands inside her clothing did nothing to arouse an interest. But looking at this man did arouse feelings, and although she did not recognise them, they were the classic 'butterflies in the stomach' type.

She resolved to make every effort to go to the museum whenever she had opportunity, at the same time and on that day if possible. With her scant knowledge of flag tours and their frequency she assessed the chances of meeting again as next to zero, and if it did happen what was she or he supposed to do?

SIX

The civilised presence of Charles coming into Sophia's life as her friend and lover was neither by accident, chance or good luck, although she would be first to admit that she found him immensely attractive and an excellent and attentive lover. Her life had been in turmoil for the 18 months before she met him on that fateful evening. Her quiet and unremarkable existence in Rhineland-Westphalia was entirely genuine, but once she received a phone call from a man who referred to himself as Dieter, a blunt and rough voice thanking her for responding to the advertisement he had placed in a local newspaper for a chief of administration for a branch of his pharmaceutical company in West Berlin and would she like to attend an interview in nearby Munster, her life changed irrevocably. She prepared herself very well for the interview but was surprised that she was appointed given her age and previous limited experience. However, the prospect of leaving the sleepy backwater that she had grown up in, and lived and worked in for many years and moving to what seemed like a thriving and very different city excited her greatly.

When she arrived in West Berlin, she was very happy indeed with the pleasant and comfortable Charlottenburg apartment. She took some time to settle into her new position, especially at management level, but was soon enjoying it. The working environment was very organised and busy, and the small team under her co-operative and hardworking. Life seemed good.

One day her manager approached her and informed her that Dieter, the managing director, would be visiting West Berlin and that he had requested a private interview with her the following morning. She of course acquiesced but wondered what it might be about. He turned out to be like his voice, blunt and rough. He was also grossly overweight, pink and sweaty and thoroughly unattractive to look at. With no preamble he informed her that he wanted her to be engaged in a 'special assignment'. There was a need to assist the East German authorities in gaining certain information about specific activities in West Berlin and, because she was from Dresden and her family were still living there, she would be required to do this. She was dumbstruck.

'Are you saying that you wish me to spy for East Germany against the west?'

'Yes.'

'What if I refuse?'

'Two things will happen. Your parents and sister will feel the full force of the state against them and you will lose your job in West Berlin and face an uncertain future.'

Sophia went very pale and felt very sick.

Before waiting for an answer, Dieter ploughed oafishly on. 'In simple terms, and you will be briefed in more detail later, you will initially be introduced to some American officers in West Berlin. From then on you will use your undoubted talents to extract information from them and pass it on to a nominated contact. A third consequence of you not doing as we wish will be that you might find yourself back in East German for *re-education*.'

Sophia managed to whisper, 'There are many, many Germans living in the west who have relatives in the east.'

'You are one of the most exceptionally attractive women that the organisation has seen in its trawl of potential candidates. You have no criminal record. You have never been involved in dissent or politics and to date you have led an entirely unremarkable life. You are not interested in forming relationships with men but you enjoy sex. We have also detected, whilst looking closely at you over the past months, that you possess a certain hardness about your character that will be ideal in your future role. Your manager has your West German passport and we will retain this for the foreseeable future.'

Sophia's heart sank. In a few minutes, her cosy world had been turned upside-down by this bastard.

'You have 24 hours. If your manager does not receive a reply by then, we will assume that you have refused and the actions that I have outlined to you will take place. However, if you do agree your rewards will be substantial and you can stay in the west.'

He left abruptly, while she continued sitting numbly with images of her family incarcerated in a Stasi prison, or probably worse in the hands of the KGB. It was an unbearable thought. She also suspected that even if she was forcibly removed to the east, she would not see them again. What to do? She had no one to turn to as she had made no friends since arriving in West Berlin and could not divulge what she had been asked to do anyway. She alone would have to make the decision.

She went straight home with her mind blank, opened a kitchen cupboard, took out a bottle of schnapps and poured a glass. Normally she would enjoy a small tot in the evenings but today she intended to drink the whole bottle and then see where her mind and desires would take her.

SEVEN

She arrived at the American barracks by taxi and having shown the gate guard her invitation was directed to the officers' mess after showing her ID card and passport. She realised that the checkpoint was at the gate, not the officers' mess, and that this check was indeed cursory. It also crossed her mind that her appearance might have had something to do with how easy her entry was. All this must be stored away for possible future use.

She did look stunning, her natural beauty complimented by her tight-fitting black dress, immaculately applied make-up and her golden mane of hair. Heads turned as she entered and having secured a glass of champagne from a very attentive waiter she was led, as a matter of protocol, to the Major General to say good evening. Behind that smooth military mask, she detected a flicker of interest in his eyes but then he was gone. Almost immediately she was surrounded by a number of the younger officers. Smartly attired in their military dress uniforms, they were friendly, polite, serious and gauche. She found their conversation stilted and it seemed that they were constantly on their guard as what they should or should not say. Perhaps their superior officer was keeping a close eye on them? A number of them had a glass in their hand but they did not drink and most did not have a glass; they were on duty.

As she stood there being admired but not feeling the slightest interest in those around her and their banal conversation, her mind wandered to the events of her immediate past. In those few short weeks she had gone from a reasonably happy and relaxed woman with no real concerns less thoughts of her family in Dresden, to someone who was constantly wary, stressed and with feelings of guilt and inadequacy. The clandestine meetings with the mysterious, unattractive, abrupt and rude German contact by the name of Annette, the telephone calls and codes to remember by heart, the information which was to be memorised, the clearly identified target and setting up of the situation in which she now found herself all proved to be an alien experience for her and she hated it.

SHE RECOGNISED him immediately and quietly congratulated herself. He was tall, slim, good looking in an all-American way and, as it turned out, certainly different to his serious and sober young peers. She politely excused herself from her gaggle of admirers and walked over to where he was propped up against a pillar in a corner of the large and, by now, very crowded and noisy reception room.

'Hello,' he said with an attractive smile.

'Hello.'

'My name is Brad,' he said, holding out his hand.

'And my name is Greta,' she said, smiling and taking his hand. His skin was cool and dry.

They began to exchange pleasantries and she quickly noticed that he was very handsome and polite but his eyes were unfocussed and his speech had a faint slur. He was not sober like his fellow young officers. As they talked waiters were summoned at frequent intervals, and as he drank he became more garrulous, amusing and irreverent. Sophia now realised why this young man had been selected as the target. But he was attractive all the same.

As time progressed, he introduced her to his nightmare world of service in Vietnam. In time, she would become used to his incoherent ramblings on this and many other subjects, none of which she could make much sense of.

Having drunk her self-imposed maximum of two glasses of champagne and passed on to Brad her contact details and secured his, she departed with disappointed male and relieved female heads following her to the door. She had achieved her first step in the game and in a perverse way felt quite pleased with herself.

She called Annette that evening from a phone box on the street where she lived and was given one of the codewords as to where to meet the following morning before work. She met Annette at a bench in the Tiergarten and recounted the evening's events. Annette, a woman of few words and fewer smiles, seemed pleased with the information but hardly showed it.

'Thank you for the information. Please contact me after you have met him again. Remember that the aim will always be to seduce him and to extract information from him at opportune moments, whether he is sober or not.'

The meeting was short and to the point. They always would be.

Brad called her at home the following evening. Whilst initially confused to find a note with her name and telephone number in his pocket, he soon remembered the vision he had met.

'Hello Greta. This is Brad. How are you? I apologise for my inebriated state last night. I hope you'll forgive me?'

'Very nice to hear from you, Brad. I have forgotten about it already,' she said with false sincerity. She clearly recalled that by the end of their first meeting he was becoming a bore and seemed to be incapable of noticing that he was irritating both her and those around them.

'Would you like to meet up? Tomorrow is Sunday and we could go for a walk down by the lakes and then have some lunch.'

'That would be lovely. Thank you.'

They made arrangements and the next day spent a pleasant morning strolling along the lakeside of the Wannsee and Brad ventured to hold her hand, a move Sophia did not resist. He was charming and amusing and told her about his position at the headquarters. He was one of three junior officers assigned to support the General and his staff in the planning, preparation and application of the defence of West Berlin, information that Sophia logged carefully in her brain. Another reason why he had been selected. He did most of the talking and she smiled and pressed the side of her body against him as they walked and talked. All was pleasant until they stopped for lunch at a lakeside restaurant.

They ordered food but Brad also ordered a bottle of wine and before that a beer. Sophia drank mineral water but made no comment on his obvious desire to drink alcohol. She felt that perhaps he wished to rid himself of his hangover. She had also decided that she would never discourage him, or make any comment on his drinking. One bottle of wine turned into two and then three. He became steadily more talkative, noisy and embarrassing. His loud voice caused staid West Berliners to turn and shake their heads. Eventually he paid up and they left, much to the relief of the restaurant's clientele and staff. On the way home he sat slumped in his seat on the tram whilst Sophia, sitting next to him, closed her mind to his condition and concentrated on getting him back to her apartment.

Later, looking at him sleeping she saw a young, handsome and fit young man who, when sober, was charming, attractive to be with and wholly non-threatening. When not sober he clearly showed symptoms of a troubled mind and, it seemed, a desire for alcohol which turned him into a different person. But he was not aggressive or abusive which was a relief; he merely fell asleep when he reached a certain tipping point. A pattern was emerging and she must not discourage it, no matter how distasteful she found it.

She was sitting in her dressing gown when he emerged from the bedroom, bleary eyed and bedraggled. He smiled weakly.

'I am so sorry.'

'I am glad that you were able to sleep well.'

She stood up and let her gown fall to the floor. She was naked less her high-heeled shoes and his eyes focussed very rapidly. Her body was sublime in every respect. She came to him and held him close.

'Now that you have had a look, what do you think?'

'You are completely beautiful.'

His hand caressed her back and moved down to her perfectly formed bottom. She kissed him on the lips and slid her tongue into his mouth. He did not resist initially, but then pulled away to hold her by her shoulders and look at her.

'I must be going. We have important meetings tomorrow and I need to get my act together this evening and have a good night's sleep.'

'Would you like to come to dinner on Wednesday evening? I can cook something delicious.'

She put her gown back on but not until she was sure he had seen between her legs as she bent down. She showed him to the door, giving him a fleeting kiss as he left, dressed and waited for 30 minutes and then walked out to another phone box to call Annette.

SHE MADE the very best effort to produce a classic German meal. She decided that it would be Schnitzel with pomme frites, peas and carrots with a complimentary pepper-based sauce, followed by Black Forest gateau with cream. She was happy with cooking the main course but decided that the pudding was beyond her. That would have to be bought and like everything else, including three bottles of wine, the receipt would land on someone else's desk.

Brad was on time and dressed casually. She was happy that he was not wearing a baseball cap that he would have undoubtedly worn inside even when eating. He was pleased to see her and she kissed him on his lips. He had bought a bottle of wine and therefore Sophia was confident that by the end of the evening she would be able to persuade him to stay the night. When she was in the kitchen and he on the balcony, sipping his first glass of cold white wine, she thought what a strange man he was. A Jekyll and Hyde character. In normal circumstances, and if he did not rely so much on alcohol, she would have been happy to try a meaningful relationship. But this had to be different and she hardened her heart and focussed on the knowledge that his position must be at the centre of the American military presence in West Berlin.

Brad ate everything put in front of him, threw back the wine and talked with enthusiasm. Sophia stuck to her two glasses only rule but as the line of empty wine bottles grew longer, Brad descended into the now familiar pattern of behaviour; loud and noisy, more incoherence, more incomprehensibility and finally asleep in the chair he was sitting on at the table.

This time Sophia undressed him and put him to bed. She looked at his body and it was obviously hardened by constant exercise. Like his handsome face, it was very attractive but she noticed on his lower back three scars that had obviously been caused by bullets entering his body. As it was still relatively early she cleared up, got undressed and slipped naked into bed beside him. He did not stir and he did not snore which was a relief. It was strange to have a man's body next to her and as she dozed off she thought how ironic it was that here she was, the seductress, lying with a man who probably had had much more experience than her in these matters.

He awoke early, pattered to the loo and returned to bed, discarding his boxer shorts as he did so. He ran one hand gently over her back and she turned to face him. They embraced and kissed in a languorous manner. Feeling his hardness against her she straddled him, sat up with her hands on his hard, muscular chest and without further ado made love to him. He looked at her with passion and marvelled aloud at her perfect breasts and hips. She did not change position and it was not long at all before their mutual desires were spent and, as a new phenomenon for both of them, at the same time. She lay back and stared at the ceiling, knowing them that she had achieved the first step in her seduction. She felt that he was hooked and it surprised her that she could be so cold-hearted about it because she genuinely liked him. Now she had to begin the far, far more difficult task of turning his drunken ramblings into some form of coherent sense by beginning the process of carefully and slowly probing around the questions that were firmly planted in her head. Or maybe he would be so enamoured of her that information could be gained without the need for alcohol?

Their relationship blossomed to a point where she knew she could not encourage it further. She neither encouraged nor discouraged his drinking; physically they were well matched and the lovemaking became more passionate and more adventurous. She did not hold back and not only acquiesced to his desires and requests which were moderate, but also took the lead on many occasions. But she never lost sight of why she was doing this and remained an actress, and a very good one at that. She briefed Annette regularly and the response was always favourable, if somewhat muted and certainly lacking in warmth. As time passed, she began to know him better and he proved to be an unusual man. When sober he was decent, kind, considerate and displayed all the signs of an educated and civilised man. He was obviously good at his job, seemed to hold a considerable level of responsibility, and he possessed a remarkable ability to show no signs of his prodigious drinking habits the next morning. He normally stayed at her apartment when they were together and always left in the early mornings bright and breezy and showing no signs of the excesses of the previous evening.

Brad was an American patriot. He had no doubt that the real evil lay beyond the wall and all the way back to Moscow, and that the duty of America and their allies was not only to counter this clear threat to democracy and freedom, but to aggressively display an intention to use their military might, including the use of nuclear weapons, to counter and defeat that evil. His fellow American officers in West Berlin in the early 1970s also believed this and the military culture that emanated from this belief made for a dedicated group of young men where duty came before all else. But Brad was also different to his fellow officers. His experiences in Vietnam as a young infantry officer, where he won the Bronze Star for gallantry, had affected him mentally and significantly and he sought solace in drink, whereas many others used drugs to alleviate the constant fear of death or injury or worse, the fear of capture by the enemy. When a burst of machine-gun fire ended his active service in Vietnam, it did not end this need both during recovery in hospital in Japan and then back in Maryland, and on his return to active duty. The posting to West Berlin and the position he was assigned to showed that his drinking habits had not been noticed by those who might feel that he was both unprofessional and a security risk. His adeptness at rapid recovery, a dedicated approach to masking his addiction and an ability to work long and hard with intelligence and distinction saw him through. West Berlin, with its endless parties and vibrant nightlife, was a paradise for someone like Brad.

'You never talk about your work. Is it interesting?'

They were walking and holding hands in the Grunewald on a Friday evening. He stopped and turned to her.

'I never talk about my work except when I am at work,' he said, smiling thinly.

'I expect that you are under some form of security restrictions?'

'Yes. Up to the highest level of military classification.'

Later that evening, they went to their favourite restaurant in Charlottenburg and after Brad had consumed his normal intake of a number of martinis followed by at least two bottles of wine they made their way back to her apartment. He was mellow, not too drunk and very attentive. On arrival he sought further alcohol in the fridge and Sophia could see the usual pattern emerging. He rambled on about Vietnam, his family back in America, his fellow officers and their strengths and weaknesses in his opinion, and their relationship and how wonderful he thought it was. But never once, even when she would have thought that the amount of alcohol he had consumed would have loosened his tongue, did he speak about anything to do with his work. He eventually fell asleep in his armchair and she left him there. She began to feel that this was rapidly developing into a dead end.

The morning lovemaking – it was always in the morning with Brad unless they had sex outside, which happened very occasionally – was particularly enjoyable, varied and passionate. He never spoke a word during the intimacy or afterwards, but his eyes told her he was in love with her.

The meetings with Annette became less frequent as there was nothing to report. It seemed he was a closed book when it came to his work and she was at a loss as how to proceed. She was also becoming increasingly irritated by his incessant drinking, a feeling that she showed from time to time but he ignored. She knew that she was probably third in his private list of priorities; his job and then alcohol and then her.

One morning, following yet another mammoth weekend drinking session, Sophia decided enough was enough. She contacted Annette.

'I am afraid to tell you that you have selected the wrong man. I know him well enough now to know that he will not furnish you with any of the information you seek. I have been patient and although I have not asked him any direct questions, I have tried very hard to find a chink in his armour. There is none. My only suggestion to you would be to try to find another target. What about the British or French? They would surely be privy to the same information you are seeking?' She sighed loudly. 'I did my best but he was the wrong man.'

THREE DAYS LATER, she was summoned by Annette who informed her that a way forward would be to persuade Brad to seek invitations to social occasions from the British. The French were no good. The Americans withheld information from everybody and the Americans and British withheld information from the French. The French regarded their American and British allies with a certain disdain, borne of a possible inferiority complex, and sought to maintain their independence from both. France was not part of NATO and although this, in theory, should not have precluded them in any way from full participation within the tripartite partnership in West Berlin, it did in certain areas. This could be traced back to the war where, having proportionally done little fighting compared to the Americans, British and Canadians the French demanded and got what was considered by many as a disproportionate share of the victors' spoils, including their own sector in West Berlin. In any case, Sophia did not speak French and therefore language was bound to be an obstacle given the French determination to always speak it rather than English.

Sophia invited Brad around for supper and asked, in passing, if he knew any British officers in West Berlin. He said he did as they often met during joint staff exercises and social events.

'I would love to visit a British officers' mess. I have heard that they are full of history and elegance.'

'Better than the American version then,' he said with more than a hint of sarcasm.

'Go on, darling. It would be fun and I have read that they are always generous hosts.'

Brad and Sophia were duly invited by Giles Hackett to a dinner and dance at the officers' mess of Smuts Barracks.

EIGHT

Annette, Sophia's handler and not her real name, was a classic product of the all-encompassing socialist system that was rapidly introduced into East German once the Soviets had successfully imposed the government of their choice on that country and its people. However, unlike the majority of other Eastern Europeans who found themselves under the Soviet yoke in those early years after the end of the war, the East Germans, with their population haemorrhaging to the west at an alarming but not unsurprising rate, and their former industrial base stripped to the bone by the vengeful Russians, embraced the communist creed with an enthusiasm that was unnerving. This enthusiasm spawned a society where the state, with all its classic Germanic efficiency, exerted its control over the people in many ways, not the least the creation of their own secret police, the Stasi, and with it a policy of creating an extensive web of citizen informers that could and did spy and report on any fellow citizen whose words or actions they considered detrimental to the wellbeing of the workers' paradise. Hence the Stasi became synonymous with the development of a system that would ultimately directly affect and control the entire population of East Germany, in both subtle and not so subtle ways.

Hailing from Rostock and four when the war ended, Annette found herself in an orphanage and then a state-run institution that sought to train ardent and committed communists for inclusion into the state system. Life was grim, grey and utterly devoid of any form of human love or affection. She was the true product of a system where the needs of the state and its avowed policies covering all aspects of life always came before the needs of the individual. She almost inevitably found herself in the employment of the Stasi and with her unseeing devotion to the cause rose rapidly within its ranks to reach her current position in East Berlin; an agent controller who was trusted to work in the west and report directly to Soviet masters. Although union with a member of the opposite sex was not discouraged by the state, she did not attract men. Indeed, she frightened them away with her ruthless focus on the task in hand. She remained confused about her sexual orientation but never asked herself why this might be.

Colonel Victor Sokolov considered her one of his best middle-order agents, with her devotion not only to the critical cause of undermining the west in every conceivable way, but the way in which she was so thorough in her approach to work and, as she had progressed up the slippery pole of promotion and mistrust within the Stasi, her ruthlessness and cruelty in her dealings with those that, through the informant system, had proved not to be worthy of the workers' paradise. Ruthlessness and cruelty were characteristics to which Victor Sokolov could entirely relate.

If there was ever a man who could exemplify the Soviet Union and the way in which they had successfully changed human nature in millions of Russians, Victor Sokolov was a perfect example. Despite communism, Victor was still a Russian first and foremost; his ancestors had been serfs in Romanov days but post-1917 his family had embraced Bolshevism through the desire to shake off their harsh peasant past where life was considered primeval, vicious and short. There existed a constant appetite for violence and a belief in the brutal overthrow of the Romanov dynasty. Despite their lowly peasant ancestry, his parents had found themselves as stalwarts of the new order where all were equal, but some were more equal than others. His parents gravitated to the cradle of the revolution, Saint Petersburg, soon to be renamed Leningrad, where the young Victor grew up. He too embraced communism although he had little or no choice, and in his formative years displayed all the norms of both a Russian and a dedicated Bolshevik. Further in Victor's case, and although he was not particularly clever or intellectual, he possessed a wealth of experience in the arts of manipulation and cunning.

Victor Sokolov had fought as a young officer with the Red Army throughout the Great Patriotic War and survived. He was amongst the first of the Soviet troops to enter Berlin and was decorated for bravery on a number of occasions. Hardened utterly by the barbarity of the German assault and occupation of his motherland, he considered the rape of German women and girls once he had entered East Prussia as a duty, and also a duty to be obeyed by the men he commanded. The lives of Germans, young and old, meant nothing to him and their fate even less. His war also taught him that disregard for human life was a virtue and that the west, in the form of the Americans and the British, were soft and contemptible in the manner in which they viewed a free and democratic post-war Europe. This contempt for the west was to remain a cornerstone of his bigoted and dogmatic thinking thereafter.

On leaving the Red Army on demobilisation at the end of the war, Victor's exemplary war record gave him access into the lower ranks of the KGB where he began his long and distinguished career working within the murky world of a secret service. Most deeds of most secret services are murky, but the modus operandi of the KGB at the height of the Cold War in Europe reached a level of callous disregard for any human norms that might impinge on their determination to undermine and eventually destroy the west. Torture and murder were considered part of the equation and the display of any emotion towards the morality of what they were doing would be met at best with derision, and at worst with disgrace and dismissal, normally to a 'corrective' environment deep in Soviet Russia.

Victor Sokolov was a short, stocky and overweight brute. He possessed great physical strength and a capacity for energetic hard work and attention to detail that more than compensated for his lack of mental agility and intellectualism. As head of the KGB section in East Berlin he was responsible for all surveillance and counter-surveillance operations in West Berlin and, where there was cause, into West Germany as well. It was he, on orders from the Lubyanka, who laid the plans to groom Sophia Voight and thereafter to put her in a position she was unlikely to resist. They needed answers to questions that were considered of strategic importance to the Soviets in their never-ending quest to gain the upper hand over the west and their plans to defend West Berlin, both internally and with assistance from their forces in West Germany.

While Victor Sokolov's long-suffering wife lived in Moscow with their teenage son, he spent most of his time in his office, a space dominated by portraits of Lenin, Stalin and the current incumbent, Nikita Khrushchev, all glaring down approvingly on the bull of a man behind the imposing desk, chain smoking and running an efficient organisation. He was a prodigious drinker of vodka, and only vodka with never anything added, and yet this all day and most of the night drinking seemed to have no discernible effect on his drive and energy. He liked to drink on his own and ensured that there was always a cache of bottles available in his office and living quarters. He hated official embassy functions, particularly when western diplomats, East Germans and other worthies were present. Victor Sokolov was also an addicted womaniser, whether embassy staff, East Germans or any other unsuspecting female that might cross his path. In planning his conquests, he aimed for the use of his desk or the nearby small conference table as the ultimate in achieving his essential but unfeeling sexual gratification. He was surprisingly successful given his unappealing appearance and his coarse, ill-mannered approach; but he exuded power and an animal-like attraction which generated in some women equal parts fear and fascination.

Victor Sokolov's carefully manufactured plans to honeytrap a member of the American general's staff right at the centre of the allied presence in West Berlin took a hard knock when he heard the American officer had proven to be a dead loss. His ever questioning and suspicious mind asked if perhaps the agent tasked with extracting the desired information might be at fault but Annette, with her equally suspicious mind, felt confident enough to tell him that this was indeed a blind alley.

Even by the standards of the paranoia existing within the Soviet system, Victor rarely felt vulnerable. He lacked imagination and this, coupled with an unshakeable confidence in his own abilities, endowed him with a self-confidence that was rare in the world in which he lived and worked. But he felt vulnerable now given the critical importance of the information that his masters in Moscow were demanding. The Lubyanka was not a pleasant place to visit in an unofficial capacity. When Annette suggested that the agent should try a different approach with the British, he readily agreed and gave Annette carte blanche to pursue this new line, with the caveat that time was of the essence.

Victor Sokolov had wasted no time in identifying the newest arrival to the embassy; the assistant doctor who was a young and stunning beauty, and in his over-confident perverted one-track mind, ripe for conquest. Subtlety with women was not Victor's game. His success rate had told him that playing the long game with women with a mixture of charm and patience was a waste of time and effort. If his blunt and bull-like tactics did not work, he would move on to the next intended victim, and it seemed that there was no shortage.

In the case of the young doctor, his efforts to secure a quick conquest with the possibility of having regular access to sex on his doorstep for the foreseeable future were met with a polite but firm rebuff. He could see that there was steel in this woman and no apprehension in her eyes. This made him more determined to persevere. However, none of his further efforts met with any progress at all and he finally gave up and moved on. But he did experience an almost unique twinge of regret which lingered and was not helped by seeing her every day in the corridors and canteen of the embassy.

NINE

L ife for the armoured squadron continued to be hectic and hard work, if unvaried. The constant cycle of training, manoeuvres and briefings, as well as the need to ensure that the vehicle fleet was at one hundred percent readiness 24 hours a day, kept everyone busy. The now not so new squadron leader had overturned Buttocks' divisive regime and welded the squadron into a happy and effective team. All were appreciative and this was clearly shown in the energy and interest they displayed in their work and play.

Charles knew that an army career was for him and he continued to excel in his job as a Troop Leader. He also occasionally spent time in the evenings after dinner in his room studying the art of armoured warfare, as well as reading widely on military history. Despite this he could never be considered by his fellow officers as a bore and swot because when he was in the mood, he was in line with the best of party animals. He was a man who could hold his drink to a remarkable degree and would think nothing of staying up all night, either in the mess with his fellow officers and perhaps a few initially coy but ultimately willing young ladies, or touring the night spots of the city, a city that never seemed to rest. With the beautiful Greta as his constant companion, it seemed that life was good, but there was always a nagging doubt. He knew that he could not have chosen a more beautiful and pleasing woman and that he was the envy of every other male he had encountered whilst with her. But his feelings persisted that there was something missing in their relationship. Perhaps it was a cultural thing but he always felt that she was holding something back. He often told himself that it was his imagination and that he was being over-sensitive, but it worried him that she only focussed on the present and never the past or the future; even decisions on the next day's or week's plans were difficult to discuss.

Coupled to this doubt were his constant thoughts about the woman from the museum. Much as he tried, he simply could not get her out of his mind. Their meeting of eyes was only a fleeting glance, but it was enough to hook him entirely, and her look in return convinced him that the feeling was mutual. Consequently, he was in danger of making a nuisance of himself by constantly attempting to be included on as many flag tours as possible. He had adjusted his carefully crafted note to her many times.

I do not know if you speak English but I hope that you do.

You are quite the most beautiful woman that I have ever seen and I so much want to meet you and get to know all about you. I know that this will be difficult, if not impossible, but I will try my very best to make it happen.

As I mentioned in my very short note to you, if you could come the same spot in the museum as much as you can during weekdays then I will do the same and perhaps we may see each other again. It may not be possible but we can try. If we do meet then I will pass you this message.

Perhaps you may be able to suggest the best way to meet in the future? I realise that I must come to the east using my diplomatic military status as you cannot come here.

I am British, twenty-five years old, and my name is Charles.
I hope that we meet soon
With all best wishes to you,
Charles

He knew that what he was trying to do was probably the longest shot in history, but being ever the born optimist, he believed it might be possible, given a large dose of good luck.

OVER THE COMING MONTHS, Charles partook in three flag tours and on each occasion, he insisted on a visit to the Pergamon Museum. He stopped inviting Jamie to be his fellow officer on these occasions. There was the problem of the Hombergs following them and what they surmised as to this obvious pattern. Orders were that flag-tour routes were to be varied and unpredictable to the 'enemy', but these were not. On each occasion, he was disappointed. She was not there. He began to think he was being unrealistic and ridiculous and that he should be happy with what he had and forget about her. He decided he would give it one more try when he was able to secure another place on a flag tour, and if she was not there he would call it a day. His head told him that this was the sensible way ahead but his heart could not accept that he would never see her again, let alone meet her, know her name or anything about her.

He did not know what nationality she was but if she was East German or any other nationality from Eastern Europe the chances of striking up any form of connection in the deeply paranoiac, suspicious and watchful atmosphere that pervaded every corner of society in East Germany at the height of the Cold War were virtually nil. He also knew that it was forbidden for any East German to speak to someone from the west and, given the almost all-encompassing influence of the Stasi-informer network, virtually impossible to avoid being seen in those circumstances. Even should they be successful in being able to pass notes at agreed places and times, any chance of actually being together in a normal environment were again next to zero. But he found he must see where this whole mad and hopeless escapade would lead.

Working on the basis that if this was his last throw of the dice he might as well look good for the occasion, he spent an inordinate amount of time preparing himself and making sure that he looked immaculate, then sallied forth to the Brigade headquarters at the Olympic Stadium and then on to Checkpoint Charlie and into the east. This time he was accompanied by a young officer from the Royal Engineers squadron, and being an 'old hand', had been instructed to show him the ropes. The driver was also relatively new to the game but nevertheless a very good driver and seemed to know most of the main roads within the city. Charles' request to stop at the Pergamon museum drew little interest from the pair. The black car and the Homberg had dutifully slipped in behind them once through Checkpoint Charlie, and when the British vehicle stopped outside the museum, one of them followed the officers inside. The rule was that flag-tour officers must always remain together. However, once inside Charles explained to the young officer that he wished to see a certain artefact and that it would be fine if they met up again in 20 minutes by the entrance. The young officer, although having been briefed to the contrary, accepted this and before the Homberg was inside Charles had taken his familiar circuitous route, turned right and then left and made his way to the spot where he had first seen the lady. He was right on time. He felt for the envelope in his pocket and folded it into his hand.

She was standing there in exactly the same spot as she had been when they first saw each other. He had checked behind him on a number of occasions and the Homberg had obviously followed his young companion. There seemed to be no one around in this distant corner of the museum and, knowing that time was of the essence, he walked straight up to her.

'Hello. My name is Charles.'

'Hello. My name is Anna.'

Apart from being almost bowled over by her beautiful face, he was taken aback by her English.

'Please take this.'

He quickly gave her the envelope and she equally quickly put it into her handbag. She in turn handed him a piece of folded paper which he stuffed in his pocket. For a brief moment he allowed his eyes to rest on her lovely face, her blonde hair and her neat, small and shapely body, accentuated by the tight-fitting coat belt. She in turn looked him in the eye with a smile on her face. His heart melted and he thought that he might look foolish in front of her.

'The best way to meet is through a diplomatic social event,' she said in accented but excellent English. 'Goodbye.'

She gave him one last lingering look and then turned and was gone. He stared after her and felt both elated that he had finally met her, and deflated that she had abruptly left. At least he now knew her name. He felt for her note in his pocket and then hurried back to the entrance to see the young officer approaching from the opposite direction. The Homberg appeared and was looking both perplexed and annoyed. Charles and the young officer strolled unhurriedly to the car waiting outside.

'Not very interesting,' said the young officer. 'Afraid I'm a bit of a peasant when it comes to that sort of thing.'

'It can be interesting,' said Charles with a half-smile on his face. 'Depends which part of the museum you visit.'

The remainder of the tour passed in a haze for Charles. He kept thinking about what her note to him contained and could not wait to get back to the privacy of his room in the mess to read it. He occupied himself by explaining to the young officer as much as he could about East Berlin as it passed by their windows, and in particular the manner in which the majority of the German population lived their grey, dull and poverty-stricken daily lives. Once the rubble of the war had been cleared and the east of Germany had been ruthlessly stripped of all its remaining industrial worth by the Russians, the emphasis had been on providing the ever-dwindling German population with the minimum to live on. Many of the older buildings of pre-war Germany, if they had survived the bombing or Russian onslaught, were dilapidated and bullet marked, whilst those that had been hurriedly thrown up since were faceless and depressing tall blocks of concrete. What you could not see from the lifeless, neglected and dirty streets was what conditions were like within; rat-infested rabbit hutches where there was intermittent electricity and water supplies and lavatories were shared. There was normally no refrigeration and the closely packed and uncivilised living conditions in these tenements meant that although there was little violence, people drank a lot and there was normally little love lost between neighbours. To add to this misery was the ever-present awareness of the Stasi and their informer system. Apart from loyal and trusted top party members, and even they were normally under surveillance, and the Stasi themselves, no one in the workers' paradise was exempt from the eye of the state. Charles couldn't think of a worse place to live.

The flag tour was not a success because Charles was almost wholly preoccupied with the note he had in his pocket. The debriefing was short as little intelligence or useful information had been gained, but the young Royal Engineer officer was effusive in his thanks to Charles for giving him such a useful and informative insight into the realities of East Berlin.

On arrival back at the mess, Charles poured himself a cup of tea and went up to his room and changed into mufti. He opened the note and in its very fluent and grammatically correct English, he read:

Dear English Gentleman,

When I met you and saw you in the museum, I was very shocked. Never in my life have I seen such a beautiful man. I wanted to see you again and try to get to know you.

I am Russian and come from Leningrad. I am a doctor and work at the Soviet embassy in East Berlin. I shall be in Berlin for at least two years, maybe longer. I have time off to myself and try to visit all the places of interest but sometimes I think I am being followed.

I thank you very much for passing me your message. It made my heart very happy. I went back to where we met as much as I could but that was not very much. As I write this message, I have decided that if you are not there this time I will not go again, which makes me very sad. I also worry that someone may notice my trips.

If I meet you again I will give you this, but to be seen with you and to talk to you is very dangerous for me. I would be sent back to Russia in disgrace and my family would suffer.

In my opinion, the best way to meet is at an official embassy function as I have to attend all of them. Therefore, if you can find a way, I would be so happy.

Yours respectfully,

Anna Nazarov

He read it three times and what he read warmed his heart greatly.

Thereafter, Charles took it upon himself to discreetly inquire as to the frequency of British diplomatic and military links to the Soviet embassy in East Berlin and how this manifested itself in such events as official receptions or other types of liaison activities. He was well aware that given the poisonous diplomatic and military atmosphere that existed between east and west at the time, these events might be few and far between. He also realised that in order to progress he needed to secure a contact in the

British Consulate. He had met such a person some weeks ago at a party thrown at the consulate and he now saw an opportunity to invite him for dinner at the mess. Once a week it was required that all officers, married or single, dine in and that black tie was worn. These formal evenings sought to further enhance an esprit de corps. Guests were encouraged and this seemed an ideal opportunity to further his discreet inquiries.

TEN

Despite Charles' determination in his efforts to meet Anna, and his unlikely success so far, he continued to spend most of his free time with Greta. His naturally kind and pleasant persona meant he continued to treat her with great respect and consideration, as well as being an energetic lover, as was she. They were never lost for words but could also easily spend many quiet times together. They both enjoyed a party and in West Berlin there were many of those. You could go out every night if you wanted to but Charles and Sophia, because of their respective jobs, chose the weekends as the time to carouse and arouse. Both enjoyed good food and wine, as well as the company of others in small doses. Both worked hard and kept fit. Sometimes they went running together through the Grunewald or Tiergarten, followed by a very intimate shower together. It seemed to others that their relationship was perfect; two handsome young people who were friendly, engaging, sociable and obviously very much in love.

The truth was different. Both in their own ways were living a lie. Sophia was living a big lie, a lie she knew she could never divulge despite her ever-growing feelings of affection and harmony towards him. Unlike Brad he was straight, decent, affectionate but a man who was never out of control, although sometimes a little unfocussed in a rather charming way. He had a style and presence about him. She always wanted to be with him but could never let herself go to the point where she could tell him all. She felt constant guilt but this did not subsume her determination to honour and protect her family. If the situation was different and she was free of this Sword of Damocles hanging over her, she would be ready to be with him forever.

Charles' lie was that he convinced himself his actions were not dishonourable but rather because he believed he could love more than one woman at a time, and they could happily love him back. Only later experience would tell him otherwise.

ON ENTERING THE OFFICERS' Club in West Berlin, one entered a different world in a different time. The club was run on the lines of a rather shabby and gentile gentlemen's club in London but where elderly Polish waiters in stiffly starched white coats served drinks to seated members and took orders for lunch or dinner. There was nothing so vulgar as a bar. Lunch or dinner could be taken in the dining room, a room stuffed full of oil paintings of grim-looking military types, and tables elegantly laid out to enable guests to enjoy the hardly edible food but rather excellent wine cellar. Meals could also be taken in the main hall which contained a dancefloor surrounded on three sides by tables and there one could eat the hardly edible food listening to the elderly Polish string quartet and their superb music. Dinner could be followed by dancing but nothing more energetic than what the quartet could muster. It was all very civilised and relaxed and the parties that the club put on from time to time were equally civilised and enjoyable, although they could turn noisy and riotous dependent on the clientele and amount of alcohol consumed.

The party Charles and Sophia attended could have been no more exciting than normal, but on this occasion, for no apparent reason, it had attracted a number of like-minded younger officers and their ladies who were determined to have a good time. And a good time they had; dancing on tables, champagne by the bucket at midnight and beyond, a number of failed attempts of strip-tease and all accompanied by a continuous cacophony of raucous and high-spirited voices and laughter.

Charles and Greta got back to her apartment at three in the morning. Greta had restricted herself to her normal two glasses of wine although she did allow a glass of champagne to slip through her net. Charles, however, was in his cups and talkative and amorous at the same time. This was the first time she had seen him like this. She calculated that if she asked a few questions he would probably answer her and not remember what he had said the following morning. She poured him a nightcap and they sat close together on the sofa.

'You hardly ever talk about your work, Charles. I know you're with the armoured squadron but what do you actually do on a day-to-day basis?'

He rambled on about life in the squadron, information that she stored in her brain but knew would be of little interest to her controller. But then he said, 'The most interesting part of the job is knowing about what we would have to do in an emergency. You know, if the Russians invaded West Berlin and West Germany. It is all very secret, you know, but very interesting.'

With slurred speech and some incoherency, he proceeded to tell her about how the British brigade, in close coordination with the Americans and the French, intended to defend West Berlin until such time when NATO in the west could relieve them. She had to concentrate hard on absorbing all the information that flowed from him. From time to time, she went into the kitchen to refresh his drink and managed to write down many of the main points. In the interim, he continued to ramble until eventually falling asleep. She put him to bed, marvelling as always at the perfection of his body. She went back to the kitchen and wrote down what Charles had told her. Not being a military expert, it was not easy but at the end she believed she had made a good fist of it all. She secreted her notes and slipped into bed beside him, feeling the hardness of his chest and looking at his gentle face, breathing easily and soundlessly.

The following morning as they sat having breakfast, she asked him if he could remember what he had talked about when they came home. He confessed that he could not. She smiled her sweet smile and told him he had burbled about how much he loved her and other nonsense, most of which she could not understand.

ELEVEN

On leaving the museum, Anna tarried for a while to make sure she was not being observed or followed. It seemed no one was aware of what had just happened but she knew that if someone was, she would know soon enough once she was back inside the embassy. However, she had an advantage. There was an acknowledged disconnect between the day-to-day activities of Russians working in East Berlin and East Germans and their ever-prying fellow citizens. The Stasi kept well clear of the Russians.

She went straight back to work although it was her one day off a week and made sure that all medical records were in order, listed what needed to be followed up on in the morning and ensured that all appointments for the following week were logged and either herself or Anton were assigned to each patient. She worked diligently, though her mind was in turmoil. She had had a chance to study him a little more closely and what she saw she liked very much. Tall and athletic in build with a very handsome face. He seemed to smile a lot and his eyes were eyes of kindness and thoughtfulness. She knew that what she was doing was completely forbidden and against all rules and regulations, of which she had been exhaustively briefed since her arrival. But this could not stop her heart ruling her head and yearning to see him again.

When she had made sure that all was in order in the clinic and that she had left a note on Anton's desk explaining to him what she had done and with a list of his appointments for the next day, she ate briefly in the canteen and then went to her room.

Sitting on the loo, she opened Charles' note with trembling hands and read the contents with a growing sense of pleasure and excitement. When she had thoroughly absorbed the contents, she carefully burnt the note and made sure that the ashes had disappeared down the lavatory.

TWELVE

Following a curt greeting from the normally severe and humourless Annette as they sat on a bench in the Tiergarten, Sophia produced her report. This provoked an immediate rebuke from Annette, who reprimanded her that any information gained must never be written down, only memorised. Sophia listened to this young harridan and decided that she was not going to take this type of rude and dismissive treatment any longer. She was worth a lot to them and that this had been borne out by the manner in which they had willingly agreed to allow her to try again following the debacle with Brad.

'I would rather you did not speak to me like that. It is very rude and unnecessary.'

Sophia noticed a very slight shadow of doubt in her superior's eyes.

'I have no knowledge of military matters and it would have been impossible for me to remember everything I heard. The information you have asked me to find out about is difficult for me and therefore I will continue to write it down. If you do not like this, so be it. Please do not be unreasonable.'

There was a moment's silence.

'Shall we further discuss this or would you like to take it away with you and we can decide on our next meeting now,' said Sophia, no longer prepared to accept the other woman's abrupt attempts at dominance.

Annette carefully placed the papers into her inside breast pocket, stood up and said in a gentler voice, 'If you could call me at seven o'clock in the morning on Tuesday, that would be appreciated.'

Sophia looked at her back as she walked quickly away. She had a half smile on her face because she had defied this unpleasant woman and met no resistance, but thought little of the monumental importance of the information she had provided that might prove to be so vital to foes of the west, and how damaging it could be to the west's defence of West Berlin and ultimately Western Europe. She had no idea that she, a mere pawn in the great Cold War game of espionage and counter-espionage, had possibly passed on information that was of the utmost importance to the Kremlin itself. Her only concern was for the safety and well-being of her parents and sister. As a young German bought up in West Germany where the young wished to forget the Nazi regime, the war and the inconclusive and dangerous present, she had little knowledge and even less interest in the day-to-day tripwire dangers of the military face-off between the opposing forces in Europe.

She called Annette at the appointed time on Tuesday and received the meeting-place code. They met at a seedy café in Wedding and sat in a corner out of earshot, not that this café had many people in it. Sophia was immediately struck by the change in Annette's demeanour. As they greeted each other, she actually offered a wintry smile and ordered two coffees.

'I have passed on the information you gave me and my Oberhaupt wishes you to know that they are very pleased with what you have achieved.'

'Thank you.'

'He inquired as to why you had disobeyed instructions as to the nature of your report. I informed him of your reasons. He accepted this but asked that you be very careful when passing information on.'

There was no apology and nor did Sophia expect one.

'I will.'

'My Oberhaupt also told me that because of the importance of this mission, you are to be given as much freedom of action as is required to achieve our aims.'

'Thank you. Do you have further instructions for me?'

'We are particularly interested in the detail which gave us a certain strategic understanding of military deployment plans in West Berlin. What we would be interested in now is the where, how, when and numbers and types of equipment and numbers of men of these deployment plans in the time of crisis. Looking to the future, and as mentioned before, we are very interested in the alert system employed by the western forces in Berlin and the plans around how NATO intends to relieve Berlin in the event of war.'

Sophia nodded and carefully stored this information. 'I'll be in touch when I have something. The less we communicate the better.'

She felt that she was the one that was now being able to exert some dominance over this woman and it pleased her to do so.

With coffee hurriedly finished they parted company, both ensuring that they were being neither watched nor followed, as far as they could tell.

Afterwards, she called Charles and asked him if he would like to come to dinner in West Berlin on Friday evening. She would book a table at the Wintergarten and they could enjoy a relaxing and romantic evening together.

THE CHRISTMAS of 1972 came and went. Charles took a week's leave and travelled home to his parents in England. The interminable grey and freezing German winter gave way to a more gentle and changeable west-country climate. He resisted the urge to make contact with a couple of old flames and returned to Greta with impatience and bearing gifts from Fortnum & Mason. He noticed that she never went away from West Berlin and when he had asked her would she like to come with him to England, or take a holiday somewhere else in Europe, she politely declined. He thought this odd but surmised that perhaps she was waiting to see how much further their relationship might develop. In essence he avoided thinking too hard about it all and, like her, he focussed on the present. His time in West Berlin would eventually come to an end and what might happen after that was too difficult to contemplate.

THIRTEEN

Charles prepared himself very carefully for the evening. Mess kit was required to be worn and this pleased him as it gave him an undisputable air of an officer and gentleman existing within an organisation where an officer and a gentleman could feel at ease in a regimental world that encouraged that existence, and jealously guarded it whenever necessary. Mess kit was indeed a lady-puller but Charles disliked the obligatory spurs which he considered anachronistic. Where were the horses? More like donkeys these days. He didn't like horses anyway but he supposed there was always the possibility of a young lady of a certain type who might enjoy them. Charles was hardly hirsute but he shaved again that evening just to make sure that he was looking his best. He had told Greta he had to attend an official function but did not say where and she did not question him. He had grown used to her artlessness in these matters.

Three official cars flying the Union Jack took the British party through Checkpoint Charlie and on to the Soviet embassy on the Unter den Linden, dutifully followed by a car full of Hombergs taking up the rear. On arrival they were checked against a list and led to the grand ballroom where the reception was being held. By this stage, Charles was in a state of nervous tension. There had been many times in his life where he was to meet a young lady, but any previous feelings of nervous anticipation paled with his feelings this evening. He suspected that it was a combination of the unknown, the forbidden and not a little desperation.

It took him about two minutes to recognise her across the already crowded room. She looked stunning in a short, close-fitting, black dress, her blonde hair shining and her face radiant. As he walked towards her, but not to her, he knew then that whatever happened in the future this was the woman that he wished to be with. Their eyes met and they both smiled. Despite the all-pervading atmosphere of stiffness and formality of this uniformed occasion, where the tensions and suspicions of Cold War Berlin were ever present, those smiles conveyed a desire to rise above all that and forge a relationship that counted friendship and love between east and west, and probably more, as a hope for the future, a future together although at this stage that was little more than a pipe dream.

He carefully manoeuvred himself so that he became part of a group of American and French officers being hosted by a number of Russian officers who could speak passable English, and one with good French. She was in the group next to his and he had his back to her, so close he could have reached out and touched her. Charles decided to move and joined her group. He introduced himself formally to the six of them, including Anna whose firm handshake came with skin that was cool and dry. She smiled at him, as he to her, but both were acutely aware that any trace of any emotion might well be picked up by the ever-watchful Russians scattered around the ballroom. There was bound to be a number of KGB men amongst them.

Charles fixed himself with this group and so did Anna. Others came and went, which gave ample opportunity for them both to engage in trivial but animated conversation without actually talking to each other. Hopefully that time would come later but he found it very difficult not to cast furtive glances at her. Every time he did this, he saw that she was looking directly at him and her lovely smile remained on her lips.

The evening wore on and as it did the consumption of alcohol became more evident. Vodka, the staple Russian drink of choice, was very popular. The decibel level in the room grew, only punctuated initially by the Soviet Ambassador's short welcoming speech followed by a toast to quadripartite co-operation and friendship in the divided city. Many other uninvited toasts followed by various unknown hosts and guests and these were invariably followed by the throwing of glasses into the nearest fireplace or corner. The time had come for Charles to face up to his urgent need to engage her directly.

'Thank you for your message,' he said as he sidled up to her, standing next to her rather than looking directly at her.

'And thank you for yours. It was so nice to read it.'

The noise levels hid their words and they became emboldened.

'I have discovered that I can probably come over to East Berlin on the either the second or fourth Tuesday of every month, or both and starting in August. Perhaps you could suggest a place to meet which is less public than the museum?'

'The best place is the museum exactly because it is public and because it is relatively easy to shake off your inevitable tail,' said Anna.

Charles nodded and felt relief that the essential information had been exchanged. Both had drunk little but as they talked, they gradually inched closer together until they could have kissed with ease. The urge was there but with difficulty they resisted. They had been together for too long and they needed to move apart and engage with others.

As they shook hands, Charles slipped her a very small note folded into two. *You are beautiful. Until we meet again. Charles x*

As he moved reluctantly away he noticed a large, bull-necked Russian looking at him from halfway across the room. The look turned into a stare but Charles also noticed that he did not look at Anna when she had moved away from him. This was a relief. This man could stare at him as much as he liked and it presented no threat to him. But if he had noticed his badly disguised intimacy with Anna, this could present a threat to her. He re-joined another group, most of whom were talking in loud voices and swaying slightly. The Russians were bellowing and hurling back the vodka. The British were in control, just. The Americans, under orders, were sober and the French, not under orders, were sober and looked with barely disguised disdain at the antics of the mob surrounding them.

Charles spotted Duncan McIntyre amongst the melee, the staff officer who had engineered his presence at this august occasion, and keeping bull-neck in his sights, asked him if he knew the large man with the cruel-looking red face. Duncan, who had enjoyed his evening and who always worked on the basis that the partaking of any liquid hospitality from the Russians was probably the only thing that they were going to get out of them, chuckled.

'That is Victor Sokolov who masquerades as the Head of the Economics Department, but is in reality Head of the KGB for East Germany. A powerful and dangerous man.'

Charles suddenly wanted to go home. He was not sure whether this dangerous man had noticed his and Anna's mutual interest in each other, but felt uneasy. If she was subsequently questioned and the truth revealed by foul means or fair, Charles would never see her again.

FOURTEEN

Victor Sokolov sat at his large and imposing desk and was surprised that his head ached slightly. Despite his prodigious and regular intake of vodka he never suffered hangovers, although he did know that at the reception the previous evening, and then long into the night drinking alone in his quarters, he had perhaps gone over the top. This did not, however, dull his capacity to exercise his cunning intelligence in pursuit of his objectives. The young British officer that he knew was to attend the reception and whom he had seen there was the focus of his interest. Following the failure of trying to recruit an American, this young man was now their main potential conduit to provide the vital information the Kremlin so badly needed. Much more work on this was needed and time was of an essence. However, he was not aware of the liaison that occurred between his object of interest and the embassy doctor who had previously rebuffed his advances. In this instance, and very unusually, alcohol had dulled his senses.

Victor Sokolov was a man of experience who worked at a slow and measured pace, ensuring all angles and avenues were covered before taking any action, and also satisfying himself with the sure knowledge that in the murky world of espionage and counter-espionage things moved at a pace that reflected the need for accuracy and a system of check-backs that would eliminate mistakes. The fewer the mistakes, the fewer lives would be lost, not that the loss of human life was any concern of his. He often wondered why his masters were in so much of a hurry and could only surmise that an attempted military takeover of West Berlin may be imminent. A Soviet invasion of West Berlin would undoubtably trigger a NATO response that could herald full-blown hostilities between the west and the Warsaw Pact, and probably World War Three. To take West Berlin was a pleasing thought for Victor Sokolov, despite the grave implications that this action would surely provoke.

As he sat there, like an overweight communist tsar, he smiled to himself about how he had directed the recruitment of Sophia Voight, the woman who he now counted on to produce the vital information so demanded by the men in Moscow. It was a masterclass of cruelty and deception. The start point was to discover links between families who lived in East Germany but who had close relatives that now lived in the west. Families that lived in the east needed to have good communist backgrounds and needed to be able to be trusted. A trawl of current Stasi direct employees, not informers, who had relatives living in the west produced a significant list. He then narrowed this down to a list containing only sisters living on the opposite sides of the Inner German Border. He then considered the need for the potential agent in the west to be both intelligent and beautiful and, after lengthy and painstaking deliberations, came up with what he considered a perfect match.

Sophia's sister, Bertha, was born in 1941 where a combination of Nazi incentives to encourage German women to have many children for the Reich, and a feeling that Germany would win the war, were a staple for a Greater Germany. Sophia followed three years later when the military, political and social landscape had changed beyond recognition and imagination for those, like the sisters' parents, who believed in Hitler, the Third Reich and ultimate victory, especially against the Soviet Union, the arch and feared enemy. Like many good German citizens of that time, they possessed little concept of what the German armed forces and associated units such as the Einstazgruppen and the SS had inflicted on the peoples of the Soviet Union, Poland and the Baltic states. Initial stunning military victories were one thing; barbarous brutality and the planned and deliberate murder of millions of innocent people was another, and people like the Voights had little concept of what was going on, and that this would lead to their ultimate demise and the destruction of Dresden, and Germany.

Bertha and Sophia's father was of ill health and was attached to an anti-aircraft unit in Dresden during the war. When the Russians arrived, his wife, mother and an aunt were raped frequently and with a callous disregard by Russian soldiers. A group of Russians forced him at gunpoint to watch as they, in turn, raped his wife who did not, like many, commit suicide but never recovered and spent the rest of her life in a state of deep depression and shock. This traumatic experience, and the general brutality and venality of their Russian occupiers, created a deep and lasting hatred of all things Russian and communist in their souls. The girls' childhoods were dominated by hunger, deprivation, fear and lack of love from their traumatised and desperate parents. They grew up in a world of want, both physical and emotional, and in all its manifestations.

In the recruitment of agents, Victor Sokolov always worked to find a combination of human need and misery to suit his plans. In the Voight family he found the perfect combination. Bertha and

Sophia's parents were dead. They had taken their own lives together, holding hands and embraced in death through poison when in 1954 they could no longer stand their broken, miserable, pointless and shattered lives.

Bertha had been taken to an orphans' institution in Dresden where, like Annette, she had grown up to be indoctrinated with the unquestionable advantages and joys of being able to serve her communist country, the workers' paradise that she so eagerly embraced at a young age. And like Annette, she joined the Stasi as an obvious choice to fulfil her dedication to the state. She was physically attractive, intelligent and enthusiastic to please and show her worth. She made an ideal Stasi operative as a member of the Dresden team tasked with the control of informers and the role of turning information gained into intelligence that could both have undesirables arrested and further the control of the people through this all-encompassing state system. She enjoyed her work and thought little of the morality of what she was engaged in.

Sophia had escaped this grey and unhappy world and had grown up reasonably happily with a loving aunt in the peace of the West German countryside, a countryside that rapidly improved and prospered as time moved on through the 1950s, 1960s and into the 1970s. She always thought that her parents and sister were still in Dresden, and as she grew into adulthood wished that one day they would be reunited. She never heard news of them but believed it was the east—west barrier that prevented them from communicating.

Victor Sokolov smiled again as he reviewed his method of the recruitment of Sophia Voight. Once he was fully aware of the Voights' family situation in East Germany and that were no other known relatives either in the east or west, his man in West Germany had diligently shadowed her for months to ascertain her way of life; her relationship with her aunt, her beauty, her interest in sex but not love and commitment, her job and her intelligent and outgoing personality. The set-up for the attractive job in West Berlin was the easy part, and after a false start with the American Brad that had aroused no suspicions, he waited for the results of his endeavours.

PART 2: DEFECTION

ONE

Outwardly, Charles' busy professionally satisfying life continued apace in West Berlin. Life in the squadron was never boring and as a committed military man he continued to revel in the day-to-day demands, successes and a few failures of commanding an armoured troop. He had no doubt that his merry band of fifteen soldiers were happy to have him as their leader and he, in turn, was committed to their well-being and professional development. He was very lucky to have Sergeant Booth as his right-hand man in the troop, a Troop Sergeant who knew exactly how to bridge that gap between the officer and the soldier, not an easy task given the experience the troop had gained in both the United Kingdom and West Berlin. They worked as a team and it showed when it came to the squadron inter-troop competition. Designed to test all aspects of a troop's operational readiness, it was held over two days and knowledge of armoured tactics, communications, driving skills, gunnery drills, readiness states, vehicle bombing-up exercises, fitness and a final troop armoured manoeuvre exercise on the Grunewald were tested to the limit. Charles' troop came top by a margin but poor Jamie ended up at the bottom of the pile. He was naturally disappointed but Charles told him kindly that it was not him but the poor quality of his NCOs that had let him down. What Charles did not mention was that Jamie had a tendency to be idle and, at times, slipshod in his application. Jamie was a likeable, gung-ho and practical-minded fellow with a good brain that he seemed to rather not want to use, and he lacked that streak of ruthlessness that was essential in developing a successful army career.

Charles could be ruthless if he saw it would benefit him, but he hid it well behind an urbane and charming exterior. This would stand him in good stead for a period of his life that he was about to enter, but not in a military sense. He was very pleased to be promoted within the squadron to second captain as the previous incumbent had to attend a long course in the UK. A new, wet behind the ears Second Lieutenant appeared to take over Charles' troop and there was a collective but discreet groan from his men when he arrived. The new subaltern proved, in time, to be a 'good 'un' and worth his rank, and Sergeant Booth took him under his wing immediately.

Charles was then subjected to the inevitable troop farewell party. It was held in the back room of a local Gasthaus where the friendly patron laid on a splendid buffet, German style, and as much beer as could be drunk. Sergeant Booth arranged no-frills transport (a 4-ton lorry) to and from the venue and a good time was had by all. Speeches were made and copious thanks given and both Charles and Sergeant Booth welcomed warmly the new Troop Leader. Towards the end of the evening, and on more than one occasion, Charles was serenaded by groups of soldiers telling him that he was 'the best troop leader they had ever had'. It did not occur to them, though it did to Charles, that the majority had only had him as their troop leader. A very good time was had by all and it was a jolly, well-oiled and noisy troop that piled into the back of the 4-tonner at the end of the evening.

In his new position within the squadron, Charles was one of

the Squadron Leaders' right-hand men. His role was one of coordination, training regimes and liaison which he relished. He sat in an office, well away from the dirt and grime of the tank park, although he did miss the banter of the soldiers and their admirable and irreverent outlook on life. With access to the operational plan and numerous other pertinent documents to hand, including some that were classified, he was responsible for all transport, movement and training programmes, both in West Berlin and externally back in England and West Germany, and liaison with the myriad of different units and agencies. His key point of contact was the British Brigade headquarters based in the Olympic Stadium as the Squadron Leader answered directly to the Brigade Commander. He also enjoyed close liaison with his American and French points of contact on an informal basis.

Charles enjoyed his new job. He had been given the temporary rank of captain and his Squadron Leader had told him that his promotion was in recognition of his excellent work as a troop leader over the past two years. He applied himself to the challenge in his typically logical and studious way and enjoyed it. It seemed all was well in his professional life and he could look forward to a successful army career if he stayed on this course and did not allow himself to step or fall into the numerous potential 'poo traps' that might come his way. In an organisation as large as the British army in the 1970s with its broad scope of maintaining an effective, efficient fighting force across many parts of the world, and in particular in West Germany, potential pitfalls for ambitious officers were in abundance. Even at this stage of his career, Charles was well aware of the danger of finding himself on the wrong side of a superior officer. If that superior officer did not like a face, the manner or the cut of one's jib, and despite an officer's talents, both real and potential, then although many would totter on to the end of an unsuccessful and disappointing career, it was curtains for the hope of high rank. It was a ruthless world, a world just like business, but without the requirement to clear one's desk that day, or the money.

If Charles' professional life bought him satisfaction and enjoyment, and where decision making came easily for him, the same could not be said of his personal life. Here, he knew that he was behaving like a weak, two-faced rat who had deliberately involved himself with two women, both of whom seemed to adore him. What to do?

He spent many hours in his room in the mess trying to decide. His indecisiveness centred on the knowledge that a future with Anna was still a pipe dream, whereas Greta represented a relationship that was here, enjoyable and gave both of them great satisfaction. He could see her when he wished, whereas even the chances of seeing Anna again were less than slim. Why not forget about Anna and concentrate on Greta? She was beautiful, excellent company, wonderful in bed and he could see that her initial interest was turning into something more. Yet his constant thoughts of Anna would not leave him and he knew that unless he strained every sinew in his body to be with her, his soul would never be able to rest. In his heart of hearts he knew that he loved Anna although he hardly knew her, whereas he did not love Greta. He was very fond of her but he knew that he did not love her because when he compared his feelings towards them both, there was always only one winner. Love was an odd thing, or it seemed to be if your name was Charles Bowater.

AFTER A WEEK he came to a momentous decision in the privacy of his own mind. He would do everything to persuade and then smuggle Anna to the west. How he would actually do this and how long it would take he had to formulate but the decision was made, a decision that if successful would change his life forever.

However, he also decided that because the outcome of his decision could never be guaranteed until Anna was physically in the west, he would continue to see Greta. He would settle down to his position of sitting firmly on the fence. Although Charles could not deny the almost overwhelming desire to see and be with Anna, he saw his plan as a practical and sensible compromise in a difficult situation, an approach in which he saw no wrong. A man for all seasons, and a rat to boot.

Having set his course, he knew he would have to follow a number of key principles if his plan was to have any chance of success. Firstly, he knew that he must never assume that Anna would wish to come to the west. He had not asked her. She was a professional woman with a good job and probably had a family in the USSR. He would have to find a way of asking her and if her answer was yes, the morality of his decision would be more than justified – if it worked.

If she declined, so be it.

Secondly, he must never allow this plan to interfere with his work with the squadron and his life in the mess. Thirdly, he and only he would know about this until such time as he needed help. He knew that it would be impossible for him to succeed on his own and that at some time, the right time, he would need help from others. Fourthly, his relationship with Greta could not be affected. He was the first to admit that he needed her; her companionship, her laughter, her tolerance and her body. He really was a rat.

From now he would run his life along a number of parallel tracks. With his mind made up and after a good night's sleep, he felt as though a weight had been lifted and he went forth the following morning with a spring in his step.

WHILST HE CONTINUED apace in his new job, making sure to never be anything other than what his fellow officers and soldiers had become used to, he began to formulate his plan to bring Anna to the west. He immediately saw that it presented formidable obstacles and difficulties. He had heard that there were Germans in West Berlin who had the means to attempt to smuggle people out from the east and through the wall, but he discounted this option very quickly. If she agreed to his plan, she would be placing herself and her family in grave danger, and therefore he would not allow her to be in the hands of possibly unscrupulous people smugglers who viewed their charges as profitable cargo, and whom he did not know or trust. This would have to be an inside job and the only way that could be done and where he was in complete control would be by using a flag tour.

This would mean bringing into his confidence two other people; a fellow officer and the driver of the flag-tour vehicle. He also knew that what he was planning to do was against every known rule and regulation imposed on all allied forces in West Berlin, against the letter of the law and the spirit, such as it was, of the Quadpartite Agreement, and that if he, and his fellow conspirators, were caught or failed in their quest, punishment would be swift and severe. As a minimum, it would end their careers in the army.

In the evenings after dinner and back in his room, he made lists of what he needed to think about and what need to be done to make his plan as watertight as possible. He was a complete novice at this game and it worried him. But it did not stop him from ploughing on.

JAMIE BUCKINGHAM'S room was just down the corridor from Charles' on the first floor of the officers' mess. The mess, along with the remainder of the barracks they occupied, was built in Prussian times and Charles often wondered who had slept in his room over the past century.

'Come in.'

'I need to talk to you about something very serious but which you might consider to be bonkers,' said Charles as he sat on the bed.

Jamie offered him an after-dinner glass of port. Charles decided to dive straight in.

'You may or may not have noticed that I have been taking a particular interest in a museum whilst we have been on our flag tours. In fact, I have met a young lady over there and who I have also spoken to at that reception I went to the other week at the Soviet embassy.'

'I *had* noticed.'

'It's all horribly complicated. She's Russian and works as a doctor at the embassy. I am utterly fascinated by her. We both want to be together and I want to smuggle her to the west. I have not asked her this yet but when we meet again I will, if indeed we ever meet again. In the meantime I have been doing quite a lot of research and planning as to how I can do this and how dangerous it will be, primarily for her but also for me.'

Jamie looked at him closely. 'What about Greta?'

'All I can say is that when I compare my feelings towards Greta to those towards Anna, by the way her name is Anna, there is no comparison.'

'Why are you telling me this?'

'Because you are the only friend I can trust,' Charles lied glibly. 'I have come to the conclusion that the only way for this to work is by taking her out in a flag-tour car. You, and hopefully Corporal Hancock, would have to be in with me on this and this is why I am here now. To ask you if you would be prepared to help me?'

'You would be violating every rule in the book. If we were caught, it would be curtains for all of us.'

Jamie sat back and thought for a moment. He had known Charles for a long time and he greatly liked him. But he also knew well enough that Charles was a loner at heart, would never come too close and was adept at using people if he felt it would be to his benefit. Even good-hearted Jamie could see that. This was a straight request, not a plea.

'Count me in – but your plan better be a good one, which I know it will be given your irritating love of detail and your terrier-like determination once something is in your head.'

'I still have to ask her and she may well say no. Of course, nothing will be done until I have that answer.'

Charles breathed a huge sigh of relief. One step forward. 'I will arrange a meeting between myself, you and Corporal Hancock as soon as possible and let you know. Thank you, Jamie. I won't forget this.'

They shook hands in a very old-fashioned manner.

CHARLES, Jamie and Corporal Hancock, having approached the Gasthaus from different directions and entered at different times, met three evenings later for a beer and something to eat. Corporal Hancock was mystified but curious as it was not usual for officers to invite JNCOs out for a meal. He was equally mystified by the instructions he had received with regards to how he should approach the Gasthaus and at exactly what time. West Berlin Gasthauses were always warm and cosy and tended to have few customers at that time of evening.

They ordered beer and wurst and once settled Charles explained to Corporal Hancock in a quiet voice what he had told Jamie some evenings before. He placed emphasis on the caveat that until Anna had agreed to all of this, nothing would happen. Corporal Hancock listened intensely and when Charles popped the question about being in or not, he looked carefully at him. All he could see was a sincere and open request from a sincere and open man whom he respected and knew was a very good officer. He was being asked to be a vital part of a team which would be engaged in an activity which could end his army career. But there was a bloody-mindedness and sense of adventure in him that told him that to be involved in this type of madcap scheme was just up his street.

'Count me in, sir,' he said, rattling his empty beer glass.

A further sigh of relief as Charles ordered more beer. He had his team.

'We must all understand that this plan must be at all times completely secret and no one else must know about it, ever, and especially after we have got Anna back to the west, if indeed she will agree to the plan in the first place. Once that has happened and she is safe in West Berlin, your part in this escapade will be over.'

They ate their meals, drank more beer, which was paid for by Charles much to Corporal Hancock's approval, enjoyed a good evening together talking about anything other than the reason they had met up, and then departed in different directions for home.

THERE WAS to be the annual Brigade cocktail party and Charles and Greta, along with the other squadron officers and their wives and girlfriends, permanent, fleeting, temporary, serious or otherwise, had been invited. Knowing that it was a cocktail party where one had to be on one's best behaviour, the squadron bachelors had organised an impromptu follow-up party in the mess afterwards. The cooks would leave out some light cold dishes and there was no requirement for any of the mess staff to be present. It was a Friday and the weekend stretched before them.

Charles knocked on Greta's door. She opened it, wearing only a short see-through nightie.

'What if I had been the milkman?' he asked.

'He would have been equally welcome,' she said, giggling, putting her arms around his neck and kissing him.

A certain pattern had developed in their relationship. If they were going out either to a party, or a dinner or just by themselves he would go to both collect her and make love to her before she dressed. This occasion was no exception and their habit was to have energetic but quick sex in a room of her choice. It was incredibly sexy and he often marvelled at her abandonment and naughtiness.

The cocktail party was predictable but fun. Any chance to squeeze copious amounts of champagne and some very good canapes out of the brigade coffers was always taken up with enthusiasm by the assembled throng. It was a beautiful and warm late-summer evening and the military band marched and counter-marched on the immaculate lawns outside the officers' mess, playing stirring martial music before the marquees and cheerful gathering. It was a classic colonial-style event in the middle of Europe and in the middle of a Cold War. Perhaps only the British could pull off this sort of thing? Perhaps the French as well, but their bands tended to be terrible and the music ear-shattering. The Americans remained aloof and hypocritical when it came to the question of colonies and colonisation.

The Brigade Commander met guests at the entrance to the mess but a small glitch was apparent. Being of an Irish infantry regiment, he had ordered an Irish piper to stand next to him to serenade guests as they approached and were welcomed. It soon became apparent that because of the bagpipes' noise, neither the

Brigade Commander nor the guests were any the wiser as to who was who.

The Brigade Commander give his obligatory speech where he welcomed all, especially the Major of West Berlin and other German dignitaries, the Commanders of the American and French forces and various worthies from all walks of official life within the city. He made a joke about how good it was to see so many from 'within the city walls', but this was not necessarily understood by those who were not British. The Brigade Commander always delivered any speech as early as possible so he could then enjoy his twin social habits of drinking champagne and looking at women. He was a highly intelligent and capable soldier with an enviable record, especially from Normandy to the Baltic and Korea, and an engaging manner, but unlike many of those of his ilk and seniority, he was human. But his 'humanity' did not extend to the opinions of his wife, who had always to keep him under a tight social leash, much to his disappointment.

The squadron officers, in various stages of happiness, mounted the bus to return to the mess. The noise in the bus was deafening and secreted bottles of champagne were handed round during the short journey.

The mess chefs had anticipated that the numbers would increase five-fold and had aimed off accordingly. They had produced a magnificent spread laid out on the balcony and which was devoured rapidly by the hungry assemble. All drinks were available but champagne and wine proved to be the most popular, that is until late evening when whiskey was produced, a lethal combination. The Squadron Leader, single, sober as always, and alone that evening, but always entertaining and cheerful, had asked his officers that this should be a 'civilised affair', and thus it proved to be. He had heard of some of the wild shenanigans that occasionally went on in the mess and although he understood, he did not want this party to be one of them. His officers duly complied, even when the worse for wear.

Once the Squadron Leader had left at around midnight, Charles, who had drunk more than he should have, went upstairs slowly and steadily with exaggeratingly careful movements in a vain attempt to hide his inebriation, not that anyone in the ante-room below would have noticed. Greta was in the loo but he knew that she'd follow when she couldn't find him. She found him sitting in his armchair, drink in hand and grinning like an idiot.

'Hello, darling. Fancy seeing you here. Have a drink.'

She poured herself a very small glass of wine from one of the half-empty bottles on his desk.

'I love my job and I love the army and I love you.'

'In that order?' she laughed. 'What do you love most about your job?' she asked indulgently.

'Being in the middle of things and a part of history. For example, this past Tuesday I attended a seminar about how we would defend the city against attack. It was very detailed and although I had heard it all before, it was still interesting.'

He waved his finger towards his desk. 'If you look in the top drawer, you will see a plan. It is most interesting and all on one page.'

He closed his eyes and she gently took the glass from his hand. He was doing his normal thing when he had imbibed too much, which was very infrequently indeed. Falling asleep at his tipping point.

She opened the drawer quietly and saw an unmarked buff envelope which was not sealed. Inside was a single piece of paper and depicted was a map of West Berlin, and superimposed on that map were a host of information windows packed with graphs, symbols and writing. Despite her almost total inexperience and lack of knowledge of military matters, she could see that this could be what her masters were looking for. She also realised that if she could get this information to them, it might be her passage to freedom from their grip on her life.

She looked over to him. He was fast asleep, his handsome and pleasant face a picture of contentment. She undressed him and put him to bed. He hardly stirred except for one brief moment when he reached to kiss her but failed. He fell back and was fast asleep.

With the envelope in her handbag, she caught a taxi outside the main gate, instructed the driver to drive to her apartment, rapidly gathered the key to her office, further told the driver to take her to the office and wait outside, opened the offices and went straight to the copier machine in the hallway. She made two copies, placed the original back in the buff envelope and the two copies into a A4 envelope from the office. The taxi driver took her back to her apartment where she hid the two copies between her clothes in the wardrobe, and then returned to Smuts Barracks. All this took no more than one hour. The guard, who knew her, were not unduly surprised to see her back. They had become used to the strange comings and goings of ladies to and from the officers' mess. She stepped over a number of bodies in the ante-room, placed the buff envelope back in the desk drawer, undressed completely and squeezed herself into the narrow, uncomfortable army-issue bed next to his slumbering body. He shifted so that their bodies were like two spoons pressed together.

Despite her exertions she was ice cold calm but within minutes, as she lay awake, she could feel that familiar surge of desire for him. He was hard but asleep and unlikely to wake. She also fell asleep but not before beginning to realise she was probably falling in love with this man.

In the very early morning as dawn was breaking, she slipped out of bed, dressed silently, wrote him a brief note saying she would call him later and left, closing the door silently behind her.

SOPHIA WASTED no time in retrieving the documents from her wardrobe, placing one in an envelope in her handbag, calling Annette from yet another call box and arranging a meeting that very day. They met at another seedy café in Wedding. As usual, there were no pleasantries exchanged and no preamble.

Sophia pushed the envelope across the table and Annette immediately placed it into her bag.

'I hope that you will find that very interesting.'

'I will send it on and you will be contacted very soon,' Annette replied.

As there was nothing more to say, coffee was abandoned and they departed their separate ways.

THE ONE-PAGE CLASSIFIED document quickly found its way onto the desk of Victor Sokolov. He had its contents enlarged and translated into Russian by his team. What he then read amazed him. It showed the operational dispositions of the British as well as the liaison links with their American and French counterparts to their south and north. This was exactly what they had been seeking. At first sight, it seemed to fill a large gap in their current knowledge of allied intentions and plans. He dispatched it by the fastest possible means to Moscow and then briefed the ambassador. It did not occur to Sokolov to act the other way around. Diplomatic niceties were not the KGB way. He did not think too much about what Moscow might do with this information but he doubted that it would generate the start of World War Three, at least not in the immediate future.

He then sent a message to Annette through his own channels showing appreciation but asking for more. He always wanted more. In particular, they needed detailed information on how the allied alert system operated in the time of crisis. Annette duly briefed Sophia but little did she know that Sophia had decided to take another direction.

She now knew that this unpleasant, almost ridiculous woman was merely a message passer to someone on the other side of the wall, that she held no authority or power and that she, Sophia, was now in the driving seat. She was not sure where this would lead or how she could extract herself from this trap that had been laid for her, but she would bide her time, focus on Charles and try to win his heart.

TWO

D*ear Anna,*

    My fundamental question is would you come to me in the west, for us to be together? For me, this would the very best thing that could ever happen.

If your answer is yes, I will make a plan to do so. My second letter gives you precise details as how we will do this. This will be a time of great danger for you so you will need to think carefully about it. If you decide to do this there will be no going back but you will never regret it.

With my love to you dear Anna,

Charles

He then composed his second letter with no frills attached.

Dear Anna,

There is a street in the Lichtenberg District called Guntherstrasse, which is off Rudigerstrasse. If you go down Rudigerstrasse from the centre and turn into Guntherstrasse you will see almost immediately on your right a narrow alleyway. If you wait in that alleyway at 1130 hours on Tuesday 9 October, you will see a black car pull up. The driver will get out, open the boot and you must get in immediately.

Bring nothing except your normal handbag and certainly no documents, not even your passport if you have one. Only wash with

water and no soap or shampoo for two days beforehand and do not use
any deodorant or perfume for that time. Wear trousers and clothes that
will allow you to move freely and quickly. Shoes must be flat. When you
are in the boot, you will find a foil blanket and a cushion for your head.
Wrap yourself in the foil and remain completely still for the whole
journey until I tell you that we are in the west and have arrived at your
destination. I will be in the back seat and will be able to tell when we are
approaching the crossing point, when you must freeze. I will also tell
you when we have arrived and the boot will be opened. I will say
nothing else and you must not reply or speak at all.

If this date and time does not work for either or both of us, the
next time will be Tuesday 23 October with exactly the same
arrangements.

Charles

HIS NEXT STEP was to find a potential safehouse for Anna. He
studied the map of West Berlin and decided the best area of the
city would be the French sector. The British or American sectors
were out of the question given the need to maintain complete
secrecy whilst Anna was in West Berlin. He chose at random a
letting agency in Reinickendorf and went there on a Saturday
morning. The attractive young woman behind one of a number of
desks was helpful and showed him a number of possibilities. He
liked the look of one in particular. It was a top-floor one-bedroom
furnished apartment which, as far as he could tell, was not
overlooked because of its height. It was situated in a nondescript
street called Kreuztaler Weg. He could afford the deposit and
monthly rent if he cut down on the champagne.

'Would it be possible to look at this today?' he asked.

She made a call and the answer was yes. They made their way
by foot and on inspection he told her that he liked it and asked if
she could reserve it for him until he could confirm. A small

deposit was required to secure this arrangement, which he duly paid once back at the office.

Monica was a chatty lady and very good looking. As he bade her thanks and farewell there was a look of regret in her eyes, but she cheered up when he told her that he would hopefully be back periodically. Being Charles, he knew that he could have asked her out with all the possibilities that might bring. He resisted the temptation.

———

HE ARRANGED his next flag tour specifically with Jamie in two weeks' time on a Tuesday. He prayed that she would be there but had no way of telling. He had the feeling she could always be relied upon, no matter what the circumstances and the dangers involved.

They passed uneventfully through Checkpoint Charlie. The Hombergs dutifully slotted in behind them but strangely none followed them into the museum. Perhaps their orders had changed? With his heart in his mouth and butterflies in his stomach, Charles left Jamie in the museum and made his way to the normal spot. She was there! It took a great deal of effort for both of them not to embrace and kiss. He looked at her and she him and from then on there could be no doubt in either mind. But they knew they had little time.

'Anna, will you come to me in the west?'

'Yes, I will Charles.' It was said without hesitation.

'Take this. It just confirms what I have just asked you. And also take this, which gives you all the details you will need.'

She took the letters and quickly put them in her handbag. She smiled at him.

'It will all be fine,' she said and, walking up to him, kissed him firmly on the mouth and then was gone.

He stared after her as she disappeared behind a column. Every time he saw her only confirmed his determination to be with her. He would not wash his face or clean his teeth for a week.

———

CHARLES RETURNED to the letting agency and the ever-attentive Monica and secured the contract for three months. He now spent time making sure it was perfect for her arrival, should it ever come. He stocked the kitchen with food and drink, made up the bed with the linen provided and ensured she had everything she would need in the bathroom. He familiarised himself with the heating and water systems.

He knew she would have nothing with her so sallied forth in typical fashion to buy her a few clothes. In an area where he was wholly inexperienced, this was not easy. He chose the KaDeWe and this proved to the right choice. He did not know her size but through a combination of using his charm and looks, as well as comparing Anna with the stature of various blushing shop assistants, he bought jeans, shirts, a jersey, a coat, a beret, socks, a pair of sensible shoes and lastly, underwear. The lingerie department presented him with a large array of different styles ranging from the ultra-naughty and sexy to the bullet-proofs that nothing could penetrate. He guessed her bra size because further attempts at comparisons would not have been appreciated. With a whole month's wages spent, he took time to lay the clothes out neatly in the wardrobe. All was ready as far as his bachelor mind could manage.

Despite his gathering and almost overwhelming feelings for Anna, temptation proved too great and he met up with Greta one evening before departing for England. They had dinner together at her apartment. She cooked a delicious meal. It was a pleasant and relaxed evening and he told her that he was going on leave to

England to see his parents and would be away for nine days. When he returned he would make contact but it might be some time until they could see each other again as he would be busy for a few days.

It had not been difficult for Sophia to notice that they were seeing each other less and less recently. She had also noticed a change in his interaction with her. He seemed less attentive, more distant and certainly less talkative. Again, and as her feelings of love for him grew, she put this down to her over-sensitivity and that he was very preoccupied with work. She could never forgive herself for what she had done to him and also knew that she could never tell him. As before, she reverted to the present and was determined to enjoy the rest of the evening.

To Charles, she remained as beautiful and desirable as ever, but she was no longer number one and had not been for some time. He had remained oblivious to the real purpose of their first meeting and subsequent relationship. She certainly looked lovely this evening and he had every intention of staying the night. It might well be the last they would spend together.

After dinner they sat together and chatted in a desultory way, as well as kissing occasionally. Her whole body seemed to be on fire for him, and sensing this he slipped his hand between her lovely legs. She, in turn, undid her shirt and gave him her breasts to kiss, whilst feeling his hardness. In no time at all they were both naked and making intense love on the sofa. It was breath-taking and beautiful and it should have lasted much longer than it did.

They went to bed and slept as only the young can do. In early morning, and before dawn, they woke and made quiet, passionate and gentle love. He looked into her eyes intensely and realised then that it was not going to work despite the loving looks that she gave him. He got up and dressed. She offered coffee or breakfast but he declined and left with a fleeting kiss.

AFTER HIS BUSY military and social life and the hustle and bustle of West Berlin, Charles greatly enjoyed his week in the peace and quiet of the English countryside where his parents lived. As their only child, he held a very special place in the hearts of his indomitable mother and gentle father and they made sure that he was well looked after. Apart from the odd foray to the local village pub with his father, he stayed at home and caught up with all the news and gossip, an activity in which his mother was particularly adept. He went for long walks with Henry the dozy Labrador and enjoyed his mother's splendid cooking and father's well-stocked wine cellar. It was a relaxing and enjoyable time, but at the end of it he was ready to return to the fray.

During their numerous discussions he told his mother that he had met a very special woman in Berlin and that one day, if it lasted, he might bring her home to meet them. Jane Bowater, ever interested in her son's all too infrequent mentioning of possible liaisons, was delighted to hear this news but said nothing more.

THREE

Despite the best efforts of the Royal Air Force to make his return trip as uncomfortable and frustrating as they could, Charles was happy to be back in the bosom of the squadron and West Berlin. He did not contact Greta, indeed thoughts of her were few and far between and he had no intention of meeting her, possibly ever again. He focussed his mind on catching up on his work, of which there was much, and which necessitated him putting in some long days in the office; and on the forthcoming flag tour where he knew his future would be made, or destroyed.

The day arrived and his nerves were jangling, although when Corporal Hancock appeared on time at the barracks to pick them up, he seemed as cool as a cucumber and entirely unfazed. After their obligatory briefing at Brigade Headquarters, they passed yet again through Checkpoint Charlie into East Berlin. It was one of those cold Berlin days and all before them looked leaden, grey and depressing. The Hombergs slotted in behind them as usual and they made their way through and around the *mitte* before ending up strolling in Alexanderplatz to pass the time of day. They had no intention of using this particular tour to gather information or intelligence. In any case, it might be the last one for all of them.

They set off again at ten forty and after driving for some time at dawdling pace, Corporal Hancock suddenly deployed his full range of offensive driving skills in order to lose the Hombergs. At times his speeds were excessive, his sudden turns spectacular and the double, double backs bewildering. After twenty minutes of draining mayhem, he drove to a halt in a nondescript and shabby street somewhere within the labyrinth of nondescript and shabby streets on the eastern outskirts of East Berlin. No word was spoken as they waited with engine off. No Hombergs appeared. Corporal Hancock had done the first part of his job.

It was quarter past eleven when they moved off, taking a circuitous route that would enable them to arrive at the designated pickup spot at exactly eleven thirty.

THE MOTOR TRANSPORT pool at the embassy was managed by an overweight and drunken individual whom Anna knew well through his frequent visits to the medical centre. He repulsed her but she dealt with him and his alcohol-induced complaints with her normal professional and sympathetic air. He, in turn and like many others, was in love with her.

She walked down to his dirty and untidy office where she knew that there was a large street map of East Berlin on the wall. He leapt to his feet with surprise and pleasure at this unexpected visit. She told him she was not only interested to see where he worked but that she hoped that he was now feeling better after yet again treating him for the tremors and horrible skin rashes brought on by his latest bout of drinking. He stammered his thanks and sat down as she examined the map on the wall. In his confusion and a terrible headache, he did not object but sat there staring at her beautiful bottom. Anna quickly found her street and then worked backwards to the embassy and made a mental note of the route. Her phenomenal memory placed the route firmly in her mind's eye. If she left the embassy early enough, she would be able to walk, thus avoiding any form of public transport and prying eyes.

'Thank you, Vladimir. I will not forget this,' she said, giving him her sweetest smile.

Anna followed Charles' instructions to the letter. Her background, within a system that normally demanded unthinking obedience through fear of retribution and had made her what she was despite her innate resistance to such a lifestyle, ensured she did what he wanted. But on this occasion, she was also doing it because she wanted to do it more than anything in the world. She trusted him implicitly.

The day dawned grey and cold. She prepared herself and then ate breakfast in the canteen as early as she could. She thought that she might be nervous but she was not; she was ice cold and her mind entirely clear on all details of what she had to do. She returned to her room, made sure all was neat and tidy and then signed out and left the embassy through security where the lecherous looks of the guards never changed. In her mind she had worked out how long it would take her to cover the approximately ten kilometres to the pickup point on foot. Her fast walking soon covered the ground; she had judged her time and space well; and she arrived with two minutes to spare but not before checking that she had not been followed and that Guntherstrasse was empty, which it was. She could not vouch for people taking an interest from within the tenement blocks lining the street, but all seemed quiet. She stood in the dingy, foul-smelling passageway and waited.

At exactly eleven thirty, a black car pulled up opposite the passageway. It had no markings. The driver, dressed in a dark overcoat, got out, walked quickly round to the rear and opened the boot. She jumped forward and was in within seconds. The boot closed and in seconds the car moved off. She felt for the foil blanket and with some difficulty wrapped herself entirely in it and, with her head on the cushion, she lay very still. Her heart was pounding but soon her adrenalin rush subsided.

'Stay still and calm Anna. Do not talk.' Charles' calm voice came through the small gap Corporal Hancock had made behind the back seat to the boot.

The car stopped for a few minutes as Corporal Hancock replaced the Union Jack in its holder and took off the dark coat inside the car. Twenty minutes later, the car slowed.

'Coming to the checkpoint, Anna. Try to freeze until I tell you we're across.'

The car stopped. Papers were taken, guards looked in. Dogs sniffed. The tension was almost unbearable. What if the Hombergs had warned the checkpoint of their disappearance? It seemed the longest seven minutes of their lives before the guard reappeared with the papers and opened the barrier. They checked in with the Americans and were then through and in West Berlin.

Charles tried to keep his emotions, euphoria and voice under control.

'Welcome to West Berlin, Anna. Please keep still and quiet until the boot is opened and you can get out.'

AFTER WHAT SEEMED AN AGE, the car came to a halt and the boot was opened. Corporal Hancock had stopped the car in a quiet street and had removed the Union Jack and changed back into his dark overcoat, as had Charles and Jamie. They all removed their hats. She was helped out by the man in the dark overcoat. Charles got out and without a word walked her quickly to the entrance to an apartment block where they took the lift to the top floor. He did not look at her. He opened the front door and they went in. He avoided her questioning eyes.

'This is your home for the time being. Do not go out. Do not answer the door unless you hear two knocks followed by a further two knocks and that will be me. Do not stay by the windows looking out. There is food and everything else in the kitchen, a fully equipped bathroom with hot water and a bed with clean sheets. I'll be back this evening.'

He left abruptly and she marvelled at his self-discipline and the way he had almost barked his wishes at her. His young face showed great strain and he looked very tired.

She went to the kitchen and discovered that it was indeed well stocked. She made herself some instant coffee and a ham and cheese sandwich. They tasted different but very good. She sat down on the sofa and within minutes she was asleep.

When she awoke after an hour, she took a closer look around the apartment. It was more luxurious than anything she had experienced before. The bathroom, the kitchen appliances, the layout of the elegant living room and bedroom; everything seemed new. She smiled at the way he had organised and arranged things for her. He had obviously bought everything he thought she would need in the bathroom and she smiled again when she looked at his women's clothes buying attempts. Amazingly, and when she had enjoyed a long, hot shower and pampered herself, the clothes fitted well. The jeans were tight and the lingerie delicious to wear. The shoes were the wrong size so she padded in bare feet. She waited impatiently for the secret knocks on the door and in the meantime busied herself in the kitchen trying to work out how the appliances worked and what they could eat that evening. Although her culinary skills were limited, she was confident something could be done. She found wine and although she hardly drank, opened a bottle and had a glass. It went to her head but helped soothe her nervousness.

HE STOOD there with red roses in his hand and a broad smile on his face, seemingly recovered from the momentous events of the day. Putting the roses down, he took her in his arms without a word. They must have kissed for five full minutes, or it seemed like that. With difficulty they let each other go and both became shy and quiet. She placed the roses in a vase; no one had ever given her flowers before and she loved them. As she was busy, he came up behind her and pressed himself against her. She could feel his hardness and wondered what it would be like. Charles obviously did not know this but she was a virgin and it seemed strange to her that she was not at all nervous about what both of them knew would happen later. Charles finally spoke.

'You were fantastic today. I was a nervous wreck but I am so incredibly happy that you are now here and that we are together. It has been a very, very long day,' said Charles with a catch in his voice. There were tears in his eyes.

'If you are happy then I am overjoyed to be with you, to have you standing next to me and with no one else to worry about,' she replied with an equal quiver in her voice.

'The next few weeks, or even months might be tough for you but I will do my very best to work out a way of getting you back to West Germany and then England. I love you, Anna, and have done since the first moment I saw you.'

This was not his normal glib talk. If this was not love, what was?

'I am a terrible cook and have no idea what you like or how to cook it, but I can try.'

'I can stay the night if you wish,' he ventured nervously.

Her answer came in the form of a long, deep kiss and of her pressing her body fully against his with an urgency that almost delayed the possibility of something to eat and wine to enjoy.

The meal was simple but well-cooked and wholly adequate. They drank wine and talked and talked and talked. Missing out nothing, he told her all about his life from start to finish and she reciprocated. If there was ever a better example of the stark differences between the systems they lived under and the beliefs that had been instilled into them from birth, these two virtual strangers coming together in open and honest discourse, exemplified it all.

She told him that because of the Soviet system she was almost completely ignorant of the west but that she would make every effort to learn fast. At least her English was excellent and would present no problems, although her Russian accent was marked. She effused about the apartment and thanked him constantly and in a manner that was almost childlike for doing all of this for her. Blushing red, she told him she was a virgin but that she had no fears about it.

He told her that until very recently he had a girlfriend in England but that had been over since their meeting at the reception. She believed him without question.

He asked about her concerns for her family in Leningrad. Her answer clearly showed beyond doubt that she saw her life with him from now on and that fate would determine how things would work out. Charles would discover that fate was deeply embedded in the Russian psyche and that communism, for all its faults, had skilfully used this national characteristic to ensure stoicism, patience and acceptance, no matter what the provocations. He also quickly saw that she was a strong minded, intelligent and gentle person. With her stunning looks, to him she seemed perfect and he was determined to keep her no matter what.

As they talked, they edged closer together, the shyness evaporating and soon they were in each other's arms on the sofa. They kissed; her lips were perfect, and his hands found his way to her breasts which again, seemed perfect. He cursed himself for buying her the jeans she was wearing but it hardly mattered. He led her by the hand to the bedroom but not before taking a towel from the bathroom to place on the bed. Ever the organised man.

'Would you like me to undress you and then I can undress myself?' he asked gently.

She nodded, unable to find words that might hide her fierce desire. He had difficulty with the tight jeans and she giggled at his urgent efforts but helped enthusiastically. He recognised the skimpy lingerie and this only served to heighten his desire.

She screamed with pain as he entered her, but it was a scream more of pleasure and as he moved inside her, her scream turned quickly a moan of desire and very quickly it was over. Charles had never experienced such desire and love as he looked into her eyes. This was so completely different to Greta. Where there had been pure sex and lust now there was just love with sex as a complement. They lay beside each other and he stroked her beautiful face. She smiled that sweet smile and within seconds they were both asleep, worn out utterly by a day during which they had experienced, it seemed, every human emotion: hope, fear, even terror, tension, relief, exhaustion, happiness, adulation, desire and a very special togetherness.

He woke very early in the morning and for a second was not quite sure where he was. He turned and her naked body was facing him and her wideawake eyes looking at him. She had obviously been up because the towel was gone and she smelt of soap and a hint of perfume. He marvelled at her beauty and then began the very gentle and slow process of teaching her the art of love as he knew it. She was a quick learner; very compliant and eager, as well as showing a mixture of ardent passion and gentleness. She allowed him to lead and do what he wished with her body. He, in turn, was constantly aware of the need to be purposeful but instructive, so by the time he had to get up to dress and return to work, they both felt that first wonderful evening and night together was only the precursor to a life to be spent in mental and physical harmony.

As he drank a hurried cup of coffee and sat next to Anna who was dressed only in a shirt, he switched back into what he called his functional mode. He gently reminded her that she needed to stay in the apartment and remember the rules, that he would be back that evening and would bring her some books to read, and that they could then discuss the next moves and how he intended to go forward with this. They kissed and he walked out into the cold early morning air, looked up at the apartment windows and thanked God he had met her and that he had done what he had done.

FOUR

It had been 36 hours since Anna had left the embassy on foot and with no indication that she was intent on anything other than her normal walk through the *mitte*. When she did not appear at work that Wednesday morning, Dr Anton Orlov was obliged to inform the First Secretary. He then retreated back to the medical centre knowing full well that should she have disappeared he would be called to give his opinion. He knew in his heart what she had done because his finely tuned antennae told him that because of her recent lightness of heart she had met someone.

This information inevitably and very quickly reached the desk of Colonel Sokolov. With his daily reports on the attitudes of all staff within the embassy, including the ambassador, she had always been shown as an exemplary comrade dedicated to the cause and to her job. His internal monitoring system within the embassy was a mini version of the Stasi system outside the embassy walls and it did the job of keeping everyone in line.

He thought about this but decided to leave it for another 24 hours before he told the ambassador and probably Moscow. He told security, where she had not signed back in, and Anton Orlov that they were not to mention this to anyone. He knew his orders would be obeyed. He examined the possible scenarios. She had defected to the west. She had found a lover in East Berlin and was holed up with him. She had been attacked and either injured or killed in East Berlin. His gut instinct told him that she had defected, but how? If this was true, it would be unprecedented. East Germans tried and did escape but not Russians, especially those from the embassy. He checked with the Volkspolizei and all the hospitals but there were no reports that she had been seen or was ill or worse. He then spoke to the Stasi and they were none the wiser. He told all that at this point they were not to do anything and that what he asked was classified.

A DAY PASSED and there was still no sign of her or reports from the East German authorities. Sokolov now knew it was almost certain she had defected to the west. How she had managed that was still a mystery but he was determined to find out by deploying all the resources at his disposal. He informed the ambassador and the Lubyanka, again emphasising confidentiality at this stage, and assuring them that he would find out how she had done this and what the next steps should be. Colonel Sokolov was nothing if not careful, cunning and calculating.

He knew Anna Nazarov did not have any access to classified material within the embassy, military or otherwise. If she had defected to the west it would not be to give the west secrets because she didn't have any. So why had she done this? The answer must be that age-old issue of love, an alien concept to the Colonel but nevertheless one whose power he understood. And if it was love, or even infatuation, who had facilitated her treachery?

Working on his faith of his own conviction, Sokolov wrote down the framework of a plan to expose the culprit. But he was also acutely aware that if he was right, this situation could be turned to his and his country's advantage. After all, he had very recently deployed the same tactics elsewhere. His next port of call was a check on Anna Nazarov's family connections back in Russia. A routine visit revealed a middle-aged couple living in Leningrad, both patriotic, loyal, dedicated members of the party and wedded to the system. Indeed, they both worked for the party and both had proved themselves in the Great Patriotic War. There was a sister living with them who was also a dedicated comrade and worked within the government. The perfect Soviet family and unaware of the current situation.

He knew that East Germans ran, or attempted to run, escape networks from East Berlin to the west but would they entertain a Russian? He knew she spoke German but she did not look, act or speak like a German. He discounted this possibility. Carefully controlled and accompanied groups of tourists came to the east but it would have been impossible to secrete anyone amongst them given the level of checks and surveillance. Again, he discounted this possibility. That left the Western Allies and their access to the East through their Flag Tours. To Sokolov, this was the most likely option.

He sat there ruminating. American, British or French? His instinct told him not the French, although it was a possibility. The language barrier would have proven too great. He was well aware of the strict, almost puritanical regime that the Americans adopted in West Berlin when dealing with the Russians, so unless there was a real maverick amongst them this again was unlikely. That left the British who, in Sokolov's opinion, were probably the most professional of the three but were certainly the most independent in spirit.

He made three calls. He instructed the Headquarters of the Grenztruppen to provide him with all logged British Flags Tours going in and out of East Berlin though Checkpoint Charlie over the past six months, what officers and drivers were involved and if any patterns became obvious. He then called Stasi Headquarters and instructed them to do the same except with their obligatory Flag Tour monitoring patrols. Ignoring the ambassador as usual, he then called the Lubyanka and told them what he was doing. The conversation with his superior was terse and short. They were not pleased with the current situation and wanted it resolved one way or another, and quickly. In KGB speak he knew that if necessary, liquidation was to be considered. He knew that the answers to his questions would take some days, so he settled down to wait. He had plenty of other business to attend to.

CHARLES KNEW that he had to face the music with Greta within the next 24 hours, and the sooner the better. Like many men who considered themselves strong and resolute, when it came to the affairs of the heart, he was a coward, and if he could put it off he would. But he knew he had to tell her. He did not love her but was very fond of her indeed. He suspected that she loved him but there was no escaping the fact he had to honour Anna. After all, they had risked their necks for each other and created a bond that could not be denied.

He decided the best way to do it was head-on and so the following evening he made his way to her apartment unannounced. She was pleased to see him.

'Greta, I will not stay long. I have to tell you straight that I have met someone else whom I have fallen in love with. You know that I never loved you although I tried my very best. I wish you the very best and happiness in life. There is no point in continuing this conversation. I will say goodbye and let myself out.'

He was gone. She stood there in the hall for a long time just staring at the closed door in front of her. The crying took some time to come, but when it did it came in floods. She went to the kitchen, reached up and found the bottle of schnapps that she always kept. When she finally composed herself with great effort, she knew that she was the one in the wrong, not that sweet, gentle man with the lion's heart whom she had duped and betrayed from the beginning of their relationship. She drank all the schnapps and fell onto the bed very drunk.

When she woke in the cold light of dawn, she knew she had to get out of West Berlin and out of the mess that she found herself in. She resolved to speak to Annette and tell, not ask her, that she would be released and allowed to return to West Germany and the safety of her aunt's comfortable home in that sleepy German village. Using one of the codes she had memorised, she called Annette and arranged a meeting for that evening. She then drank cold, white wine at six o'clock in the morning, something she had never done before but it helped on this desperate morning.

They met and Sophia wasted no time.

'The Captain told me last night that he no longer wishes to see me and that he has met someone else. I doubt very much that I will ever see or hear of him again.

'In light of this, I request that you release me and allow me to go back to West Germany,' she continued. 'You have my family in your grip so there is no chance that I shall do anything stupid. I also suspect that I have provided you with useful information for which you should be grateful.' The word 'grateful' was not in the Stasi dictionary.

Annette was her normal taciturn self and promised to get back to her as soon as possible. Her masters were not going to like this at all.

Sophia's heart was heavy and she found herself constantly sobbing with a feeling of almost overwhelming loss. She went over and over in her mind all the wonderful times they had spent together. She vowed that she would never love again. She wanted to contact him so badly but knew that that would probably only worsen the situation. She had to stick it out and slowly things would get better. She must focus on the present and getting out of West Berlin.

VICTOR SOKOLOV GREETED the news and request provided by Annette with ill-disguised anger. First the doctor and now this! But this mood was short. His long years in service of the Soviet State had taught him that any type of human emotion was a waste of energy and time. His survival instincts immediately kicked in as he began to consider the possibilities and options that might allow him to turn these events to his advantage, and save his skin.

The results of his inquiries were beginning to come in and they bought with them some interesting, if not conclusive, developments. British flag tours into East Berlin over the past six months showed one particular pattern which was of interest. Normally flag-tour personnel of two officers and one driver never came together for more than two, and a maximum of four, times. But the records showed that the names Bowater, Buckingham and Hancock had completed no less than eight flag tours together. This was excessive and possibly, from a western perspective, against quadripartite rules. In addition, when he examined the Stasi report on the routes taken by those particular tours it seemed that they set a clear pattern in firstly visiting the Pergamon Museum at about ten in the morning, and always on either a Tuesday or a Friday. The report did not mention that on each occasion the two officers involved had hoodwinked the Homberg following them by splitting up and disappearing into the maze of rooms and alcoves.

The name Bowater preyed on his mind. Where had he seen that before? And then he remembered. The name was on the list of allied officers who had attended the last embassy reception, a name that stood out because he was a lieutenant and the youngest. This was unusual because normally the minimum rank allowed was captain. He checked the list again. There was also something he couldn't quite put his finger on.

Sokolov instructed the Head of the embassy security to examine the signing-out book in the guard room for the past three months and see if Dr Anna Nazarov had set a pattern. The information came back in double-quick time that yes, she had. She always went out for a walk on either a Tuesday or a Friday and she normally left at about nine in the morning and returned by midday.

What if this young British officer Bowater and the young British officer that Annette's agent in West Berlin had been dating and extracting information from were one and the same? And what if that same officer had been meeting the beautiful Anna Nazarov in the Pergamon Museum on those Tuesday or Friday mornings and had then managed to smuggle her out to the west where she could be now? And was it merely a coincidence that at this time Sophia Voight had been unceremoniously dropped by this young officer? To Victor Sokolov, it now all added up. Anna Nazarov was in the west and she had been taken there by this young officer. He could be entirely wrong in his supposition but his gut told him he was probably right. Too many of his strands of thought and the facts presented to him came together to be a coincidence.

To save his neck, he needed to be able to present to the Lubyanka and the ambassador a plot to use Anna Nazarov's presence in the west as a potential long-term sleeper agent, but a plot with a difference in that she would not be aware of her status until the time was ripe. He was taking a risk because the three key elements to his plan could only be based on assumptions. The first was that Anna Nazarov would be with and remain with this

British officer into the future. The second was that this young officer Bowater, given that he would be with her into the future, would rise in the British Army to positions where he had access to classified information that could be of use to the Soviet Union. Thirdly, that he, Sokolov, would be able to exert pressure on Anna Nazarov at the right time in the future through a combination of threats; placing her parents and sister in danger, exposing Bowater to his passing of secrets to the Soviets through Sophia Voight, and exposing his illegal smuggling of Anna Nazarov out of East Berlin into the west. She, in turn, would, he hoped, pass these threats onto Bowater who would, again he hoped, decide that he would pass on classified material and thus avoid a collapse of his relationship with Anna Nazarov, and save his career.

Would it work? He did not know but until his plan had been approved, or otherwise, there could be no pursuit of Anna Nazarov in West Berlin or further afield; there could be no official complaint by the Soviets to the Western Allies, and the whole affair must be kept absolutely secret. With the ambassador's approval, he sent out a notice to all embassy employees that Dr Anna Nazarov had returned to the Soviet Union for personal reasons and that this was no longer a subject for discussion. Older members of the embassy staff grimaced when they read this, knowing full well what it likely meant for the sweet and smiling Anna Nazarov.

Victor Sokolov then encapsulated on paper all that he had spent the last 48 hours planning. He gave the situation, his overall aim, his assumptions, his reasons for these assumptions, the actions needed and what would be the benefits if it worked. He stressed the importance of realising that this was a long-term project that could, if handled correctly and with a bit of luck thrown in, bring great benefits in the future. Once he had done this and checked it carefully several times, he took it to the ambassador who spent some time examining it closely. He was no fool and could see the benefits the plan could bring if it worked. He also correctly surmised that the risks were negligible because if she was never activated in the future, no one would be any the wiser.

Victor Sokolov then asked the ambassador if he could personally take his plan to Moscow and present it to his masters. He added that it had been some considerable time since he had seen his family. The ambassador concurred.

Victor Sokolov had one further piece of business to attend to before he departed for Moscow. He was aware that the agent Sophia Voight had requested that she be released from the position he had placed her in and wished to return to West Germany to resume her life there. This was very unusual but even Sokolov could see that she had provided him and Moscow with some vital classified intelligence which, if it had been used, could have given the Red Army a military advantage over at least the British should an attack on West Berlin be envisaged. He also knew she believed her parents were still alive and living in Dresden and that even if she returned to the west, he could still use them as a lever against her if she decided to talk. If she had been prepared to spy for the east to protect them, she would surely be prepared to be silent about all of this once she was back in West Germany living with her aunt. He informed Annette that she could be released, but only on the proviso that she understood the dire consequences should she decide to talk to the West German authorities. He then went ahead and arranged his visit to Moscow.

SOPHIA STILL CRIED at night and she hardly ate. Since Charles' visit, she had not returned to work. She drank, but it only made her more depressed and bereft. She waited for a week and then called Annette. The loss of Charles was a devastating blow to her but if it now came to pass that they would not allow her to leave West Berlin, she felt she may well contemplate suicide.

It was not to be and she was released.

At their next and final meeting, Annette spoke without emotion.

'Please make your own arrangements for travel. Your West German passport and sufficient money will be put through your letter box within the next 24 hours. Please do not return to work and please attempt to leave the city as soon as is possible.'

With that, she was gone. No word of farewell, no word of thanks and no wishes of good luck for the future. Sophia looked after her and thanked God that very soon she would have no more of this nasty world. She hated Annette and she hated herself.

VICTOR SOKOLOV'S relationship with his family was a poor thing. His marriage of 20 years to Svetlana had never been based on love and understanding. She was a beautiful woman when he met her and she remained so today. At the beginning, it was lust rather than love that bought them together but that inevitably palled. The relationship today relied on the practicalities of life in the Soviet Union. As a senior KGB officer, Victor Sokolov enjoyed a privileged position in society and as such lived in a three-bedroomed apartment in one of the better districts of Moscow. Most Muscovites would be happy with one bedroom and shared washing facilities. He and his wife were able to shop in special stores set aside for the elite where most goods could be bought. They could holiday on the Black Sea, staying in secluded dachas and send their son to a school for the elite. Svetlana was prepared to put up with her husband's boorish drunken behaviour, as well as his indiscreet womanising, to continue to enjoy these material benefits. In Soviet Russia all were equal, but many were more equal than others.

She too was prone to seek sex and there was an army of discreet admirers who were willing to oblige. Victor Sokolov's long periods away, postings she knew he deliberately engineered, gave her time to enjoy something to which she was very partial, and the more variety the better. Her suitors normally knew who she was and who she was married to and never caused any trouble, whilst living in some trepidation.

They had a son, an insipid and callow youth who displayed none of the communist virtues Victor Sokolov cherished. He was physically weak, prone to illness and idle. Due to enter compulsory military service at some stage, Victor Sokolov hoped that this might generate some life into him, but he doubted it.

When he arrived in the official car, there was no happy homecoming welcome. There never was. He busied himself preparing for his meeting that afternoon and then left for the Lubyanka to present his plan. He knew this could be the making or undoing of him and that he would have to deploy all his persuasive powers to convince them that in the longer term it was sound.

Even to a man as brutal as Victor Sokolov, the Lubyanka was an oppressive place. He wasted no time and made his way to the office of his immediate superior. Victor Sokolov counted Major General Alexei Gushchin as a comrade-in-arms during the Great Patriotic War and as a friend with whom he had grown up with in the MGB and the KGB after victory. But Victor Sokolov also knew that his 'friend' could be as ruthless as he and was capable of disposing of him if required in order to protect himself and the agency.

He presented his plan in a careful, concise and judicious manner. There was silence when he had finished. Alexei Gushchin smiled his thin smile.

'It is a good plan and you have my permission to implement it in accordance with your own arrangements. You will also be the officer responsible for monitoring it into the future.'

Victor Sokolov had saved his neck and probably even enhanced his reputation within the service. He had two days left in Moscow before returning to East Berlin, so it gave him time to celebrate with some old chums. Not once did it enter his mind to spend time with his family.

Before he poured himself onto the Antonov to return to East Berlin, Victor Sokolov spent long hours and many vodkas reminiscing with old friends, either at their homes or in the KGB Officers' Club. He was drunk most of the time and only returned home to sleep a little and eat occasionally. He was sullen and mostly silent with his wife, apart from the occasional grunt. His son stayed in his bedroom. Victor Sokolov left without saying goodbye.

SUFFICIENT MONEY and her passport were placed through her letter box that very evening. The next morning she wasted no time in visiting the nearest travel agent and booking a flight on British European Airways to Hamburg for the following day. She returned to the apartment, packed and ensured all was neat, tidy and clean. She would deposit the front door key, along with the office keys, at the office very early the next morning before going on to Tempelhof Airport. Nothing more to do except to eat out at a local restaurant and drink wine.

Leaving Berlin was a relief and her journey uneventful. A bus from Hamburg to Osnabrück and then a taxi to her aunt's small and sleepy village saw her knocking tentatively on the front door mid-afternoon. Her aunt's surprise turned to delight as she enveloped Sophia in her arms and ample bosom. She was a gentle and kindly soul and had always loved her favourite niece.

It took little time for Sophia to settle back into the routine of this large, warm and comfortable house. Her aunt was a good cook who produced traditional German fare, her bedroom was comfortable and there was an air of permanence and quiet. He aunt was an unobtrusive and private person. This was what she needed but it did not prevent Sophia from crying every night and moping during the day, Charles constantly in her thoughts.

Aunt Gertrude had been married to a Wehrmacht officer who had served in Hitler's war. She kept a large photograph of this handsome man in uniform by her bed. In 1939 he had entered Poland and was engaged in that five-week war, the details of which have since remained largely unknown. What is known is that the Wehrmacht, along with the SS and other special units, committed numerous barbarous and brutal atrocities against the Polish people, a people that they considered to be Slavic and therefore racially inferior. Gertrude's husband remained garrisoned in Poland after hostilities but was then engaged in the build-up and invasion of Soviet Russia in June 1941. He met his Valhalla at the seminal battle of Kursk in the summer of 1943 and his body was never found. During his short periods of leave during his time in Poland and Russia, he never spoke about what he personally might have done to the peoples of those countries, but few Wehrmacht officers or their men remained untainted, if not in deed then by association. Almost to a man they followed the Fuhrer's dictate that they must 'close their hearts to pity'. Gertrude remained convinced that he was an honourable soldier doing his duty for Germany.

Unlike her sister and her husband, the war did not touch Gertrude until the very last days when the British and Canadian Armies were sweeping through Northern Germany. A group of SS men came to the village and hung three men, including the village elder, from trees as a warning that there could be no surrender. Since then, and although not entirely silent, Gertrude had, like so many other Germans of that generation who had survived, steadfastly maintained an attitude of denial of any form of guilt about the crimes the Third Reich had committed. As a younger woman she had greeted the ascension of Hitler and the Nazis with adulation and joy. She had witnessed the early triumphs that had made her Germany great again, and she had seen the utter disaster of total defeat that befell her nation.

Sophia and her aunt never discussed such matters. Sophia, like most young Germans, wanted to look forward, not back. Forward to a better life and a safer future where the extremes of the Nazis would never be allowed to rise again. In any case, and unlike her aunt, it was not something that occupied her mind.

Time passed in the slow pace of village life and she started to recover. Charles was no longer always in her thoughts but nights were still difficult. She decided she would try to find a job. Her Volkswagen Beetle was still in the garage and she started to venture out to search for a position. She was in great luck because the agricultural firm that had employed her before was looking for a senior secretary and interpreter. The company was close by and soon she had settled into a rhythm of a life that suited her. She enjoyed her work, especially when providing interpreting services for a number of new contracts with the UK. She was provided for in a comfortable home and she was once again amongst the company of others. Life slowly but surely improved.

THE BUFF ENVELOPE came through the door addressed to her. The postmark showed that it had been posted in Bremen. She was puzzled and opened it. Inside was a single sheet of typed paper.

Dear Sophia,

Please be aware that despite what you might believe both your parents died in Dresden in 1954. They took their own lives together. This is the truth.

You cannot follow up on this news and must take this information as absolutely genuine.

There was no indication of who had sent her this.

She stared at the paper for a long time and then slowly sunk to her knees, her back against the hall wall, and put her head in her hands. No tears came. There was nothing, only numbness.

When she stood up, she forced herself to think clearly. The first thing she must do was to never show any emotion in front of aunt Gertrude or to tell her about this – ever. Aunt Gertrude was too elderly to be presented with news like this. The second was to accept that it was probably true unless, in the future, it was proven otherwise. The third was to also accept that those bastards had duped her in the knowledge that she believed her parents to be still alive. She had done what she had done to her beloved Charles for nothing. She hated them with a passion.

She had taken a few steps forward in her life but this news, should it be true, had forced her ten steps back. She sunk into a kind of depression but knew that her outward appearance at home and at work should not portray her inner turmoil. Start again she told herself, and she did. She was a woman of steely determination and once again set her sights on recovery. She had now lost everything except her sister of whom she not heard from for many years and had no idea what she was doing, or even if she was alive.

She started running in the evenings and venturing into Osnabrück on occasions where she could enjoy a break from her aunt and her cooking, as good as it was. All this took a long time but as before, life once again began to get better. She believed in the maxim that time can normally heal most things, but not all. One day, remembering her previous life where she had lured unsuspecting men into casual sex, she tried it again. With her beauty, it was not difficult to achieve, and purely as an act to engender pleasure she found it not impossible, although she never allowed the eager young men to know anything about her and her heart remained hard and cold.

FIVE

Charles worked diligently at his job and continued to impress. He did not arrive late, leave early or cut any corners. Although he recognised the very real dangers of keeping Anna in West Berlin for any longer than it was absolutely necessary, with her presence so close to him, his evening visits to the apartment and the unremitting love that they felt for each other and which continue to grow made him a much happier and more relaxed man.

He made a point of arriving to be with her after dark and leaving before it got light. He visited the British Forces library and took out many books for her, some of which she read and some of which she didn't. They compiled food lists together and he shopped. She gave him precise instructions and measurements on clothes and he dutifully went out to buy what she would like. She cooked for him and startled him one evening when he arrived and heard her in the kitchen. She was there wearing only an apron, holding a wooden spoon and smiling that sweet, enchanting smile. She certainly was a fast learner and loved her new-found sexual freedom with a man that equally shared her passion and sense of adventure, even when a wooden spoon was involved.

They talked and talked and talked until they felt that they knew everything about each other, but there was always more and there was hardly a quiet moment, except when they were asleep. Her English improved rapidly although the accent remained, an accent that Charles found sensuous. Both were happy and revelled in that happiness neither had known before. What both now experienced was a love for each other where sex was only part of the whole, a truly satisfying position and one which they found, at most times, sublime.

Charles and Anna knew that their temporary Nirvana in their love nest could not last. She was powerless, could do nothing to influence future events and relied entirely on him. The more Charles thought about how he could get Anna out of West Berlin and home to England without the authorities knowing, the more he realised this was not something he could do alone. Anna had no identity and no papers. Any attempt to move her illegally, even with false papers, was fraught with danger and the possibility of exposure. He assumed the Soviets were on the hunt for Anna so he must do something now, not linger and hope for the best, a position he was adept at.

Anna told him that she possessed an intimate knowledge of the workings of the Soviet embassy in East Berlin and therefore, by association, every other Soviet embassy. She could have talked for hours about the few good points and the more than numerous facets of an organisation shackled to a top-heavy system that denied efficiency, effectiveness and a progressive working atmosphere. She also told him that as a doctor she had the opportunity to visit many Red Army units based in East Berlin and East Germany and observe closely their personnel and methods used in welfare of the soldiers, their morale and their methods of healthcare. Many, many young soldiers, faced suddenly with a beautiful young woman to confide in, did not hold back in their condemnation of all that was wrong in their worlds. They normally painted her a picture of low morale, brutality, cruelty, gross negligence towards soldiers, corruption and an army that lacked any form of good leadership from the officers. Leadership was not by example. Leadership was by coercion and threats. She went on to tell him that she could offer an excellent and detailed insight into life in Soviet Russia and how it all worked – or did not, as the case may be.

Charles took all this in and wondered if it might be enough to rouse interest in the right circles. He realised he had no option but to try.

PETER ROGERS WAS DELIGHTED to accept Charles' invitation to dinner for the following Thursday. Over the time they had both been in West Berlin they had grown to become friends, as much as Peter Rogers could allow or be allowed.

Thursday evenings were when officers could invite friends to the mess for a black-tie dinner and on this occasion, it was a full house. The food and wine were excellent and the assemble enjoyed themselves. The Squadron Leader gave a short speech welcoming all to his mess and making the point that it was important that the British contingent in West Berlin worked together for the common good. Charles drank little and was preoccupied, but he looked after his guest very well. After dinner, Charles took Peter aside.

'I have to tell you something that you might find extraordinary, but I ask that you listen carefully and try to understand.'

'Absolutely no problem,' said Peter, who had enjoyed the wine and was mellow.

'Nine days ago, when I was in East Berlin on a Flag Tour, I smuggled someone out into the west.'

Peter stared at him in amazement.

'It is a she and she is Russian. In fact, she worked as a doctor in the Soviet embassy until I made my move. I met her by chance at the Pergamon Museum and then later at an Allied reception at the Soviet embassy. A fellow officer and the driver are the only other people that know about this. Her name is Anna Nazarov and she now in hiding here in West Berlin.'

Peter continued to stare at him. Charles ploughed on, with everything to lose.

'I tell you all this now not only as a friend but also because I know you might be prepared to help. Anna has no military or other secrets to offer but she does possess a unique and detailed insight into a number of aspects of Soviet life including the diplomatic and military worlds here in Berlin, and Soviet Russia itself.'

By now Peter had become very sober. He knew what Charles was driving at. Information exchanged for a passage to the west.

'What is your relationship with this Anna, Charles?' he asked.

'I completely love her and have no doubt whatsoever in my mind that I want to be with her. Her feelings are equally strong.'

Peter could see and sense the sincerity, almost desperation, emanating from Charles.

'I'll see what I can do.'

Charles' heart lifted. Not an outright no and no further questioning. This could represent progress.

They parted with thanks coming from both. Peter, for Charles' hospitality and Charles for Peter agreeing, at least, to give his revelation some thought.

IT TOOK Peter Rogers two days to discover where Charles had hidden Anna Nazarov and from that moment on she had an unseen watch and guard on her and her apartment. When it came to espionage tactics, Charles was a novice. He had set a pattern in his going to and leaving the apartment and this was very easy to pick up by experienced operators. He had also naively given the letting agencies his details.

In the meantime, Peter Rogers had his Secret Service hat on and was considering the startling news that Charles had imparted. On one hand, because this woman very probably had not had access to any classified material, military or otherwise, she could be considered of no use and in the 'spirit of quadripartite harmony' should be handed back to the Soviets with an apology. Or she could be used as bargaining chip and used for an exchange. Or she could be interviewed to see if the general information she possessed might be of interest to the British, and the western allies. All information was useful and the defection of a Russian employee of the Soviet embassy in East Berlin was unheard of. At no point in his considerations did Peter Rogers include thoughts on Charles' professed love for this woman.

He needed to try to ascertain what the Soviet reaction had been to this defection.

All was quiet. There was no apparent reaction, although it was difficult to judge. There had certainly been no official accusations that the west had deliberately smuggled a Russian citizen out of East Berlin against her will. Nothing. Were they embarrassed by this development, desiring it to disappear into the ether of the Cold War? Was it a set-up and did they have other plans for the future? There was no way of telling.

He then contacted separately and privately Lieutenant Buckingham and Corporal Hancock and summoned them separately to the Consulate. He debriefed them on what part they had played in the defection and it became clear to Peter that they had been mere pawns in Bowater's scheme. They were sworn to secrecy and made to sign the Official Secrets Act.

He briefed the Consulate General, who in turn briefed the

Ambassador in Bonn. A decision was made. She should be allowed to come to the west to be debriefed in Bonn and then on to the UK where she would be given a new identity and a new life. Peter Rogers assumed that this new life would be with Charles Bowater. However, and if it was deemed necessary and prudent, they would retain a string on her life and continue to monitor her into the future.

Peter Rogers then imposed a complete blanket of secrecy over the whole episode. He called Charles and asked him to meet him in a car park in the Grunewald. They sat in his car.

'You have been very lucky, Charles. What you did was completely against all that we, as members of the quadripartite agreement in Berlin, stand for. Normally you would have been exposed, sent back to England and probably court-martialled in camera. Your Russian friend would have been exchanged for some equally insignificant person that they may be holding and sent back to face the music. We all know how nice the Russians can be to those who defect.'

Charles nodded gravely.

'However, it has been decided that because of the potential information your friend may be able to impart, and because she represents no discernible security risk to us, and because this has caused the Russians embarrassment even if it is unspoken, she can remain in the west.'

The relief on Charles' face was palpable but he said nothing.

'We know where your lady lives and we have placed very discreet 24-hour protection on it. You will not notice and don't try to look. However, we have also observed that the Russians are not even bothering to look for her. I must emphasise to you that this whole game is under a complete wrap of secrecy and you must never mention it to anyone, including your Russian friend. Your flag tour co-conspirators have been warned and have been made to sign the Official Secrets Act, something which you too will do very soon. Do not talk to them about your little escapade again. Come and have supper at the Consulate tomorrow evening at about seven and we can do all the business beforehand. Must go, old chap, and do not worry. You and she are in safe hands and the army will never know about this. You can carry on with your illustrious career.'

Charles walked back to Smuts Barracks. Although it was a freezing Berlin winter afternoon, there was a warmth in his heart. So far, so good.

CHARLES MADE his way to the apartment that evening and studiously avoided trying to locate the protection. Anna greeted him with her normal enthusiasm and passion. A long, lingering kiss followed by a meal she had lovingly prepared. He could plainly see she was completely in love with him and he knew that he was with her.

He told her that very soon she would be able to leave the apartment and Berlin. Arrangements were being made and he would probably be able to tell her the plan in the next few days. He also told her that everything he said to her about this was secret and must only be between them and no one else until she was out of Berlin.

She was so happy. The rapidity of their eating thereafter meant that the table and the kitchen were left as they undressed each other with wild abandon between there and the bedroom. Their lovemaking was desperate and afterwards they lay in each other's arms and dozed pleasantly, saying nothing. Even at this early stage of their relationship, periods of silence between them were periods of contentment and peace together.

WHEN CHARLES ARRIVED at the Consulate, Peter Rogers took him to his office where he duly signed the Official Secrets Act, a commitment that was for life unless officially revoked. Charles was then briefed on what was going to happen next. The day after tomorrow, Anna would need to be ready to move at six in the morning when a car would take her to Gatow airport. She would fly to an RAF base in West Germany and then on to the British embassy in Bonn where she would stay during her full debrief. This could take some time. Dependent on the debrief, she would then be moved to the UK.

'Please be well aware that after tomorrow evening you must not contact your friend again until you are informed that you can do so. It is likely that you will not see again for at least six weeks, maybe longer. You can tell her all of this and I hope that you have warned her of the need for complete secrecy.'

They enjoyed a very pleasant supper together in the company of other Consulate staff and Charles then left and returned to the mess. As he walked, he thought about Peter Rogers. In his line of business there could be no doubt that he could be ruthless, probably as ruthless as his counterparts on the other side of the wall but with the added ingredient of operating under the guise of an English gentleman. But Charles also thought of him as a good friend who was doing him a favour.

Their farewell night was one of physical gentleness and sleep. Before sleep he made sure that she understood what was required of her; do as she was told, don't question anything, provide every single detail of what she knew, answer all questions honestly and in full, remain calm and composed and keep positive. He also told her that she could wholly relax about him because he would always be with her forever, no matter how long the separation might be, and would see her again in England.

LEAVING the apartment early the next morning was Anna's first contact with the outside western world. The two men who accompanied her to RAF Gatow were very polite but said little. The military flight was uneventful but again she was acutely aware of how polite and quietly efficient everybody was. There was no atmosphere of surliness, distrust or an underlying feeling of threat that she was so used to. This was a new experience for her and it gladdened her heart.

She was taken directly by car to the British embassy in Bonn. She marvelled at the sleek autobahns and evident prosperity and neatness of the German countryside and the towns and villages that swept past. On arrival, she was booked in and shown with courtesy to her quarters in the embassy grounds. It was a suite of rooms that was small but comfortable and tasteful. She was then given a tour of the facilities she was welcome to use; the dining room, the gym and the library. Taking her back to her quarters, the gentleman told her that the following morning she would be collected at nine o'clock for a meeting. It all seemed too good to be true.

WITH A LIGHT HEART, Charles went back to doing some serious soldiering. It seemed to him that he had cleared his decks and that the worry and stress of the past months was behind him. Now he had to wait and be patient. There would be no contact with Anna but he had her constantly in his mind's eye.

He worked hard, kept fit and partied on occasions. He also received some further very good news. His Squadron Leader informed him that his next posting had come through and that it would begin in January. He was to be a Platoon Commander at the Royal Military Academy Sandhurst, a position which was always filled with the very best of young Captains and was generally recognised as a stepping stone to greater things. Apart from his pleasure on hearing of this news, he would be back in England – hopefully with Anna! That Friday evening he celebrated in the mess with the other young officers that he had spent so long with in West Berlin, and with whom he was close as only comrades-in-arms can be. He had six weeks left in Berlin, six weeks of waiting but at the same time keeping his standards up at both work and play.

Charles also saw Peter Rogers socially on a few occasions during this time. Taking him aside, Peter told him that all was well with Anna and everything was going according to plan and he was not to worry. Charles thought how good this was of him but did not venture to press him further.

THE INTERVIEW ROOM, a room that Anna would become very used to during the coming week, was functional. She always faced two interviewers, one female and one male, both of whom were never anything other than professional, calm, pleasant and polite. Voices were never raised and emotions never shown. She never knew their names as they were never offered. Anna felt comfortable and relaxed in their presence, even to the point where she looked forward to the next session.

The interviews were conducted in an atmosphere of calm politeness, aspects of life she was still getting used to but learning fast. These people were, on the face of it, decent and understanding. She had been very close to Charles as an Englishman and everything she had experienced and seen since she had liked. A gentler world. It would take time, but time that she was very willing to give to enable her to become fully a part of this new and still strange world.

She always responded positively to their questions. She gave them a probably unique picture of how a Soviet embassy worked from the inside with all its positive and negative intricacies. She was extremely detailed in that she tended to concentrate on people. She could not help but concentrate mainly on their failings. The alcoholism, inefficiency, corruption and sheer bloody-minded disregard for people and their wishes. The fear, mistrust and paranoia as part of life. The maxim 'the less you know, the better you sleep'. The Soviet system in microcosm but with the added spice of her incisive and telling mind. But she also expounded the good side of the Russian character. Their inherent decency when they could feel free to express themselves, their patience, their humour and their romantic and emotional beliefs where fate played such a great part in their lives.

Anna explained in detail how she, as part of a small medical team from the embassy, took part in a number of visits to Red Army units based in East Berlin, and some in East Germany. Again, she focussed on how she interpreted the people she observed and met and again she painted a sorry tale. The interviewers were well aware that they were speaking to someone who had no previous experience of the west and that what she was telling them was based on what she saw from a Soviet point of view. And yet the insightfulness and truthfulness of her observations was remarkable.

One of her main tasks during these visits was to conduct briefings to assembled soldiers, sometimes as many as two hundred at a time, on the importance of personal hygiene. Her briefings were practical and full of good advice but she soon became used to almost total lack of interest displayed in the myriad of faces she addressed. She also noticed how sallow and underfed they looked and, when leaving the lecture hall, how they seemed to shuffle with no enthusiasm for life. Many had bruises on their faces. The overall impression they gave, and she emphasised this to her interviewers, was one of low morale and a general lack of interest. She had a chance after she had given her lectures to talk to some of them and this confirmed to her that they were not happy soldiers. With their officers hovering nearby, they were not prepared to tell her what she suspected might be the truth about their existence as part of the 'elite' Group of Soviet Forces in Germany, or GSFG, but they were very happy to have the chance of being in close proximity to a very beautiful woman. The whole atmosphere permeated a drabness and lack of purpose that was depressing and pervasive.

Anna also talked for some days about general life in the Soviet Union, and in particular about her life in Leningrad, the cradle of the revolution. Again, she pulled no punches in her descriptions and opinions. She gave insights into living in a close-knit family that held dear the principles and way of life of the Soviet system. She described at length and in detail the daily grind and how the system ensured that everyone, or certainly everyone she knew, was kept in a state of permanent servility. There was no real friendship outside family life because of the mistrust the system generated in everyone. No one spoke to give opinions or complaints about daily life in case they were reported on. There was no civic pride or willingness to be involved. Everyone kept themselves to themselves and said as little as possible. She said that, in her opinion and in the knowledge that she had known none other, it was an almost unreal existence, and one which she hated but could not influence at all. To try to do so would invite retribution.

The interviews went on for almost a week. The information she imparted over that period was, in a holistic way, very useful indeed as an inside personal picture of the Soviet way of life and how it impacted on people's lives and made them what they were. She had no military secrets to tell, and she had no startling revelations to give but what she did give was something that helped to fill in some of the pieces of the jigsaw that gave the west further intelligence about what their enemy was really like, and especially their weaknesses as one of their own honestly perceived. May Day parades in Moscow or Berlin were fine spectacles of military might and intention, but they did not portray the brutality of barrack-room life in East Germany or the alcoholism so prevalent in the Soviet embassy in East Berlin.

———

THE POLITE INTERVIEWERS finally informed her that they were happy with what she had given them and that she could now relax and wait for further information. She waited a further two days and enjoyed relaxing in the embassy. She ate well, visited the library frequently, attempted to improve her English by increasing her vocabulary, and slept well. She managed she borrow some sports kit from a member of the staff and visited the gym each morning.

On the third day she was taken to see a gentleman who did not give his name when they met but sat her down and informed her in measured tones that they were extremely grateful for all in the information she had given them, that there may be occasion in the future for further interviews but that in the next days she would be taken to England where she would be required to remain at an address for some time. He assured her that there was nothing to worry about and that she could now consider England her future home.

———

THE TRIP to England the following day, again by military aircraft, was uneventful. She was then driven to a detached house in a quiet tree-lined avenue in a suburban area. She had no idea where she was and no one told her. The two gentlemen in the car said nothing during the journey and she ventured no questions.

On arrival, she was introduced to a further young man whom she was told would be looking after her during her stay. He was a pleasant and polite person but she detected a certain hardness about him. He certainly looked physically hard. He showed her around the house which had been modified to allow 'Jake' to occupy a very small, self-contained apartment at the front overlooking the street and the remainder to accommodate 'guests'. It was spacious and comfortable with, it seemed at first inspection, everything she needed. There was a small, very enclosed and secluded garden at the back with a high wall and much shrubbery. What she didn't see were the discreetly placed cameras on those high walls.

After she had settled in to her comfortable bedroom, Jake briefed on the dos and don'ts of life in the house.

Never go out except into the garden. Do not venture to the front of the house where he lived. Food would be bought to her and she could cook what she wished. Stay away from windows upstairs and keep bedroom blinds down at all times. No contact with the outside world. If you have any concerns or questions at all, and of any nature, ask me and I will sort it out for you. Every three days there will be a changeover. I will go and my colleague will take over for the next three days and so on. And by the way, may I take some pictures of you for security purposes?

This was not a request and he took some photographs of her face and upper body.

She settled down to wait. There were many books in the house and a small gym where she could use an exercise bike and a rowing machine, as well as some weights. She resolved to read as much as she could and get fit. Charles would like that because he had told her how keen he was on physical exercise. She had no idea how long she would be in the house and did not ask. Patience and stoicism were the order of the day.

The peace and silence of the house gave her ample

opportunity to mull over what she had done and why. The 'why' was easy to answer. She had fallen completely in love with a stranger where the urge to be with him overwhelmed her. He was now no longer a stranger and their short time together in Berlin had only served to confirm beyond doubt that her initial feelings were right. She had done it for him, and herself, but what had she left behind?

She reasoned that some aspects of her previous existence were easy to discard. Although she had had nothing to compare it with, she instinctively knew that the system under which she lived was wrong and contrary to the human spirit. She was not sorry at all to leave that behind. She was not sorry to leave behind the almost zero prospects of meeting someone whom she might wish to be with in the future, although she was sure that there were probably some good men out there somewhere. She was not sorry to leave behind the almost mind-numbing and predictable banality of life in Russia, with little prospect of real improvement.

What she was very sorry indeed to leave behind was her family whom she loved dearly and greatly missed. She knew that the authorities would now place all three of them under suspicion. She also knew they would not tell them what had happened, or what they thought had happened. She assumed they would still imagine her as working as a doctor in East Berlin and that all was well. She also knew she would probably never see them again.

MIKHAIL AND ALEKSANDRA NAZAROV, who lived for the state and their two daughters, in that order, were surprised when two plain clothed-officers from state security visited them in their apartment in Leningrad. This was not a usual occurrence unless they had done something wrong. The KGB knew that the Nazarovs had an impeccable Soviet pedigree worthy of great respect but because of their daughter's mysterious disappearance in Berlin with a possibility that she had defected to the west, they were there to blank them off from the situation and its possible ramifications.

'Comrades. We are here to inform you that your older daughter Anna Nazarov has been moved from the embassy in East Berlin to a closed city in the Urals. Her work in Berlin has been exemplary and therefore she has been promoted to be the doctor for a research facility in that city. We are here to inform you that once she is there it will be some time before you see her again, maybe years.'

Mikhail and Aleksandra Nazarov greeted this news with pride. Their daughter was going up in the world. They knew many comrades whose children had been away from home for years. It was a way of life in the Soviet Union.

CHARLES' last weeks in West Berlin passed very slowly. To be completely out of touch with Anna was rather like when she was in East Berlin, but he resisted the urge to approach Peter Rogers for an update. He had no idea where she was or what had happened exactly since he last saw her but he had little or no doubt in his mind that all would be well. Life remained very busy as usual and he focussed on his work. He was pleased when his replacement arrived a week before he departed and he enjoyed his farewell parties, both with the squadron and in the mess.

Both were informal affairs. The Squadron Sergeant Major spoke warmly of him at the squadron party and presented him with a brass model of a chieftain tank. Soldiers in various states of inebriation were complimentary, but one ventured to tell him that he didn't think much of him, to which Charles smiled and thanked him for telling the truth. A good time was had by all and was helped by free beer all round for the whole evening.

In the Officers' Mess there was a small gathering of the squadron's officers and their wives and a smattering of female friends. It was a quiet affair and after his speech, which was short but kind, the Squadron Leader presented Charles with a superb etching of the Brandenburg Gate. He emphasised the point that this etching was done well before the wall went up.

It was time to pack up and go. He wanted to get back to England but before he departed that divided city he called Peter Rogers and asked if they could meet very briefly. Peter told him that he was going to call him anyway and they met in a café close to the Consulate.

'The message is that Anna is safe and well and in England. I cannot tell you where she is but can say that you need not worry.'

'Does this mean she can remain in England?'

'Probably yes.' Never a straight answer, but a good enough one anyway.

'I would like to keep in touch, Peter.'

'I hope that we can.' Never a firm commitment given.

CHARLES LEFT West Berlin with a light heart. Not a great one for reflecting too deeply on the past, no matter how recent, he nevertheless recognised as he travelled what a tumultuous time it had been in that wonderful but fractured city. He had been lucky to serve there. He also recognised in his own way that what he had done with Anna would probably change his life forever. He seemed, on the face of it, to have got away with it, at least in the short term, and his posting to Sandhurst had proven that. The Foreign Office knew because he had told them, but the army apparently did not.

Before he left Berlin, he met up with Jamie and Corporal Hancock in a nondescript bar to thank them for their support during that nerve-racking time. Their reaction surprised him. They did not speak about it but merely nodded and changed the subject. He realised that for them it was an episode they wished to forget.

As he disembarked at RAF Brize Norton there was a spring in his step; indeed, spring itself was in the air. He had so much to look forward to. For the next three weeks he would be living at his favourite place, his parents' home in Wiltshire. He would be beginning his new job which he looked forward to immensely and lastly, but most importantly, he would be seeing Anna again soon, he hoped.

Jane Bowater was there to meet him. They drove home to the sleepy village in Wiltshire where the family home was situated. Time for a new start, thought Charles, as his mother chatted away cheerfully.

PART 3: CONTENTMENT

ONE

The Bowaters' house was tucked away down its own drive on the edge of a pretty Wiltshire village nestling on the banks of the River Wylye. It represented the epitome of Englishness. Georgian by age and design with a classic symmetry of windows and doors, mellow stone and a beautiful garden with lawns sloping gently down to the river. It was large and spacious inside, had been recently wholly renovated and modernised and was a delightful haven of peace and tranquillity. It could have been described as 'picture postcard', although all the Bowaters would have hated that description.

In Charles' view, the best part of his home was the peace and gentleness of the English countryside that surrounded the house. He could look out of his bedroom window and see green fields and small woods and coverts with trees just blossoming. If he stood still and listened, he could hear nothing but the birds and the odd mooing cow, and at night owls and the occasional badger's cry. So different to the hustle and bustle of Berlin. He knew that one day this would be his as his father had constantly told him and this gave him a feeling of permanence and inner contentment.

Unpacking was swift. He knew where to put everything and

most of his kit had been sent direct to Sandhurst to await his arrival. He went downstairs to the spacious kitchen and found his mother preparing lunch, a lunch that would no doubt be delicious and ultra-healthy. Jane Bowater was a very accomplished cook, an art that she had learnt many years ago as a young woman in London as a cordon bleu chef. Not the usual heavy, unappetising food from her. It was a Mediterranean diet for the Bowaters whether they liked it or not.

Jane Bowater was a very attractive middle-aged woman with immense energy and joie de vivre. Being what the English called 'well off', she ran her house with an efficiency and style that was sometimes alarming but always charming, convivial and friendly. It always seemed immaculate no matter what was happening and she never seemed to flag, be ill or complain.

Jane Bowater's relationship with her husband of 30 or so years was based on a close and mutual understanding that it was the comfort and practicalities of life that counted. She doubted that she ever loved him in the truest sense of the word, unlike he who adored her and remained after all these years completely in love with her. She had bought their house and she kept him. He knew this but it did not make him feel guilty. He did his bit for their partnership.

David Bowater was a gentle soul and always had been. However, this gentle nature had always hidden a steely interior. He had spent a career in the army, and in particular serving with an illustrious infantry regiment. He had enjoyed the delights of a pre-war colonial existence in the far east including Hong Kong, Singapore and Malaya. But he had also experienced, at first hand and at the end of a rifle and a bayonet, the terrifying heat of combat, in North Africa, Italy and North West Europe, and then in counter-insurgency operations in Malaya and Borneo. In North Africa, Italy and France and Germany the foe were the Germans; well led, competent, organised, ruthless but hopelessly flawed in that they represented and mainly supported a wholly repugnant cause. In Malaya it was communist-backed insurgents; unseen, brutal and committed to another wholly odious cause.

David Bowater's two Military Crosses and five Mention in Despatches bore testimony to that steely interior. Guests were shown the row of shell fragments that adorned a shelf in the downstairs loo and told that they used to be in his body. He also delighted in telling them there were others that remained inside him. He saw his army career out and after a number of gratefully received and sedentary postings in the south of England, gracefully retired as a Lieutenant Colonel. His promotion was met with some surprise by those who knew him well, but they were happy for him because more than most, he had proved himself in his wars.

Having retired five years previously, David Bowater honed his life down into a number of passions. First and foremost was his one-acre garden which he tended with loving care every day of the year, through the changing seasons and in all weathers. The second was his dog. Henry was, like his master, gentle and unassuming. A black Labrador who despised walks and aspired to the easy life. His third was his son and finally was his wine cellar. In that mix, and it was a mix rather than a list of priorities, Jane Bowater appeared from time to time.

David Bowater's affection for alcohol was an accepted part of family life, and the reason it was accepted was that alcohol never made him loud, boorish, aggressive or argumentative. It merely sent him to sleep, even, on occasions at lunch or dinner parties, of which there were many. He drank too much but Jane Bowater accepted this because he was always so gentle, kind and accommodating, whether he was in his cups or not. Tucked away in a corner of his garden was a wooden hut where he kept a myriad of tools and appliances. He also kept a cache of whiskey to fortify himself during his long hours of horticultural endeavour.

This cache was kept in a water barrel where it could be drawn up using a piece of string. When chums appeared, they would retire to his hut and reminisce over a dram or four.

He also loved to entertain Charles over a bottle or two, regaling him with tales of derring-do. Not for him was the 'I never talk about the war' syndrome. Not only would he tell all, but his ability to embellish remained undimmed.

Grateful for the rest at home, Charles went for long walks with a reluctant Henry, rediscovered his favourite pubs in the area, made contact and met up with various chums and generally relaxed and waited, impatiently. During his first week at home, he ventured to warn his parents about the impending arrival of Anna. He was in the kitchen with his mother.

'You remember I mentioned a girl that I met in Berlin, mother?'

'Yes, I do. Is she coming to see you here?'

'Yes, but would it be alright if she stayed for some time? It is rather a delicate situation that I can explain to you later.'

'When will she arrive?'

'I'm not sure yet but I will give you as much warning as possible.'

Jane Bowater smiled. 'She can stay as long as she likes and will be most welcome.'

She realised she might be sticking her neck out here. There was only one other occasion when Charles had bought home a 'friend' and it had proved a disaster. She had never asked where Charles had found her. She wore few clothes, swore constantly and her table manners were non-existent. She made serious inroads into David's wine cellar and turned Charles' bedroom into a tip in no time at all. She appeared never to wash and would frequently disappear into the garden, returning smelling of something strange and unknown to Jane. She did not stay long and Charles never mentioned her again. He had spent most of those five days either acutely embarrassed or exhausted due her insatiable appetite for sex. Jane Bowater viewed it as an aberration and had cast the episode from her mind.

'Thank you, mother. I know you'll like her and she will like you.'

David Bowater was not consulted because both Jane and Charles knew that he would not mind at all. Indeed, he would welcome a potential drinking partner. Charles did not tell him that Anna hardly drank.

After two weeks at home and with the time drawing nigh for him to report to Sandhurst, the telephone rang.

'Is that Captain Charles Bowater?'

'Yes.'

'Your friend will arrive where you are tomorrow at about midday. The transport will be by car to your location.'

The telephone went dead. Charles sat down for a few minutes, his mind racing. So, Peter Rogers had been true to his word. What a fantastic man he was. Charles leapt into action.

TWO

Anna's minders changed over every three days as promised and both were equally discreet and polite. They kept themselves to themselves and remained in the front of the house although she could sense that they were constantly there, ever watchful and available if she needed anything or was worried or concerned.

One morning, Jake came to her.

'Tomorrow morning, you will have a visitor. This gentleman will explain to you everything you will need to know about the immediate future.'

'Do I need to do anything beforehand?'

'No. He will explain everything to you.'

The visitor was a slim, very dapper young man who bore an air of authority. He greeted her but did not proffer a name. He carried a slim briefcase. There were mutual pleasantries.

'I have come to give you instructions and issue you the necessary documents for you to remain in the United Kingdom. These documents include a British passport and a National Insurance Number which will allow you to move freely and give you access to all the medical and social services this country offers if you need them.

'Once you have left this house, you must never again mention what you have experienced here, and to that end I will be asking you to sign the Official Secrets Act which essentially binds you to that requirement under the pain of imprisonment should you choose to ignore or abuse it at any stage.'

He went through the paperwork with her and she signed the necessary documents with alacrity and a heart that was becoming lighter by the moment.

He went on in his precise and clipped tones.

'You should have everything packed and be ready to move tomorrow morning at six o'clock. A car will take you directly to a house outside London where you will be re-united with Captain Bowater. Do you have any questions?'

She shook her head dumbly. He stood up, shook her hand and was gone.

She sat down and thanked God, whoever he may be in her hitherto Godless world.

She carefully examined the documents she had been given. In her passport her name was given as Hanna Novak. She was born in Prague in Czechoslovakia on 8th May 1946. She wondered how they had worked that one out. Best not ask or even mention it again.

Her mind in a happy turmoil, she busied herself with lunch and supper, packing her meagre belongings and making sure that she looked as beautiful for him as she could. She greatly amused Pete by asking him to buy her some makeup, a subject that was alien to him but which he did nonetheless through Jake , who did rather well although the lipstick was a bit too red and bright for her liking. Never mind. Charles would probably like it.

THE JOURNEY WAS comfortable and silent. There were two young men, both bearing the same hallmarks of Jake and Pete, who sat in front and she in the back seat. The journey took about an hour and at no time did she have a clue of where she was. All she knew was that the green English countryside that they passed in the early morning mist and gathering sunlight was beautiful and peaceful. Small villages with their ancient churches represented a world that she was entirely unfamiliar with but which she liked greatly.

The car turned off the main road, passed through a village, entered a short drive lined with trees and came to a halt in front of a beautiful, mellowed-stone house of some size. The front was all drive and beyond that neat lawns to the border with the road. To the sides were walls adorned with an array of climbing plants in full flower, displaying a rainbow of colour.

Charles stood next to the front door and just behind him she could see what were obviously his parents. She was very apprehensive and her heart beat loudly as she thanked the two silent young men, one of whom helped her with her suitcase. Charles greeted her with a stiff formality and shyness she had not seen before, but she too was reticent and showed no emotion.

Charles then very formally introduced her to his parents, a handsome and elegantly dressed couple. Anna immediately took to them both, and in particular Jane Bowater whose welcoming warmth was very evident. David Bowater was bowled over by the beauty of this woman, and amazed that his son could possess such good taste. She had an elegance and poise about her which he very much liked.

Whilst Jane busied herself with breakfast, Charles showed Anna to her room, a room that was large, en suite and tastefully decorated and furnished. It faced on to the large garden at the back of the house and as she looked out on to the well-kept lawns, many trees and borders full of what seemed like an enormous variety of flowers and shrubs, she felt a peace descend on her. This seemed like heaven after Leningrad and East Berlin. To cap it all, it was the beginning of a beautiful early summer's day.

Over a very English breakfast, shyness evaporated as they came to know each other. Both David and Jane Bowater were respectful enough not to delve into Anna's past, although they had quickly picked up her accent and knew that she was not English. Perhaps this was a good thing, given their last experience.

Anna thought it best that at the earliest opportunity she gave them a quick resume of her past and then hopefully there it would rest. This was going to be news to Charles as well, as she had not had either the opportunity or time to explain to him her new identity. The evening before, she had concocted a plausible story about how she had ended up in West Berlin where they met.

Her name was Hanna Novak, not Anna as Charles had introduced her as and which raised a momentary David Bowater eyebrow, and she originally came from Prague in Czechoslovakia. When young, and before the 'Iron Curtain' descended across Europe, her parents and their only child fled to West Germany where she had lived ever since. They lived in a city called Kassel where she was educated and trained as doctor. In time she was offered a position in West Berlin where she met Charles. In the meantime, both her parents had died and she had no living relatives, as far as she knew.

This short narrative, given in her gentle, quiet and sweetly accented voice, was met with acceptance by the Bowaters. There were no questions or intrusive probes. That was the way of the Bowaters. They had always respected other people's privacy and had never been intrusive. Hanna seemed to be a blessing and that was that. Charles smiled to himself. She had cleared the air in one stroke.

IT WAS a relief to be alone for the first time in six weeks. They went upstairs, Hanna to unpack and Charles to chat. They had so much to talk about but as soon as her bedroom door was closed, he took her in his arms and they kissed, deeply and passionately for a long time. As their bodies pressed against each other, the passion turned to a fiery desire. They fell onto her bed and as they continued to kiss, his hand found her knickers, the knickers he had bought her in Belin, and urgently pulled them off. She giggled and held him closer. Without further ado he took her with a desire and passion he could not have thought possible. Her body arched eagerly for him and within thirty seconds they were spent. She stifled a scream of pure pleasure as she came with him, staring into his eyes with love.

As they lay there, Charles simply said, 'Will you marry me?'

'Yes, I will.'

'Shall we unpack and organise your room and then we can go for a walk and talk about all the things we need to talk about?'

'That will be lovely.'

THEY WALKED for two hours along bridleways and footpaths so expertly signposted. Charles knew them all well but to Hanna this was another revelation; a recognition of and subsequent provision for the countryside to be used by the public for their enjoyment. Henry came along and was unimpressed by the distance they covered, but he was privy to their conversations.

Ignoring the earnest instructions she had so recently received, Hanna told him all about her time in Bonn and then the safe house in England. She had surmised that during that week in Bonn she had given them enough information for them to agree that she could stay. In any case, and in her opinion, they were happy that the Soviets had been embarrassed by her disappearance. She told him about her new identity, her registration in England and how she had concocted the story to tell his parents. She told him many times how much she loved him and how she looked forward to their life together. She said that she would always have a dark cloud over her which was her family in Russia but that it was nothing compared to her love for him.

Charles in turn talked about his farewells in West Berlin, his new job at Sandhurst beginning in ten days' time and how excited about it he was, his wish for them to be married in the late summer and of his almost overwhelming love for her.

During the next ten days, and before Charles departed, Hanna and Jane Bowater spent many hours in the kitchen together where Janes' ability to cook delicious, healthy food at all times gave Hanna a new interest that was to remain with her. Much of the fresh produce came from David's spectacular vegetable and fruit gardens, but trips with Jane to the local supermarkets also amazed Hanna. There was so much of everything and everyone was so friendly and helpful.

Hanna quickly noticed David's fondness for wine but liked him anyway because he was so gentle, kind and understanding, even at the end of dinner when he got out the legal whiskey bottle. Charles indulged him to a point but held back in the knowledge of the lovemaking upstairs that would inevitably follow.

The Bowaters entertained at least once a week. Jane loved to organise supper parties and produce an enviable fare, often alfresco on the terrace during the summer months. Hanna always helped and loved the atmosphere in which these events were held. She marvelled at the easy openness of the conversation that ranged through politics, to the economy, to scandal if there was any, to family, to shooting and much more besides. Most had an opinion and all listened. There was none of the suspicion or fear she was so used to.

Each day they would walk long and hard through the

delightful countryside, sometimes with Henry but sometimes not if he was snoring by the Aga surrounded by a green haze. When supper in the evenings drew to a close, a heightened sense of anticipation fell over them both.

They had both agreed that their lovemaking meetings should remain clandestine in respect of his parents as it was their house. The most distant from his parents' bedroom was Hanna's, so it was agreed that he would make the furtive trip during the night. He soon discovered every creaking floorboard and how to avoid them, and once he had very carefully closed her bedroom door he was in her arms. She normally wore nothing as she waited for him in bed in the fading summer dusk, but sometimes she wore stockings and suspenders, something she knew he liked. As time went on, and in many ways like West Berlin, their lovemaking varied between total desire and lust to gentleness. But no matter what the feeling of any particular night, and no matter what they did, their love for each other was a constant.

David and Jane Bowater knew exactly what was going on but cared not one jot. Charles could never avoid all the creaking floorboards or, in his ardent haste to dive into bed with his beauty, close the bedroom door with the required silent gentleness.

———

THE DAY before Charles was due to depart, and over lunch around the kitchen table, he decided to broach two subjects that both he and Hanna wanted them to know and hopefully accept.

'Firstly, Hanna and I would like to get married in the late summer this year. I hope that you will not object. Secondly, would it be alright if Hanna was able to stay here until such time as we are married and can live together wherever the army will take me?'

Over the ten days since her arrival, Jane Bowater had grown exceptionally fond of Hanna. She loved her gentle, kind nature, her willingness to help and do anything asked of her, her acute intelligence and her obvious love for Charles. Not only did she want her to stay, she would have been very sad if she had left when Charles had gone. In turn, Hanna adored this strong but kind woman.

David Bowater's reaction was typical. A broad smile followed a mellow nod. As always, he left the talking to his wife.

'We are so delighted for both of you. In fact, we were hoping for this and late summer would be perfect. As for you staying with us, Hanna, you are completely welcome and you can stay as long as you wish. You are part of the family already.'

She got up from the table, walked round to Hanna and took her in her arms with a big hug, a most unusual occurrence from this indomitable woman. She then hugged her son. David Bowater looked on with a smile and a chuckle.

Charles knew that his mother would attempt to start the wedding planning immediately, but quickly interjected.

'Shall we wait until I have settled into my new job before we start discussing plans for the wedding. I will have to see what my programme is and then we can decide on a date.'

He did not mention a possible location but in his mind he saw the Royal Military Academy as a perfect spot to be married. He pictured the Memorial Chapel, magnificent, and the potential locations for the reception. Its splendid reception rooms in Old College, as well as the beautiful lakeside could all be used, especially as he would then be a serving member of staff there. But he also knew his mother would be more than disappointed. He knew she would want nothing more than for her only son and this beautiful and charming woman to be married in the village church and have the reception in the grounds of their own home. He also knew that in the end she would get her own way.

THREE

C harles had done well in West Berlin and his annual reports reflected that. They noted he was always well prepared, confident and competent in all that he was required to do, but that he was also a good leader of men, innovative, unassuming and an attentive listener. There was a box at the bottom of each report where the reporting officer was able to give an estimate of what rank the officer he or she was reporting on might reach in his or her career. In Charles' case it was Brigadier, which was very pleasing but not what he wanted. He wanted to reach the very top and nothing else would do.

It did not take Charles long to settle into his new position. He focussed entirely on his role and what he had to achieve and mostly put thoughts of Hanna aside for the time being. His new intake was of 30 rather insipid youths whose average age was nineteen and who appeared to be an unprepossessing lot. Few, if any, had university degrees and most had come straight from school after passing the Regular Commissions Board's four-day test at Westbury. They then found themselves in the torturous maelstrom of the first term at Sandhurst. It was a rude awakening and designed to be so. The whole British army logic of testing bodies and minds to the limit and seeing if they would break was applied. If you survived the first term it was likely, barring mishaps, that you would receive the prized Queen's Commission at the Sovereign's Pass Out Parade two years hence.

Over that two-year period, Charles revelled in his role and took great pride in how he moulded these young men into young officers who would hopefully become competent and professional leaders of men, both in peace and in war as many of them would find out when they went to their regiments and corps. He loved the structured atmosphere of Sandhurst where everything from early morning runs, drill on the square, tactical studies, exercises both home and abroad, church services, academic studies, visits, sport and many other activities besides was conducted to the highest standards. The physical setting of Sandhurst was also maintained to the highest standards. It was very hard work but not once did he not enjoy it. He also greatly appreciated the company of his fellow officers and academics, all of whom had been selected, like him, to show to the army and indeed the world that the Royal Military Academy Sandhurst was at the top of the pile in all respects. He enjoyed a sound relationship with the two Company Commanders that he served under; one being a stern Guards officer and the other, in contrast, a relaxed cavalry officer. Appearances can be deceptive and these two majors knew their business.

When time allowed, he made inquiries as to the possibility of being married in the Memorial Chapel and hold his reception either in Old College or within the grounds and preferably down by the lakeside. He was told that all was possible and everything could be arranged. He was also told that the reception would be expensive but magnificent with marquees, food and drink provided. In short, he would have to do little and nor would Hanna or his parents. The prospect was encouraging.

HE WAS in a state of nervous anticipation when he arrived at the railway station.

As always, his mother was there to meet him. With her was this vision. He had not forgotten, but seeing Hanna again made his heart jump. He held her and looked at her intently, and she him. He once again vowed that this woman could never be anything else but with him for life.

There was much to discuss. Both Hanna and Charles were eager to be on their own once they arrived home. They had not seen each other for four weeks, and apart from a number of quick calls, had not spoken. Jane Bowater sensed this and disappeared into the garden to find her husband and, perhaps, catch him out in his lair.

As before, and it would always be, there was the lust and sex that drove them to the very heights of pleasure. They both wished that it hadn't happened so quickly but time did not detract from the intense feelings they both experienced for each other at the moment of climax. They also knew a long night of love and passion lay ahead.

Hanna told him in detail all about her time at home and how much she loved it here, and how much she loved his mother and respected his father. He could see that she was very content. He then told her all about his first four weeks at Sandhurst, how much he enjoyed it and how much he wanted make his army career a success, not just for him but for both of them.

The conversation moved on rapidly, each trying to get more words in, but the main topic of the day was finally reached. Charles suggested to her a date, Saturday 24th August, and then talked about his feelings concerning the location. He explained to her the delights of holding their wedding at Sandhurst and how he thought it would be the best solution. They would be married at the Memorial Chapel and he would wear uniform. He probably extolled the virtues and advantages a little too much, but Hanna listened quietly and attentively.

Lunch was a lively affair. David Bowater delved into his impressive cellar and produced some Moet to welcome his son home. A couple of bottles of excellent Chablis nestled in the fridge. Conversation ranged far and wide, bringing in home, garden, village gossip and, much to her embarrassment, how wonderful Hanna had been and how she was now part of the family. His mother obviously adored her and his father nodded sagely in agreement at every opportunity.

Inevitably, after champagne had been partaken and the wine opened by the expert hand of David Bowater, talk turned to the wedding. Charles opened by suggesting the date he had in mind and this was agreed with no fuss at all. If there ever was going to be a disagreement, it would be about where. Despite his glowing explanations, Charles could see that he was on to a loser from the start. In his absence, Hanna had been got at by his parents. They had taken her to the beautiful and capacious eleventh-century Norman church in the village, she had met the charming but eccentric vicar and it had been explained in detail to her how the reception would be held in their own beautiful gardens. She was convinced and Charles lost the vote by three to one. This vote was greeted with a great deal of laughter and the clinking of glasses. He did not mind at all and at least he could wear morning dress which he much preferred.

Their short time together was bliss. A short walk after lunch with Henry was followed by further animated discussion about the wedding and who they should invite. This was a one-sided affair as Hanna had no one to invite, so Charles trod carefully. She was not perturbed at all about this but Charles realised it would be crass of him to use the wedding as an excuse to invite all his army chums, of which there were many. He mentally scaled down his list to an absolute minimum. An elegant, quiet wedding was the order of the day – despite the many noses that would be put out of joint.

The following morning, after a lazy breakfast which Hanna prepared, they all attended communion at the village church and afterwards discussed the date and arrangements with the vicar. The date was clear in his diary and so it was to be.

Charles returned to Sandhurst after lunch, his mind full of Hanna and their night of love, and of their wedding. Before he left he could see his mother beginning to move into top arranging gear with a willing and able Hanna by her side. David Bowater retired to his shed but knew that on the day his responsibilities would be considerable; an immaculate garden and the very best in the copious amounts of fine champagnes and wines that would need to be served. He undertook his initial planning over a dram or three of illicit whiskey retrieved from the offending barrel.

Once he was back in his comfortable rooms in the Officers' Mess, Charles clicked back into military mode.

The end of his first term at Sandhurst was nigh and when he returned after the summer break, he would be a married man. The thought filled him with a mixture of delight and apprehension. He had discussed with Hanna their post-wedding plans and both agreed that the best solution would be for Hanna to remain in Wiltshire for the time being. Jane Bowater had been more than delighted.

'I would not have it any other way and I know it will be the best for both of you until you decide where you want to live. I am sure that there will be married quarters available at Camberley, but do you really want to live there?'

She had lived in too many army married quarters in her time and David Bowater nodded sagely in agreement.

THE GUEST LIST had been pared down to absolute maximum of 40, and that included the vicar. Charles felt it prudent to invite his Company Commander, his Squadron Leader from Berlin, a number of his fellow platoon commanders at Sandhurst and a few other friends from Berlin, the army and beyond. His parents invited a few village worthies and a couple of David's old fighting and drinking chums to keep him happy. Jamie Buckingham would be best man. Morning dress would be *de rigueur*.

Jane Bowater insisted that Hanna wore her wedding dress – at which Hanna burst into tears. In general, and as the day approached, Hanna became more nervous. She even banned the amorous Charles from her bedroom for the last few days but promised him that after the knot was tied she would make it up to him tenfold.

David Bowater, commander of the garden, marquees, dance floor, band and drinks flow had excelled himself. His in-house wine tasting had produced the best from his cellar and more was ordered. The garden gleamed and the marquee company produced the best including everything that went inside. The local yokel band were hired and warned to keep it civilised or they would be out on their ear.

'We have a perfectly good stereo system we could use instead,' he warned them.

Jane Bowater hired a catering company and scoured the village for willing young people who would be happy to serve as waitresses and waiters and be paid handsomely. She ensured flowers were in abundance everywhere and she did those herself with the help of Hanna, who again was on a steep learning curve.

WITH CHARLES and Jamie at the altar, there was a just discernible gasp as Hanna entered the church on David Bowater's arm. None had seen her before, let alone met her. She radiated beauty and the dress fitted her to perfection.

The vicar was splendid. He portrayed a benign and calm exterior although those that knew him in the parish were well aware of his approach to non-believers and anyone else who didn't attend church regularly. Many, including his wife, considered him slightly bonkers and certainly eccentric.

The service went without a hitch and the happy couple were whisked by horse-drawn carriage back to the house followed by the congregation on foot, led by the vicar in the role of the shepherd guiding his misguided flock.

If the village church and the service therein set the scene then the lawns and gardens of Vine House, the white marquees, the delicious late lunch, the splendid wines and the excellent service from the coterie of young waitresses and waiters, well briefed and drilled by Jane Bowater, only served to complement it. To cap it all, it was a beautiful late summer day.

The reception and lunch were civilised throughout, if not necessarily sober. David Bowater gave a gentle, quietly delivered speech on behalf of the bride extolling her sweetness and his delight that she was now his daughter-in-law and part of the family. Jamie Buckingham spoke without resorting to any form of bawdiness as is sometimes expected at these occasions. His speech was short and succinct, perhaps reflecting their not so close relationship.

'I have known Charles for many years and we have grown up together in the army. I count him as friend, and a very good friend but he is a man of independence and honour. I wish him and the beautiful and captivating Hanna the very best, a wonderful future together and that all their times will be happy. Let's raise our glasses to them both.'

The gathered throng, seated on round tables of six, murmured their appreciation and congratulations. It was all very English.

Hanna looked even more radiant and happy, although she couldn't help thinking of her parents and sister. How far away they seemed and in such a different world to the one to which she now belonged.

The vicar excelled himself at the reception. Despite the beady eye of his long-suffering wife, he entered with gusto into the patronage of the Bowaters. He was adept at exchanging an empty champagne glass with a full one each time a waiter or waitress passed by so that by the time all were seated for lunch he was in full flow about the inequities of the modern world, which obviously did not include partaking excessively in alcohol. He was amusing rather than aggressive, and like David Bowater tended to sleep when in his cups. As lunch progressed, and in between bouts of noisy opinion alternating between happiness and despair, he slowly nodded off, much to the relief of his wife and his table. He nodded off so well that he slowly slipped beneath the table where he mercifully remained throughout the speeches and toasts. The band woke him up and with a bottle in his hand he staggered off into the gathering dusk to face the wrath of his long-departed wife.

Whilst after lunch most lingered and continued to enjoy David Bowater's largesse, Hanna and Charles slipped away for her to change out of her wedding dress. They were kissing fervently when Hanna pulled away, hoisted her wedding dress up and knelt on the bed. He was vaguely shocked to see that she was not wearing any knickers but recovered quickly enough to engage in the most blissful of sex, and did well to stifle her screams in a cushion. It did not last long but it was spectacular and a memory that would last for ever. Flushed and laughing, she changed quickly and hurried downstairs to join the fun.

The elders eventually drifted or hobbled away and the young waited impatiently for the appearance of the Turnips, a band none of them had ever heard of and, following their performance, would not want to hear of again. They tried to model themselves on The Wurzels but failed. However, alcohol had loosened everyone's inhibitions and tongues and they danced the night away to the sounds of the sixties and other delights such as 'I got a Brand-New Combine Harvester and I'll give you the Keys'. The young waitresses and waiters downed their trays and joined in with enthusiasm.

WITH NO NEED TO sneak quietly back to his room at five in morning, avoiding the creaking floorboards, Charles lay quietly looking at his new wife as the early morning sun streamed into the room. She slept peacefully on her back and he marvelled, as he always did, at her serene beauty. He did not disturb her although he was sorely tempted to do so, got up and went downstairs to make tea. His mother was already in the kitchen and even at that early time following the reception was as spruce as ever. He wandered outside in his dressing gown and surveyed the scene. He woke up a dishevelled George recumbent in the marquee and after a grateful cup of tea sent him on his way. He chatted to his mother and they agreed that breakfast would be the time to break the news of their honeymoon to Hanna, a honeymoon that had been gifted them by Jane Bowater.

Hanna was stunned by the news. That afternoon they would leave for the Amalfi Coast in Italy. They would fly to Naples and then on by taxi to the small coastal town of Positano where their small, elegant hotel overlooking the sea awaited. Her amazement turned to excitement and she hugged her mother-in-law, their bond complete.

Positano proved to be as romantic and Italian as the pictures suggested. Their hotel was perfect for them and their rooms spacious and comfortable. The views were splendid, especially in the early morning. Their ten days went by in a flash. Neither were interested in lying on a beach. They loved the sea and swam every morning before breakfast, and they loved the Mediterranean diet in which they indulged fully, sampling all the local ristorantes. They visited the island of Capri to savour real romance, Pompeii for drama, Sorrento for elegance and Salerno for Charles to look at the landings, battle memorials and military cemeteries. The menacing Vesuvius loomed over them. They drank the crisp white wines of the region and enjoyed a brief siesta after making love. They sat on the hotel terrace and viewed with interest the other guests. It was a sign of the size of Jane Bowater's chequebook that there was not a single unrefined person amongst them. Not surprisingly, many were Italian who were charming and friendly. The days of 'La Dolce Vita' were fading fast but these people epitomised the inherent elegance and taste of that nation. Music, food and wine were more important now than making war, following recent wars that they were never really very enthusiastic about anyway.

It all too quickly came to an end but the experience left a memory that would not dim for many years to come. Both Hanna and Charles were amused to see on their return that Jane Bowater had used their time away to rearrange matters upstairs. Hanna's bedroom and bathroom, the bigger of the two, had been turned into their bedroom and bathroom, and Charles' room reverted to a guest room. All his kit had been neatly moved and the bedroom of his boyhood was no more. A larger bed had been installed and furniture rearranged to accommodate a married couple. She had also had the room redecorated and a new loo installed. In all it told a story about Jane Bowater; kind and loving but determined to make things the way she wanted them to be. By doing what she did she was being genuinely kind and thoughtful, if a little bit of a bulldozer.

Although they would be spending periods apart in these early months of their marriage, a fact that army couples become used to, they had entered into a love match that they were both convinced would stand the test of time.

JAMIE BUCKINGHAM RETURNED to his regiment after the wedding, looking forward to further operations in Northern Ireland with his normal enthusiasm and keen, as always, to prove himself. On his first patrol his short life was obliterated by an IRA roadside bomb that exploded under his Land Rover, instantly killing all on board. Charles read the message in his office. It saddened him greatly but not enough to stop him almost immediately attending to his duties. Life went on and his coldness to those male friends whom he counted as close could be nothing less than indifference, whilst those whom he loved were to die for if necessary.

He gave the eulogy at the funeral and delivered it in a matter-of-fact but sympathetic way, but there was little warmth and he left soon afterwards.

FOUR

Charles was now entering into a period of his private and military life where he wanted to consider the way forward to career success. Those of lesser ambition would have sneered at this approach, arguing that as a young officer you should enjoy your soldiering and life in general and leave the serious parts to later, if at all. But Charles knew his situation was different. He had done something that, if discovered, would end or seriously restrict his career and if that were to be the case, how would his marriage to his adorable wife work out?

What Charles also did not know, and would never know, was that Peter Rogers had, through the Foreign Office and the Ministry of Defence, ensured that what he had done in Berlin had been erased from the records, less those held by MI6 which remained under lock and key until 50 years hence at least.

What neither Charles, Hanna, her parents, the Foreign Office, the Ministry of Defence or the army in particular, imagined was the dossier on Charles Bowater that lay neatly in Victor Sokolov's saferoom, a dossier which was waiting to be enacted, however long it took.

FOR AN OFFICER OF CHARLES' abilities and professional dedication, his career from the time he arrived at Sandhurst to the time he attended the Army Staff College some seven years later took a predictably upward trajectory. He had set his initial sights on qualifying for and attending the Army Staff College, the acknowledged passport to greater things. Thereafter his greatest desire was to command his regiment. Thereafter he planned to progress to the very top. His officer peers might have scoffed and called him an egotistic lunatic, but he was deadly serious. He knew he possessed the capability and the capacity.

In Charles' mind, there were two key elements to success: never make a major mistake, or even a minor one if possible, and always develop a good relationship with you superiors. Friendship was not the answer; mutual professional respect was. A certain distance would protect from any form of emotional involvement, a sure way to corrupt a relationship within a close-knit organisation.

Making a major mistake in the army, either professional or personal, could mean the death knell for any promising career. A series of smaller errors could also spell disaster in the longer term. An officer could be highly intelligent, an excellent leader of men and well capable, but if he is sleeping with the Commanding Officer's wife, this will not help his career. If he drinks too much and then loudly voices his opinions to his Brigade Commander, again this would not go down well. However, unless it was a particularly heinous crime worthy of a court martial and dismissal, the officer would not necessarily be aware his career was slowly draining from him.

Ambitious though he was, he never showed it; Charles had the ability to focus and project his energy and rapidly gained experience into the right channels without being boorish or irritating. He sought to maintain good relationships with all without appearing to be unctuous, enjoyed himself at parties although now he drank a lot less, and was always polite and charming. He also had a beautiful wife to live up to and look after.

Whilst at Sandhurst, Charles decided that he would seek to follow a career path that was entirely armoured centric. Unlike many of his peers, he did not hanker after 'special forces' roles and he had not been posted to Northern Ireland since being commissioned. His focus would be on the conventional European battlefield and NATO. His genre would be the art of armoured formation manoeuvre and the enemy would be the armies of the Warsaw Pact. His regiment was in Osnabrück in West Germany and it was likely to stay there for the foreseeable future, and although his immediate goal was to attend the Army Staff College, he also had his sights clearly on the command of his own regiment in due course.

MARRIED LIFE SETTLED INTO A PATTERN. Hanna stayed on at Vine House where her relationship with Jane and David Bowater blossomed, her culinary skills improved to the point where she and Jane shared the cooking, and she continued to work hard on her English. Henry became her firm friend and companion and even perked up when a walk was in the offing. She came to know well all the byways and paths for miles around and loved the English countryside. She was content.

Charles came home whenever he could and the Sandhurst holidays between terms were always welcome. Early on after their marriage, they decided that the current arrangement was better that Hanna moving up to Camberley and living in a married quarter. Charles had gone to view them and was not encouraged. Their decision was also greatly influenced by a suggestion from David Bowater. Right at the back of the garden and close to the riverbank, was an old barn which had been left in a sorry state. Previously there had been vague plans to convert it into a cottage and let it out, but these came to nothing. With the enthusiastic support of Jane Bowater, ever keen to keep Hanna by her side, David suggested that now was the time to convert and turn the barn into a home for his son and wife. Charles and Hanna were bowled over, and even more bowled over when Jane Bowater stepped in and told them that she would pay for the conversion herself. After all, apart from creating a home for her son and his wife, a conversion would be an investment and would increase the overall value of the property, not that they would ever move.

And so, for the remainder of the time that Charles was at Sandhurst the barn was converted into a very comfortable three-bedroomed cottage. Hanna loved being intimately involved in everything and proved beyond doubt her ability to absorb English tastes and norms rapidly. She supervised the decoration and furnishing of the cottage with style and elegance so that when they finally moved in it was their perfect home.

Married life was bliss. Charles' absences only fuelled their love and desire for each other and it was perhaps a good thing that they were now well out of earshot from the main house in their new abode.

Hanna made the occasional trip to Sandhurst to attend various functions. She enjoyed the mess nights and parties but her favourite was always the Sovereign's Parade, a spectacle she found both fascinating and impressive. How well the British did things! She turned heads wherever she went and even the poker-faced Commandant smiled in appreciation when he met her.

Charles' time at Sandhurst was coming to an end and he had received notice that he would return to his Regiment in West Germany as Adjutant, a progression that pleased him. Farewell parties at Sandhurst were muted but at his final mess night very good things were said about him by his College Commander and he was congratulated by the Commandant during his final interview. He left and, in typical fashion, only looked forward to the next challenge, and not back to that which had already passed.

He and Hanna agreed that initially he would move to Osnabrück alone, settle into his new job and do a thorough recce of the married-quarters situation before making any decisions. Coming home frequently would be more problematic but not impossible. Charles had acquired a Saab convertible that could eat up those autobahn miles and over the next months he became well acquainted with ferry crossings to and from Dover.

THE CASE of Charles Bowater and Anna Nazarov did not currently occupy a great deal of Victor Sokolov's time but when it did, it always presented him with a difficult conundrum. How to track Bowater's career and thus be able to strike at a time when he would be occupying a position that would allow him access to the maximum number of military secrets? This was not going to be easy and although Victor Sokolov knew he had time, he needed to find a solution.

FIVE

Apart from a year and bit at the Army Staff College at Camberley, Charles spent the next nine years of his career in West Germany, a situation which he found to his liking. Northern Ireland and the Falklands War passed him by but his career and reputation prospered. As his experience grew, so did his confidence and abilities. Before attending Staff College, he spent two years with his regiment as the Adjutant and then moved down the autobahn to Paderborn to work as a staff officer in a Brigade Headquarters. After passing a very tricky exam to get to Staff College and passing out well, he was sent back to West Germany as a Brigade Major, followed by a further two years as Squadron Leader back with his regiment. It was considered by most as a classic path to the top. He made no mistakes of any significance and managed, often in the face of provocation, to maintain harmonious relationships with all, and good professional relationships with his immediate superiors and peers.

The only concern he had in his meteoric rise was the question of Hanna and his vetting profile. He was beginning to have direct access to not just British, but many NATO plans for the defence of Northern Germany against a Soviet invasion. He was vetted to

Top-Secret level but not once during their interviews with him did the Army Vetting Service refer to his wife and her background. This was unusual but it never seemed to prevent him from being cleared. He could only surmise that that the hand of Peter Rogers was somehow involved.

He was always busy, sometimes very busy indeed and the demands on his time sometimes impossible. But he always enjoyed it, always looked forward to the next day, even in the dead of another German winter on manoeuvres. By getting up early, he kept himself fit through his running and continued to be sociable and engaging away from work, but drank less and less.

During this period of his life, two joyous events occurred. Hanna gave birth to two daughters some fifteen months apart. The first, born in 1978, they named Eleanor Aleksandra, a very English first name and a very Russian second name after Hanna's mother, and the second little bundle of joy Viktoria Jane, a very Russian first name after Hanna's sister and a very English second name belonging to a certain lady. They were both Christened at the village church presided over by their favourite vicar and both were the apple of Jane and David Bowater's eyes. The vicar was his normal jovial self although, like David Bowater, now looking a little frayed around the edges. He hoovered back the champagne and asked for more. Eventually his wife took him home early.

Predictably, the babies grew up into beautiful looking little girls. They had certainly inherited their mother's looks, helped a little by Charles. It all seemed so perfect. Perhaps too perfect.

Hanna and Charles had worked out that the best way to tackle the living together or apart issue in the army was to combine a mixture of both depending on the location he might find himself in and the benefits of living at home in their cottage at Vine House. Married quarters in Germany were normally superior to those in England. When he moved within Germany they would stay together, but Hanna and the girls would take long breaks in the England enjoying their cottage and the adoration of Granny and Grandpa. Henry was jealous but sadly ailing fast. Whilst Charles was at Staff College, Hanna and the girls remained at home. It all seemed to work very well but both missed each other badly when apart. It seemed that would never die and the passion remained alive and well.

ON TWO OCCASIONS whilst he was stationed at Osnabrück, once as a captain and then as a major, another dark cloud briefly passed over his life. It was before Eleanor was born and Hanna and he were in town on a Saturday morning. It was a habit. Café und Kuchen followed by the wonderful market followed by lunch, a habit that would be abruptly curtailed for a while once Eleanor appeared on the scene. They were sitting outside drinking coffee when Sophia walked past. She had not changed. She was beautiful and for a moment Charles' heart skipped a beat. She looked directly at him and he at her. Their eyes met. She looked at pregnant Hanna and then walked swiftly on.

On the second occasion, some seven years later, Hanna and the girls were back in England permanently because of schools. He spotted Sophia walking towards him on a busy street. She saw him too and he stopped, hoping to engage her in conversation. She looked at him intently but walked on, her beauty luminous, as though the intervening years since Berlin had not been.

The passing years had only served to enhance Sophia's beauty, and despite some unenthusiastic attempts to find romance she could not find it in herself to do so. Wholly casual, unfeeling and robotic sex on a few occasions meant nothing to her. She remained single and resolute in her love for Charles. On the two occasions when he saw her and she him, her feelings were in turmoil. She desperately wanted to talk to him but the sight of a pregnant Hanna made it impossible for her to do so. She therefore carried on as before and resolved to cherish his memory. Little else mattered to her.

CHARLES AND HANNA rarely argued but one heated discussion involved the question of schooling for the girls. Charles, knowing full well that his mother would foot the bill because she had already said so, wanted the girls to go to Pre-prep, Prep and Public school, like he had done before. In his blinkered and class-driven English way, he saw no other alternative. When he tried to explain to Hanna that this would mean the girls boarding and away from home, she put her foot down very firmly – saying she had never heard of such a barbaric system. Charles tried to argue but failed. As always with them, when there was a disagreement a compromise was reached. The girls would go to private schools but always as day girls, but this meant that from that from the time they started at school Vine House Cottage would be their home. Everyone was happy, not least Jane Bowater.

THE RUSSIAN SOUL is deep and runs very deep when it comes to family. The Soviet state system had attempted to break the family in the interests of the state but, like religion, had failed miserably. In many cases the bond was too great and the Nazarovs were no exception. Would her parents ever see their granddaughters of which they knew nothing, and would they ever meet her beloved husband? These thoughts, when they came, cast Hanna into depression and she knew that she could not share this with anyone but Charles. Charles knew what she was going through but was determined to look forward, not back and give his family the best possible life that he could. She was often tempted to come clean with Jane Bowater and tell the truth about what her background really was and how she had come to the west, but she could not because she was terrified that it would sully their wonderful relationship, a relationship she valued so much. So, Hanna kept things to herself and in true Russian manner faced it with stoicism and patience, always hoping for better times. As she often said to herself, 'It's a life.'

No one, not least Charles, was surprised when, at the end of his two years as Squadron Leader with his regiment, he found himself on the infamous 'Pink List', named after the colour of the paper it was printed on. This gave him promotion to Lieutenant Colonel at the earliest possible opportunity. He suspected he was probably the youngest on the list for that year. He then waited for news of his next posting. He knew that he would have to wait for command of his regiment because the present incumbent had only just arrived. He would remain in West Germany and go to Corps Headquarters as a Staff Officer Grade 1 responsible for operational planning, a key appointment and definitely in line with his ambitions and desires. An added bonus was that he was granted three months of 'gardening' leave before he had to take up his next posting. Charles wasted no time in heading back to his family in England, leaving his kit stored in the mess waiting for the next appointment.

Jane Bowater, in her usual efficient manner, had helped with securing places for the girls in a small pre-prep school in the local market town, and their names were down and places secured at a nearby girls' public school that catered for both prep and senior pupils. Her other immediate goal was to get Hanna on the road. As with everything, Hanna was a fast learner and soon mastered the intricacies of the motor car, although Charles had suggested that when she passed her test all drivers in Wiltshire would need to be warned that there was a brand-new driver on the roads and to be very careful when approached. Hanna passed at her second attempt and was then able to ferry the girls to and from school.

IT WAS DURING HIS THREE MONTHS' gardening leave that Charles heard the sad news of Corporal Hancock's demise. The army jungle drums always work well and he was informed by one of the Corporal's former friends from Berlin who had been in his troop. The details of his death were very sad. He had left the army after his tour in West Berlin came to an end, and unable to find a satisfactory job or enjoy a stable personal life, he drifted, eventually ending up living on the street or in hostels for the homeless in Bath. In the end, alcohol killed him. Charles went to his funeral which was very sparsely attended. The man had such good qualities – all wasted.

THE MONTHS PASSED by far too quickly but they managed to fit in a lot, both essential and non-essential. A few loose ends in Vine Cottage had to be completed, then they went on a bucket-and-spade holiday for ten days to Cornwall and took the opportunity to visit a number of Charles' friends around the country, in particular to introduce Hanna and the girls to them. For the rest of the time they enjoyed each other's company in the peace and quiet of the English countryside. Why go away when you had everything on your doorstep?

Life for the Bowaters had reached a high point where contentment and happiness were constant and seemingly inviolate.

PART 4: ENSNAREMENT

ONE

Victor Sokolov had spent ten years in East Berlin. This length of time in one post was unusual within the KGB and although they never told him, perhaps they valued the work he did, work that needed continuity, especially when running agents in West Berlin and West Germany. Victor Sokolov preferred to be where he was. He hated Germans and he hated the western allies and he felt that he was in a position to do something about his paranoia. He also enjoyed the lifestyle that the embassy in East Berlin offered him. He was his own boss and the ambassador rarely bothered him and certainly did not ask as to his activities. He reported directly to Moscow, geographically a long way away but with the power to recall him at any time. He also enjoyed being remote from his family. The prospect of having to live in Moscow with them did not appeal. He assumed that he was doing well enough to remain in this plum post for some time to come.

During his time in East Berlin, Victor Sokolov had enjoyed some success. Despite his intense dislike of Germans, he had forged very close links with the Stasi leadership. He and they knew who was the organisation at the helm and this helped him to direct many espionage and counter-intelligence operations in West Berlin and West Germany using East German agents belonging to the Stasi. He had also reorganised his slice of the KGB so it could operate more effectually. He had managed, with some considerable difficulty, to keep the Lubyanka reasonably happy with progress. The British military operational plans for the defence of West Berlin were a good example. But his snippets of useful intelligence that could be used against the west in general were few and far between. He was adept at bluff, procrastination and delay and towards the end of his tenure he was only just able to keep his drinking habits under control. He was certainly drunk every night and it was slowly beginning to impinge on his ability to do his job effectively.

The KGB's First Chief Directorate at Yasenevo just outside Moscow could clearly see the bigger picture when it came to Victor Sokolov's overall performance. Despite his minor successes, he had never been able to deliver intelligence that would put the Warsaw Pact on the front foot in the event of a war in Germany. It was all small fry as far as they were concerned and it did not change one iota the Cold War status quo, something that the KGB were constantly trying to bring about to give the Soviet Union an advantage in any future war with the west. In their eyes he was a failure and a liability and the only reason they had kept him in East Berlin for so long was his war record, his loyalty to the cause and a number of low friends in high places.

But the time had come for fresh blood and the war in Afghanistan had conveniently provided an opportunity to get rid of him. He was to go to Kabul in the same rank and take up the post of Chief Liaison Officer to Operation Cascade. Operation Cascade involved KGB operatives in direct combat operations against the Mujahidin using local tribes. Victor Sokolov's job was to direct liaison between the KGB and these local tribes. This involved him travelling all over Afghanistan, and it was during one of these visits that he was killed. The local tribe he was visiting had been infiltrated by the mujahidin and they shot him and his escort without warning and out-of-hand.

Victor Sokolov despised and hated the Afghans as much as he did the Germans. He also hated that wild and uncontrollable country and rapidly realised this was a 'punishment posting' and probably his last. His job invited great danger and so it proved to be. No one mourned him, not least his family or the legions of women he had seduced and used. His body was recovered and taken back to the Soviet Union where it was buried quietly and with no ceremony. He was forgotten about and in private his wife and son each breathed a sigh of relief.

ALEXEI VOLIKOV WAS Victor Sokolov's replacement in East Berlin. He represented everything that Victor Sokolov was not. A career KGB officer who had risen rapidly through the ranks and had not been tainted by emotions generated by the Great Patriotic War. He was a young, highly intelligent and dedicated teetotaller. His seemingly only weakness, like his predecessor and indeed many men of his ilk, was women but his approach to them, like his work, was entirely different. Careful, cunning, smooth and snake-like. Few could resist his charm and focus. He also had the ability to appear affable and urbane, but beneath that approachable exterior was a ruthless man who would stop at nothing in achieving his and his superiors' needs.

Victor Sokolov and Alexei Volikov did not meet, but Alexei Volikov soon discovered that although Victor Sokolov enjoyed a reputation for getting things done and thinking on his feet, his administrative organisation was a shambles. He was so secretive that he refused to entertain an assistant and the result was ten years of chaos. It took Alexei Volikov six months of hard work with his assistant to insert any form of order and prioritisation into his domain. Many folders languishing in the filing cabinets had to dusted off and carefully examined. Most were burnt as being out-of-date, irrelevant to the overall aims of the KGB or useless. Some were kept as cases to be continued or resurrected and one of those was the file on a Captain Charles Bowater. Because of his embarrassment, and indeed his country's embarrassment over the disappearance of Anna Nazarov all those years ago, Victor Sokolov had shied away from even looking at the file. Indeed, he had forgotten about it.

The file was placed in the 'to-do' tray and very near the top. When Alexei Volikov read it in full, he did feel a tinge of admiration for his predecessor's chain of thought, a chain of thought brought about by years of experience in his murky world of trying to stay one step ahead of your enemy and your superiors, and gaining maximum advantage from doing so. He agreed with the long-term approach and that the case needed to be resurrected and used at the right time, a time when Captain Bowater would be at a position within NATO where the highest level of military secret might be able to be extracted from him. He agreed with the supposition that Captain Bowater and Anna Nazarov would still be together, and he agreed with the list of pressure points that could be applied.

What Alexei Volikov also knew was that there was a considerable amount of work yet to be done before this case could get off the ground, if indeed it ever could. However, he felt that there was significant merit in beginning the process of trying to make it work. The potential intelligence gained could be great, and possibly a game changer in the Cold War. Using a serving British Army officer as a spy had never been done before.

THE FIRST TASK was to ascertain if Captain Bowater was still serving in the British army and if so, what rank had he reached and where was he serving. If he had left the army, there would be little point in pursuing the case. However, if he was still serving and had had a successful career to date, he might be in a position to provide them with vital intelligence in years to come.

The second task was to find out whether Bowater and Anna Nazarov were indeed together and had even got married. In Alexei Volikov's mind, if Bowater had been determined and foolish enough to smuggle her successfully out of the east, he would be equally single-minded enough to take her back to England and probably marry her. Again, if this was not the case there would be little chance of success.

Alexei Volikov needed to establish the facts on these two counts before anything else could be done. Realising the potential gains for both the organisation he represented and for himself he set about devising a plan with a focussed zeal, but knew it would not be easy.

His first task was to select a dependable and effective KGB officer working at the Soviet embassy in London who could organise a covert search for Bowater and his assumed wife or girlfriend. He knew of this person, an old friend of his who had sensibly held onto his shirt tails as they progressed through the ranks. Nikolay Kalugin was not a patch on Alexei Volikov when it came to intelligence but he was a reliable, conscientious and efficient officer on whom Alexei knew he could rely. Having cleared the initial first part of his plan with Moscow, he contacted Nikolay Kalugin securely and explained carefully what he wanted him to do. He also emphasised the importance of complete confidentiality, whilst at the same time perhaps having to bring in a British scout loyal to the cause and who could be relied on absolutely. Alexei Volikov was right in realising that for Nikolay Kalugin to attempt to do this himself would be far too dangerous.

The British were too clever and too alert to members of the Soviet embassy moving around the country or trying to ascertain information from sources that were publicly available. After some discussion, they opted for using a British scout to try to find the information needed to begin the next phase of his plan, if indeed he would ever be able to do so.

Alexei Volikov then sent a secure message to Nikolay Kalugin giving him all the details he could muster on Captain Bowater, which were sparse. Details on Anna Nazarov since she disappeared were non-existent. It would not be an easy task and it would probably take many months, if not years.

IT WAS WELL KNOWN from previous attempts that trying to break into the records of the British army, or indeed the Royal Navy or Royal Air Force, was nigh on impossible unless you had an insider working for you. This was not an option as it would immediately arouse suspicion. Therefore, in true KGB style, the information had to be gained from the line of least resistance; the family, and then by a process of working up to the target itself.

Kenneth Bateman worked as civil servant at the Home Office. He was a lonely, disillusioned man who could not bring himself to search for a woman and who drank too much. He lived by himself in a grubby flat in Stoke Newington and drank at the local pub. He was socially gauche, had no friends and kept himself to himself at work. He was conscientious and efficient but never showed any inclination to attempt to gain promotion.

Five years ago, in his local pub he fell into conversation with a man who was obviously foreign but friendly and generous. He bought him many drinks and as it was a Friday night Bateman did not hang back and became very drunk. The foreigner escorted him back to his flat where they shared a bottle of whiskey. In the morning, Bateman had no recollection of what had happened but in the following days it soon became obvious that he had been the victim of a set-up. Lurid pictures of him with this man in bed came through the letter box, accompanied by a note telling him to be at a different pub in the local area at a certain date and time or his employer would be sent the pictures.

Thus, Kenneth Bateman was reeled into the uncertain world of being a person that could be used for the purposes of the Soviet state. Surprisingly, rather than being resistant and terrified he actually enjoyed the thought of being someone at last and waited for his first 'assignment'. Having previously had no interest in politics, he now took an unhealthy interest in the Soviet Union and its political systems and objectives. He fancied himself as becoming a master spy on par with the likes of Kim Philby or George Blake. The reality was somewhat different. The KGB recognised his minimal strengths and significant weaknesses and played on them. From their perspective, his strengths lay in firstly his position at the Home Office. He was a member of a team which was responsible for liaison between the Home Office and the Metropolitan Police. This could be useful. Secondly, he was a grey man; innocuous and bland and would never stand out in a crowd. No one would suspect him of anything. Thirdly, and over the coming months and years, he proved himself to be a skilled ferret well able to find information they requested that might be turned into intelligence that might be able to be used against the UK.

Kenneth Bateman's weaknesses lay in his addiction to alcohol and from that the possibility he would talk about what he did to either colleagues at work or anyone in the pubs and bars he frequented, and that he was a very small man in the wider scheme of things. The KGB recognised he would never find himself in a position where he would have access to information that could be of real value, but to have people like Bateman hooked in and at their disposal was sometimes very useful. He could be used for low-grade assignments that were normally put in place to find out the basics that could, in turn, allow them to make decisions as to pursue a line using more mature and seasoned agents. He had been allocated the code name Badger.

Following his discussion with Alexei Volikov, Nicolay Kalugin planned to use Bateman to ferret out the information requested on Charles Bowater and Anna Nazarov. A nominated contact met with Bateman and he was given the task to find out where the parents or relatives of a certain Charles Bowater lived. It was likely that his family had a military connection but this was not confirmed. He was to tread very carefully and take his time. If successful, he might be required to undertake further tasks relating to this mission. As usual, he would be financially rewarded. He needed the money because on his paltry pay he could only just afford to fuel his alcohol addiction.

BATEMAN WAS ENTHUSED by his new task. In his fantasy world he saw no wrong in what he was doing because he was convinced it was for a good cause, a cause that always sought to help the common people, not the elite. At this point in his long relationship with his masters, it did not occur to him that he could never again escape their hold and that what he was doing was illegal.

His first port of call was the British Records Office at St Catherine's House in Aldwych, where he hoped to find out how many Bowaters there actually were in the country. There were many of them and many of them were eminent, which was depressing. He then went on to do some research at the British Library but again he drew a blank. There were many historical records of Bowaters through the ages but he could find nothing that pointed him to specifics.

Bateman then sat down to think about the best approach that

would enable him to begin to pinpoint the target. He considered using the information he had at his disposal at work but dismissed that as too risky. He was keen to retain his job and even keener to remain a very important and key spy for the cause. He did not relish being in prison.

Captain Bowater was in the army. In traditional English families such as the Bowaters, it was often the case that son followed father into the army. He had noticed that many of the Bowater tribe had been in the armed forces, and in particular the army. Perhaps Bowater's father had been in the army? It was a line of inquiry worth pursuing.

Following his failed attempts to ascertain information though public institutions Bateman worked out that probably the best way to narrow down his search was through Telephone Directories, and the best way to do that was to take a trip to the Holborn Telephone Exchange in London where all telephone directories, historical or current, were held.

Bateman sought to narrow down the areas within the country that he should concentrate on and prioritise. He knew that the most army-heavy counties in England were Hampshire, Wiltshire and Dorset and therefore he would start there. Wiltshire was to be his first port of call. The microfilmed current directories for Wiltshire came up with a total of eight Bowater numbers and he made a note of all of them plus the location listed. Sometimes it was just a town and sometimes an address was listed.

Bateman's next task was to call each of the numbers from a public telephone box and not always the same one. His line would be:

'Good morning. May I please speak to Mr Charles Bowater?'

On the sixth attempt, a very refined English female voice answered the phone.

'Good morning. May I please speak to Mr Charles Bowater?'

'I am afraid he is not here. This is his mother. May I ask who is calling?'

'I am an army friend from Berlin days. I am very sorry to have bothered you.'

'He is currently serving in Germany with his regiment.'

'Thank you very much for your help, Mrs Bowater.'

He hung up and exited the telephone box with a smirk. The question of any sort of information security was obviously not considered by the likes of Mrs Bowater, living her cosy and safe existence in the English countryside.

Bateman re-checked the address given against the number and carefully noted the details and the gist of his conversation with Mrs Bowater. Vine House was located in a small Wiltshire village on the edge of Salisbury Plain, a well-known army stomping ground. His hunch had been right and it was time for some fieldwork. He headed straight for his local pub to celebrate.

All of Bateman's efforts had taken some time as he had to go to work as well. He had researched at the weekends and had taken days off as holidays from time to time. He thought rightly that at this juncture he should report back to his masters. His contact seemed unconcerned about the time he had taken and over a cold lager at opening time put Bateman's detailed written report in his pocket.

They chatted in a desultory way about the weather and other inanities until the contact departed and Bateman ordered his second cold lager to further temper his hangover.

Bateman took a weekday train down to Westbury in Wiltshire armed with a small rucksack in which was his issued camera and binoculars, an ordnance survey map of the area and a waterproof jacket with a hood. Despite his newly bought walking boots, he looked incongruous in the country with his pallid, spotty face, ill-fitting city clothes and unkempt appearance. He set off to walk the three miles to the village.

When he arrived, he asked at the village shop where Vine House was.

'Ah! The home of the Bowaters,' said the elderly old dear behind the counter and gave him directions.

He then walked a further mile until he stood outside the gates to the house. He could see it from the road and even with his untrained eye he could see that it was a classic English country house.

Bateman had studied his map and had marked a route which enabled him to take a circular way around the house using public footpaths and bridleways. After an hour and the frequent use of his binoculars and camera, he felt he had a good feel for the place and much evidence. He then came off the marked paths and made his way closer over a small, enclosed field. On the other side of the river but with an excellent view onto what was obviously the large back garden and the entrance to what looked like a converted barn, he settled down to wait in a small copse which provided good cover.

An attractive middle-aged lady came out of the back of the house and walked down to the barn. Parked outside the barn was an Austin Metro. He made a note of the make, colour and registration number. After a while she came out, accompanied by a most beautiful young woman. He managed to take a few long-range pictures of the two of them. He couldn't hear what they were saying as they stood outside the barn but after a while the young woman got in the car and drove off through the archway in the wall and down the drive. He settled down to wait for her return. After a while a tall, elderly gentleman came out of the house and made his way down the garden and disappeared out of sight.

The stunning young woman reappeared some one hour later with two little girls. From their pretty frocks, flowers in their blonde hair and cake and balloons in their little hands it was obvious even to an unworldly oaf like Bateman that they had been to a birthday party. He took pictures and retreated. He had done enough for one day. He walked back to the station along empty country roads and caught the next train back to London. On arrival, he telephoned the number given to him and stated that he wished to pass on information of some importance. He then went home and wrote up his report and removed the film roll from the camera. His contact appeared at the agreed meeting place in a local park and he passed over the information, and in return was given an envelope which contained £200. The rest of that Friday afternoon and evening developed into a lonely blur, a condition he was well used to.

NIKOLAY KALUGIN carefully examined and assessed the information before him. He knew all about Bateman and his habits but had to admit that what he had produced was impressive. He had obviously approached his task in a logical and sensible way, using his brain to narrow down the possibilities until he could produce photographs, annotated with accompanying notes of the targets they sought to identify.

Bateman would be further tasked to confirm that Vine House was indeed the home of the Bowaters, and in particular Charles Bowater. Additionally, he was to confirm that a marriage involving Charles Bowater had taken place within the last four years and that the village church was the starting point for that line of inquiry. He, Nikolay Kalugin, would be easily able to confirm that the pictures of the beautiful young woman at Vine House were indeed those of Anna Nazarov. And he, Nikolay Kalugin, would ask Alexei Volikov to confirm the name of the British regiment that was stationed in West Berlin during the time that Bowater served there, and then trace where that regiment was now in West Germany, or elsewhere. Once it was confirmed that the regiment was based in West Germany, agents there would be used to confirm the presence of Bowater at that location.

Once Bateman had completed his inquiries, hopefully successfully, his further involvement in the case would be terminated. He would be debriefed, warned directly that any mention to anyone of what he had been involved in would have very serious consequences, and he would be recompensed generously for his work. What Nikolay Kalugin meant by 'very serious consequences' was quiet liquidation.

Once again tasked, Bateman threw himself into the role and in a short space of time had confirmed that Charles Bowater had indeed married a Hanna Novak in 1974 in the village church. Bateman even became involved in conversation with the vicar who, recognising a fellow soak, suggested that they wander down to the village pub and enjoy a drink or three. One thing led to another and at the end the vicar drove Bateman to the station, dumped him there and wove his way erratically back to the vicarage to face the well experienced wrath of his wife.

It took Bateman even less time to confirm that Vine House was indeed the home of Lieutenant Colonel (Retired) D S Bowater MC and Bar and Mrs Jane Bowater, parents of an only child Charles, parents-in-law to his wife Hanna and grandparents to Eleanor and Viktoria. His task complete, he received his warning in no uncertain terms, gratefully accepted an envelope containing £450 and was told to lie low until contacted again.

CHARLES BOWATER'S regiment was stationed in a former Wehrmacht Barracks in Osnabrück, a barracks that had been built in the 1930s to last a thousand years. Like many of these types of barracks that the British Army had occupied at the end of the war, it was well laid out, substantial and could easily accommodate armoured, infantry, artillery, engineer and air corps regiments, as well as a host of different level headquarters and logistic support units.

In peacetime Germany in the 1980s, it was not easy to gain entry to these places if you were not a military person and did not hold the necessary passes. However, in general security was lax and most installations could be physically penetrated away from the main entrance point which was always guarded. It would take less than a determined intruder to achieve this. Married quarters were not guarded at all, and when British officers and soldiers and their families ventured out in civilian clothes to enjoy shopping, entertainment and exercise in the many cities and towns in which they were based, there were no controls in place. Single officers and soldiers living in the barracks had to sign out and in but that was all.

Alexei Volikov was well aware of the security precautions, or lack of them, that the British Army practiced in West Germany and felt confident that he would be able to confirm where Bowater was stationed, but he was not so confident when it came to what position he held and whether or not he had access to military intelligence at a level that would be of significant benefit to him and his masters.

He appointed three of his agents living in West Germany to firstly confirm that Bowater was indeed currently stationed with his regiment in Osnabrück. He held a photograph of Bowater taken when he was entering East Berlin through Checkpoint Charlie all those years ago and this was issued to them. The agents knew they could not enter the barracks to seek him out but they could position themselves outside the barracks to attempt to monitor his movements when off-duty. This they did in shifts on the road that led away from the barracks and into Osnabrück. For many patient weeks this tactic proved to fruitless but then they recognised him in a car with two other men driving down to the town one Saturday morning. The agent followed and watched them as they did some shopping, drank coffee and then disappeared into a Gasthaus. Whilst the three men had sat drinking coffee, he managed to take some pictures whilst looking like he was interested in the surrounding architecture. He then retired to write up his notes, brief the other agents and develop the photographs in the dark room at the back of his humble and innocuous house. They compared the photographs and indeed one of the three was Bowater. In the ten years that had passed, he had changed little but at least they now had an up-to-date photograph.

Alexei Volikov had gained the confirmation he had sought but now he had to construct the next part of the plan. What was Bowater's job? In true Soviet style, he reverted to a classic ruse. He would use a beautiful young German woman to engage with the target, or the target's friends whilst he was present and gently attempt to extract information from them in the time-honoured way.

On the following four Saturday mornings, the three friends followed the same pattern. It was an indication of how little they considered personal security as important in this safe and prosperous country. On each of these occasions they followed the same routine, ending up going into the Gasthaus Albersmeyer for lunch and a beer. On the third occasion the agent followed them in and positioned himself so that he could observe what they did. They ordered beer and food, ate and drank and then drank more. Three hours and many beers later, they paid and left whilst the agent drained his one and only small beer. He followed them carefully to their car, took a note of the vehicle's details and saw that Bowater, despite being seemingly the worse for wear, took the wheel and drove off.

DURING THE COLD WAR, the Soviet Union controlled many active and sleeper agents in West Germany, and there were a number of these who operated at the highest levels of the West German political administration. At the lower levels, current and useful information was constantly being sought. The case of Charles Bowater was no exception but with a potential far greater than most. Alexei Volikov selected two women whom he knew would draw the interest of the band of three. They always operated under their assumed names.

Emelia Lang was tall, slim, blonde, blue-eyed and beautiful. She was also very socially engaging but quiet, possessed excellent English and was an almost rabid communist sympathiser. She was intelligent enough to be able to hide her beliefs whilst living in a country she wished to destroy. Her parents had been persecuted by the Nazis for their communist beliefs but had miraculously survived and been reunited at the end of the war. In East Germany she grew up to believe in everything communist and was an immediate candidate for the furtherance of the aims of that creed. She had lived and worked in West Germany for nearly ten years, waiting for the call which now came.

Mia Schuster came from the same historical background and was of the same political persuasion. Small, dark haired and with a striking figure, she gave off a permanent air of sexual voluptuousness. Her English was fluent and she attracted men wherever she went. She too had lived in West Germany for nearly ten years but unlike Emelia had been tasked on a number of occasions to extract information from selected targets through the giving of sexual favours. Her pillow talk was accomplished and her success bred success to the point where she was considered one of the Soviets' most valued agents.

ALEXEI VOLIKOV'S selection process proved to be almost faultless. The two women were briefed in detail together and then sent to Osnabrück, staying in a small hotel for the Friday and Saturday nights of the chosen weekend but with an option to keep repeating the routine until they could take the opportunity to corner their quarry. Emelia and Mia came to like each other. They had much in common.

The first two Saturdays proved fruitless and it was surmised that the band of three were either on manoeuvres, on a course, were taking leave out of the country, or were otherwise engaged. On the third Saturday, the two women were sitting in the favoured coffee house when the band of three walked in. Emelia and Mia had seen the picture of Charles but the other two looked interesting. One was George, one of Charles' old chums from Berlin days who was now a major, a rank he would not rise above. He understood and accepted his limitations and was a happy man who enjoyed soldiering but had no ambition. He had always remained unmarried but was certainly more than interested in the opposite sex. The other character was Andrew, whom Charles had been at Sandhurst with and was on attachment from an infantry regiment.

They drank coffee and eyed the two attractive women across the room, a gesture that was reciprocated. Judging their moment, the two women left the café and entered the nearby Gasthaus Albersmeyer. Inevitably the three men followed and took their normal table, a table that Emelia and Mia had been briefed on beforehand. As the beers and food were ordered and drank and eaten, glances and smiles were exchanged. On their third beer, George got up.

'Good afternoon. We were wondering if you would like to join us at our table?'

He had done this so often in the past that there was no nervousness in his approach.

'We would love to. Thank you,' said Mia.

It was an animated and amusing conversation that became more animated and amusing as time passed. George was particularly struck by Mia, so much so that he managed to end up sitting very close beside her. He could feel her sexual energy and liked it very much. Charles, very attracted to Emelia, fought the inner battles that he always experienced when faced with inebriation and female beauty at the same time and place. Nothing could come between himself, Hanna, his girls and the life he had created and cherished, but his weaknesses were always present. Would one night of passion make a difference?

George now had Mia in his sights and she appeared to equally have him in her sights. Charles won his battle and resisted and Andrew drank more beer. George asked Mia if she would like to have lunch tomorrow and she readily agreed. Now all rather drunk, George paid the bill and they unsteadily left. Tomorrow was another day, and luckily a Sunday.

GEORGE WAS in a high state of excitement when he met Mia the next day for lunch at a restaurant in central Osnabrück. He much preferred small and voluptuous women and Mia fitted the bill perfectly. Lunch was long, slow and boozy. George felt that he had made a suitable impression and was therefore not surprised when Mia invited him back to her hotel for a 'digestif', surely a euphemism for something else. He was in love again. This would have been for at least the hundredth time.

Emelia had left and returned home in disappointment that she had not contributed to the cause. Charles Bowater was certainly a very attractive man, both in mind and body. She would wait patiently for her next assignment, should it ever come.

The sex was wild and uncontrollable. Mia deployed every trick in her extensive book and George attempted, mainly unsuccessfully, to keep up with her. At the end, he lay exhausted as she lay right on top of him and gazed into his eyes. Eventually he fell asleep and she carefully and quietly checked the contents of his wallet. He was a major in the regiment she had been briefed on but she gained no other information. She asked if they could meet again that next day for dinner and he readily agreed, inviting her to have dinner at the Officers' Mess.

THURSDAY EVENING DINNER AT THE OFFICERS' Mess was always an enjoyable occasion. The men wore black tie and the ladies generally opted for the fashionable 'small black number'. The food was delicious, the wine excellent and the conversation both highbrow and lowbrow depending on who you were sitting next to. Mia loved it. She had never been to an Officers' Mess before, let alone to enjoy such an evening in the name of the cause. She looked stunning and every young, and certainly older officer including Charles, accompanied by their wives, girlfriends or nobody, lusted after her beautifully formed body. George couldn't take his eyes off her and spent the evening longing to take her to his room to repeat the delights of the afternoon before.

Again, the sex was lustful and abandoned. George was no slouch in these matters and having got the measure of her desires and needs, took the lead. She complied entirely, offering herself in every possible way. He only hoped that her moans, shouts and screams did not carry beyond the walls of his room. The entire Third Reich barracks had been built to last and consequently the walls were very thick. Afterwards they lay together in the narrow, uncomfortable army officer's bed and enjoyed the bottle of champagne that George had brought upstairs when they had skulked off early.

'I am glad to have met you, George.'

'I am more than glad to have met you, Mia.'

'I hope that we can continue to see each other.'

'Why not. I will be here in Osnabrück for at least another year.'

'I liked your friend Charles. He is very good looking and charming. I was not sure about the other one, though.'

'Andrew is a strange fish but he is not part of our regiment. And as for Charles, yes, he is a very good man. We call him the boy wonder because of his meteoric rise. He is about to be promoted to Lieutenant Colonel and will be posted away from the regiment in a couple of weeks' time. When he is promoted he will be the youngest Lieutenant Colonel in the army, so they say. I have known Charles for at least 12 years.'

'Emelia was very interested in him.'

'He is married to a beautiful woman who lives in England because of their children's schooling. Sadly for Emelia.'

'When he moves, will you still be able to meet up?'

'Oh yes. He is only moving up the road to Bielefeld to take up a very high-powered job in our Corp headquarters.'

George was at this point feeling more than comfortable, drowsy and slightly drunk. The narrow bed forced their naked bodies together and he could feel her nakedness pressed against him, and she his awakening hardness. It would no more occur to George that he was probably saying too much to a woman whom he hardly knew than if he was talking to the man in the moon.

Mia decided that she had asked enough questions for now and with the information gained firmly stored in her mind she mounted him and rode him to the finishing line. Further sex very early in the morning was followed by arrangements for the weekend and a rapid departure. The guard at the barrack entrance smiled as this very attractive woman tiptoed barefoot past in her evening finery and holding her high heels at six o'clock in the morning. An ever-present taxi waiting outside the guardhouse whisked her away. These German taxi drivers knew their business.

MIA'S TACTICS were working well and to plan. The very nice but gullible George was hooked and in the weeks that followed their relationship blossomed and he was happy. To Mia it was a different story. She carefully cultivated him by giving him amazing sex at every opportunity, encouraged long, slow lunches at the weekends, cosy evening meals and as much drinking as he wished. George was not a great drinker but when he did it affected him rapidly, and when it had loosened his mind and tongue, he, like Charles, could be indiscreet. However, this indiscretion was only the product of a general approach of the British to their German friends amongst whom they lived and whom they befriended frequently. It would never have occurred to George to question his relationship with Mia, let alone have a background check run on her.

Mia's experienced judgement told her that the time had arrived to nail down some more details on Charles. She could see that George was besotted and she also knew that he had visited Charles in Bielefeld the previous weekend and stayed in his officers' mess.

They went out for dinner the following Friday and then retired to her flat. He was very merry and she gave him the very best she could with her body. Afterwards they lay in the large comfortable bed and snuggled up.

'How was your time with Charles last weekend? How is he? How is he enjoying his new job?'

'You seem to like talking about Charles. Perhaps you would rather be in bed with him than me,' he pouted. 'He is certainly enjoying being a colonel and as always is taking his new job by the horns so to speak. But he told me that there is so much to learn and he is very busy. I could see that. He looked tired and lacked his normal *joie de vivre* at dinner. But it was good to see him.'

She took the plunge. 'What does he actually do?'

In normal circumstances this question should have rung alarm bells, but lying next to her his mind was running on a single track.

'He works in operations and plans and it's all hush-hush and top secret.' He ran his hands over her lovely body.

'Sounds interesting,' she purred. She knew that her masters could work out the rest. They had their man and now extraction needed to be handled carefully. To suddenly disappear might invite suspicion and even with George's limited imagination he might attempt to work it out. In any case she liked him, certainly enjoyed sex with him and found Osnabrück and her hotel to her liking. She would ease out slowly and at the end find a suitable excuse. Then she would disappear and he would not be able to trace her.

She spent the best part of a day writing up her report giving all details and then very discreetly delivering it the nominated contact in the middle of Osnabrück's very busy main street. Her job was done and now she could relax and really enjoy George's company for a few more weeks.

ALEXEI VOLIKOV WAS WELL pleased with Mia's detailed report. It answered the key questions.

Recently promoted Lieutenant Colonel Charles Bowater was stationed in Germany. He held a position in 1 British Corps Headquarters in Bielefeld. That position involved operations and planning, which at that location undoubtedly meant that he would have access to highly classified British and NATO military material.

There were still questions that could not be confirmed but Alexei Volikov felt confident that he was now ready to implement the third part of his plan. His next task was to nominate two controllers; one for Hanna Bowater in England and one for Charles Bowater in West Germany.

TWO

U rsula Thompson was yet another agent from the Soviet stable. She was in her forties and had lived innocently in England for 25 years under her own name, married an English university professor whom she had met when a student, did not have children but lived a quiet life in a leafy suburb. She was urbane, civilised and seemingly very English with a slight German accent. She blended in well. What no one knew, including her husband, was that her background before being sent to England was that she was from Leipzig in the east of her country and had, from an early stage, been indoctrinated into the communist cause. Some potential agents carried their responsibilities lightly, sometimes almost irresponsibly, but not Ursula. Her parents had been persecuted by the Nazis to the point of death, but survived. The arrival of the Russians was initially terrifying but when their true credentials were revealed and the urgent need to create a vasal German state became apparent, they began to enjoy the benefits of their life-long beliefs. Ursula was born and educated into this sordid world, indoctrinated and turned into what she was now; an agent of the Soviet system that sought to overthrow the west. Because of her dedication, looks and inherent worldliness she was sent to West Germany and then to England to study and then wait for her turn to come. Her marriage to the professor was not through love or luck, but by design.

Adam Neumann's background was very different. He had always lived in West Germany and had enjoyed the benefits of the economic miracle and beyond. He was a well-educated and clever man, although cunning and shifty in character. His greatest personal gift was his ability to talk in a persuasive and earnest manner. He was always looking for the main chance to make money to feed his alcohol and drugs addictions. He lived alone in a very untidy and dirty apartment and worked for the Bundespost as an administrator. He never had enough money. He drank large amounts of alcohol every day and at times had difficulty in holding down his job. His habits came to the notice of the inevitable recruiter and he was drawn in carefully with the promise of being handsomely recompensed for 'services rendered'. The only comeback for him would be his body found floating in the Elbe but this never occurred to him. His recruitment was backed up with the passing of an envelope containing 2,000 deutschmarks. He was easily hooked.

Alexei Volikov believed he had the right people to do his dirty work in the field.

He had long mused over the approach. The moment of the initial point of contact in both cases was the most dangerous time. It had to be engineered to seem and sound as normal as possible, but then followed up rapidly with the facts, accompanying direct threats and the laying out of the consequences to them both and their families should the demands not be met.

In both cases, the initial approach method would be the responsibility of the agent. Ursula Thompson would be tasked first to approach Hanna and gauge the reaction. If there was an indication that it would be positive and that Hanna would be willing to approach her husband, Adam Neumann would be warned off and then tasked to make contact with Charles Bowater. His would be the easier task because by then Bowater would know the dire position he and his family found themselves in. Adam Neumann's task thereafter would be to ensure that the information passed to him by Bowater on an irregular basis was executed in a secure manner, and then transmitted to his own controller in West Germany.

They now needed to be briefed separately in detail as to their tasks and this was duly done. These agents would not be aware of the other or what the other was doing. Ursula Thompson was not interested in money and was driven purely by ideology. Adam Neumann was driven purely by money and had little interest in the meaning or consequences of what he was about to embark on.

HANNA HAD DEVELOPED a habit during the week and term time when Charles was away. She would drop the children at school in the morning and go into the small market town, do her shopping and then if the weather was clement drink coffee outside her favourite café. In her safe world which she felt could never be disrupted or spoilt and within which thoughts of her past were rapidly fading, she would not have noticed a respectable looking woman sitting at a table inside in a corner.

On the third occasion she drank coffee, the woman sat down at the table next to hers and smiled at her. Hanna smiled back and they engaged in conversation about the weather and other topics of no importance. They introduced themselves. A very pleasant woman, thought Hanna, as she departed with the promise to perhaps meet at the café at a later, undetermined date. Although she was more than content with her life, the one thing Hanna lacked was a friend with the same interests to spend time with on a mutually relaxed basis. She loved Jane Bowater as a mother but at times felt the need to enjoy an extra female dimension. Hanna had not had the opportunity or inclination to make friends in England but it seemed to her that this engaging woman Ursula might become one. How she hoped so.

Ursula Thompson was staying for the duration of her mission in a small hotel discreetly tucked away down a side street of the market town. It was comfortable and the food was good. She had been instructed to remain there until she had achieved the desired result. All bills would be met through a cash delivery dropped at the hotel. Her husband was none the wiser. She had told him that she was going to Spain with a girlfriend for a number of weeks with an option to extend the stay if they felt so inclined. Piers Thompson tried to hide his pleasure at this news. Possibly a month without Ursula and therefore the unhindered opportunity to be with his favourite student, a 21-year-old beauty 30 years younger than him. Bliss, but he was well aware of what type of degree she was aiming for.

They agreed that they would have lunch together that next day and so Hanna, having deposited the girls, returned home and then ventured out to the market town to meet her new acquaintance. The small restaurant was excellent and they shared a bottle of wine. Neither had anything to hide as to their current lives in England and this drove the conversation. Neither ventured into the past before the first day of their marriages and the wide range of topics discussed centred on the present. They got on well together and agreed to go shopping in Bath the following week.

Shopping in Bath was always an enjoyable experience. Clothes were tried on and sometimes bought, Hanna bought items for the cottage and the day was rounded off with lunch in one of the many restaurants where they discussed husbands. Ursula could clearly see how much Hanna was in love with her husband, whereas she explained that her relationship with her husband was conducted more on the basis of a mutual happiness to avoid each other if possible. Hanna liked Ursula and felt the feeling was mutual, all those years of living and working within a society that, by its very nature, generated and encouraged mistrust and suspicion having fallen away.

They both agreed that the visit to Bath had been a great success and planned to meet up again at their favourite café. Hanna invited Ursula home for lunch where she also met Jane Bowater who was suitably impressed by this newcomer. After lunch Hanna suggested a walk through the many public byways and paths that surrounded Vine House and this is when Ursula decided to strike.

They walked and chatted in a desultory manner until they came across a bench conveniently placed by the River Wylye, a spot with dappled sunlight and secluded.

'Hanna, I have to tell you that I am not who you think I am.'

Something stirred in Hanna's subconscious. She turned pale.

'I have befriended you for a specific purpose and I would be grateful if you could hear me out.'

'Yes,' whispered Hanna, seeing no escape. Who was this woman?

'The organisation I work for, and have worked for many years, wishes you to carry out a certain task. We know that your husband in Germany has direct access to information on NATO and British Army operational plans for the defence of West Germany and classified as top secret. We also know that your husband smuggled you out of East Berlin using an official car when you were working as a doctor at the Soviet embassy, which was illegal and against the quadripartite agreement in that city. We also know that your husband, when he was a young officer serving in West Berlin, conducted a long and passionate affair with one of our agents and passed to her military secrets about the defence of West Berlin to be used if hostilities were to break out. He only ended this affair when he made plans to smuggle you to the west. We are also aware of your background and your family in Russia. What we want you to do now is to firstly inform your husband of this situation and secure his agreement that he would be willing to pass certain information to us in Germany on an irregular basis and when he can gain access to it and be able to pass it on. Do you understand me?'

Despite her rapidly sinking heart, Hanna was able to understand clearly and answer in the affirmative.

'I want to spell out the consequences if you do not agree to do what we wish. Firstly, your parents and sister, despite their allegiance to their country, will be banished to Siberia and you certainly shall never see them again. Secondly, your husband will be exposed with regards to the classified military information that he passed to us in Berlin, and this will destroy his glittering career. Thirdly, your escape from East Berlin will be published and sensationalized and your whereabouts in England will be exposed. Finally, I suggest that you keep a much closer eye on your children should you not comply. Again, do you understand?'

At this stage, Hanna was able to begin to gather her thoughts and again she replied in the affirmative.

'We will give you two weeks from today to decide what you wish to do. Whatever the answer please call this number on that day, no sooner and no later.'

She passed Hanna a small card on which was written a telephone number. Ursula then stood up and walked away down the path they had just used.

Hanna's urge to do a number of things almost overwhelmed her. She wanted to weep uncontrollably; she wanted to rush home and call Charles immediately and beg him to come home; she wanted to take the next flight to Germany and be with him; she wanted to find her children and protect them; she wanted to fall into Jane Bowater's protective arms; she wanted to kill herself.

She sat there for a long time, quiet tears falling down her

cheeks. She was devastated but she was also still capable of clarity of thought. Since coming to England she had, with Charles and the girls, created her perfect world. But before that her world was far from perfect for all the reasons that she was well aware of. She was now back in the world of the Soviet Union. The system she had been bought up in, had hated and then rejected, was now acting true to form. Revenge, threats, espionage and ruthless manipulation were their staple fare and here it was now right in front of her and her family in the peaceful English countryside. She would not let them beat her and take away her cherished life and family.

After a little while, she got up and slowly walked home. She composed herself at home and then went up to the house to ask Jane to collect the girls and look after them for the evening until bedtime.

Hanna went back to the Vine Barn and sat at the desk, drew out a sheet of paper and noted down all that she would do over the next few days, dependent on her communication with Charles. By this time her mind was clear, unemotional and determined. She was a tough woman when she wanted to be. It was time to take the battle to the enemy.

She recognised that the key to the response to this outrage lay in their ability to plan and work as an unbreakable team. She also recognised that the freedom and lifestyle they all enjoyed here in England was more than partly due to what Charles was doing in West Germany. Even as a Russian, to abuse those privileges she and her family enjoyed, would be unthinkable.

She wrote:

Book flight to Germany.
Tell Charles absolutely everything.
Must not succumb to this blackmail under any circumstances.
Must find another way to turn it to our advantage.
Charles must tell me everything.

Speak to no one else.

With flights booked and her mind ice-cold clear, she went up to the house and enjoyed supper with the Bowaters and the girls. She drank some wine and felt much better and more relaxed. They had time but not too much. It all depended on her weekend with Charles.

Charles was delighted she was coming to see him but mystified as to the short notice as they had only seen each other two weeks previously and had spoken on the phone most evenings.

'There are some important matters that we need to discuss, darling,' said Hanna.

'OK, no problem but I'm mystified. Can't you give me an inkling?'

'Not really. I will see you at the airport on Friday. Do not worry, darling.'

Hanna was putting on a brave face, but felt that with Charles she could face anything. After all, did they not achieve the impossible in East Berlin and cock a snoop at those Russian and East German monkeys?

THREE

In Bielefeld, Charles soon came to realise that the position he held was one of importance, not because it offered the opportunity to adjust and change, but because it needed a firm hand on the tiller of that which was already in place. The NATO armies in Western Europe had been deployed for decades and had readjusted and redeployed constantly over that period to meet the threat, that of a possible Soviet intent to invade Western Europe. This threat had not really changed since the end of the war but it needed to be constantly monitored and reacted to if it did. There was now a certain equilibrium and the plans in place were probably as good as they were ever going to get.

Along with other staff officers, both senior and junior to him, he found himself at the centre of this constant process of ensuring readiness to meet the threat posed, and it continued to be a very real threat in late 1984. One of his key duties was liaison up and sideways which meant frequent visits to SHAPE at Mons in Belgium; the Northern Army Group Headquarters in Monchengladbach in Germany; and the German, American, Dutch and Belgium Corps headquarters in the northern part of Germany. All Corps had their strengths and weaknesses but it was generally agreed by all that the Belgium Corp Headquarters produced the best lunches and finest wines. Charles also liaised less frequently with the French as they were not part of NATO and found them, as usual, somewhat aloof. He found it difficult to understand their attitude but it was not for him at his level to make judgements. His job was to foster good relationships and improve liaison and cooperation within a separate set of security classifications.

His other key duty was, with others, to ensure that the Corps armoured divisions were constantly at a state of readiness that would allow them to deploy to their battle positions within their sector and within a certain timeframe. Again, constant meetings, briefings, conferences, workshops and, most important of all, everything to do with the physical practice of the operational plans, both indoors and in the field, often for weeks at a time, was the relentless training cycle in which he found himself, and at the centre.

Charles' work meant that he had direct access to all NATO top-secret operational plans, not only for the British Corps but all others in Northern Army Group. His personal vetting was the highest obtainable, a fact that sometimes made him feel uncomfortable given his past and who he was married to. The Ministry of Defence continued to appear to wish to ignore these concerns he harboured. During these moments of doubt, the face of Peter Rogers appeared.

The day-to-day round was busy enough to ensure they did not persist for long and sometimes the workload became wearisome. But he enjoyed it all immensely and was soon making his mark through his hard work, knowledge, focus and intellect. He also discovered that he was a good public speaker in front of large audiences. He was well set for a professionally satisfying two years in Bielefeld, firmly supported by Hanna and the life he had created back in England. He was a happy man.

WHEN HE SAW her coming out of the arrivals gate at Hannover Airport, he was filled with joy. She was so beautiful. They kissed and held each other very tight for longer than they realized. He could see that her face bore a worried and strained look, which was unusual as she was normally radiant especially when they met again after a separation, no matter how short or long.

It was very cold and raining as Charles drove along the autobahn back to their favourite Gasthaus in the wooded hills around Bielefeld. Herr and Frau Beck welcomed them warmly and with enthusiasm. Over the past months they had become *bervorzugte gaste* or favoured guests, which meant that they always found themselves in the best room and received undivided attention. The Becks were a kindly couple and their hospitality beyond reproach.

As the rain continued to fall heavily outside, they ate a delicious meal prepared by Frau Beck and then retired upstairs. Hanna, normally so bubbly and talkative when she was with her beloved, was strangely quiet but Charles did not push.

When they lay in bed, she told him all with no detail left out. When she had married Charles she had vowed to herself that no matter what happened in the future, she would always be completely honest with him and always tell him everything. She did this now and asked him not to interrupt until she was finished. She started at the very beginning when she had first met Ursula and finished as she described her feelings sitting on that bench and what she had resolved to do. There was silence for longer than a moment. He stared at the ceiling and felt weak and helpless. It had all caught up with him, and parts of the story had caught up with him that he didn't even know about. It had also caught up with them as man and wife. As always, he outwardly controlled his emotions but inside he was in turmoil.

He turned to her and looked into her eyes. She pressed her finger against his lips and smiled that lovely smile.

'Two things you need to know and believe before we go any further,' she said. 'Number one. I will never, never leave you or be anything other than your devoted and loving wife. Number two. We are in this together and together we will turn this to our advantage and beat these swine at their own game.'

Charles stared at her. How on earth could he have been lucky enough to have met a woman like this? She was unlike anyone he had ever met before. Beneath that lovely exterior was true steel and a love for him that he did not believe could ever be possible, even after all these years together.

She drew him to her and pressed herself against him, stroking his neck and back. He felt the inevitable urge rising in him.

'We need to relax and sleep. Tomorrow is another day and we can talk then.'

Surprisingly, he slept soundly and perhaps that was because she was beside him. She was the quietest sleeper and never disturbed him at night. In the morning, he woke at his normal time, a time that had always been six o'clock, and lay there listening to the rain beating against the windows. It was unlikely that there would be any long walks in the woods today. He was warm and cosy and turned to look at her. She slept soundly. He forced himself not to think about what he should do. This had to be a joint affair and he vowed then that he would not do anything in the future that might jeopardise her wish that they must face this together, and that he would never lie to her. It must be the truth and nothing but the truth. They had two days to make a plan. He dozed off again and was awoken by the feel of her silky body close to his. He opened his eyes and her face was close to his, her eyes looking intently at him. Their lovemaking was gentle, warm and quiet. No words were spoken but the intensity of feeling was the same as ever.

With Frau Beck fussing around them, breakfast was taken and they then retired to their room. It was time to come to terms.

'I did some very stupid things whilst I was a young man in Berlin. I drank far too much and behaved at times in an irresponsible way – mainly, though not always – due to the alcohol. I am very sorry.'

She smiled but said nothing. She let him tell it all without interruption.

'I would like to tell you a number of things, darling. The first is that I did conduct a long and passionate affair with a German woman whist I was in Berlin. I was still with her up to the point when we took you from the east, but terminated it that same day. I am sorry.

'The second is that I never had any inkling of who she really was and why she suddenly appeared in my life. I now know. I was deliberately targeted but never realised it. That woman was probably right when she told you that this Greta woman had taken secrets from me. I have no recollection of when or how but do know that I was many times drunk with her and may well have talked. I was also very lax with security and on more than one occasion flouted the rules over the protection of documents. Sometimes I kept them illegally in my room in the mess. I was, after all, the holder of the keys. I'm so very sorry.'

Hanna smiled again and let him continue. She could see that he needed to get all of this off his chest.

'I engineered your escape entirely on my own with no other assistance, and far as I am aware the army knows nothing about it. The people who do know about it are the British Secret Service and I know the secret will be safe with them. I know this because being married to a Russian, I would never have been allowed to do the jobs I have done and the job I am doing now with all my direct access to very secret classified documents without their help and support.

'So, you see my darling, I have been very foolish and unwise in my youth but in the case of the relationship with the German, not intentionally. I want you to know that from the day that I took you to that flat in West Berlin to today you have been my life and I will never, ever let you down. Bringing you out of East Berlin was the best thing I have ever done. For everything else I am truly sorry, and I hope that you will forgive me.'

Hanna looked at his sincere, handsome face and smiled once again.

'What you have told me, dear Charles, matters not one jot for our relationship. It makes no difference at all and my feelings and thoughts for you now are the same as when I looked into your eyes standing in that museum. I loved you then and I love you now. You must never think that it will affect anything. It will not.'

The relief on his face was palpable.

'What I suggest we do now is start thinking about how we together are going to play this new situation. I can tell now, and being a Russian, that they will never let it rest because they feel they have an advantage, but we must never allow them to control either of us or our children no matter what happens. But I do think that we need to approach this whole thing in a clear, logical and unemotional way and come up, if possible, this weekend, with a plan that will work. I suggest we think about it separately at first and then come together here after lunch and discuss. What do you think?'

'I think that is a good idea.' She seemed to be taking the lead in this but a thought had already crossed his mind.

The rain had eased and, suitably clad, they ventured out into a blustery, damp and cold morning for a short walk, a walk taken mainly in silence, a most unusual occurrence. In their relationship there had never been a shortage of conversation. Back at the warm and cosy Gasthaus, they drank coffee and sat by the fire in the main room until lunch. Charles continued to develop the thought that he had had and the more he thought about it, the more of a possibility it seemed to become.

The rain had come back in earnest and turned that afternoon into sleet and then snow. They went to their room, held each other and kissed with an intensity that was only broken when they both realised that they had to come to grips with what was probably the most important decision of their lives, and of their children's lives.

PART 5: DEFIANCE

ONE

S itting opposite her and looking at her lovely face set in an expression of combative determination, Charles realised he had not seen his wife in this light before. She, in turn, continued to be impressed by his composure with a situation that must have shaken him to the core.

'Any thoughts?' she ventured.

'Actually, yes, I do and it is the only one that I could come up with that, if it works, will do a number of things which may solve our problem. The downside is that it carries risk but I have worked out that whatever we decide to do will carry risk. It is the way it is going to be from now on, I am afraid.'

Charles clicked into military mode.

'It seems to me that we need to come up with a scheme that will do a number of things. Firstly, we need to negate the direct threats that have been levelled at us and therefore protect our family. Secondly, we need, if possible, to turn their demands to our advantage, or should I say our side's advantage. And thirdly, we cannot do this on our own.

'I am sorry that I am being so military, but it helps me think along straight lines. On the first point, and in my opinion, the best way to negate the threat to us is to give to them what they want.'

Hanna's face dropped and she was about to open her mouth.

'But giving them what they want can be done differently. What we will really do is to give to them what they believe is what they want, but in fact is not. Subterfuge is never easy and one mistake in that game could have serious consequences.

'My first point leads directly into the second. If we can achieve that and they believe it all we will not only be screwing them big time but we will be doing our own country and NATO a serious favour.'

This time Hanna did open her mouth, but only to come over and kiss him and then sink back into her chair opposite him.

'The third part, which is the management, support and backup, would have to be put into place before anything else and I know who I have to speak to. His name is Peter Rogers and he is the man who made sure that you ended up at home after your escape and time in Bonn and England before we were together again all those years ago. I suspect that he is now quite senior in the service. I intend to make contact with him as soon as possible – unless you disagree with this whole idea.'

She was astute enough to see the dangers but if they were to avoid the long arm of the Soviet system ranged against them, an arm that could be ruthless and murderous, then she could also see that her husband's plan, if successful, would not only protect them but also satisfy her desire to strike back at those who had threatened her family and way of life in England, and whom she hated with a passion.

'We must try to do it,' she replied with alacrity.

'You would become a double agent?' she ventured.

'In a rather odd way, yes.'

Charles rather liked the idea of being a man of mystery operating in the dangerous and murky world of espionage, whilst at the same time taking part in and upholding the defence of the free world. In retrospect this felt rather corny, but never mind. Even in his late thirties he could remain at times detached from the real world and would dream, although he was far too clever and worldly wise ever to be suspected of being a Walter Mitty.

He was also rather surprised by himself. He could hardly describe himself as a George Smiley and apart from his brush with the world of espionage in Berlin, he was a novice.

Charles found his ever-present notebook and jotted down a number of 'things to do', although to a prying eye it would have made no sense.

'By the way darling, everything we do and say with regard to this subject from now on must be treated in the utmost confidence. No one else must know less those who are in charge of what we do. Security must be paramount.'

Hanna nodded and smiled. In her previous life that was all she ever did – keep her mouth shut and her mind sharp to the ever-constant possibility of slipping up. All secrets were safe with her.

'There are many details that I have to think about, but I will always tell you everything that I think and do, and what is planned to happen and what will happen. I am going to make a call now to try to send a message to Peter Rogers. When he hears who it is from, he will almost certainly call back at some stage in the near future. After I have done that, we must try to enjoy the rest of our time together this weekend.'

Charles went downstairs where there was a public phone set aside in a small booth. He called the FCO duty number, a number he had kept on him since Peter Rogers had given it to him in Berlin all those years ago, and left a very brief message.

'Please tell Mr Peter Rogers that Charles Bowater wishes to speak to him as a matter of urgency.' This was acknowledged and he rang off. He knew that Peter Rogers would find out where he worked and make contact. Time to enjoy the rest of the weekend with Hanna.

They had been married for ten years but time had not dulled their passion for each other. The remainder of that very wet weekend was spent enjoying Frau Beck's solid but excellent German cooking, drinking Riesling, sitting and talking or making love. Hanna continued to be surprised by Charles' relaxed approach but Charles' mind worked in very organised lines. Until he heard back from Peter Rogers and then met him, there was nothing he could do to influence the situation; therefore, he could relax and enjoy the companionship of his wife. It was an attribute that served him well in the army. Thinking in straight lines and compartmentalising his life when necessary helped greatly.

They were always like young lovers when they met and said goodbye. He kissed her passionately and held her tightly at Hannover Airport as they parted. This time it would only be a week apart as they had booked with the Becks for the following weekend.

'When I speak to Peter, I think he will be interested in meeting before next weekend but I do not know yet. Of course, I will call you as soon as I know.'

'I will wait.'

'We need to remember to use veiled speech whenever we talk about this.'

It was not a term Hanna had come across before, but she soon understood. As always, she would surpass Charles in the art of keeping secrets.

'Give huge kisses and hugs to the girls.'

'I will. Goodbye, my sweetest man.'

Back in the officers' mess, Charles slipped easily back into military mode. He made sure that the week ahead, packed with meetings, a divisional conference and a pile of paperwork, the majority of which would be of a highly classified nature, was clear in his mind before going to bed and dreaming of his wonderful wife.

He waited patiently until Wednesday, but in reality had little time to dwell on it. The pressures of work continued unabated. Peter Rogers called him in his office and said that he could come to Germany that weekend and meet him at a place and time of his convenience. Charles said that he would meet him in Bielefeld and gave a landmark and a time. Peter Rogers agreed and rang off. The call lasted no more than two minutes. Hopefully it had been made over a secure connection, but knowing Peter it would have been.

Charles called Hanna, who gave him her flight details for Friday evening.

'I am glad I will be there with you.'

'Even if you weren't there physically, you would be there in my heart, as always.'

'And you in mine.'

CHARLES MET Hanna at the airport. He asked that they spend a short time sitting by the arrivals gate so that he could explain something to her.

'I do not know if I am being watched but I am very aware of the possibility. As we sit here, let me know if you feel that there is someone close by who might be taking an interest in us.'

Hanna glanced around her in a casual manner.

'Not that I can see,' she said, taking his hand.

'From now on wherever we walk or drive or visit places either here or in England, you will need to be aware of this possibility. When we are together, I will always make sure that I can confuse them if they are there, but I suspect that until you give that woman our answer next week, they will leave us alone.'

She nodded. Their situation was coming into sharper focus and she did not like it. But for Charles, their girls and their life together she would do anything and must adapt and make it work.

They drove back to their favourite Gasthaus where the Becks greeted them enthusiastically.

'I think it would be best if we just enjoyed our evening together, because tomorrow will be a key day for us.' Straight lines again.

Charles explained to Hanna about Peter Rogers arriving the next day and that he would go and collect him and bring him to Gasthaus where he would stay the night.

Frau Beck produced an excellent meal as they sat in a near empty dining room looking intently at each other. Even after only spending a week apart, the passion and desire could not be dimmed.

———

As AGREED, Peter Rogers and Charles met in a small café down a side street in Bielefeld. Charles was a novice at the espionage game, but he did know that if he was being tailed he had to shake them off. He left the Gasthaus alone after breakfast that Saturday morning and in his 15-minute drive to Bielefeld *Mitte* he constantly checked in his rear-view mirror. He was not followed and nor did he note anything untoward once he had parked the car and doubled back three times during the walk to the café.

Peter Rogers was already there and they shook hands. It had been well over ten years since they had last met, but Charles saw no real physical difference in his friend less a greying of the hair. He was still the quiet, astute and competent operator he had always been. They drank coffee and chatted about nothing in particular. The serious talk would come later. They drove in silence to the Gasthaus, where Peter was shown to his room. They agreed to meet downstairs after lunch and go for a long walk in the woods where Charles planned to break the news to him and present to him his proposal. Woods do not have ears and Charles knew that Peter Rogers would approve.

Hanna and Charles took a light lunch in their room and Charles cleared his mind as to how he was going to approach this, making sure he would leave nothing out.

The weather was kind and unseasonably mild. The woods were all but deserted. After introducing Hanna to Peter Rogers, they set off. Once clear of the Gasthaus complex and having walked for some ten minutes along a forest path, Charles opened the discussion – or what he hoped would be a discussion.

'The reason I have asked to meet is because they have found out all about me, all about Hanna and who she really is, where we live and where I work now. One of their female operatives met Hanna in England, befriended her and then issued a number of direct threats against us both.'

Charles explained all and gave as much detail as he could. Peter Rogers was all ears but said nothing.

'That is all the background. Over the past week or so we have been giving this and what we should do about it very much thought and have come up with a proposal. That is why I invited you here.'

Peter Rogers was silent for a moment and then said, 'The only part that seriously worries me is what you told me about how you passed military secret information to the Soviets via a German girlfriend, something that you did not tell me and that I was unaware of. You suggested that she was a honey trap and that you had done these deeds when you were drunk. Is that correct?'

'As far I am aware yes, but whatever I did say or do all those years ago has made no difference to the status quo in Europe. I only had access to immediate plans that detailed the British part of things in Berlin and none of the bigger picture. I was small fry in those days. I should know, given my present position and responsibilities.'

Peter Rogers nodded. The Ministry of Defence had provided him with all the details of Charles' meteoric career, exactly what he did now and what access he had to classified material. Since those days in Berlin, there had been no real change in the east—west face-off in Europe so one could safely assume that no damage was done at the time through Charles' indiscretions and immature behaviour.

'I could hardly do the same thing now. I hardly drink, am happily married and have two lovely daughters and a good career. Things have moved on.'

'So, what is your proposal given this fix that you now find yourself in?' asked Peter Rogers.

'If you could hear me out, I hope you will find it of interest. When we discussed this last weekend, we saw clearly that we had a number of options. Do as they asked, pass classified intelligence to them and save our necks. Pass them disinformation when they believe they are receiving the real thing, or do nothing and see what happens. We opted for the second and that is why I invited you here.

'If this is a direction that you would be interested in, I am sure you would agree that this could give us a number of advantages, both collectively and individually. The most important would be that we would be one step ahead of the Soviets because they would believe that they were now in possession of NATO operational plans in Northern Germany, but these would be false. Secondly, my family and I would be safe and can continue our lives, albeit under great and constant strain. Hanna and I have decided that what we can do for our country is so important that we are prepared to live with this. In Hanna's words, and despite her being one, anything to screw the communists would be a good thing for her.

'I realise that the detail would need to be very carefully handled. One false move which could arouse suspicion would put me and possibly my family, as well as Hanna's family in Russia, in a dangerous position, something I would certainly not want. But the bottom line is that I am prepared to do it if you think it is feasible. Please always remember Peter that I am doing this for my family and our future happiness together, and not for my career. I am also doing it for my country.

'In principle, what do you think?'

Despite his considerable experience of living in a world where espionage in all its guises alongside human courage, emotion, frailty and competence and incompetence were its driving forces, Peter Rogers was taken aback by what Charles had just told him. He had not imagined for one moment that this was why he was walking in a German forest with a man whom he liked and trusted but was an officer in an institution where he doubted this had ever happened before. Certainly not to his knowledge. It was probably unique. Indeed, it was unthinkable that a serving army officer of Charles' rank and position would propose such a thing.

But to Peter Roger's fertile mind what Charles had said to him all added up, from the escape of Hanna to the west, to the affair with the beautiful German agent in Berlin, to his current predicament. The Soviets were showing classic tactics in this affair and he recognised all of them. Charles, through his actions, either inadvertently or deliberately, had put himself in a position where they could use a number of direct and very real threats to turn and use him to their advantage, a situation without precedent.

As they walked on in silence, Peter Rogers carefully thought about Charles' proposal. Would it be worth it and would it be able to be made to work to gain advantage over the Soviets? Both questions were not easy to answer at this stage, but given the need for Hanna to contact this woman next week there was an element of urgency in this. Peter Rogers knew he was now senior enough in the service to be able to make a decision himself and his gut instinct, always useful, told him that they must give it a go. But this gut instinct was backed up with logic and a desire to use Charles for the benefit of the country, his service but certainly not the army. If it faltered or failed, he also knew that it would then be his responsibility to look after Charles and his family, even to the point of giving them new identities and moving them well out of the way for an indefinite period of time. At least the Americans would probably be happy because he had surmised that Charles' handlers would be seeking far more than just the British military plans and dispositions in West Germany.

He needed 24 hours back in London to clear it with his master and then put it all together before giving Charles the nod, or otherwise. After that, there would have to be a defined period of planning on how disinformation was to be formulated and on what basis. It had to be believable and look genuine, but at the same time not be vulnerable to exposure as being something it was not. This would be very difficult but not impossible if approached in a wholly logical way.

They enjoyed a very pleasant evening together at the Gasthaus. Frau Beck excelled once again and there was a relaxed or perhaps relieved atmosphere. Peter Rogers was more than taken by the beauty and poise of Hanna and now saw more clearly why Charles had taken that huge risk all those years ago in Berlin. She certainly seemed more than worth it but now those events, and others, had caught up with them.

Charles drove Peter Rogers back to the train station the next morning. Peter Rogers handed Charles a slip of paper.

'On Tuesday morning at nine o'clock UK time, call this number from your office and I will call you back. Please do not talk. I will do all the talking by firstly telling you yes or no and then to give you instructions on what will happen next, either way.'

'Thanks Peter. I will do that. Safe trip.'

Peter Rogers was never one to say goodbye and, in a moment, he was gone.

Hanna and Charles tried to enjoy the rest of the time they had together that weekend, but it was difficult. They were both tense and were not looking forward to either the next two days leading up to Peter Roger's call, or to the time when Hanna would have to either call the woman who called herself Ursula with an answer, or ignore it which both felt unlikely. Hanna returned to England and they waited, and whilst they waited they both thought separately about what they had done in the past and both rued their current situation, a situation which they had bought upon themselves and from which there seemed no way out, whether Peter Rogers agreed with their proposal or not.

CHARLES CALLED the number at the time he had been given.

'Good morning. I will call you back,' was the answer. Charles recognised the voice.

Peter Rogers called him back immediately and was, as usual, spare with his words.

'The answer is yes for a number of reasons which we can talk about later. Are you planning to come back to England soon?'

'I wasn't but I can.'

'Do not worry, I will come to you and shall be bringing a colleague with me. We will make our own travel and accommodation arrangements. Details on where we will meet will follow within the next 24 hours and we should be with you this weekend. In the meantime, please tell your lady H that she is to agree to the demands made and then wait to see what happens. All understood?'

'Yes, understood.'

The phone went dead. This news filled him with a sense of relief, tempered by thoughts of what might come next. In typical fashion, Charles then compartmentalised this information in his mind and burrowed himself in his work, which was plenty enough to keep him very busy. Tomorrow was another day, but that evening he called Hanna. As they had agreed, they both waited for twenty seconds before speaking to listen for the tell-tale click of the telephone. There was none and Charles assumed that at this stage of the game their detractors were merely content to wait and not rock the boat.

'You need to contact that woman and give our answer as yes but say no more at this stage. No need for you to come to see me here and I will plan for some leave in England for Christmas.'

'I understand, darling.'

'We are having another meeting here in the very near future. I want you to carry on as normal, or as normal as you can, look after the girls and be patient. Once you have passed that information, let me know and then it will be up to me to get on with it over here.'

'OK, darling. I will be patient. I love you with all my heart.'

'I love you too, my sweet and wonderful lady. I kiss you and send my love to my parents and the girls.'

He rang off and went back to waiting for Peter Rogers' information to come to him.

The next morning, his phone in the office rang. Without preamble: 'On Friday, book into the Hotel Zur Stemmer Post in the town of Minden for one night. I will meet you there the following day about mid-morning.' The telephone went dead before Charles could answer.

Charles knew Minden. The British Army had troops based there and he had visited it often. He called the hotel and made his booking. More waiting.

TWO

Hanna made the greatest efforts to focus on her life, their house, their daughters and Charles' parents. It was a life she loved not only because it was so far removed mentally, physically and materially from the life she had known in Soviet Russia and Berlin, but because it represented to her happiness, stability and a future with those she loved. She had forgotten about being a doctor and felt no real loss despite all those long years of training. She felt comfortable in England and her skills in the English language had reached a point where she was fluent but still with that slight East European tinge to her accent. She was always aware of her own parents and sister in the background but as time passed she grew used to being without them in either word or presence. The occasions when she used to sit down and sob quietly were growing fewer but she would never forget them and would always wait for the time when they would meet again.

Although the protection of Charles and the girls were and would always be her main priority, she also prayed that her actions in Berlin had not given the authorities in Russia an excuse to punish them in some way. She was also astute enough to know that this latest turn of events would be a further excuse for the authorities to act against them should she and Charles refuse to cooperate. Although the current president of the Soviet Union had relaxed the regime's grip through glasnost and perestroika, the country's security apparatus was still well capable of acting with brutality and disregard to its own people should they believe that the aims of the state were being threatened.

Having dropped the girls off at their much-loved school, she called the number the Ursula woman had given her. There was a nervous tremor in her hand as she listened to the ringing tone.

'Hello.' She recognised the voice.

After twenty seconds. 'The answer is yes.'

'Excellent. Your husband will be contacted in due course.' The phone went dead.

Hanna immediately called Charles on his office number.

'Hello darling. I passed the message to her and she said that you will be contacted in due course. That was all.'

Charles sounded upbeat and cheerful. Those early-morning runs always did the trick.

'Thank you, darling. There is no need for you to do anything else but keep a close watch on the girls. From now on it is all up to me. Please try to relax and enjoy yourself as much as you can. I will be fine and as you know I am more than capable of looking after myself and handling this in the right way. After all, I have everything to play for. I have had my leave for Christmas approved and will be with you on 22nd December. Details to follow but I will catch a train to Westbury.'

He was right, she thought. From now on, even as he stepped into the unknown world of espionage, she knew he would be the one who would be in control, not the people she hated. Having met Peter Rogers, whom she liked very much, she was also confident that her husband would be fully looked after and supported. Peter Rogers exuded reassurance and professionalism.

Her mood lightened and she wandered up the path to the Vine House and had a chat and coffee with Jane Bowater. They never tired of each other and there was never a lack of animated conversation between them. David Bowater wandered in. He had aged prematurely to look at but had never lost that gentle, charming quality, that twinkle in his eye and his slim and dapper appearance. The doctor had warned him that it would be wise if he cut down on his drinking or even stopped. He greeted this with a dismissive wave and carried on as normal. It is probably a truism to say that to men of his generation, and with the experiences he had endured in his life, his reaction to this 'granny' advice was not uncommon. He went out into the garden and headed for the shed and a little relief. It was ten o'clock in the morning. Jane Bowater knew exactly what he was doing but smiled and ignored it, as she always did.

'Charles tells me that he will be home for Christmas for two weeks, which will be wonderful,' said Hanna.

'That's very good news. You should make a plan and of course include many suppers over here with the girls.' She was as hospitable as ever.

'As it is the middle of winter, we will probably stay at home and enjoy Christmas with you and even the vicar in church, certainly for the carols and the Christmas Day service, take lots of walks in the countryside and perhaps some trips to a few places of interest nearby. Or perhaps he would just like to stay at home and unwind. I know that he works incredibly hard.'

'I can see that he is doing so well in the army but I hope that all this success will not spoil him.'

'He is the same lovely man as when I first met him. He is so good at dividing his life between work and family and friends. They never seem to interfere with each other.'

They chatted on for a bit and then Hanna went back to the cottage. She felt so much better and the tension had lifted. Time to wait for Charles and in the meantime carry on with her life – Eleanor and Viktoria as the priority as always, improving her English, being an active member of the Parish Council, attending the local shoot as a beater in the season and keeping fit. Childbirth had made little or no difference to the beauty of her body and she wanted to keep it that way, not only for Charles but for herself. She swam, went to the gym, walked miles and was careful with her diet. The English weather suited her and she looked radiant. When she had time, she read voraciously and slept well. It was a busy life and even without Charles there all the time she was happy. The dark cloud that had passed over her seemed to have dispersed, perhaps temporarily, and the reason was that she had so much belief and confidence in her husband.

THREE

Charles sat in the foyer of his small but warm and comfortable hotel in Minden that Saturday morning and drank coffee.

Peter Rogers came in, accompanied by a younger man.

'Good morning. I think you may have some information for me?' he said without preamble.

'Yes. She made contact and H passed on the affirmative and was told that I am to wait.'

'Shall we go for a walk.' It was not a request and there was no introduction to the other man.

Charles' hotel was situated on the outskirts of Minden and backed on to wooded hills with many paths. It was very cold and the forest was deserted. After ten minutes and having checked that they were alone, Peter Rogers pointed at his companion. 'This gentleman is codenamed Cyclops. He will be your controller here in Germany and you will deal only with him. No one else will be involved.'

Charles looked at his controller, liked what he saw but thought that his codename was faintly ridiculous. Cyclops was a mythical monster with only one eye. This man was not a myth or a monster and he had two eyes. Obviously a service man, he exuded an air of quiet confidence and ability. He was young and looked fit. He had a calm and pleasant face and Charles took to him immediately. They exchanged nods but nothing more.

'We will now spend the next hour or so talking about the system we will employ to pass disinformation to those over there.' He pointed towards the east.

'This will be divided into two parts. The relationship between Cyclops and yourself and how you will interact and pass information to and fro, and the manner in which real information is developed and formulated into disinformation before being passed on to the other side. You are not to take any notes or ever write anything down. You have to carry it all in your head. You,' he nodded to Charles, 'will obviously have to pass on disinformation to the other side but apart from that there will be no written evidence at all of our activities. All understood so far?'

They both nodded.

Peter Rogers then said something which took Charles by surprise and which he wasn't expecting.

'You will never take anything out of the Headquarters in which you work. There will be no need to do this and I will explain why. A team is being set up in London consisting of people from the armed forces of all the countries of Northern Army Group and the Americans. They will sit beside members of the relevant secret services and this team's task is to create the disinformation from the real plans and then pass it on to me. I will then pass it on to Cyclops who will, in turn, pass it on to you. You, in turn, will pass it on to the other side through methods they must dictate, not us.'

Charles realised at this point how vital this all was and how important it was to the west. He had naively thought he would be involved in formulating the disinformation through the manipulation of the truth that he had, on a daily basis, at his fingertips and smuggling it out of the headquarters in true spy mode, before passing it onto the other side. These fanciful notions had been dispelled. Having absorbed this, a sense of relief came over him. His job was merely to be an 'information mule'. He would be given the information by his controller and his task was merely to pass it on to ensure that the Soviets could see that it was he who was gathering the information they knew he had access to. He would not even have to know what it was he was passing on, and he would be expected to carry on with life and work in the headquarters as normal.

'It is important that the information given will arouse no suspicions with the Soviets if it deviates from the real plans too greatly. But it will make sure that if they decide to attack, which in today's climate is highly unlikely, they will be deceived as to where the strengths and weaknesses are in our defences. In addition, there are other methods which will be deployed to further deceive them such as tactical nuclear options, strengths of forces, types of equipment and the systems used in the alert states. This detail is no concern of ours.'

Peter Rogers went on.

'Furthermore, this disinformation passed on must reflect the difficulty in recording or removing it and getting it physically out of the headquarters. It must be given in drips and drabs and at times perhaps not at all. It must all seem very real and as I have said, must never rouse any suspicion. This will all take time, perhaps years. We must be prepared for the long haul. The overall aim is to keep the enemy happy through the provision of information that is entirely believable and credible to them. We know that they have no method, apart from SOXMIS which can be easily monitored and thwarted, of verifying the information we will send them. All happy so far?'

Again, they both nodded but said nothing.

'We will now return to the hotel and I will depart. I will now step back from coming again to Germany in respect of this mission. Both of you are now to work out a plan on how you are to liaise in the future and how you will pass on information. Do not worry Charles, Cyclops is an expert at these sorts of things and will school you in no time at all. Remember, the whole mission is classified top secret and should not be talked about to anyone, including your wife Charles. Finally, this will not be forgotten Charles so stay calm as I know you will. You will always have our full support and if it gets tricky, we will react immediately, not only for you but for your family as well. Good luck.'

He strode off down the hill leaving them together in the gloomy, dank forest. They walked back to the hotel where they had lunch together. There was no one else in the main bar where they ate. They eyed each other and there was already a feeling of trust and even friendship, though all the while Cyclops never offered any information on his background, what he did, his family if he had one, or where he came from.

FOUR

dam Neumann was both pleased and relieved when the call came through that he would definitely be required for a task and this task would start in the very near future. He found his humdrum life with the Bundespost and living in his grubby flat tedious, but at no time did he make an attempt to improve his lot. He had half a dozen favourite seedy *kneipe* close to his apartment where he occasionally mixed with others such as himself and where he drank large quantities of beer. Not surprisingly, he suffered from health problems, but this did not deter him from his chosen lifestyle. The only personal quality he did retain was his intelligence and ability to think on his feet in a quick and logical manner. When sober, he was a very different man to when he was drunk.

When he returned from work one day in early December, he found an envelope that had been slipped under his front door.

'Meet me in the Gasthaus Feuermelder tomorrow evening at seven. I will be sitting in the corner by the fire wearing a red jersey and drinking a beer. I know what you look like.'

Adam Neumann went out as usual and drank his usual beer, but not quite so much this time. He was consequently unusually bright and breezy the next day and made his way to the Gasthaus Feuermelder that evening, arriving exactly at seven. It was a seedy dive, dark, smoky and overwarm. A few men sat at the bar. He immediately saw his contact and approached his table. The man sitting there was to become an ever-present part of his life for the foreseeable future. He was thick-set, even fat, badly dressed with a fleshy, unpleasant looking face. His eyes were black and constantly darted from point to point. Adam Neumann did not like the look of him at all.

He nodded and pointed to a chair. In a low voice, he spoke.'To you, my name is Lutz. To me your name is Fridof. Please remember. Have a beer and look normal. Do not worry. All will be well.'

Adam Neumann ordered a beer.

Contrary to his physical appearance, Lutz's personality and voice were pleasant, persuasive and generally agreeable. He was not threatening and as time went by Adam Neumann realised that he was in possession of sharp intellect which he used in a careful and logical manner. Throughout their relationship, he never found anything more about him and never asked.

'You will need a clear head for your task which could last for some time. You do not need to stop but you drink too much and you will need to cut down. Can you do that?'

'I think so. Yes, I will,' said Adam Neumann, knowing this would be enormously difficult.

'I will meet you tomorrow evening at the same time at the main entrance to the Nordpark here in Bielefeld. All understood?'

Adam Neumann nodded and with that Lutz stood up and left, leaving his nearly full glass of beer behind. Adam Neumann didn't like waste so he poured it into his glass and, with a number of others thereafter, drank to a more lucrative and liquid future.

BOTH LUTZ and Cyclops understood that the mechanics of making this work on the ground was not going to be too difficult or particularly dangerous for either side. For Lutz and his agent Fridof, the task was to collect the information and pass it on to their master in Hamburg for onward transmission, and to relay to Bowater any questions that may come back. For Cyclops, his agent would not have to smuggle anything out of his workplace but collect the disinformation from himself and deliver it to the other side. Both sides realised that the key to success would be not to interfere with each other's tasks and queer the pitch of either. It therefore followed that in the benign democratic atmosphere of West Germany in the mid-eighties this espionage would be conducted in an atmosphere of mutual understanding and non-interference, an unusual occurrence in the broader scope of Cold War hostilities.

However, this particular atmosphere did not detract from the critical importance both sides placed on what was happening. At the tactical end of the mission the low-key, functional nature of the proceedings belied the fundamental and potentially game-changing stakes that were being presented to the leaders of the NATO countries and the Soviet Union. This was unprecedented and those leaders knew it. But because of one man, what he had done in his youth and what he wanted to do now, the continued but lessening threat of conflict in Europe could well be diffused. Western leaders were also well aware of the precarious economic, social and military position that the Soviet Union was beginning to discover itself to be in. There were also unmistakeable and distinct rumblings amongst their so-called allies within the Warsaw Pact. A wounded bear could be at its most dangerous and despite a seemingly progressive President there were enough hawks and unreconstructed Stalinists amongst the Council of Ministers and serried senior ranks of the Soviet forces who would not hesitate to strike if the moment was right, and before it became too late. The information Charles Bowater was providing might well be the excuse they urgently sought to press the trigger. In time, and as the information filtered through to those in the Moscow Military District and Wunsdorf in East Germany, the headquarters of the GSFG, they now believed that they held, for the first time, a tactical, operational and strategic advantage over the west. Such was the impact of this information as it was slowly filtered through, information that was false but believed. This belief was based purely on an overriding conviction that the pressures engineered by Victor Sokolov and implemented by Alexei Volikov would be more than sufficient to make Bowater do their bidding.

The major concern of the NATO team in London as they devised their deception and formulated it into bite-size pieces was that the information they gave might be enough to generate a GSFG first strike. It was therefore imperative that this information was very carefully compiled. It needed to deceive but also seem entirely credible. This was no easy task, but it always had to be a work of fiction. At this they were adept, and possessing some of the best military minds in NATO they ensured there would always have to be an acute balance between what could be seen as operationally and strategically sensible but not the truth. It proved to be a very difficult act, but with the overriding imperative that the information could never be enough to give the Soviets the absolute certainty and confidence to strike first and gain a quick victory, though if they did that, they would fall into a NATO trap along their main prepared military thrust lines in northern West Germany.

It was also assumed the disinformation they produced would have to be in the form of camera films. They knew the favoured cameras were the Minox Mini camera produced in Latvia, a Leica and a Zenit F-21. They would need to know which one Charles Bowater would be given.

ADAM NEUMANN NEEDED to make contact with Charles. He knew where he worked and he knew what he looked like. He thought long and hard and finally came up with the simplest of solutions. He would deliver a letter to the guardhouse addressed to Lieutenant Colonel Charles Bowater. The letter would contain nothing less than cheery greetings from a friend and could they meet up at the Brauhaus *kneipe* that Thursday evening to discuss the social activities for the coming weekend. All entirely innocent sounding. At the end it was signed 'Stefan'.

Adam Neumann shaved, smartened himself up and strode purposely across the street to the guardhouse. In English, he asked the guard at the gate if he could speak to the commander. The guard did not view him with suspicion but called to the guardhouse and a corporal came out. Adam explained the situation and that he fully understood he could not come in, and handed over the envelope. The guard commander was polite and promised to deliver the envelope. Adam Neumann thanked them politely, made his way back across the street and went on his way.

THE BRAUHAUS WAS, like all the *kneipe* that Adam Neumann frequented, a seedy dive. Charles arrived on time and whilst standing at the bar ordering a drink was approached by a man who simply said, 'Charles Bowater, I am Stefan.'

They sat down and drank in silence for a time.

'This is the number you can use to contact me when you have things to pass on. We can then arrange a time and place. There are numerous bars around the city and each time we meet it will be at a different place,' Adam Neumann said in his excellent English.

The noise in the bar was considerable, which was ideal. Their conversation went unheard and unheeded.

'We need not call each other by a name or anything else. I know your voice and you know mine. That number can only be used in conversation between us and no one else.' This was Adam Neumann's decision, not Lutz's.

Charles nodded.

'I fully understand that all this is going to take a lot of time for you to avoid suspicion. I will not push you for information. I will be very patient.'

Adam Neumann had worked out that the longer this job could be stretched out, the better it would be for his bank balance. Oddly, this purely selfish, personal non-idealistic approach coincided with Cyclops's intended *modus operandi*.

Charles nodded again. He had taken a good look at Neumann and could see the dissipation in his features. He did not look well and he drank very quickly. For Charles' one beer before he left, Adam Neumann had consumed three.

Just before he rose to leave, 'Stefan' handed Charles a small brown square-shaped package. He said nothing and departed.

As 'Stefan' was on his way to report back to Lutz, Charles walked back to the car park, sat in his car for some time to see if he noticed any unusual activities in the dark and then drove back to the officers' mess. He opened the package warily and found inside a Minox Mini camera and many rolls of film. He stored them in the lockable desk drawer and then lay on his bed and thought things over.

The circle had now been completed. On his side, Cyclops would provide the information in a highly controlled manner and he would deliver it in accordance with the instructions from Stefan. Stefan would pass it on to persons unknown. He would never know, and nor would he have to know, what was contained in the information he passed on. The danger point was his relationship with Cyclops and when and how they met. He was relying on Cyclops to come up with a solution.

He got off the bed, went downstairs and called Cyclops from the public phone box.

'Met up and contact arrangements made.' Charles took a risk. 'It's a Minox Mini camera.'

'Very good. I will be in touch.'

'I will be back in England for Christmas for ten days so can we reconnect in the New Year.'

'Yes,' and he rang off. No 'Happy Christmas'. Nothing.

With four days left before he took the well-trodden path to Zeebrugge, Charles felt he had done all he could for the time being. The Corp's officers' mess was almost empty, populated mainly by officers who had families back in the UK with a few bachelors thrown in. He went to the bar and drank wine whilst continuing to contemplate his position. He was not going to be a traitor; indeed, he was directly contributing in a major way to the defence of the west and he was protecting his family and himself, in that order. In his normal blithe manner, he did not regret what he had done in a past that had caused this current delicate situation. Greta was a graceful companion and someone he was genuinely fond of but not in love with. That was until he first saw Hanna and then it all changed and time had proven that the decision he made then was the right one. Now he had to focus on her and his daughters' future happiness by doing the task required of him and for which he had volunteered, and doing it well. But like all things in Charles' life, he would find a way, on a daily basis, to accommodate both without an overlap.

ALEXEI VOLIKOV WAS PLEASED with progress. As with Charles, the circle had also been completed with the mechanisms now in place in West Germany to expedite the vital military information they craved from Bowater, a man whom he believed was now in his pocket. Alexei Volikov also knew that this operation would be lengthy and he was not expecting any movement until after Christmas at the earliest. He had ordered his operatives in West Germany that from the Soviet side this operation was not to be initially monitored at all but that it must be allowed to develop in its own way as long as the intelligence started and continued to be delivered.

Alexei Volikov, never short of ambition, reported the situation back to Moscow and received a rare congratulatory note from the head of the KGB himself. This was indeed an honour. It generated enthusiasm in him but he well knew that this was going to a long game and he would need to be patient. He was enjoying his job in Berlin, made easier by a compliant ambassador who viewed the presence of the KGB with unease, like the majority of Russians, and his relationship with one of the secretaries in the main typing pool. She was his type. A voluptuous figure, striking by her curves, and a ready, flirtatious smile. She had been the focus of many a frustrated embassy employee before the arrival of Alexei Volikov, who soon claimed her as his own. From that moment on no one dared even look at her. She was his property and he ensured that with her all his dubious sexual fantasies were played out, fantasies that his wife back in Moscow refused to participate in. Whether she enjoyed the situation she found herself in, no one dared ask.

ON THE LAST day of term before the Christmas holidays began, Hanna picked up the girls. They seemed subdued and not their normal bubbly selves, especially as they now had two weeks of holiday ahead of them and Christmas to look forward to.

'Everything alright, darlings?' she asked.

'No Mummy. During our break this morning a lady came up to Viktoria and I and said we needed to be careful and to tell you that she would be back after the holidays,' Eleanor replied in a rush.

Hanna's stomach turned but she drove on with the sole aim of getting home safely.

'Let's talk about it all when we get home, darlings.'

She took them straight inside and sat them down in the kitchen.

'We need to be very serious about this. Can you remember exactly what she said to you?'

Viktoria was too young to really comprehend, so Eleanor took the lead.

'She said that we both needed to be careful and that we had to tell you Mummy and that she would be back after Christmas. That was all she said. She then turned around and walked very quickly away and out.'

'Can you remember what she looked like?' said Hanna, taking great effort to appear unconcerned.

'She was a little older than you I think and had a nice face and she was wearing a very nice pearl necklace. And she had a funny accent.'

It had to be that woman who called herself Ursula. How on earth had she managed to get into the school?

Despite what had happened, Charles' ten days at home in England with his family were bliss. Both he and Hanna had decided and were determined not to allow what had taken place to spoil this very special time with their family. On Christmas Day, the little girls discovered their stockings and then they all opened their presents under the tree amidst great excitement. The whole family went to church where the now doddery and forgetful vicar struggled through the service and must have delivered the shortest Christmas sermon in history, much to the relief of the congregation. Carols were sung and a truly festive spirit hung in the cold, frosty air. Charles and Hanna, Eleanor and Viktoria and David and Jane Bowater strolled back to Vine House to enjoy a traditional Christmas lunch which had been assiduously prepared and cooked by Jane Bowater, with Hanna's help.

Turkey was eaten, wine drunk, crackers opened and silly hats worn. David proposed toasts to Charles, Hanna and the girls, Henry the dog (just still alive) and Richard, the bone idle and haughty cat. The lunch went on and the girls decided to escape back to the cottage as they had many new presents to play with and didn't want to listen to all this boring grown-up stuff. More wine and then port were partaken and David Bowater became jolly and then sleepy, eventually slumbering peacefully by the fire with Richard content on his lap. Jane Bowater and Hanna cleared up and Charles went back to the cottage to be with the girls. It had been a fine day.

The remainder of his short break from the rigours of his job in Germany were taken up by doing as little as possible save to be with his family. Recent events had made him more acutely aware not only of his love for them all but how much he was responsible for protecting them and their lives in England into the future. Hanna and he spent long, languid and sometimes wildly passionate nights in bed together, whilst during the day the warm, comfortable cottage provided the perfect setting for the family to be together. The weather was cold and it began to lightly snow. They did little but always went for a walk in the afternoons, taking old Henry if he was in the mood. Walks with Henry, taken to sniffing every blade of grass, took twice as long as when he was younger but no one minded. David and Jane Bowater were more than hospitable without being overbearing and a number of very social lunches were enjoyed by all.

The New Year was not, by tradition, seen in by any of the Bowaters. As the clock struck midnight, all were fast asleep. In the morning, Charles and Hanna lay in bed with tea and talked quietly about what 1985 might bring. They decided it would not be wise to try to guess but rather keep their goals firmly at the front of their minds and take each day as it came.

There were tearful goodbyes from Hanna and the girls as Charles left the following day. He had said goodbye to his parents where there were no tears. David and Jane Bowater scorned the modern-day habit of everybody wanting to blub, especially on television. What fools these people made of themselves as they showed no dignity or decorum. However, if you had the temerity to disagree with their behaviour you would be branded cruel and unsympathetic, and probably a fascist as well.

Charles' trip back to Bielefeld was uneventful. Having spent most of his army career in Berlin or Germany, he knew the route intimately and arrived back in the mess in time for supper. Once back in his room he clicked into military mode once again, ready for the coming inevitable deluge the following morning would bring in the office. He also thought about Cyclops and knew that Cyclops would be well aware of his movements. He would wait for him to make contact and in the meantime he had a job to do.

FIVE

The call came two days later and they agreed Cyclops would come to dinner but arrive an hour early so that they could discuss their plan of action in Charles' room beforehand.

'I'll need to give the guard a name before you arrive,' Charles said.

'OK. Let me know,' and he rang off.

More espionage. He needed to think of someone that he knew, or had known who had no connection with anyone else. Then it came to him. Corporal Hancock. Charles had not known his Christian name until he attended his funeral. It was John. John Hancock would be Cyclops' name. He called back on the mess public phone.

'Is that Mr John Hancock?'

A slight hesitation.

'Yes, it is.'

'I look forward to seeing you soon,' and put the phone down. He felt that he was getting good at this.

They met as planned and went up to Charles' room. The first

thing Cyclops did was hand Charles a brown envelope which was of a size you could place in coat or jacket inner pocket.

'That's the first instalment. It will be some time before the next one is produced but the information in that should keep them happy.'

Charles put it in a drawer in his desk and locked it.

'Do not tarry. Hand it over as soon as you can. Please be aware that the information contained therein is not classified at all but you need to treat it as though it is. It is designed to whet their appetites and promises that the next assignment will be the beginning of the information they desire, information that will continue to come for a long time yet, and until there is no more to give.'

Cyclops produced another brown envelope from his pocket.

'In here is a list of locations in and around Bielefeld. They vary in nature but all tend to be off the beaten track. Against the name of each location is a number so when I call you all I will give is a number, date and time. When you have delivered to your contact on the other side, no need to tell me then. Tell me when we next meet. That's all that is needed. All clear?'

Charles went to his desk and took out the camera and film. He handed them to Cyclops.

'This is what they wanted me to use so can I assume that this is what will be used by your people in producing the information?'

'Yes, it will. Thank you.'

Charles nodded.

'Shall we go down to dinner?'

Charles made sure he placed Cyclops next to a pleasant officer who was known for his endless chatter about nothing in particular, and for his drinking habits, which were considerable. He was the headquarters' Motor Transport Officer. Sitting on his other side Charles was impressed that Cyclops had his cover story down to a T, not that his other dinner companion would have been particularly interested. He was too busy explaining the intricacies of his newly built conservatory back in Scotland. The food and wine were reasonable and the evening passed pleasantly enough. At the earliest polite moment, Cyclops took his leave. Both were relieved that this form of meeting would not be repeated, but its objective had been achieved. Vital information had been passed and they were now set up to begin the process for which they had been brought together in the first place.

Later that evening when all was quiet in the public rooms of the mess, Charles went downstairs and called the number he had been given by 'Stefan'.

'Can we meet tomorrow evening?'

'Yes. Come to the Gasthaus Scharze Pumpe at seven.' The voice sounded slurred.

———

IT WAS AN EXTRAORDINARY MEETING. Charles walked in at seven and immediately saw 'Stefan' sitting in a corner nursing a beer. He ordered a small beer and sat down next to him at the table. He put his hand in his inner coat pocket and placed the envelope on 'Stefan's' lap under the table. 'Stefan' put it his coat pocket, drained his beer, got up and left. Not a word was spoken between them. Charles finished his beer and also left. As he walked back to his car, he doubled back twice and kept a very sharp eye on what was going on around him. There was nothing he could see. As he drove home, one eye constantly on the rear-view mirror, he thought about 'Stefan'. He had looked terrible. Bleary eyed, unshaven and scruffily dressed. Was he the genuine article and should he be giving him this type of vital disinformation without really knowing who he was? He needed to talk to Cyclops again, and soon.

They met at one of the coded spots where Charles conveyed his concerns to Cyclops. Cyclops listened intently.

'We'll get him checked out but it might take some time.'

'He has reacted in the way in which we wished but there was something about him that didn't quite add up. I may be wrong but I feel we need to be very careful with him. He is definitely a drunk and probably alcoholic. I expect he's doing this for money to fuel his drinking and possibly drug habits.'

'I'll follow up as a matter of urgency.'

Cyclops left and Charles often wondered where he went. He assumed that he worked through the embassy in Bonn but stayed somewhere nearby. What was his real name? Did he have a family? Charles was sure Cyclops knew every single detail about his life, past and present. He placed all these thoughts to one side. It did not matter at all that he knew nothing of Cyclops or what was in the envelopes he would receive and would pass on. It was not his concern, though if he had been aware of the contents of the envelopes he would recognise immediately what they meant and why they were being sent. He had only been in his job for three months but he lived and breathed the strategic and operational plans of First British Corps, and the plans of their allies in northern West Germany. He was already an expert due to his diligence, hard work and application. He was only happy that he had not been called upon to smuggle real information out of the operations and plans secure area. That would have been difficult and highly dangerous, but not impossible because he was well aware of what security there was in place. Access to the secure operations and plan area situated deep within the headquarters was strictly enforced but because he was in the secure area every day, he was beyond suspicion. No one would have imagined that a serving and well-respected British Army officer of Charles' rank would be engaged in espionage. It was unheard of.

CYCLOPS WASTED no time in making contact with the Bundesnachrichtendienst, or Federal Intelligence Service, or BND, and within the BND the case officer for Operation METTLE, the code name for the disinformation mission. All of the nations represented in NORTHAG had afforded the highest priority to providing the necessary assets to METTLE, including their intelligence services.

Over the secure line, he passed on all the information he knew about 'Stefan' and was told this would be investigated as a top priority. Knowing well the German propensity for efficiency, he had every confidence that this would be the case.

Four days later, the BND case officer called him back and asked for a meeting. They met the next day. In good English: 'His name is Adam Neumann. He lives in Bielefeld at an address we can provide if you need it. We do not think you will as we now have him covered. He works for the Bundespost in Bielefeld. He is well known in his local area and the pubs for his drinking habits and, at times, disorderly behaviour, but he has never done anything to warrant an arrest. We gather that although his wages at Bundespost are not great, he never seems to be short of money. He has no criminal record, has not been engaged or shown interest in any political or subversive movement and has not been noticed by us before. We can of course dig deeper but as I understand it you do not want this and you do not want us in any way to take this further at this stage?'

'Thank you very much. This is very useful. You are right. At this stage this will be enough.'

The last thing Cyclops wanted was to frighten the horses but as an SIS man he worked on the maxim that all information had its uses, even if it seemed banal or irrelevant at the time.

He called Charles.

'Number 3. 28 January. Seven o'clock,' and having received a yes put the phone down.

They met at a petrol station on the outskirts of Bielefeld.

'Carry on with Stefan. If his behaviour changes or you suspect something else, let me know immediately. It is imperative he suspects nothing. The next, or should I say first, batch of info will be with you within the next few weeks.'

They parted company. All seemed to be going to plan.

SIX

Charles' two-year posting flew by. He was always busy, sometimes almost snowed under with work, but he never allowed it to get to him. He always remained even-tempered, diligent and thorough. Although never said, he recognised that his superiors, including the Corps Commander, were pleased with his work and what he was delivering and achieving. The future could have looked bright and Charles would have been more than happy to focus entirely on his family and his career. But he knew he could not do that because if he did not keep feeding the enemy, danger would loom and he may have to be made to disappear with his family to God knows where.

Therefore, and in typical Charles style, he created three separate compartments during his life in Bielefeld; his family, his job and being an agent. He was capable of being able to focus almost entirely on one at any one time without allowing the other two to impinge. It was a useful skill to possess in his circumstances.

Charles always took all of his six weeks leave for a year and divided it up between going home to England and taking an annual holiday to the Continent, preferably either Italy or France.

Neither he or Hanna's idea of an enjoyable holiday abroad was to stay in a tourist-style hotel and lie on a beach. They liked to do things that involved history, architecture, music and culture and Italy and France had more than enough. Both enjoyed staying in very good country hotels off the beaten track. Eleanor and Viktoria tagged along, never complaining and always happy, but Hanna often wondered if they would rather be on a beach and swimming in the sea.

Holidays in England were mainly lazy affairs with the opportunity to visit friends, or for friends to visit them. Spending time at Vine Cottage with his girls was Charles' idea of bliss and each year Christmas time was sacrosanct. Hanna would come to see him in Germany frequently, much to the delight of the Becks. At times she would lengthen her stay to include a dinner in the mess which she always enjoyed, as did most of the male attendees when she was there. She never seemed to lose that radiancy that surrounded her and as time went by, she certainly did not lose her looks. Indeed, as time passed she became more alluring and attractive.

It was when Cyclops made contact that Charles became more alert and aware of the absolute need not to make any mistakes during the collection and delivery of the 'information'. The collection system Cyclops devised worked well and there were never any problems. They met at various discreet locations, always either in the evening or at night and the meetings were brief and to-the-point. Only once did Charles relay a message from Stefan back to him. It was a question regarding a certain operational disposition which Cyclops took in and informed Charles during their next meeting by telling him that the answer was contained in the latest envelope that he handed over. Charles did not know what it was and nor did he need to know. It was a strange situation. Over that two-year period he collected and handed over what must have been reams of disinformation, but he never knew what the film rolls therein contained. He knew all about the real thing, of course.

The part that Charles did not enjoy was his meetings with Stefan. The meetings always took place in seedy and down-at-heel pubs. It seemed that Stefan could only operate if he had a full glass in his hand and Charles soon became wary of this unpleasant, rude and dissolute man who was normally almost drunk or seemed to be intent on going that way.

Charles had worked out that if he arrived slightly late Stefan would always be there and tucking into the beer. Once he had handed over the envelope without a word, Stefan had the habit of leaving abruptly leaving Charles to look casually around to see if anything was amiss. In the nine meetings he had with Stefan over that two-year period he never noticed anything unusual, or a face that he might have recognised from a previous pub. Nor did anyone follow or approach him either inside the meeting place, or when he was walking back to his car, or driving back to the barracks. Both sides had backed off and that's the way they both wanted it to be. One was feeding with pleasure and the other accepting with gratitude.

SEVEN

I t was every ambitious officer's greatest wish and desire to be given command of their regiment or battalion and Charles was no exception. A successful command was undoubtably a major and essential stepping stone to greater things. Conversely, failure or unforeseen disaster could end a promising career at that point. There could be no mistakes, or certainly very, very few. Charles coveted this prize like no other and was confident he would be selected for command before his tour in Bielefeld ended. In his relative naivety he did not realise or know that his current circumstances and the vital role that he was playing in the Cold War game was about to take precedence over his career.

On invitation Charles sat down with Colonel Julian Goodsake, his immediate boss, in his office. Charles liked him and Julian Goodsake liked Charles. He also thought Charles Bowater was probably the most competent operator he had come across in the army and respected him for it.

'I am afraid I have rather bad news for you, Charles,' he said.

'As you know, the command "Blue List" will be published next week and I am afraid your name is not on it. The command of your regiment is going to a contemporary of yours who you will know very well. I have not been made aware of the reasons for this decision but it will mean that for the next two years at least you will not be commanding your regiment. I had better go on. You are to be posted to Headquarters Northern Army Group in Rheindahlen as one of the Chiefs of Operations. You will be promoted to the rank of full Colonel because that is what the position demands and you will have a group of six Majors under you from all the participating nations in NORTHAG.'

Charles was downhearted when he left the office. A promotion so early on in his career was more than welcome but to have to wait for another two years at least until he could return 'home' and to the regiment he loved was a blow. He was sure he knew why this had happened but would wait until it was explained to him, and not through army channels. When he got back to his office, he called Cyclops and arranged a meeting for that evening.

They met this time in a small and dingy café down a side street in Bielefeld and Charles told Cyclops about his latest news in hushed tones. Cyclops listened to the disappointment in Charles' voice.

'I was going to suggest that we meet up with Peter Rogers as soon as possible. He will come here within the next two to three days and explain the situation to you,' he said.

They left at suitably staggered intervals and Charles waited impatiently for news of the meeting. He had already surmised what this was all about and once again he could plainly see that his past had come back to haunt him. It was depressing and he decided that on this occasion he would not tell Hanna until all was clear.

THE THREE OF them walked in the extensive wooded hills that surround Bielefeld. It was freezing cold. It was a Saturday and

Peter Rogers had appeared the evening before and was staying in yet another small hotel on the outskirts of Bielefeld. He was his normal pleasant but careful, calculating self.

Once they had walked far enough to shake off any vestiges of buildings and people, Charles was put rapidly in the picture.

Peter Rogers explained, 'The situation in which you find yourself in now and which was originally caused by you is considered to be of the highest importance to us. You have of course done an excellent job. That is why we have engineered it so that you will not command your regiment but be posted somewhere where you can continue to feed disinformation to the Soviets, albeit at a higher level.'

Charles nodded. He'd been right.

'I know you're disappointed but as I said your situation is of your own making, a situation that could have turned you into a spy for the Soviets, or turned very nasty for you and your family should you have refused to cooperate with them but not come to us.'

Charles nodded again. There was nothing new here but it had served to confirm to him his career path for at least the next two years.

'As your posting is due in six weeks, there will be no further tasks for you until you have settled in to your new job. Thereafter, Cyclops will make contact with you and the cycle will start again. Are you happy with all this or do you want to opt out now?'

Charles was surprised he had been given an option, although both he and Peter Rogers knew he could not take it. To do so would mean the end of life as he knew it and this did not appeal to him at all. It would mean a life of living in the shadows for him and his family.

'I am disappointed but I fully realise the importance of what I am doing. The answer is of course I wish to continue.' He gave Peter Rogers a sideways, wintery smile, to go with the weather.

Over lunch they chatted in a desultory manner about nothing in particular. With these two Charles knew it would be unwise to attempt to converse about family, friends, where they lived or what they did in their day-to-day lives. No information would be forthcoming and it would only irritate, even anger them.

After Peter Rogers had departed for Düsseldorf airport in his hire car, Cyclops handed Charles a small piece of paper on which there was a telephone number.

'You know the score. Once memorised, destroy by burning. When you have settled in your new posting, let me know and we can begin again. In the meantime, you will need to make contact with Stefan and inform him of where you are going and when, and that when you are settled further information will become available. You will need to type this and place it in an envelope and give it to him. The less talking the better. Given his apparent unreliability, he may forget the information if it is given to him verbally. All clear, old chap?'

The following day, Charles called the number for Stefan and awaited the call back giving him a date, time and rendezvous. It came and once again Charles found himself walking into another grubby bar. He sat down next to Stefan and placed the slim envelope on his lap. Stefan secreted it in his jacket and took another large gulp of beer whilst Charles sipped his carefully. Once again, Stefan got up and left with saying a word.

Back out on the narrow street, Charles felt a sense of relief. He suspected Stefan was running out of places to meet that suited him and his habits, and from a security point of view a completely different city would offer greater safety from inquisitive and prying eyes. He also knew there would probably be at least two to three months before he would be required to collect and pass on the next batch of film to the contact, whoever he or she might be. Time to relax and focus on the job and his family.

When he arrived back at the mess, he called Hanna and asked

if it would be possible for her to come over to Germany for the weekend. She was delighted and made the arrangements. They spent yet another blissful weekend enjoying the hospitality of the Becks who were, as always, very pleased to see them and made sure that their normal rooms were made available. The weather was unkind, but it did not deter them from walking in the woods. They ate well, loved and generally relaxed. Charles loved these interludes from what had been, and continued to be, a taxing job, both intellectually and, at times, physically when the headquarters was required to deploy into the field on exercise. He had excelled over the past two years and had made up his mind that he would equally try to excel in his new posting. Showing disappointment and sulking were not his game and he needed to get on with his life. After all, he had been promoted and although he suspected this to be a sop, he would probably be the youngest full Colonel in the army.

He was also still completely in love with his wife and never tired of her sweet gentleness, charm and beauty. He constantly reminded himself how lucky he was and there was never any doubt in his mind that the Berlin episode had been the right decision. Hanna would also confirm to him from time to time that she felt exactly the same way about their meeting. And then there was his daughters. Growing up rapidly with different characters and of independent minds, they were his pride and joy. They never complained about anything, always did as they were told and obviously adored their parents and grandparents. They were happy little girls and both Charles and Hanna wished to keep it that way. He knew they led privileged lives and was quite happy for that to continue. Not for him feelings of guilt over the have and have-nots.

It was Saturday morning. Hanna was flushed and her eyes still full of desire. They fell asleep and woke to a room of complete quiet and peacefulness. Hanna always loved, even insisted, that they make love in the shower and almost always got her way. Charles could hardly refuse her soapy body pressed against him. They went down to breakfast and Charles decided to tell all. There was a lot to tell.

'I didn't tell you before because I wanted to do it face to face. It is always better in my opinion. I am not going back to Osnabrück to command the regiment. They have decided to send me to Rheindahlen to the NATO headquarters there for the next two years or so. I was very disappointed at first but have now resigned myself to it. My new job will be interesting and challenging and I am now looking forward to it. The good news is that I will be promoted to Colonel. So, it means yet another two or more years in Germany which I think suits us fine, don't you think?'

Hanna nodded and smiled. The army with its ranks and organisations and protocols had always been a bit of a mystery to her. She was always happy that her husband was doing so well and never queried the ins and outs of his career. In the days when they lived together in Germany she had always been a charming hostess when they entertained, a frequent occurrence, and always captivated the hearts of the officers who knew her, not only the young subalterns and captains but many a married man and even a brigadier or two.

'The reason I am not going back to the regiment and instead to Rheindahlen is because they want me to continue with the work I am doing against those people that you "love" so much on the other side. They asked if I wanted to opt out but I said no. The alternatives were not what we would want and which you know about, and this mission that I am on presents very little danger and is easy to carry out. I have been given very good support by those who look after me and feel I can continue into the future with little or no repercussions on our or our daughters' lives. That's the situation, darling. What do you think?'

Hanna sipped her coffee and thought for a moment. He was so

balanced and even, considerate but focussed and above all always honest with her to a fault.

'I am happy that it is clear where our path lies for the immediate future. It will never be ideal but we have learnt to live with it and we need to continue to do so to protect ourselves and the girls. You know I'll always be by your side and support you in everything you do.'

He got up. Walked around the breakfast table and kissed her fully on her upturned lips, leaving a smudge of lipstick on his. No words were needed.

He took her to the best restaurant in Bielefeld that evening. Their long walk in the woods in the cold rain and blustery conditions had given them an appetite and they enjoyed the food, the wine and the German hospitality. Charles liked Germany with its cleanliness, efficiency and orderliness. What he did not particularly like was the Germans' ability to blank out a short period of their history which would leave forever a stain on their nation and people. None of them talked about it and no one ventured to express shame or remorse. He doubted that many of them felt it either. It was probably one of the best examples of collective amnesia ever. In his next job he would be working with Germans and would have to put these opinions to one side for the sake of professional harmony, something that did not concern him at all.

Charles drove Hanna to Hanover airport, by now a well-trodden route. Their passionate goodbye always took those in the departure entrance by surprise. They were both happy that in two weeks' time Charles would be home for leave between his postings. A well-deserved leave, they both thought.

Charles was dined out in the officers' mess where no less than the Corps Commander gave a speech extolling his efforts and achievements. He spent a week handing over to his successor. He spent a day or two organising all his kit and sending it on to one of the messes in Rheindahlen, and then headed for the channel ports and home. It was 1987 and spring was in the air. Another chapter in his life had closed. It was a good feeling and he savoured a moment of satisfaction for what he had achieved and what he was about to look forward to. But always at the back of his mind was a nagging concern about how his 'mission' would end – if it ever did.

EIGHT

A lexei Volikov was well pleased with life. His plan to ensnare Bowater and his traitorous wife seemed to be working to a tee. The information he was receiving in the diplomatic bag from the Soviet Union's embassy in Bonn, albeit in an irregular and irritatingly slow manner, was gold dust to the Lubyanka, the Red Army Military District headquarters outside Moscow, the GSFG headquarters in Wunsdorf and, no doubt, the Politburo. In return he had received numerous notes of congratulation from worthies of various military and civilian hues, most of whom he had never heard of. But Alexei Volikov was astute enough to ensure that before passing on the information received to Moscow, he always made a copy for himself. This he did by taking photographs of the film shots and storing them away for a possible rainy day. Like most Soviet Union government servants, he needed an insurance policy, something that the majority of Russians did not have. How he could use this information to his advantage in the future was unclear, even to a fertile mind like his. He could not predict the future and remained wholly wedded to the Soviet cause and way of life.

He also enjoyed life in the embassy where he was secure in the knowledge that even the ambassador would not dare to question what he did. He answered to the Lubyanka and no one else, and they were a long way away. His methods were ones of quiet menace, methods he found far more effective than those of his predecessor; blunt, bullying and openly threatening. The information coming from his agents in West Berlin and West Germany was minor in nature compared to what was being produced by Bowater.

His other interest lay in the voluptuous and desirable form of Olga, his typist lover. For Alexei Volikov their relationship was based entirely on his need for sex with her, whilst she always hoped for something more tangible based on tender feelings for him. She was a simple girl originally from Ufa who saw in Alexei Volikov an opportunity to improve her lot. He was having none of this and almost nightly subjected her body to his desires. He never actually marked her, a sure sign of his former training, but he forced her to do as he bid. She accepted it all in the hope that he would eventually want to be with her. A forlorn hope and something that was never discussed. Their conversations were always extremely limited as he wasted no time in having her as he wished as soon as she was in his apartment, and then dismissing her. There was no pillow talk in this relationship.

Alexei Volikov's life in Berlin took a further turn for the better when he received the information that Bowater was to be posted to a position that would able him to further provide highly classified military intelligence, but at a level one up from the Corps' operational plans in Northern Germany. Moscow was delighted with this news, thus placing a further feather in Alexei Volikov's cap. The long arm of the KGB did not, however, extend to knowledge about the British Army's promotion and posting policies. If it had, suspicion might have been aroused concerning Bowater's posting from one staff job to another, and at a higher level.

In turn, Alexei Volikov now turned his attention about how best to run his top agent from his new location near Monchengladbach. Lutz had warned him on a number of occasions over the past year and a half that although Fridof had always passed on the information when he received it and there had been no problems or indications that he had caused any security issues, he was an alcoholic whom he considered too much of a risk because of his inherent unreliability and possible susceptibility to 'other pressures'. He was also not politically or ideologically motivated. His beliefs lay in a beer glass and the means with which to fuel this addiction. Fridof had been paid handsomely and it was this that was driving him, not his beliefs, of which he had few. Lutz recommended that when Bowater moved to Rheindahlen, Fridof must be removed and a more politically reliable agent found to run him.

In his latest report Lutz also alluded to the need to probably eliminate Fridof altogether, a thought that had already crossed Alexei Volikov's mind and to which he was not adverse. These Germans meant nothing to him.

BY THE BEGINNING OF 1987, the Bundespost had finally run out of patience with Adam Neumann. His direct manager had received numerous complaints about his lateness, his terrible hungover state in the mornings, his drinking at lunchtimes and the foul odour that emanated from him because of alcohol. Often, he was still drunk when he came in to work and this made him both abusive and incompetent. He was dismissed with a generous pay-out, three months' wages and a small pension.

From the time he was dismissed, Adam Neumann did not receive any further calls from Bowater to arrange a meeting. He was unaware that Bowater was about to be posted and leave

Bielefeld. He sank into a nether world of drunkenness and dependence. One day in that spring of 1987, he was in a pub and drinking heavily. He kept himself to himself and focussed on his glass rather on those around him. When he could hardly stand, he left and stumbled outside. Two men came up behind him in the darkness, picked him up bodily and forced him into a waiting car which drove off at a leisurely pace. In the car Adam Neumann was gagged and held firmly on the seat by his two minders. They drove out of Bielefeld to a carpark which served a forest area used by the public. They dragged his barely conscious body into the trees, lay a large plastic sheet on the ground, pushed him down and stabbed him three times in the heart. He died instantly. They then forcibly removed all his teeth and cut both his hands off. They removed all possible identification from him and then wrapped him firmly in the sheet – with the teeth and hands placed in a separate bag – included some rocks to both that they had bought with them in the car, tied the sheet and bag up securely, placed them in the boot of the car and drove off sedately. This all took about 30 minutes, so well had it been planned.

The drive was long but eventually the car reached a remote spot on the Elbe, north of Hamburg, where Adam Neumann's body, weighed down with rocks, was deposited at the bottom of the river. The other bag was similarly disposed of five kilometres further north. No one missed or asked about him as he had no known family and no friends. He simply disappeared.

The main task now was to identify a new handler for Bowater. He or she needed to be ideologically pure with a deep belief in the cause, wholly reliable and well trained in the arts of an agent operating in West Germany. He or she needed to be German and needed to live in the Monchengladbach area, thus being geographically close to Bowater. Lutz ran many minor agents in West Germany, but given the obvious importance of this task he needed to make sure his selection, unlike the last one, was absolutely right.

After much deliberation, he decided on Irma Huber. He studied her details carefully and felt he had made the right choice. Her photograph showed her to be extremely good looking at 43 years old, which gave her maturity and hopefully a balanced approach to life; she had received some cursory training by one of his team in West Germany in the arts of being an 'agent'; she was single with no children; she had been born in the last year of the war in the village of Lobberich close to the Dutch border; and that she now lived in Monchengladbach by herself. She worked as a laboratory technician in one of the city hospitals.

The most interesting part of Irma Huber's background was her radicalisation whilst at university. Through interaction with left wing, even communist students, she herself became one of the most ardent supporters and advocates of extreme socialism although she had never been to the east and experienced the type of society that she so fervently endorsed. From university she continued to follow the student movement and then joined the Communist League of West Germany. In the 1970s and 1980s this tiny party and others started to disintegrate and were politically marginalised but she hung on, always naively believing in their Marxist, Leninist goals of a better world for all. It was in early 1980s that she was noticed by Lutz and it was not difficult to recruit her. She had carried out a number of minor tasks for him but now he believed she fitted the bill and could be used in this vital role, not that Lutz knew exactly what that role was.

He arranged a meeting and briefed her on everything she needed to know about the task. He handed over full details of Bowater including photographs and the details of his car and informed her that in the early summer she would be expected to make contact with him. He would be expecting it. She should report back when contact had been made and feed Lutz useful information about his movements, patterns and habits once he had settled into his new position. She would also be recompensed generously. She was obviously delighted to be involved and they parted in the best of moods. Lutz found her good looks slightly disorientating.

THE MOST DIFFICULT part of Irma Huber's initial task was to pin Bowater down as to his movements and routine to enable her to choose the right moment to approach him. She knew this had to be done without arousing the suspicions of the significant military presence in this major NATO and British Army of the Rhine, or BAOR, base. It was to her advantage that apart from individual specific military establishments within the base area which were guarded and secure, the roads, open spaces, messes and single and married quarters were not and afforded free access to anyone who wished to travel within them. She knew where he worked, she knew what he looked like and she knew the details of his car. However, loitering in the close proximity to Headquarters NORTHAG in her nondescript car could well arouse suspicion. But it was a risk she was prepared to take, a risk she had to take as she could see no other way.

Unlike in Bielefeld, Charles found the routine in his new job to his liking. It was seldom, unless when on exercise or attending conferences or meetings elsewhere, that his working hours would extend beyond six in the evenings, and sometimes it would be earlier. His team consisted of a German Lieutenant Colonel as his deputy, four majors from the United Kingdom, West Germany, the Netherlands and Belgium representing the army group corps in Northern Germany, and three liaison officers from Denmark, France and the United States. He enjoyed both the work and his elevated status, especially as he was still so young. As usual he immersed himself in his work and soon gained the respect of his team, some of whom were older and more experienced than he, and of his superiors. He knew that once again he could look forward to a professionally satisfying two years. Rheindahlen was a pleasant place to live, with all the facilities you could hope for at a British-run base and the Dutch border was very close. The Netherlands, with its pleasant and thriving border towns such as Venlo and Roermond, made a good place to visit at the weekends. The channel ports were closer still and Düsseldorf airport just down the autobahn. He kept to his running and joined the squash club which enabled him to maintain his fitness levels, something he had always done both for himself, but in his younger unmarried days for the benefit of whatever young lady was either on the immediate horizon or actually with him. It never occurred to him that although most women liked his fitness, they were much more likely to be interested in his mind rather than his body. That was certainly the case with Hanna. He could live with his life in Rheindahlen despite his current ever-present commitment to another master, and his missing of Hanna and his girls.

It did not take long for Irma Huber to find out where Charles lived. She had surmised, correctly, that he would be amongst those who would leave the headquarters after work in large numbers. Sitting in a nearby car park, she picked him up and followed him to his mess situated on the periphery of the camp area. She also surmised correctly that like many unattached officers at Rheindahlen it was likely that he would like to visit the Netherlands at the weekends, and in particular Saturday mornings when the excellent markets were running and a good lunch was beckoning. She could have walked into the mess and asked for him but the last thing she wanted was to open him up to suspicion. Neutral ground was the best option and especially when it was in a different country.

Three Saturdays later, she was able to pick him up and follow him across the border to Roermond. He was on his own and she followed him as he browsed through the markets, not buying anything except the delicious Dutch liquorice which he loved. He then sat outside in the sunshine and drank coffee and watched the world go by whilst she positioned herself at the next-door table. He glanced at her, noticing and appreciating her good looks, but thought nothing of it.

'Charles Bowater?'

He was startled.

'I think that you might have been expecting me,' she said with a smile.

Charles' immediate reaction was one of relief, relief that contact had finally been made. He had been expecting to be contacted by the dreaded Stefan but instead he was faced by an attractive woman, probably in her forties, who had a smiling face and clear blue eyes.

'Yes, I was,' he replied.

She delved into her handbag and handed him a small envelope.

'In there are three numbers. When you have something for me, call the first number. If you have no luck with the first then call the second and then the third if necessary.' Her English was excellent.

'The best place to meet is here in Holland. For the first time it will be here in this café. After that I will give you the next rendezvous. No need to call me about anything else.'

Charles nodded. All very clear. Her coffee arrived and she drank it leisurely whilst not looking at him or talking to him. He cast a sideways glance at her. She was indeed beautiful to look at. Was she a 'honey trap' as well as an agent? Did they suspect something was up? Best to report this meeting back to Cyclops, meet her and see what happened. With a jolt, he suddenly remembered he himself had been the victim of a 'honey trap' in

Berlin and had fallen for it. This was the reason why, all these years later, he was talking to a mysterious woman in a café in Roermond and placing the envelope in his jacket pocket. He wasn't going to fall for that trick again. With a cursory nod in her direction, he got up, paid and left.

If Charles had been unnerved by Irma Huber's good looks, the feelings were mutual. What a good-looking man, she thought, though she would not allow her mind to wander into realms of what his body would be like. He certainly looked lean and mean.

ON HIS RETURN, Charles called Cyclops on the well-known number. Time to change that, he thought. All he received in reply was: 'I will come to where you live this evening at seven.' The phone went dead. Charles assumed that Cyclops must have moved to be closer to him.

They met outside the mess at seven and went to Charles' room. He told Cyclops the details of his meeting that morning. Cyclops nodded and handed Charles an envelope.

'There is a new number in there. Please use that from now on. There is also a new list of numbers against locations in this area and over the border. It will be the same drill as before. Your first package will be with you within the next few days.'

To cover a reason for his visit, Cyclops stayed for dinner. As usual there was very little to talk about and Cyclops left as soon as he could, having consumed no alcohol.

Thus, the pattern was set for the foreseeable future. It was hardly an onerous task for either Cyclops, Charles or Irma Huber. They were merely passing on information, information that they were not privy to. Potential danger lay in the making of contact by telephone, the meetings and the actual physical passing on of information, but given that both sides did not want this system to be disrupted, the danger was minimal. There was no third-party involvement. They all did what was required of them and no more or less. Their respective masters continued to be happy with the way things were going. This would continue for the next 18 months. It was humdrum and sterile. Irma Huber continued to harbour licentious thoughts about Charles but he did not for her. Every time he looked at her, he saw Hanna and there was no contest.

NINE

T hroughout 1988 for most 1989, it was becoming more and more evident that it was highly unlikely that the Warsaw Pact would survive. There had always been dissent, dissent that had in the past been ruthlessly suppressed by the Red Army; East Germany in 1953, Hungary in 1956 and Czechoslovakia in 1968. But if a determination to maintain the countries of Eastern Europe behind the Iron Curtain was a reality then and through the seventies and early eighties, it was not the case by 1988 and 1989. The forces of this dissent were gathering pace and when in July 1989 Gorbachev declared that the Soviet Union would not intervene or use force against countries in the Warsaw Pact who wished to leave, he effectively signed the death warrant of that organisation. Poland, with Solidarity in the forefront and the holding of election in 1989, was the first to break free, followed by Hungary and East Germany. When Hungary opened its border with Austria, the floodgates had been opened. There was a chain reaction in Czechoslovakia, Bulgaria and Romania and the Pact disintegrated. The rest is history including the momentous events surrounding the breaching of the Berlin Wall in November 1989, surely the most poignant symbol of Soviet repression and aggression.

NATO in the west could only sit and watch with a sense of gathering amazement at these historical events unfolding in front of them. Many toasted a victory in a Cold War where hostilities never erupted despite much sabre rattling by the Soviet Union in its coldest days. To many more, victory was the result of firstly the deployment of nuclear weapons in Western Europe and the clear indication that they were prepared to use them if necessary, and of the belief that the Soviet Union never had the strategic aim or desire to attack the west. They wanted to hold on to what they had as a buffer against possible western invasion, a sure sign of their continuing inferiority complex when looking westwards. Some would say that it was fear, not aggression, that drove their foreign policy in the years following the end of the Second World War and up to 1989 and beyond. Subsequent history shows that the eastern European states that had suffered for 45 years under the Soviet yoke embraced the west both politically and militarily thereafter. Further, the Baltic states and Ukraine broke free as the Soviet Union broke up, thus bringing NATO up to the borders of Russia.

―――――

NOT ONLY DID Charles and his team look on with great interest at events in the east as they unfolded, but they also realised that their own raison d'etre was disintegrating. Their daily routine continued as before, as did the planning, conferences and numerous meetings with NATO headquarters in Belgium, the national divisions within NORTHAG, as well liaison with the French, Danes and Americans. NATO policy held firm for the time being until they could see that the threat was no longer there. The most worrying aspect was the continued presence of the GSFG in East Germany and the possibility of them launching a revenge attack to the west without the consent of Moscow. However, this threat was considered highly unlikely. They knew that the state of GSFG in East Germany was by now abysmal and that they could certainly never count on the support of their former Warsaw Pact allies. Indeed, it was estimated that those forces would turn against the Russians given a slither of a chance.

In this uncertain atmosphere, Charles met with Cyclops who handed over a package containing the latest military operational plans from the London team.

'I doubt very much if you will be able to make contact with her from now on.'

Charles nodded and agreed with Cyclops.

'I will try and see what happens,' he said.

Charles went back to the mess and called the first number of the three the mysterious woman had given him. There was an unattainable noise at the other end, as there was with the other two numbers. He repeated this three times with no success. It told him all. It was over. He stood in the mess phone box for a full five minutes, overcome with a sense of relief. He then went to the bar and ordered a bottle of champagne. Whilst sipping this he returned to the phone box, called Cyclops and arranged a meeting. He was tempted to 'go clear' but resisted the temptation. He finished the bottle in the bar and, feeling quite drunk, went to bed without having dinner.

They met the next evening and Charles handed back the package.

'All three numbers have been cut off. There was no response.'

Cyclops smiled; the first time Charles had witnessed this wintry contortion.

'It looks as though it is all over, then. I have spoken to Peter Rogers and he would like to meet within the next two weeks. He will come here to meet you. Are you happy with that?'

No longer orders but polite requests.

'No problem at all. I look forward to it. Do we still need to continue to use our coded system for meetings?'

'For the time being, yes. When Peter Rogers arrives he will give us both clear instructions on this and other matters. I will be in touch when I have a date, time and location.'

They parted company. Charles still didn't know anything about Cyclops and he doubted he ever would. With the situation in the east continuing to make front-page news, Charles wondered how his original initiative and subsequent involvement in the passing of disinformation to the Soviets over a period of three and a half years had helped the current situation. He would never know the details and nor did he expect to be told. He would also never know what actual disinformation was passed over to the other side or whether it made a difference to Soviet military planning or not. In fact, he didn't want to know.

In classic Bowater style, he compartmentalised this episode in his life and placed it to one side. To him the greatest achievement was that Hanna and the girls were now safe, as was he, from the threat of retribution from the people who had set him and his family up in the first place. The original fault was his, and his alone, but he felt that through his subsequent actions he had made amends and had avoided consequences that could have been unbearable. He needed to tell Hanna as soon as possible, and in person. He asked his boss, a German Brigadier, if he could take the next Friday and Monday off to attend an event in England. The Brigadier waved him away with wishes of good luck. He respected and admired Charles for his professionalism and dedication, qualities which were dear to his German heart. Charles respected the Brigadier but could never admit to liking him. Charles decided to give Hanna and the girls a surprise.

EAST BERLIN WAS no place for a senior KGB officer in 1989 and for the first time in his life, Alexei Volikov felt vulnerable and nervous. A man of cold, calculating ruthlessness with a veneer of respectability, he felt rattled. His close connections with the now defunct and reviled Stasi placed him in a very difficult position. Perhaps it was time to go? He spoke with his immediate superior in the Lubyanka and was instructed to close down his networks in East Germany, disavow the Stasi and inform his agent network in West Germany to go to sleep until further notice. He was also told to destroy all incriminating evidence with regards to his activities directly linked to engaging western spies in his network. No mention of his master coup in providing vital military intelligence to the Russians, there was an air of resignation in the voice at the other end of the telephone.

Alexei Volikov did as he was told. He informed Lutz that he was to close down Irma Huber and tell her to lead a quiet life until further notice. She in turn disengaged the lines that had been created to receive and pass information to Bowater. She was disappointed. She felt sexually attracted to this handsome westerner but knew the feelings were not mutual. Such a pity! Lutz also put to bed his numerous other agents operating in West Germany.

What Alexei Volikov did not know was that for the past two years, and despite all the gold dust they were receiving from Bowater, the Soviet leadership had never had the will, intention or capability to attack the west. The strategic level intelligence they were receiving merely confirmed the fact that they would never again be in a position to take the initiative. It would be politically and militarily disastrous, even if some of the dinosaur generals still wanted it.

Alexei Volikov left East Berlin in early 1990 and disappeared into the maw of the KGB in Moscow, an organisation that was in chaos. He was not unhappy to leave Berlin at that time. The good times were over but he would certainly miss Olga and her charms. He would have to return to his wife and her boring frivolities and a heart empty of passion. Perhaps in time he would be able to persuade Olga to come and work with him, or near him in Moscow?

CHARLES CAUGHT the early flight from Düsseldorf to Heathrow that Friday and made it home to Wilshire by lunchtime. As usual the greetings were an exciting event, but being a surprise, it was especially exciting. The girls were still at school and the Bowaters up the path were not aware of their son's homecoming. He kissed Hanna and she responded eagerly. She was so happy to see her man and held him tight. It was a rare occasion where they found themselves alone in the cottage.

'Talking can come later,' said Charles as he led her by the hand upstairs to their bedroom. The passion was as fresh as the day they married. They never tired of each other's bodies and their lovemaking was more to do with unbridled lust than love on this occasion. It was bliss.

They lay in bed, looking at each other with love in their eyes. Finally, Charles spoke.

'I am sure that you have been following the events in Eastern Europe over the past months and weeks.'

'I have,' she said dreamily.

'Because of all of that it seems our ordeal is over. I am no longer in contact with the other side. They have disappeared. I am due to be debriefed this coming week in Germany. It is over.'

Hanna sat up in bed and made no attempt to cover her wonderful breasts. 'You mean we can go back to normal? There is no more threat to us? We can lead our lives again?'

'It seems that way. I will know more about it all next week when I meet up with the boys.'

Hanna knelt up, straddled him and cupped his face in her hands. 'Thank you, thank you, thank you my darling man. I am so happy.'

The weekend passed far too quickly. The girls squealed with delight when they saw their father and except when they were asleep followed him around for the rest of the weekend, asking him the inevitable numerous and usually unanswerable questions about everything. They were growing up and blossoming and he could plainly see that in the years to come he would have to make sure his shotgun was close to hand. They walked and talked, enjoyed a splendid lunch with the Bowaters where Jane Bowater, as usual, excelled herself. The passing years had not dulled her culinary expertise. David Bowater, fraying at the edges, was still his charming and hospitable self. Warnings from his doctor and the advent of various minor medical-related ailments had not blunted his love of life at Vine House, his wife and his children and grandchildren, and his wine cellar. If you are going to die, do it with style and a glass of decent red in your hand. Sadly, old Henry had left them and there was talk of having another dog but Charles and Hanna successfully dissuaded them. The cat Richard, a lot younger, was enough for them now. The subject of age was never discussed in the Bowater household. It was considered both irrelevant and irreverent.

All too soon, Charles was on the train and then plane back to Germany, happy in the knowledge that he was leaving behind his family who were safer, and a wife who could now relax. Sitting on the plane his mind wandered to their far too short nights of love, their only concern being the noise Hanna made. She was certainly noisy. He smiled at the thought.

HANNA HAD INDEED BEEN FOLLOWING the momentous events in Europe with a growing sense that soon, but not so soon, she may be able to see her parents and sister again. It had been over sixteen years since she had said goodbye to them in Leningrad when boarding the train to Berlin. In that period they had seldom left her thoughts, but she had become adept at hiding her feelings from all, even Charles. He had given her such a wonderful new life, two beautiful daughters and a lovely home in what she considered a country worth living in. She loved England and memories and experiences of her former life in Russia and Berlin were fading.

Being Russian she knew that she would have to wait patiently for the time when she might be able to make contact with her parents, but like everything in the Soviet Union, now falling apart, there was no guarantee of that. Before the surprise appearance of Charles at the weekend she had decided that she would put her hopes to one side and get on with her life in England, her marriage and her children. Once Hanna Bowater had made a decision, she would stick to it. The decision she had made in Berlin all those years ago was testimony to this.

TEN

Seeing Charles Bowater twice in Osnabrück had unnerved Sophia Voigt. On both occasions, he had not changed physically. He was still very handsome, slim and dapper. On the first occasion he was obviously, but sadly for Sophia, with his pregnant wife. In the many years that had passed since they parted company in Berlin she had never stopped loving him and had never forgiven herself for leading him, albeit under immense pressure, into a 'honey trap'. She hated herself for it. The second time she saw him, and when he was on his own, she was sorely tempted to stop and ask him how he was. But she could not do it for fear of a rebuff.

What Sophia Voigt did not know was that Charles would never have any intention of rebuffing her. He was also fearful of what such an unplanned meeting in the street would bring but had hoped that she may have stopped to talk. As always, he was easygoing and forgiving in matters of the heart. She also did not know that he knew what she was doing during their courtship in Berlin and that she was an agent working for the Soviets. Yet he was still willing to forgive her.

Sophia Voigt had continued to lead an unremarkable life since those heady Berlin days. She still lived with her ageing aunt who was now fading fast with cancer. Her aunt had shown Sophia her will and in the absence of other relatives had left her house and everything in it to her. At least she was secure in that respect. Her job was secure and she had been twice promoted. But she continued to be unhappy in general, and certainly unhappy in love. Initially she had hoped she might find a man who would be perfect for her, but it was all in vain. She remained beautiful and alluring but the men she either met or who pursued her, sometimes oafishly, sometimes relentlessly and sometimes, but rarely, with air of the respectable were, in her eyes, a sorry lot. She immediately compared them all with Charles and they all fell well short in all departments. She missed his laid-back and charming manner, his kindness and, at times, his naivety. She missed his handsomeness and casual English elegance. These young, and not so young, German men were so different and she did not enjoy their bluntness and, at times, rough approach in trying to develop a relationship. They bored her but she needed sex from time to time and let a number of them have their way with her. It was always unsatisfactory and sometimes she found it repulsive. Her 'flings' never lasted more than three nights except on one occasion when she thought that there was a flicker of hope. He turned out to be a control freak and she quickly disappeared.

Sophia Voigt's other concern lay in the east and in particular Dresden. Since she had received that awful and anonymous letter informing her that her parents were dead, she wanted to go to Dresden and find out for herself. She also wanted to find out about her sister Bertha. Where was she? Was she still alive? What did she do? She had so many questions and no answers. But like Hanna she was following closely events in the east, and in particular the eastern part of Germany. It seemed to her that in time she would be able to travel east and find out. However, she was wary, very wary. She had once worked for either the Soviets, or the Stasi, or both. To attempt to rush would not be wise. She decided to wait and play the long game. It proved to be a very long game and it was not until German reunification some two years hence did she feel confident enough to venture east.

Sophia Voigt carried on with her humdrum life, a life that was neither happy nor unhappy. She enjoyed her job and she had developed over the years a number of much liked girl friends with whom she shared a quiet social life. Much time was spent nursing her by now very ill aunt when the carer was not there. But mostly her life was still dominated by Charles Bowater. No matter what she tried, his image and memory stayed with her.

ELEVEN

Cyclops called the morning after he had returned to the office.

'Can we meet this evening?' No longer instructions but requests.

'Come to the mess at seven and stay for dinner.'

They went to Charles' room in one of the mess annexes. Charles was aware that Cyclops was probably very abstemious but took the risk of having a bottle of wine in his room.

'To celebrate, would you like a drink?'

To his surprise Cyclops accepted and they drank a toast to success, not only for their own particular campaign but for victory in the war itself.

'Peter Rogers will arrive tomorrow. Could you meet him that evening at about seven for dinner at the Hotel Anchovis in Monchengladbach?'

Cyclops handed Charles a note with directions. Charles offered more wine, an offer that was enthusiastically accepted and in time they finished the bottle with Cyclops leading the way. Charles looked at him and surmised, correctly as it turned out, that Cyclops was one of those people who could go quite happily for months, or even years without tasting an alcoholic drink, but once he had the taste found it very difficult to stop until he woke up the next morning with a hangover. They went to dinner where Cyclops, who always talked in hushed tones, continued on his downward path with copious quantities of wine whilst becoming quite openly talkative with Charles. Even towards the end of the evening he was never indiscreet but did talk about where he came from and that he was single and liked it that way. He was, when relaxed, an engaging character and was more than happy to lampoon the Foreign Office in very general terms whilst giving nothing away. Like Peter Rogers, these people seemed to have an inbuilt mechanism that was able to shut out anything that smacked even vaguely of 'useful information'. They were masters of the art of discretion.

Charles wondered how Cyclops would be getting home. Cyclops had told him over dinner that he had relocated to an apartment in Monchengladbach in anticipation of a long stay, but did not say where. He offered him a bed for the night but Cyclops asked to use the mess public phone and called a taxi. Whilst waiting, they sat in the ante-room and Cyclops hurled back a number of whiskeys to round off his evening. He then went out and disappeared. Charles, very sober, enjoyed a nightcap and went to bed.

THE FOLLOWING EVENING, Charles found his way to the Hotel Anchovis and arrived early. He sat in reception and waited. Peter Rogers duly appeared with the faithful Cyclops by his side and they moved to the bar area. Charles noticed that Cyclops was back on the tonic water whereas he and Peter Rogers enjoyed a beer.

What surprised Charles most about this meeting was the marked change in the demeanour of Peter Rogers. He was positively friendly to him and he made a point of it. Whether it was genuine, Charles was doubtful.

'The first thing I would like to say is to congratulate you most sincerely for all you have done. We will probably never know what effect our efforts had on the overall result of the avoidance of war in Europe. However, as I was privy to the scale of the deception I will tell you that it did probably work, or was a contributing factor in making the Soviets believe an attack would not be a wise move. Well done, Charles and thank you for everything.'

He raised his glass and they drank a toast.

'What we need to do after this meeting and for some time is to lie low and terminate any further meetings or even contact between yourself and Cyclops. I assume you will be relieved to hear that?'

'I am indeed,' said Charles.

They drank again in silence.

'I have a proposition to make to you, Charles,' said Peter Rogers suddenly. 'What would be your reaction if I were to offer you a position in our organisation on a permanent basis?'

It was the directness of it that took Charles by surprise.

'You mean that I should leave the army and join the Foreign Office?'

'In a nutshell – yes. I would like you to think about it carefully rather than make a hasty decision. There would be many details to discuss but it would be useful for me if in principle you would consider it.'

'I will and thank you. I'm flattered.'

Charles realised that this was the reason Peter Rogers had made the effort to come to Germany. It was not to discuss the current mission and its future, or otherwise. He was beginning to understand that everything these people thought, said and did was as a result of careful calculation and cold logic.

They chatted inconsequently until Peter Rogers got up to

leave. He had a plane to catch. Farewells were exchanged and he was gone.

'Thanks for everything, Charles. We may meet again in the future but as Peter said I think this is the end of the road for you and I. I really enjoyed working with you.'

They shook hands and Cyclops left, leaving Charles on his own sitting in the bar area of this pleasant hotel. He ordered another beer and sat down to think about the surprising proposition that had been presented to him. He could tell that there was no pressure, but how much did he owe Peter Rogers for what he had done for him in the past? Essentially everything. Without his timely intervention and subsequent action all those years ago he very probably would not have remained in the army, and he would not have been married to his beautiful Hanna and had all that had followed from that. He owed him and Peter Rogers knew it. Charles decided he needed time to consider all the angles and consequences of his situation and so he placed the question at the back of his mind. He would need to tell Hanna and discuss it with her before anybody else and it was about time she came over, anyway. Perhaps they might spend the weekend over the border in Holland.

CHARLES MET Hanna at Düsseldorf airport that Friday morning. She looked as radiant as ever. They held each other close. How could he ever not live with this wonderful woman?

They drove to Roermond where Charles had booked them into a cosy little hotel in the centre of town. It suited them perfectly.

The tension of the past years had gone. They had seen it through and weathered the storm. The momentous events of recent history had released them and they could look forward to a more secure and happy future together. Charles was reluctant to break this idyll with the latest news, so he kept it for dinner before broaching it to her.

'I met with my friends the other day. It was a sort of low-key back-slapping exercise but Peter Rogers also had a proposition to put to me. It came as great surprise,' he said.

Hanna's eyes were sparkling and mischievous. Their lovemaking that afternoon had been spectacular and she had drunk two glasses of wine since coming down to dinner. She sat opposite him, removed her shoes under the table and proceeded to rub her toe up and down his leg whilst staring into his eyes. Charles laughed and knew that he would have to be on top of his game when they got back to their room.

'Peter offered me a job with the Foreign Office. I said I'd consider it.'

If Charles had told her he was going to become an astronaut, she would not have really cared so long as they were together. She had always admired his progress in the army but did not really understand it in its entirety. She knew he loved it and wanted to reach to the top if he could. He was certainly heading in that direction. She was not really someone you would call a dedicated army wife. Her life in England with her girls and close to Charles' parents was her ideal existence. She always missed him but reasoned that their times together were so much more poignant and alive; the savouring of every moment together. She was happy and content.

'I will always support you whatever you decide. All I would say is that whatever they offer you it will need to be a quantum leap in position, responsibility and money than what you have now. So, if you are asking me my darling then the answer is that you must do what you think is best for yourself. I am here for you.'

Charles looked at her. What a wonderful woman she was. That evening the food was excellent, the wine delicious and the lovemaking even more delicious. The weekend was bliss, the

Dutch as friendly and charming as ever and the weather like spring. Their farewells were as sad as ever but they both had a feeling that the existence they had led since they had created their lovely home and decided that Hanna and the girls would remain in England was perhaps coming an end. He would have to use this coming week to find out more.

THAT WEEK, Charles called Peter Rogers on the same number he had been given many years ago. He got straight through.

'Good morning. I would like to come and see you in the near future. I have many questions for you.'

'It would be easier if I came to see you. I can be with you the day after tomorrow. Could you meet me at the Palace St George Hotel on the outskirts of Monchengladbach at seven in the evening?'

'I will see you there.'

The brisk efficiency was still there but the abrupt, even rude approach had dissipated. Peter Rogers also seemed to have a never-ending list of hotels with which he could make a booking at the drop of a hat.

Charles arrived early and chose a quiet alcove. He needed some time to get his many questions in a row.

As usual, Peter Rogers appeared on time and they ordered a glass of wine each.

'Methinks you have given my proposal some thought.'

'I have and I have spoken to Hanna. She has no qualms and neither do I. However, I need some questions answered before I make a decision.'

'Fire away.'

'Firstly, given my wife's background, and therefore our children's, and the method of her coming to the west and the fact that her family still lives in St Petersburg as far as we are aware, how would this affect her security and well-being into the future?'

'What we had in mind for you should you come over would not affect your family at all. You may not be surprised to hear that we had thought this through and had anticipated your question. When we come on to what we had in mind for you within the organisation, it will become clearer.'

'As you know, I hold the rank of full Colonel in my present position. I am afraid I would not be able to accept anything you offered me unless I could see a significant elevation in position, responsibility and recompense from my present situation.'

Best to play it hard, thought Charles. If you don't ask you almost certainly will not get, especially if you are working for the government.

'We would ensure that your package and allowances will reflect all these wishes, and probably more,' Peter Rogers replied.

'Would I be spending time overseas? I understand that your organisation has many of its people operating in many parts of the world.'

'Apart from the odd conference either in the US or Europe, you would be based entirely in London.'

Peter Rogers lowered his voice to almost a whisper. 'We want you to be our Head of Operational Liaison with the Five Eyes Alliance and the major European Intelligence Agencies.'

Charles sat back in surprise. This was indeed an interesting proposition.

Peter Rogers, perhaps in fear that his carefully worked out plan might meet with rejection, ploughed rapidly on.

'I think you need time to think about it? Please have as much time as you need and let me know. I can promise you that if do agree, your passage from the army to us will be a smooth one. There will be none of the normal bullshit when leaving the services as we will treat it more as a permanent transfer rather than you having to separately leave one government organisation and then join another. I am an expert at bending the rules.'

This was more agreeable news to Charles.

'I have a feeling that your main concern will be with regards to the safety of your family. I can assure you that no one outside the intelligence world in which you will be working will know anything about you, and even most inside the organisation will know nothing of you either. Your job is one of the most sensitive and we will always treat it as such. You will not be an operator on the ground but the director behind how we plan and direct cooperation policy in these matters.'

'I need to go away and weigh all this up,' said Charles.

'Of course, dear chap. Take your time.' The bonhomie was not quite convincing but Peter Rogers was making a good stab at it.

They had another drink together and in the absence of not being invited to dinner at the hotel Charles took his leave, promising Peter Rogers that he would be in touch very soon. He had almost made up his mind at that juncture but needed to consider the pros and cons of leaving the army, an army which had been his life up to this point and which he had hoped would propel him to the top.

OVER THE FOLLOWING DAYS, Charles pondered long and hard. He realised he had reached a junction in his professional life and whatever decision he made would set him a path he could not deviate from again. The offer was very tempting and Peter Rogers had answered all his questions in a direct and seemingly entirely honest manner. There was no reason to doubt him. If Charles was taking a risk, so were they. He thought about the reasons why they had approached him and surmised that it must have been from a combination of recognition of his excellence in the army, his youth, his risk-taking approach whilst in Berlin and his recent performance in that great disinformation game in West Germany. It all added up.

Charles then looked at his career in the army and what leaving it would mean to him. He knew as well as anyone, that the path to the top was strewn with mines, the worst of which was the tricky, irritating, irritated boss who did not like you. This could abruptly end a career in its tracks. He hadn't met one yet but they always lurked behind the next career corner. He also knew that he had found himself at HQ NORTHAG on promotion, a very unusual occurrence, not because of the army but the Foreign Office. In fact, he was half-way in their pocket already. He had missed out on command of his regiment and knew he could not return because it would mean he would have to be demoted back down to Lieutenant Colonel. He could carry on in the army and was probably assured of promotion to Major General, no mean feat, but after that, who knew? In essence, it appeared Peter Rogers and his co-conspirators had him over a barrel, albeit a barrel of his own making.

He would miss the cut and thrust of army life, the comradeship, especially when working with soldiers, the inevitable rise in rank and importance. But his time with soldiers in the command sense was probably over and it seemed to him that he would be fighting a desk for most of the rest of his career. Not much to look forward to if you also considered the almost Byzantine staff system that the British Army was a slave to, a system Charles never understood, hated and frequently attempted to sabotage.

Charles was not a man to ponder for too long. Pondering officers in war were normally a disaster. Pondering officers in peacetime were a nuisance. This was, on the face of it, a very good offer and one that he was drawn to because of its potential for him to sit at the top table and take to the global intelligence stage. He would be based in London and that opened up all the possibilities of actually seeing his family, if not every day, at least most weekends. Whereas Hanna was happy with her lot of only seeing him monthly or less, Charles was more partial to actually sharing their bed every night. He knew he did not have to confer with her. She had given him her blessing and he also knew it was highly likely he would not be able to tell her what he did. He would also insist on her and the girls' safety above anything else.

Charles reached for the telephone, hesitated for a second and then called Peter Rogers.

'Good morning. The answer is yes.'

He almost detected an audible sigh of relief at the other end of the telephone.

'Excellent! How are you feeling about it?'

'Convinced.'

'The next stage is for you to come to London next week for a briefing day. This will be for you to confirm in your own mind that you are happy with everything and will be willing to commit. Do you have somewhere to stay?'

'I do. At my club.'

'Someone will call you this afternoon and pass on a date and time I can meet you there. We will reimburse your air ticket and any other expenses.' He hung up.

THE MORNING long briefings were interesting but hardly enlightening. Charles went away from them with the feeling they had not really told him anything but this did not worry him unduly. No doubt it would come. He had made his decision and that would not change now. The afternoon was taken up with the inevitable paperwork which ended with him carefully reading and then signing his contract. It certainly was generous with a basic salary well in excess of his current earnings and numerous and generous allowances including rent for an apartment in London. Charles had no complaints. All was set fair.

The ease at which he was 'transferred' amazed Charles. All he had to do was to hand over his position to the incoming British officer, a man he took an instant dislike to but kept his powder dry, hand in some kit to the Quartermaster, pack up the rest of his kit and send it home to Wiltshire and be dined out in the officers' mess. Several other officers were also being dined out and it turned into a rumbustious affair. Speeches were delivered and Charles came in for special praise from the general. Unlike with the other officers leaving, there was no mention of where he was going next. Charles drank more than normal and went to bed a happy man. He would no longer have to wear that uncomfortable mess kit with the throttling collar and those silly spurs, and would no longer have to bat off awkward questions as to his next posting. His answer was always that he was going on some gardening leave and did not know where his next posting would be. This was easier to say to a non-British officer such as a German or a Belgium who would show little curiosity, and he was glad about that. He left the army behind the next morning.

TWELVE

I t had been a steep learning curve for Charles during those first hectic months at Vauxhall. Gone were the certainties of peacetime NATO and the British Army facing the foe to the east. The work was relentless but incredibly interesting and rewarding. Not once did Charles regret the decision he had made, and nor did Peter Rogers. It was not normally possible to settle into anything resembling a routine and this was the way Charles liked it. He had a team of mainly young planners and analysts who brimmed with intelligence and energy. None of them would have been any good in the army but in this atmosphere and working environment, they were brilliant. He was beginning to form a firm bond with them. They liked him and he admired them. Teamwork was not like teamwork in the army with its hierarchical systems. Consensus was the name of the game and it took Charles some time to adjust to this alien way of working, but not too long. Charles had always placed respect before friendship in the working environment. He soon realised how important his job was and the weight of responsibility that lay on his shoulders. He also soon realised how senior his mentor Peter Rogers was in the organisation; very senior and near to the top.

Charles' predecessor had been removed. He was not talked of but apparently he was of the old school. Charles never quite understood what this meant in Foreign Office speak but he found out that there were two types. One was the dedicated professional who was steeped in the skills of espionage and all its vagaries, believed in the cause, never let his guard drop and despite advancing years remained a stalwart. The other normally fell foul of alcohol or women, or both, but held on because of past achievements and loyalties. In the case of Charles' predecessor, who had departed some months hence, he made the fatal mistake of being caught *in flagrante delicto* with the wife of a senior member of the firm. The empty bottle of whiskey by the bed did not help their cause. Once he had departed, people such as he were not talked of again.

Charles also became rapidly adept at the art of being able to separate his work life from everything and everybody else. It was not a particularly difficult thing to do less the need to be constantly on one's guard against a slip, either physically or mentally. His consumption of alcohol fell to almost zero during this period, not because he did not enjoy it but because the dangers of overdoing it and not firing on all cylinders, or becoming indiscreet, were obvious. He also rigorously kept up his fitness with early-morning runs, a habit he had never lost.

The nature of his position meant he was not required to attend the normal courses designed for those that operated 'on the ground' or 'in the field', frequently overseas and in positions that could be fraught with potential or real danger. He was mainly deskbound with infrequent forays to the USA and Europe. The main requirement for his job was his brain and it seemed to be serving him well. He did, however, attend a number of in-house introductory, background and management courses which were all useful

Gone were the comforts of living in an army officers' mess

where all was provided. He actually had to buy food and cook for himself, unless of course he chose to eat out. For the first two weeks, he lived in a small hotel until he could find himself an apartment which he did with his normal efficiency. It was a two-bedroomed flat just south of the river in Battersea close to the park and it suited him perfectly. Jane Bowater and Hanna scoured their combined houses for all the necessary furniture and just about all the household goods and appliances he would need and had them transported to London where a very busy weekend followed with the family unpacking and setting up his new home. The girls enjoyed getting in the way. It took some time to get himself straight but three months in he was well established and comfortable. Hanna came up every second weekend at the beginning and was invaluable in setting him straight domestically. Her much more frequent presence was a godsend to Charles, who could only see good in her and all she did. He was never a lapdog because he well understood the art of separating obsequiousness with a genuine desire to please. He would also frequently travel down to Wiltshire at weekends to be with her and the girls and all seemed well and set for the future. He did not like London much after his various army postings but found that it grew on him as time went by. He learnt to cook and decided to add 'cooking' to his list of worthwhile hobbies, not that he had many. He was always too busy at work and life went on at its normal hectic pace.

There seemed to be no clouds either overhead or on the horizon, although Charles sometimes wondered how his new masters had come to accept he was married to a Russian with a family in Russia, and actually tolerated it. The stringent vetting system under which he now existed would normally never have allowed it to happen but it had, even to the point where he held a position in which he was privy to and managed top-secret information on an almost daily basis. He never asked and he was never told. Let sleeping dogs lie was the best approach. Charles would not have been surprised to know that Hanna too had wondered about these things but she too knew it would more than unwise to even mention them. It was, and remained a moot point that never affected their love for each other, or their busy but closer lives together.

THIRTEEN

L ike the majority of Germans, Sophia Voight had followed the events of the late 1980s and early 1990s with growing interest. She had known for a long time that she could have applied to travel into East Germany before the wall came down but she never did. To her, the reason for this was simple. Her application would have been picked up almost immediately by the East German authorities and then the Stasi and then the Russians and although they had allowed her to return to the west from Berlin all those years ago, she was never quite sure what they might do to her now. To work on the edges of the espionage game in those times in Germany gave even the most naïve agent a negative, cautious and suspicious perspective to what might happen in the future. For many, this physiological burden would remain with them throughout life.

For Sophia, with her positivity, it did not affect her in such a way but she was still cautious and fearful, and was prepared to wait until she was certain that it would be safe and she would be free to travel as she pleased. That day came quicker than she was expecting; the day of German reunification in October 1990.

She needed to look and dress in a dowdy fashion. She needed

to be nondescript. She needed to blend in to what she imagined would be a colourless world. She was right. Having crossed the former Inner German Border, the long and tedious train journey to Dresden passed through some of the most depressing countryside and towns she could have imagined. It was certainly colourless and seemed weighed down with a sense of hopelessness. She did not like it at all.

Her journey through Berlin bought back painful memories. Very painful memories. His face was there in front of her as she stared out of the window at the passing city, moving from affluence to poverty and then beyond. She pictured all those wonderful times they had enjoyed together, his charm and innocence, and her hateful duplicity. She wept quietly and felt miserable. It could have all been so different.

Sophia Voight had no memories of Dresden but she had, through a friend at work, managed to book herself a room in a small hotel close to the shabby and downtrodden centre. The British and American bombing raid in February 1945 had destroyed this city of beauty and culture, 'The Jewel Box' of magnificent baroque and rococo architecture. Although the communists had made efforts to rebuild the centre, it had never really recovered its splendour of the 1930s. The place had an air of decay about it.

Sophia Voight planned to stay for a week and she had two firm aims. Find her parents, dead or alive and if dead, their graves, and find her sister. She knew her task would not be easy, and might even be impossible, but she was determined to find closure, one way or the other. She decided to start with her sister and the next morning made her way on foot to the Civil Registration Office. This office was in a state of flux but she was lucky to speak to a very sympathetic lady who had worked there since the 1950s.

'I have come from Osnabrück and am trying to find members

of my family who remained in the east and in Dresden as far as I am aware,' Sophia told her.

'I have a sister, Bertha, and my parents whom I am not sure if they are dead or alive. I was wondering if you could help me?'

This lady proved to be both courteous and helpful, a rare combination in immediate post-communist Eastern Germany. She suggested that firstly they attempt to look up her parents and see what had happened to them and whether or not they were still alive. From that, Bertha might be able to be traced. Leaving Sophia in her office, the lady disappeared for half an hour and then returned with a number of files. Her expression had changed from being friendly to being serious.

'I have traced your parents my dear and I am very sorry to inform you that they both died together in 1954 here in Dresden at their house. The reason given for death was through natural causes. They are buried here in Dresden at the Dittersbach Cemetery. I can give you directions. I am so sorry.'

Sophia sat and stared at the floor, tears in her eyes. In her heart she had known that this is what she would discover, but the news did little to assuage the pain of it being there in front of her in black and white. Whoever wrote that letter had been right.

There was a silence and then Sophia said, 'Thank you so much for your help. You have been very kind and helpful. I will visit their grave tomorrow. And my sister?'

The lady went behind her and closed the office door.

'Miss Voight, there is no record of your sister here but I have worked here for 35 years and I know who she is, what she has been doing and where you may be able to find her. You will not be happy to hear what I am about to tell you but I feel you must know.'

Sophia nodded. Was this more bad news?

'Your sister Bertha was trained by and worked directly for the Stasi for at least twenty years. Before the demise of that organisation last year, she had attained a senior position in that organisation. She has always remained in Dresden and lives here now.'

The lady wrote something on a piece of paper and handed it to her.

'That is her address as far as I am aware.'

'Thank you very much.'

Sophia got up to leave.

'This last part of our conversation about your sister. I would be grateful if you could erase it from your memory. You came here only to find out about your parents.'

'I understand and thank you once again.'

As she walked back to her hotel, her mind was in turmoil. Her sister Bertha a senior member of the Stasi! She could hardly believe it and then she remembered that she too had worked indirectly for them in West Berlin, albeit reluctantly and coerced. She had to have been taken at an early age and trained in her late teens. What a nightmare. Sophia wanted to go home now to her peaceful village in the west and put this all behind her, but she knew that she had to see it through.

Sophia ordered two bottles of wine, lay on her bed, drank and planned her next moves. She would leave things until tomorrow and then visit her parents' grave, if there was one. She would then have to face up to her sister, if she could find her. And then she would go home early. There was nothing for her here and she was already beginning to hate the place.

———

Sophia woke up with a hangover and was glad she had one. She had finished the wine and wandered down the grim street from her hotel to a bar which she had noticed that day on her way back. She sat at a table, drank beer and viewed the comings and goings of the clientele. Inevitably, it was not long before she was approach by a callow young man who asked if he could join her. Despite his unappealing looks, Gunter turned out to be a pleasant and intelligent man. Sophia saw this as a chance to gain a better feel of the place.

Having introduced himself, he said, 'You look different from the people round here.'

'I am. I come from the west but we are all Germans.'

'True, but history has not been kind to us and kinder to you.'

'Let's hope that things will improve now,' she said.

They chatted and drank more beer. She bought them. She could see that he had more on his mind than just chat. No chance of that, she thought, and managed a smile.

'What about the Stasi, or ex-Stasi now,' she ventured.

He instinctively lowered his voice, borne of habit.

'They are all bastards, and brutal. You couldn't do, say or think anything. It was total state control with their army of informers.'

'Did you know any of them?'

'No, thank God. They were invisible but what is worse now is that apart from the really senior figures in Berlin who will go on show trials all the others will just be immersed back into German society, just like most of the Nazis after 1945.'

They drank more and Gunter told her all about life in the 'Workers' Paradise' and how hideous it really was. He hated the Russians. He was not bitter. He showed pragmatism and hope for a better future. He was young enough to be able to hopefully enjoy it.

'I will have to go now,' said Sophia.

His face showed disappointment. 'May I walk you back to where you came from?'

'No thank you, but it was very nice to meet you.'

They shook hands and she left, feeling a little woozy but well in control.

THE NEXT DAY she found the graves, side by side and in a terrible state. They had probably not been tended for years. She knelt and cried again for them. She felt desperately sad. She couldn't leave them like this. She went to the cemetery office where an old man sat. Obviously, the caretaker.

'Good morning. My parents are buried here. May I pay you some money to have their graves tended by yourself, or someone?'

'Show me where they lie.'

She showed him.

'I remember the day they were brought here. There was a government official and a young woman. A very pretty young woman. That was all.'

Bertha, thought Sophia. She must have paid for, or arranged for the headstones and graves; not elaborate but solid.

'May I give you fifty Deutsche Marks to tend them?' she asked.

He was delighted and accepted the money. However, his face fell when she said; 'I will come back tomorrow to see how you have done.'

Sophia then went on to the address given to her by the lady in the Civilian Registration Office. It turned out to be an apartment in a shabby block on the outskirts of the city. The main door to the block was open so she walked up the stairs to the numbered door and knocked. Her nerves were jangling and she felt a cold chill come over her. The door opened and there stood Bertha, instantly recognisable. Like her sister, still attractive. She showed no emotion and nor did she offer any welcome.

'Please come in.'

The apartment was shabby and untidy. Bertha offered Sophia coffee.

'I knew that you would come back one day so I was waiting for you,' she said.

Sophia had somehow expected a joyful reunion and was hoping for one. None came. Bertha was deadpan and uncommunicative. They sat and Sophia told her about where she now lived, what she did and why she had come to Dresden. The responses were monosyllabic and no information was forthcoming in return.

Sophia decided there and then that she would not ask any questions about Bertha. She knew what she had been doing for the past 20 years or so and there was no point in pressing for information that would never be revealed. The woman sitting opposite her was not the sister she remembered. Here was a woman hardened by what she had done, and God knows what she had done. It was time to go.

As a last effort, she offered Bertha her address and telephone number on a card but this was refused. Without even a handshake, the door had closed behind her. Sophia was not emotional as she walked away, but she felt sadness. Apart from her aunt, her family as she had known them were a closed book.

Sophia left the next morning and having left some flowers on what were now two very well tended graves, caught the train home. She had hoped for so much more but in her own pragmatic way realised it was not to be.

Her aunt had taken a turn for the worse whilst she had been away. She died peacefully two weeks later. Now she really was on her own but strangely felt a sense of relief, even deliverance from the past. Physically she had everything she needed and more than most. All she really needed now was Charles Bowater. No one else would do but she was also realistic enough to know that the chances of her ever being with him again were very slim indeed. Perhaps she would meet someone like him in the future, but in reality she knew that it would never work.

Sophia stood naked in front of the mirror and examined herself closely. She had looked after herself and it showed. She had been blessed with startingly good looks and had developed into a handsome and desirable woman. Her long hair had lustre, her skin was cream-like and without having given birth, her figure was as it was when she was twenty. She turned and looked over her shoulder. She was pleased with what she saw. Outwardly she always dressed well and with elegance but also with a hint of daring. Sometimes she wore clothes that were too tight and which accentuated her figure. She always wore make-up, but never too much, and she always wore the lightest and skimpiest lingerie. All of this made her feel good. She was all dressed up but with nowhere to go and no one to go anywhere with. It made her want to weep, and sometimes she did.

FOURTEEN

Hanna had adapted to her family's new lifestyle with her normal calmness and energy. Unlike in the army when she accompanied Charles on some of his postings and was expected to be 'an army wife' in this new world no one seemed to care who she was, what her relationship was with her husband, and what she did. It was none of their business, but in her case of course a few knew everything about her. They no doubt still had a file on her somewhere in the hideous edifice where Charles worked in Vauxhall. But being Hanna, she cast these thoughts aside and got on with life. She was incredibly happy now that Charles was back in England and that they could see each other almost every week. If absence made the heart grow fonder, in their case togetherness did the same and more.

Hanna continued to keep a close eye on events in Russia. Naturally she missed her parents and sister as much as she did when she first came to the west but time, her own family and her happiness had dulled her desire to see them. Before the Soviet Union had collapsed, she had held out little hope of ever seeing them again, but now it seemed there was a glimmer of a possibility. One weekend at home in Wiltshire she asked Charles if it would be possible for him to find out if people with British passports would be able to travel to Russia in the future. A general and discreet enquiry. If the answer was a possible yes, it would make her feel better even if she never went to Russia. It was the knowledge that she could that counted. He did not like the sound of her question but said that he would look into it, having made up his mind there and then that he would not.

On his way back to London on the train, Charles relented and decided he would look into it in a very discreet way and hopefully just as an aside. He discovered that the answer was yes but a visa would be required. What he was sure of was that on three counts this was an impossibility. Her name would come up in lights as soon as she applied for a visa and they would plan a reception committee. If her visa application was approved, it would be for the purpose of taking revenge on her for her defection in Berlin all those years ago. This act would compromise himself and his position. He deemed it all impossible and should not be countenanced.

Charles knew that the KGB, now morphed into the FSB via the short-lived FSK, was a shadow of its former self but still willing and capable of acts of revenge against those they considered traitors. They had memories like an elephant, and probably documents to back them up. Hanna was considered a traitor and time was not a consideration when it came to acting against them. Like most Russians they had patience and could wait, sometimes for decades. It was a national characteristic. Charles also was well aware of the pain that Hanna felt about being separated for so long from her parents and her sister. Maybe there was another way? He would need to think about it, but for Hanna to go to St Petersburg was completely out of the question.

On the next suitable occasion, lying next to each other in bed in Vine Cottage one spring morning, Charles broached the subject. He told her that there was a possibility that she could go to Russia but in their circumstances, it was an impossibility. He gave her all the reasons straight and she accepted them with sadness in her eyes. Charles then said that there may be another way but he needed to think very carefully about it.

'Do not despair, my darling. We will get there just as we have on so many other occasions.'

'I know you will do your best for us. I will wait and, in the meantime...'

She drew his naked body to her with carnal thoughts in her mind. It was just about to become something more than a cuddle when the door burst open and there were two now not so small bodies sitting on top of them. Eleanor and Viktoria were in their nighties and were so happy to see their Daddy. They had been asleep when he arrived late the evening before. They were blossoming into two beautiful girls who not only had the looks but apparently some brains as well according to their school reports. They chatted and chatted, telling him everything and vying for attention. Hanna slipped into her dressing gown and went downstairs to make tea. She loved these peaceful, happy times when they were all together and with the weekend to look forward to. Nothing should be allowed to interfere with the life they had created, even it meant never seeing her parents again.

The family had been invited for supper at the house where they once more enjoyed the Bowaters' hospitality and bonhomie. Jean Bowater was her normal sprightly self, never seeming to age much or tire. David Bowater had once more been given the gypsies' warning over his health but chose to ignore it. He was not looking that good but remained his normal amiable and congenial self, always topping up your glass even if it did not need it, and engaging in animated conversation. There wasn't actually anything his doctor could find wrong with him, he just looked physically frail and worn out.

The girls went back to the cottage as soon as the meal was over.

Grown-ups could be so boring. Charles and Hanna lingered on until David Bowater was sound asleep, the inevitable Richard the cat on his lap. Hanna helped Jane Bowater as always and they then walked back to cottage hand-in-hand.

'I hope I can stay forever,' she said.

'No reason at all why you can't. This is your house,' said Charles.

'You know what my priority is when it comes to you and my parents, don't you?'

'I do but I will see if there is another way for you to be able to meet your parents without risking anything.'

'Thank you, darling. I will wait.'

AGAINST HIS BETTER JUDGEMENT, which had always been suspect, he did investigate carefully another way. Why not bring her family to her rather than she going to them? They could not come to England but they could meet in a country that would be convenient to both. Which country? None of the former Eastern Bloc countries in Europe could be possible but Finland might be the answer. Russians could travel there now and for Hanna it would be easy to fly direct to Helsinki. He decided to give this more thought as he hurried into the daily heads' meeting.

This is not sensible, he thought, as he sat in his apartment in Battersea that evening. I am putting in jeopardy everything that we have achieved over all these years so that Hanna can see her family. My new career, her life, our children's happiness at stake. His mind drifted back to that seminal moment when she got out of the boot of that shinning black car in West Berlin. For him, she was everything. The love had never waned, not even a tiniest bit. He needed to help her and find a way. It also crossed his mind that even now their past would never leave them. They were saddled with it forever.

Charles also pondered as to the mechanics of actually trying to make contact with Hanna's family in St Petersburg, but this turned out to surprisingly easy. The walls under Yeltsin were really coming down and he was able to find and give Hanna the number of the St Petersburg Information Bureau where he hoped she would be able to gain access to her parents' telephone number. It worked. Being in London, he was not privy to the almost overwhelming flood or emotion and happiness that ensued from that first tearful and emotional conversation. The happiness of at last hearing from the ones you loved, your family and parents and your sister, was almost overwhelming for Hanna. It had been 20 years with no news and this was a revelation.

Her Russian was rusty. But the sound of their voices made her weep greatly. Her mother, always the dominant one in the family, told her that all was well but that their secure communist life and probably their even safer communist-style pensions were dead. Everything was up in the air but they were lucky in that she had a secured a very good agreement with her former employer, a giant Russian gas company who had managed to ride the chaotic collapse of the Russian economy of the early 1990s. They were not destitute like many Russians but they were prey to the rampant gangster-induced crime the pervaded the streets of St Petersburg and many other Russian cities and towns.

Initial contact was delightful but Hanna managed to tell her over-excited parents that they would need to wait for further information about a possible future meeting.

'Please wait for at least three weeks, Mama. Charles and I need to make a plan.'

'What is he like? What does he look like? Is he handsome? Is he an English gentleman? What about my grandchildren? Tell me all about them. What about you? Are you still beautiful? Do you still love us all?'

There were hundreds of questions she could not hope to answer. When she put the telephone down, she had to sit and compose herself. She walked up to Vine House and asked Jane Bowater if she could collect the girls from school that afternoon and babysit as she needed to go up to London to be with Charles. Jane Bowater had babysat for them for years and never tired of it, and the girls loved it as they were inevitably indulged by their grandmother.

She was happy. She told Eleanor and Viktoria that they now had grandparents on her side. She busied herself and loved her husband even more. It was a major day in her life. She walked over to the house and told Jane Bowater all. The lady did not flinch. They hugged each other – with happiness. What her son was capable of never really surprised her.

Hanna took the train with a plan to come back down to Wiltshire with him the following day, it being a Friday. She let herself in to the apartment and busied herself in the kitchen before she heard him open the door. They held each other close and kissed like young lovers. The mutual attraction never faded.

Hanna told him all that had happened that day. He could see how happy she was. Her face virtually glowed with excitement and pleasure. They went out that evening and enjoyed a romantic dinner together. They did not talk about the next part of the plan until they got back to the apartment.

'I would be really careful about planning to go and see your family in Russia. With our backgrounds and their long memories, it would be madness in my opinion. In any case, if the firm found out that would probably be curtains for me. It really is a complete no-no.'

They were lying in bed with Charles propped up on one elbow gazing at her. She could be a temptress at times. She had let the duvet slip to show her lovely firm breasts, an act of deliberate arousal.

'If you can't go and see them, why don't they come and see you?'

'How would that work?' she said drowsily.

'Let's talk about it in the morning,' he said, switching off the bedside light. He was exhausted. The workload seemed to be increasing with each passing day but he still enjoyed it, enjoyed it more than the army and he had not regretted the move. Sleep came quickly.

HE MADE tea and they sat up in bed.

'I was thinking about meeting up in Finland as an alternative,' he said.

'Could my family get there?' she asked. Hanna knew nothing about where Russians could go and not go these days.

'I will make discreet enquires, today if possible.'

She seemed happy and whilst Charles was at work she walked in Battersea Park, did some shopping, drank coffee and relaxed in the apartment. She ate a light lunch out and waited for him. They caught a later train back to Wiltshire.

CHARLES HAD JUST ABOUT MADE time to speak to one of his team about Finland and whether or not Russians could visit there now. He couched it in a way that made it sound as if he merely interested as a passing matter of little importance and Tom, one of his best, came back with an answer within the hour. Russians could now visit Finland and many were, mainly on day shopping trips and other short periods. The visa system had been simplified.

Charles, through bitter experience, was acutely aware of the potential dangers that lay ahead should he and Hanna decide this was a possibility. Memories within the Russian security services were long, as was their global reach, and that since 1917 history clearly showed that anyone who had been or was an opponent or critic of the regime, or who had put the Soviet Union in an embarrassing position through defection, was ripe for elimination. He did not know whether the desire for revenge was strong enough for a relatively minor irritation such as Hanna's defection, but there would be no way of telling until it actually happened. It mattered not that the KGB had morphed into the FSB. The methods of operating were the same, even if their world had been severely bruised by recent events. She was a traitor and nothing would change that. Talking on the telephone to her parents in St Petersburg was the first red light. If her parents' telephone was bugged, which it could well be, to talk about meeting up in Finland could be an open invitation at an attempt of kidnapping, something which they would be capable of and well able to carry out. The whole prospect filled him with dread.

Charles thought long and hard about what to do, if anything, all weekend. He was preoccupied and Hanna, sensing his reluctance to engage in conversation, left him to it. She knew he was trying to find a solution within a situation fraught with difficulties and unknowns.

It was not until the following week that a possible solution became apparent. Charles was to travel to Helsinki to meet with his counterpart in the Finnish Intelligence Service or SUPO. It was to be an introductory meeting with an aim of mapping out future cooperation within areas of interest, areas of interest that could be fraught given the Finns' history and proximity to Russia. The meeting had been scheduled for a date three weeks hence. Charles would travel incognito and he would be in Helsinki for a maximum of two days. He would be staying at the Hotel Kamp in the centre. All had been arranged.

Could he take Hanna along with him? In itself, and if done overtly with the backing of the firm, this was a possibility. She would be accompanying her husband on a short break to a very agreeable European capital. The key sticking point would be passing the planned meeting details to her parents and sister. They would only need two pieces of information: a date and time; and a location. But if this information, when being passed, was picked up by interested ears it could spell real danger. Further thought was needed but, in the meantime, Charles went to his boss and requested his wife be allowed accompany him on his short trip to Helsinki. The answer came back as yes but with the caveat that he must ensure she was always either with him or in her room in the hotel when he was attending the meeting. Could they ever lead a life free from the spectre of that damn bear?

He was drawn to finding a solution for his beloved, even to the point of exposing himself to a raft of risk. He was not a schemer or remotely duplicitous, just a talented man who was perhaps too disingenuous for the game he had found himself in. He pressed on with his plan regardless.

In the privacy of his office he made a brief, secure call to the firm's man in the Consulate in St Petersburg, Anthony Bridges. Charles asked if he would be prepared to do him a favour. A brief hesitation but the answer was yes.

'I will send you a note in the diplomatic bag. It should be with you shortly. Thank you very much, Tony.'

The letter he wrote was short and to the point. He gave Tony the names, address and telephone number of Hanna's family. He then gave a meeting point date, time and location. He ended by stating that this message was from Anna and stressed the importance that the passing of this information should, at all costs, be conducted in a covert manner and should not be mentioned again.

Charles knew that Tony Bridges would do the business and left it at that. He dived back into his work and did what he was so good at; compartmentalising his life. The 'Helsinki' compartment had been created, the lid closed for the time being, and other compartments opened and closed according to what was happening at the time.

That weekend Charles explained the plan very carefully to Hanna. He warned her that it might not happen and they would not know until the actual time arrived. He also talked at length about the great dangers of his plan. She listened and absorbed all, but her main feelings were of immense gratitude and a feeling of excitement that very soon she might be able to see her family again after nearly 20 years.

AS HE WAS FLYING business class, Charles treated Hanna to the same and they arrived safely in Helsinki. They took a taxi to the Hotel Kamp and settled in. The hotel was a good choice; comfortable and elegant and Hanna wasted no time in heading for the spa with Charles in tow to enjoy two hours of pampering and a general cleanse. They had dinner and further enjoyed the luxurious and enormous bed.

The plan was that Charles would make his own way to an address in Helsinki the next day, attend the meeting which would probably last into the early afternoon, have lunch with his host and then back to the hotel to write up his notes. The following day – 6th June – was the date given for the meeting and Charles could clearly sense a growing tension in Hanna as the time approached. She hardly slept that night and got up early to sit quietly by the window in their room. They had to wait for another five hours.

Charles was glad that his plan had seemed to work up to that point and he had not had a sense that they were under any kind of surveillance. However, the danger point was yet to come and he had to be on his mettle throughout that day, indeed until they were both safely in the air leaving Helsinki the following morning.

THE STATED HOUR had arrived and they made their way down to the lobby. It was virtually deserted but Charles surveyed the scene carefully. He saw nothing unusual. They sat and waited. Hanna was very quiet and Charles left her to her thoughts and emotions.

An elderly couple and a younger, attractive woman entered the lobby. Hanna gave a shriek of delight and rushed to them. The next ten minutes were a flurry of hugs, kisses, crying, talking in rapid Russian. More hugs, more kisses, more crying and more rapid talking but by now interspersed with laughter and cries of delight. Charles stood quietly to one side and observed this unadulterated explosion of pure family joy. It went on for some time until Hanna, tears pouring down her face, suddenly remembered she had a husband to introduce.

She came to him and, holding his hand, introduced him.

'This is Charles, my husband,' she said proudly in Russian. Charles stepped forward and shook their hands solemnly and formally. Mikhail Nazarov smiled and greeted him warmly with a very long and vigorous handshake.

Aleksandra and Annika Nazarov stared at this tall, handsome and elegant Englishman. Aleksandra Nazarov, being Russian, could immediately sense the bond of love that existed between her daughter and this impressive looking man. Annika Nazarov just fell in love with him on the spot.

Charles had arranged for them all to have a family lunch in a small, private dining room on the first floor of the hotel. He organised that all food would be cold and placed in the room beforehand and once the family were inside that the door should be locked from the inside and hotel staff briefed that they were not to be disturbed. The food was excellent and some, but not too much, wine was drunk. It was a good plan.

Charles sat back and let Hanna take centre stage. Her face glowed with happiness. They talked and talked and talked in rapid-fire Russian. He did not mind as he and Hanna could catch up later, but he was aware of Annika's interest. Like her sister she was certainly attractive but had never married. She had told Hanna that she found Russian men in general quite rough in manner and many of them drank too much. She spoke a few words of English and so they conversed haltingly. Charles liked her immediately.

Hanna had put together a comprehensive photograph album before she had left England. It gave a record of their lives together, their girls from birth to now, their house inside and out and many happy, holiday snaps. There were squeals of delight from Aleksandra that she was now a babushka. Mikhail Nazarov, a man used to being in the background, nodded and smiled as he looked at all this evidence of his twin daughter's life, a life so different to theirs and what they had suffered. He was happy for her. Charles looked at Hanna's parents and could plainly see the goodness and genuine nature in these scions of the Soviet system, now defunct. They had a decency about them and he could now plainly see where his wife had inherited her delightful nature and personality.

Time flew by all too quickly and Charles had gathered through Hanna's translation that the family had to be back at the railway station in time to catch the train to be at the border by that evening. With sadness and many more hugs, kisses and tears the lunch broke up. Charles ordered a taxi at reception, put it on the bill and saw them outside. There were further hugs and kisses and

Charles himself got a few, especially from Annika but also from Babushka, photo album tucked firmly under her arm. They were gone and Hanna stood disconsolate. He hurried her inside and they went straight to their room. Time to calm down and recap.

Hanna was both elated and sad but the positive showed on her face.

'Thank you darling for making all this happen. You have been wonderful.'

She kissed him and held him close. She had loved the way that he had hung back and let her have all the time with her family, had arranged everything in his normal efficient manner and had shown politeness and interest despite the language barrier.

'I feel that the ice has been broken and from now on it will be easier to stay in touch and see each other more and more. My father gave me the telephone number of a friend of his which I can use to pass on information. It was so wonderful to see them all after all these years, I am so happy.'

'I am very happy for you, darling. I liked your family very much. And it is a relief that all seems well on the security front. I didn't notice anything untoward. Did you?'

'Not at all but there again I was in such a state that I probably wouldn't have anyway.'

They didn't bother with supper and went to bed early as they had an early flight back to London in the morning.

HELSINKI AIRPORT WAS NOT busy at that time of morning. They checked in and before going through to departures, Charles excused himself to quickly go to the loo. Hanna sat and waited for him. When he returned, she was not there. He assumed she too had gone to the loo and sat down to wait. He waited and waited and still no sign of Hanna. He was beginning to feel panic rising in him. He had left her alone for a very short time, something he had told himself he should not do and she had seemingly disappeared. He went over to the nearby information desk and asked there, explaining to them what Hanna looked like and what she was wearing. Perhaps she had gone through to the departures lounge by herself? He hurried through security and then on to the business class lounge. No sign. He almost ran to the gate where a queue of passengers had formed and were boarding. Still no sign. Now he was panicking and sweating profusely. He stopped and thought, trying to calm himself. She definitely wasn't in the departure lounge, therefore she must not have come through security. But why? Was she waiting for him on the other side? He found the nearest official and pleaded to be allowed back out. He had lost his wife. The man was understanding and sympathetic and he was soon back in the main check-in area where he had last seen her. He combed the whole area. Still no sign. She had disappeared. He was desperate. Where was she? He sat down heavily and put his head in his hands.

'Are you alright, sir?' A heavy Finnish accent. He looked up to see two policemen standing in front of him.

'I have lost my wife. She has disappeared. I have looked everywhere,' he said.

'Do you happen to have a photograph of your wife on you?'

He found the one he kept in his wallet.

'This lady was seen being escorted from the building by two policemen. My colleague and I are the ones who have been on duty here for the past five hours and no one else. When this was reported to us, we checked with our headquarters and they had no knowledge of this.'

Charles' heart sank. They had got her. He had left her for a few minutes and they had pounced. He had made a fatal mistake, one he would probably have to live with for the rest of his life.

'We will need to take a statement from you, sir.' They had missed their flight with all their baggage on board.

With a shaky hand he wrote his statement, making sure that he included all details, including his contact details in England.

'We will investigate this incident thoroughly, sir. Do not worry.' What they did not know, nor would know, was the background against which this had happened.

The policemen then took him to British Airways desk and he was rebooked on the next flight that afternoon. He had become an unthinking automaton going through the motions but with no feeling, only despair in his heart.

WITHIN A MINUTE of Charles disappearing into the loo, Hanna was confronted by two men dressed in the uniform of the Finnish Police.

'Mrs Bowater?'

'Yes.'

'You must come with us. We need to ask you a number of questions.'

'No, I will not. I am waiting for my husband.'

Within a further minute she had been physically propelled through one of the doors of airport building and bundled into a waiting car which drove sedately away from the airport complex. In the back, her assailants bound and gagged her. She was terrified, so terrified she could not speak, let alone shout for help. Through the terror she knew what had happened. These people were Russian and they were speaking Russian. She sat between them until they had cleared the outskirts of Helsinki and the car stopped off-road down a forest track. She was hauled out and forced into the boot of the car. There was a mattress and pillow in the boot. She was given a drink of water and told there was food there as well. They then told her that for the next ten hours she would remain in the boot and that if she made any noise she would be gagged again. The boot closed and she was left in pitch-black darkness. These men had talked to her in Russian knowing she would understand. They knew her name. She had been kidnapped and she was being taken back to Russia. There was no mistaking that. She wept quietly and sunk, like her husband, into a vortex of despair. Would she ever see her family again?

As CHARLES SAT NUMBLY on the train taking him back home to Wiltshire, he tried to clear his mind and to start thinking logically about what had happened and what he must do next. In Berlin he had engineered Hanna's escape and had been her rock ever since. He must not let her down now in her hour of need, and he must make sure that Eleanor and Viktoria were looked after and were not worried about their mother. It was time to get a grip and make a plan. There could be little room for emotion at this time.

His first decision was centred on the need to wait to see what the Finnish police could find out. It may be that Hanna would by some miracle turn up but he doubted it very much. Those bastards would not let her go even if what she had done had been done in the Soviet era. As he got off the train, he decided that he would tell his parents and the girls that Hanna had stayed on in Helsinki to be with her family for a few days and would be back soon. This would give him time to see if the impossible might happen. His mood lightened slightly as he drove home and on arrival went straight to the main house to collect the girls.

That evening when he had tucked the girls in bed and said goodnight with a kiss for both of them, he went downstairs and drank whiskey. The absence of his lovely Hanna hung like a dark shroud over him. There had always been that worry in the background that something one day might happen and that their pasts would really catch up with them and now it had happened. He forced himself not to have another drink and went to bed. He was exhausted, physically and emotionally, but slept badly.

That morning he called his boss and asked if he could take a few days off for family reasons. It would be his first days off since he had started and the answer was yes. He decided to wait for a further three days before he went up to London and told all to Peter Rogers. He settled down to take on Hanna's mantle in the cottage and kept himself busy and outwardly cheerful with his daughters.

As she lay in the darkness, terrified and desperate, Hanna forced herself to try to think logically about her situation. She drank from the water bottle and with groping hands found the food, a number of sandwiches which she ate. For the sake of her husband and children, she must not allow herself to fold emotionally. Some of the steel returned. She would not attempt to antagonise her abductors but play along with them and see what happened.

Hanna felt a change. They had obviously pulled off the main road and were driving on a rough track. After a while, the car stopped and the boot was opened. One of the three men beckoned her out. He was a brute of a man with a large beard who smelt of alcohol. She hauled her aching and stiff body out and stood before the three of them, shaking and confused. They were parked on a narrow track in a dense and dark forest. She didn't even know what country she was in but assumed that it must be Russia. She was wrong. They were still in Finland and some thirty kilometres from the border with Russia.

Without speaking or touching her, they escorted her down a narrow path through the trees to a clearing where there stood a small wooded hut. They told her to go inside. Hanna was now more than terrified. This seemed to be a classic case of a rape or murder scenario, or both. How she longed for Charles. They followed her in and indicated that she should sit at the small table in the middle of the only room.

'We have bought you here to teach you a lesson that you will not forget,' said the more urbane one. He was smartly dressed and softly spoken – always a bad sign in this type of situation, she thought.

'You know why you are here. Why did you defect from your country in Berlin?'

'I did it for love and nothing else. I loved my country then and I still do now. And you will know what my husband did for the Soviet Union in the eighties. I do not deserve this,' she said in a small, quavering voice.

'When you defected did you pass on any information to the enemy?' said the urbane one.

'As you know, I worked as a doctor at the embassy and was never privy to any classified information, military or otherwise. My husband did that for you later.'

There was a silence, a dangerous silence. It could be the time of reckoning, Hanna thought. Or it could be the time when that brute, who was looking at her closely with an expression of desire in his piggy eyes, would rape her. She sat quietly and waited.

'I want you to understand, and always understand that you will never be off our radar screens but because of what has happened since you defected and the help that your husband provided for us, we are letting you go. Never forget,' he said mildly. 'We are still in Finland. We are now going to head east and for home and you are going to find your own way back to where you live.'

They all stood up and led her back to the car on the track. The urbane one handed her her handbag and within minutes they had got in the car, turned around and disappeared up the track to what she assumed must be the main road. She stood there and savoured a sense of almost overwhelming relief. She wept a little as she made her way back up the track through the gathering gloom. After 20 minutes, she found herself on the main road. It was still light and seeing the sun lowering in the sky, she headed west in that direction. At least the weather was warm. She was dressed to take a flight back to London in an elegant dress and high heels, not to walk for miles. She took her shoes off and started to walk.

Cars and trucks passed her at frequent intervals but eventually a car pulled up. She was hugely relieved to see that the driver was a woman and there was no one else in the car.

'Where are you going?' said a kindly voice in Finnish.

'I am trying to get to Helsinki or the nearest police station,' she replied in English.

'I am going as far as Rantahaka which is about thirty kilometres. Would that be alright?' she replied in halting English.

'That would be so kind. Thank you so much.'

The lady, whose name was Helli, was not an inquisitive type. The Finns tended not to be. She could have enquired as to what an obviously well-educated and well-dressed woman was doing wandering down the highway in the middle of nowhere as night was approaching. But she did not, which was a relief for Hanna.

Whilst sitting in the car she had a good look in her handbag. Those men had obviously gone through it but nothing was missing. Her passport and money and credit cards were all there.

'Is there a hotel in your town where I could stay the night?' she asked.

'There is the Hotel Leikari which is fine. I can drop you off there?'

After profuse thanks to Helli, Hanna found herself in a small but comfortable room. She immediately noticed the telephone but decided to sort herself out first. She stripped, washed her knickers and tights in the basin, had a long, hot shower, washed her hair

343

and donned a bathrobe. She felt so much better. Charles would probably be asleep by now given his preference for early nights so she decided to call him in the morning. She collapsed and slept soundly. What a day it had been!

The morning was bright and warm. Coming down to breakfast, Hanna had made herself look as though she was about to board her flight to London. She waited a little and then called the cottage number.

'Hello Charles.'

'Hanna! Hanna!' A shout of joy.

'Are you alright? Where are you?'

'I am still in Finland in a small town somewhere between the Russian border and Helsinki. I am staying in a hotel. Shall I go to the police station?'

Charles thought for a moment. 'No, don't do that. Can you find your back to Helsinki and go directly to the airport?'

'I am sure I can.'

'Rebook a flight and let me know. I will pick you up at Heathrow. We should not discuss anything further on the telephone.'

It was a long bus, train and plane journey but by that evening she had fallen into her husband's warm and familiar embrace at Heathrow. Thirty-six hours earlier neither of them would have believed that this emotional and poignant moment could have been possible. There was a mutual feeling of almost overwhelming relief and happiness.

On his way up to the airport, Charles had come to a number of decisions. The girls and his parents would never know what had happened. He would have to inform someone at the firm and that someone would have to be Peter Rogers. He would do this as soon as he was back in London. Hanna and he would have to come to some sort of agreement as to whether or not they could continue living as they have done since they met in that museum in East Berlin 17 years ago. There was a lot to think and speak about.

Hanna told Charles the whole story with no omissions she could think of from the time that she was hustled out of the airport to when she boarded the aircraft back to London.

'How did they know that we were in Helsinki at that particular time?' she asked him.

Charles had also pondered on this and had come to the conclusion that her parents had been coerced into telling whoever they were what their plans were for that day and who they were meeting. Hanna reluctantly agreed.

'Did they do it just to give us a warning or was it something else?' she asked.

'I think they did it to tell us both that they have reach and that despite the collapse of the Soviet system they are still a power to be reckoned with. But according to them you are a very minor traitor and when they revealed that they knew all about my activities this tells me that the episode had been planned to issue a statement only. But I believe that you were incredibly lucky. They could have killed you there and then and buried you, or taken you back to Russia to a very uncertain future, both for yourself and your family.'

'Will we need to do anything else now?'

Charles told her about his decisions made on his way up to meet her. Hanna agreed wholeheartedly; he was always so logically cool in situations such as that which they had just been through.

'Will they try anything else in the future or is it all over now?' she asked.

'I really do not know. What I do know is that we must never take a risk like that again.'

This caused Hanna to remember seeing her parents and sister and how happy she had been.

Their arrival home was met with joy with the girls to the fore. They loved their Granny but they loved their mother much more. Having been warned off by Charles and knowing they would be late, Jane Bowater had prepared a light supper for all. Both Hanna and Charles were emotionally drained but their happiness kept them buoyant until bedtime when they slept like the dead for ten hours. Waking together when they thought that they never would again they made gentle, slow love. It was bliss. Charles made tea and they lay in bed talking quietly.

'I have to go back up to London tomorrow early and face the music,' he said.

'Will it be music?' she asked.

'I suspect so but I hope that Peter will be his normal sympathetic self. We shall see.'

CHARLES RANG Peter Rogers that afternoon and arranged to meet him outside the office for breakfast on the Tuesday. They duly met.

Charles wasted no time in telling Peter Rogers all. He talked quietly and succinctly with the facts and at the end put his hands up and admitted he had been a damn fool.

Peter Rogers listened to him with no interruptions, with his face showing no emotion.

'You're a strange one, Charles. At work you are competent, logical and sensible. In matters of the heart you are incompetent, illogical and behave, at times, like an idiot. I know so well that it is all part of your character but this time there is no excuse. Your behaviour was unacceptable. Your actions put yourself and your wife at huge risk and you may have opened up a pressure point which our friends may wish to exploit in the future.'

Charles felt a cold shiver come across him.

'I have protected you in the past, indeed furthered both your careers by my own interventions, interventions that were not popular at times, and now you do this to me. Please go back to continue your excellent work and I will be in touch. We eagerly await your report on your meeting with your Finnish counterpart.'

Without a goodbye, Peter Rogers got up and left, leaving Charles with the bill. No doubt they would be meeting very soon.

Back at the office Charles threw himself into his work, driven by a subconscious desire to prove himself irreplaceable. He produced an excellent report on Finland which was widely admired and commented on by the top table. There was no word from Peter Rogers all that week. Charles began to think that he had let it ride and he travelled home that Friday feeling better than he did at the beginning of the week.

AT HOME, a number of sad events had occurred. Firstly, the old vicar, who had married them and Christened their children, died. He had not been well for some time, but his illness did not preclude him from consuming more daily alcohol than was good for him.

'God will not forgive me if I was not honest with myself,' he would say as he slurped another glass of red.

His funeral was a sombre affair. The village had lost a man of God who was deeply religious, patriotic, illiberal, kind and gentle, old fashioned and old school. In his memory the Bishop actually took his funeral service and the church was packed. His successor, an insignificant figure lurking in the background, was not of the old school. It soon became apparent to all that with his 'modern' approach he wished to turn the church and its services into a circus. He was soundly rejected by the village and they voted with their feet. Whilst previous services had always been full, the church was now virtually empty.

Old Richard the cat, a stalwart of superiority and laziness, also met his end through old age. Talk of a replacement was mooted but it was decided that in memory of Richard a suitable time should elapse before a new feline friend be acquired.

The last unsettling event was the slow but sure deterioration of David Bowater. Like the vicar, he would not listen to reasoning or any medical advice in general. One evening, when the younger Bowaters were over for supper, he complained of feeling unwell and excused himself. This was very unusual behaviour so when Jane Bowater went upstairs after supper to check him, she found him lying peacefully on the made bed with arms and legs crossed and a smile on his face. She assumed he was asleep. He was dead. Some said that he missed Richard snoozing on his favourite lap in the evenings in front of the fire, but others were convinced that the whiskey in the shed syndrome had finally caught up with him. He died a man true to his values; courageous, agreeable, polite and charming, always dapper and always with a ready smile on his face for all. Jane Bowater was her normal stoic self. There were no tears, at least not in public. Before the funeral, Charles took no truck from the new vicar. The service would be held according to the King James version and nothing else and it would be appreciated if he respected the wishes of the family to the letter. The message was received loud and clear. Again, it was a sombre affair and the new vicar did not slip up. David Bowater was buried in the peace of an English village churchyard, something which would have pleased him. A few very old members of his regiment came to give their respects.

In the coming months, and at the wishes of Jane Bowater, Charles, Hanna and the girls moved from the cottage to the main house and Jane Bowater moved into the cottage. It made eminent sense.

FIFTEEN

Charles finally received the call to see Peter Rogers. He was full of trepidation and expected the worst.

'Once again you have beaten the hangman's noose, Charles,' Peter Rogers said sternly.

'Everything will remain as it is but I am telling you now that one more slip-up and it will be curtains for you. I had great difficulty persuading "C" to keep you but he reluctantly agreed. He knows all about your history including your latest escapade, and that your wife will always be a security issue, which makes you a security issue as well. For her sake and yours, you simply cannot afford to put family matters above the work you are engaged in.'

His fondness for this man, always carefully masked, made it almost as difficult for Peter Roger as it was for Charles. He went on quickly.

'From now on, Hanna Bowater and your children will not be permitted to leave this country under any circumstances. For the time being contact with the outside world for her ceases. If the situation in the coming years changes for the better then her parents and sister may be allowed to come to England to see you. But there is no guarantee.

'I suggest you return to your work and your settled life in London and at your home. Your performance to date with us has been exemplary and very much appreciated. I always knew that you were somewhat of a loose cannon, especially when it comes to women, but your capabilities and capacity for clear thinking and getting things done outweigh your foibles by a long way. Let's keep it that way. This matter is forgotten.'

Charles felt relieved as he walked back to his office. He was wise enough to know that this recent incident, and all those before, would never be forgotten, merely documented and stored away. These people had long memories. The best thing for him to do now was to heed wise advice and try to put it to one side, even if they never would. Time to work; there was much to do. He would sit down at the weekend and talk it all through with Hanna.

It did not surprise Charles at all that when he told Hanna about his interview without coffee with Peter Rogers, she expressed no surprise or disappointment, only happiness that their lives could go on as before. Her meeting with her parents and sister was wonderful and would always live in her memory but she was here with her family in England and loving it more every day. At least they had met and her mother now had an up-to-date record of her life in England and ever to be cherished photographs of them all, especially her grandchildren. Who knows, one day they may meet up again in less stressful, or even dangerous circumstances. Three things she was sure of: her love for Charles Bowater would never die, the safety and happiness of her children were paramount and she would never do anything to put her husband's job in jeopardy. She would stay put, forever if necessary.

LIFE WENT ON. The Bowaters took holidays in Cornwall and Scotland, taking Jane Bowater with them if she wanted to go, which was not always. She remained her normal energetic, loving but unemotional self who was devoted to her son and his family. She did not really know what he did and never asked. She mostly enjoyed going on trips with Hanna where they could shop and have lunch together. Bath was their favourite city.

Charles was in the United States for two weeks and Hanna decided to take the girls to Salisbury for the day.

The girls were now old enough to begin to take an interest in what they wore and what they were not allowed to wear, much to their frustration, but shopping for clothes was exciting. They endured their mother taking them around the cathedral but enjoyed lunch in one of the excellent bistros in the city centre. It was a happy day out and Daddy would be coming home the next day, a Sunday.

With the happy and very chatty girls firmly strapped in the back, Hanna drove home. On the A36, whilst passing the turn off onto the A303, their car was hit head-on by HGV which was driving at speed and veered across the central reservation and directly into their path. The driver of the HGV was uninjured but Hanna, in trying to avoid the oncoming juggernaut, died instantly as the truck sheered off the front of the car but left the rear intact. It was as though an axe had cut the car in two. The two girls in the back were miraculously unhurt but were traumatised to the point of complete speechless numbness. They saw their mother being carried away by the front of the truck.

When the police arrived on the scene within minutes and an ambulance soon after, the girls were taken immediately to Salisbury hospital where they were sedated and a close eye kept on them. Neither of them had spoken since the accident and there was at that point no way of telling what their reactions would be when were able to begin to understand what had happened.

Hanna's crushed and broken body was taken to the mortuary. She was hardly recognisable but the pathologist quickly established that she had died instantly from a massive and lethal moving force that had crushed her torso and all internal organs.

By the time the police had tracked down Jane Bowater, Charles was airborne and heading back home. He would not discover what had happened until he had arrived back at Vine House where he found his utterly distraught mother who was only just capable of telling him what had happened, but with no real detail. At first Charles could not believe it. There must be a mistake. But there was no mistake. It had happened and the woman of his life was no more.

He was the only one who could identify Hanna and he did so in a numb and hardly conscious state.

———

THE NEXT TWO months passed in a haze of inconsolable misery and sadness for Charles. He just managed to call Peter Rogers to tell him what had happened and was promptly granted two months' leave to start there and then. He was not to come to the office. Everywhere he looked he saw her beautiful, smiling face. She was there in the house all the time, but was not there. It was unbearable and at times he thought seriously about taking his own life. He took a shotgun out of his gun cabinet, loaded it and put the barrels in his mouth. But then he held back because even then he was able to exercise some logic. He could not do it because it would be a betrayal to her memory and the future of his daughters and they would not have wanted it. He also thought of his mother. She would not want it either.

The funeral at the village church was a dire affair. Charles gave the eulogy in a halting and almost desperate voice, just holding back the tears. She was buried close to Grandpa Bowater. Charles and Jane Bowater were glad when it was all over. Jane Bowater went back to the cottage to weep quietly whilst Charles went to the house with the girls and where there was little said or done.

Charles hardly noticed the flood of condolences that were sent. He was a popular man and his wife, when people had met her, was even more popular. Her charm and poise had captivated many and her ability to make all feel at ease in her presence was a special thing. All this made it doubly difficult for Charles to accept what had happened and he answered none of them.

Acting entirely independently and with no regard as to his actions, he sent a long letter to Hanna's parents and sister in St Petersburg telling all. He promised that one day he would bring the girls to them for a visit when things were better. He received a reply a month later, a reply full of sadness but also to tell him that he was their son and that he and their grandchildren would always be in their lives and loved and welcomed.

Time passed slowly. He had no desire to do anything but Jane Bowater, in her stoical manner, kept on top of things and made sure that both the house and the cottage were well kept, and a gardener regularly tended the grounds. From the outside nothing had changed, but inside and especially in the mind and heart of Charles Bowater and his sorrow, everything had changed. He knew that he could have turned to drink but he did not. He rejected it altogether. He had never had that destructive gene in his body. His overriding reaction was to consciously adopt an ice-cold persona except when he was with his girls. With them he deeply felt and portrayed a host of emotions; love, protection, apology and fortitude. Despite his grief, he forced himself to try to be positive and honest with them. They were now thirteen and twelve and understood. Their resilience, like that of most children, was remarkable. They spoke together very often about Hanna and although tears still came, they became fewer and fewer as time went on. The beginnings of a determination to get on with life for her sake began to show. They visited her grave often and laid flowers. During these months, the bond between father and daughters became unbreakable and thus it was to prove in the future.

Whereas their father gave them love and devotion, Granny Bowater gave them the rock on which to build their future. She knew that only love combined with strength would get the girls through this time and she remained her indomitable self. She talked to them about Grandpa and her sorrow and told them that time would not always heal completely but it helps so much. She told them their education was very important because their parents wanted them to be successful and so they went back to school. Charles assumed the domestic mantle and very, very slowly life settled into a pattern, but not without a few tearful hiccups along the way.

Jane Bowater always made the effort to come up to the house and have supper with the family. She often did the cooking, although Charles had made great efforts to continue to improve his culinary skills even if it was only another way to keep his mind occupied and on the present. When the girls had gone to bed they often talked into the night in a way that they had never done before, and in a way that was more intimate.

'I am supposed to be going back to work next week, mother,' he said one evening.

'Are you ready, and more importantly, capable of going back?' She was still not entirely sure what Charles actually did.

'I have been giving it a great deal of thought and in the end it all came down to priorities. Before all this happened my priorities were my family including you, my job and my home. Now it seems to me that they are first and foremost my family above anything else and at least until I am entirely happy that the girls are completely alright and able to cope, and then my home and then perhaps my job.'

'So the job is no longer important?' she asked.

'The point is that thanks to you I no longer need to work. I am financially secure and have my own lovely home.' It was true: she had paid for so much including all the school fees and many holidays. He was also worried that he would not be able to give his best if he returned and in any case the idea held little appeal.

'I have therefore decided I am going to resign and concentrate on the girls and you and the home for the foreseeable future.' A declaration delivered with some force.

'I agree and I am glad.' She wanted him at home, at least for the short and medium term.

HIS RESIGNATION WAS ACCEPTED GRUDGINGLY by Peter Rogers but he understood.

'Come back if you want to,' he said.

'Thank you, Peter. We shall see. In the meantime I will come to London and make all the necessary administrative arrangements and say goodbye.'

Peter Rogers took him out to lunch, reminded him of his obligations under the Official Secrets Act, thanked him profusely for all he had done and told him and repeated his offer of further employment if he wished. His opinion of Charles had not changed despite his indiscretions. Very clever but flawed.

Charles returned from London within a week and was back at Vine House and unemployed for the first time in his life.

The compensation for the accident resulted in a dangerous driving conviction for the driver. This bought back painful memories for Charles but he also mused on the possibility that it might have been deliberate and linked to the past. It could well have been but he decided there and then that to attempt to pursue this line would be both painful and pointless. He dropped it. The deed had been done and he could not bring back the past.

SIXTEEN

The long school summer holidays were approaching fast. Eleanor had already spent a year at public school and Viktoria was due to join her in September. Both girls had shown Charles, through their school reports and his talks to their teachers, that they were bright and industrious. Charles remained fully committed to them in all respects and made sure that whilst not spoiling them, they grew up understanding the difference between right and wrong, respect to all, no matter what their calling in life, and the importance of decency, kindness, diligence and courage. Jane Bowater added to these in her own way. Despite their loss they had once again developed into happy girls where their father and grandmother were the focal points of their lives. They were also growing up into two very beautiful, very blonde young girls who looked uncannily like their mother but had yet to show any interest in the opposite sex, much to Charles' relief. He checked his shotguns anyway.

Charles had been contemplating what to do during the summer holidays. He wanted to take them away somewhere for the duration. He decided once again on Italy, without doubt his country of choice, and the girls were beside themselves with excitement when he told them. Jane Bowater declined but insisted on paying for it all. In true military style, he planned the holiday down to the last detail. A very smart villa in Tuscany with a pool and tennis court, close to the sea and beaches and within striking distance of centres of culture and antiquity such as Florence, Pisa and Sienna. He found just the place on the internet, booked it for two months as well as a car and the flights.

It proved to be a perfect two months away from Vine House, the scene of so much happiness and then sorrow. The villa was excellent with large cool rooms, a terrace for all meals and a much used swimming pool and tennis court. They spent most of their time there where Charles honed his skills in the kitchen as well as taking the girls out to a variety of local restaurants where they could sample the delights of Italian food at its best. Charles drank a little wine, a sure sign that he was relaxing, and although Eleanor tried and liked it, Viktoria did not. Her expression of distaste caused hilarity with Charles and Eleanor.

They took a few trips to the sea and more to those renaissance gems that surrounded them. During his planning Charles had read up on what to see in Florence, Pisa and Sienna. The girls trailed along behind in the summer heat, never complaining but relieved when they made numerous pit stops along the way, mainly for ice cream. Charles could not really tell whether they enjoyed these trips or not and whether they would rather be by or in the pool or playing tennis. He was working on the basis that the splendours he showed and explained to them might generate in the future an interest and a desire to return one day and learn more.

ALEXEI VOLIKOV HAD BEEN PROMOTED and now occupied a senior position within the FSB in Moscow. His seniors, and there not many of them now, were obviously pleased with him and he was pleased with himself. He was now the number two in the internal counter-terrorism directorate. Living in Moscow had initially proved to be difficult domestically but he had decided that it would be sensible to remain with his disinterested wife whilst engineering a post in Moscow for Olga, his lover from Berlin. It had not been difficult for a man in his position and she had accepted with alacrity and perhaps a little trepidation. Once he had installed her in Moscow he saw her often and even his hardened heart began to soften towards her. He began to treat her with a level of consideration and decency that surprised him, and her. She remained as willing and pliable as ever.

In the months leading up to his promotion there was one issue amongst many that had exercised Alexei Volikov's thoughts. There had never been closure on the question of the traitor Anna Nazarov. Her husband had produced the goods during the Cold War and she had subsequently been given a serious fright and warning in Finland. But was this enough? KGB and then FSB policy on these matters remained wholly inflexible. A traitor is a traitor forever and therefore must pay the ultimate price eventually. He made up his mind. He had to harden his heart and take action.

Alexei Volikov swung into action. He briefed the Russian Embassy in London as to the requirement and the resident KGB man in turn created a watching brief on the movements of the target in order to ascertain any patterns that might emerge. He also decided that the least suspicious method of elimination was a traffic accident. He therefore lined up a truck with Romanian plates and a driver that was a FSB operative who spoke Romanian and had been issued with false Romanian documents. They waited patiently and eventually their moment came. Another chapter had been closed.

THE GIRLS HAD SETTLED back into a steady and fulfilling environment. They were now both at the same public school and despite initial tears, Viktoria was doing well. Eleanor kept an eye on her and soon Viktoria was happily engaged in school life. They both made friends easily but what they most looked forward to was to see their Daddy at the end of each day. He in turn, and supported by Jane Bowater, encouraged them to become fully involved at school and enjoy it. He was positive and upbeat with them and this rubbed off. They were bright and athletic, so becoming involved was not difficult for them. What they never saw was the quiet tears their father shed at night in bed.

Charles was in a quandary. Since Hanna's death he had worked relentlessly to ensure his daughters were as happy as they could be, had felt he had succeeded and that he would continue to always support them into the future. But what of himself?

'Do you think the girls have now reached a point where they are emotionally stable?' he asked his mother over coffee in the kitchen one early December morning.

'I think they are but it depends how deep inside that stability goes.'

'I agree. One can never really tell what remains deep inside,' he said.

'We just have to keep working on it by being strong for them and ourselves. Each day that goes by makes it better.' She was always full of good advice and never shy to voice her opinion.

'What do you think I should do now? I want to be with them and protect them but at the same time I am beginning to want to do something useful again.'

'There aren't any jobs locally or even vaguely locally that would suit you, unless you want to become a Retired Officer in some army base nearby.'

The thought did not appeal to Charles at all. He had had his army career and did not want to return to it in any shape or form, and especially on 15 grand a year.

'If I went overseas again but made sure that I came back as frequently as possible, what do you think the girls would think of that?' he ventured.

'They would be sad but I think that they would understand. They have often told me they want you to be happy as well.'

'Shall I talk to them about it?'

'Yes, and I will too.' Charles thanked his lucky stars that he had the mother he did.

Charles sat down with his girls and explained all. He was surprised by their reaction. It was very positive and they reminded him that they had Granny to look after them, a Granny they had known closely all their lives and that there was nothing to worry about. He must do what he wanted to do and enjoy it. Charles also realised that now they were both teenagers their views on grown-ups were beginning to change, not for the worse but from a different perspective. They would always love their father to distraction but there were now many other interests crowding in on their lives. It was healthy and normal. They were growing up.

Jane Bowater merely reinforced what Charles had told them and reminded them that whatever happened she and Vine House were their rocks that would never change.

ONE DAY, a friend of his from army days called in for a chat. In passing he mentioned he was feeling a bit down because he had applied for a job working within the British contingent of a mission to be deployed to Serbia and Montenegro under the auspices of an Owen and Stoltenberg initiative that would monitor any attempted cross-border movement of war material from

Serbia to support the murderous campaigns of the Bosnian Serbs in Northern and Eastern Bosnia. This mission was called ICFY or the International Conference for the Former Yugoslavia. His friend had been rejected but Charles' ears pricked up. His friend gave him the contact details to apply – they were still recruiting.

Charles was pleased when he saw that the employer was none other than the Foreign and Commonwealth Office. Might his history with them be a positive or negative thing? They might or might not be interested, but he decided to apply anyway.

He only waited two days before he received a phone call inviting him to the FCO main building in King Charles Street. They might have made the connection but perhaps they were not quite as joined-up as he had imagined. He put on his best and most sober suit and made sure he looked immaculate. The main building can be intimidating and he, like the other candidates, was made to sit outside the interview room on a very hard chair in a very long and empty corridor which seemed to echo with voices from the Britain's glorious past.

The interviewer was a young woman and Charles felt the interview went well. It did not last very long which could have been either a good or bad sign. The FCO were in a hurry to fill their contingent slots as the mission was about to start and their people needed to deploy. The Bosnian Serbs were obviously receiving copious amounts of arms and other killing machine materials from their compatriots in Serbia and the international community needed to do something about it, and fast. He was called the next day and told that he had been selected.

He busied himself with his preparations to depart and realised that they made him feel useful and content. The farewells on the day were passionate but short. Granny needed to take them to school and they had a busy day ahead of them. There were no tears on their part and only a misting of the eyes on Charles'. The strength and resolve of the Bowater clan was returning.

Along with three other individuals selected for the mission, he found himself on a JAT aircraft heading for Belgrade. JAT was the Serbian national carrier and passenger comfort and safety was not one of their strong points or concerns. The on-board meal was disgusting and the memory of rancid butter would linger for the next 18 months as JAT flew him back and forth to and from London for his obligatory two weeks' leave every six weeks, leave he would religiously take.

The plane made the hardest landing Charles had ever experienced. All the oxygen masks came out and he was surprised that the undercarriage had not collapsed. He had arrived in the Balkans during the last year of that bloody conflict to what would prove to be a fascinating and compelling six years of his life. It was January 1994 and it was time to start once again and make a success of his life.

ABOUT THE AUTHOR

James Withington spent 21 years as a British Army officer serving mainly in Cold War West Germany. His military career was followed by extensive periods spent in the Middle East, Asia and Africa working for governments, development and risk management and security companies in most of the non-tourist countries of the world. He lives near Blandford Forum in Dorset.

This is book one of the Charles Bowater Series.

If you've enjoyed this book, please consider leaving a review on Amazon, Goodreads or any other suitable forum. These are a huge help to authors.